TORMENT

DAVID EVANS

**ORCHARD
VIEW
PUBLICATIONS**

ABOUT THE AUTHOR

Born and brought up in and around Edinburgh, David Evans graduated from Manchester University and had a successful career as a professional in the construction industry before turning to crime ... fiction that is and writing thereof.

TORMENT is the second in his Internationally Best Selling Wakefield Series and was shortlisted in 2013 for the CWA Debut Dagger Award. The first in the series, *TROPHIES* and the third, *TALISMAN* are also available. A fourth in the series will follow.

His other novel currently available is *DISPOSAL,* the first of a planned series set in the Tendring area of North Essex.

Find out more by visiting David's website at
www.davidevanswriter.co.uk

or follow him on Facebook at
www.facebook.com/davidevanswriter

and Twitter @DavidEwriter

ACKNOWLEDGMENTS

I have been privileged to meet some amazing people, without whose help, encouragement, support and above all friendship got me through some occasions when it would have been easier to walk away and do something else with my time.

First and foremost, I have to say a huge thank-you to Sally Spedding who was the first in the publishing industry to take my writing seriously. I owe her a great debt for all her continued support and encouragement.

Heather Adams did an inspired editing job which improved the story's telling.

I am fortunate to have a great little band of writing friends and I would like to thank Sarah Wagstaff, Jan Beresford, Julie-Ann Corrigan, Manda Hughes, Lorraine Cannell, Glynis Smy and Peter Best, all of whom are talented writers in their own right and have made some significant contributions.

I am also fortunate to have the input of Colin Steele, ex-Detective Superintendent of the Essex Murder Squad and Tom Harper, ex-Principal Crime Scene Coordinator for the Kent & Essex Serious Crime Directorate. Both have given their time and guidance generously. Any residual errors here, are all mine.

Finally, Ger Nichol for just loving the series.

Sheila,

she would have been proud

TORMENT

David Evans

TORMENT

Prologue
Monday 6th March 1989

He carried the lifeless burden down the creaking wooden staircase. The door at the top had closed behind him and the only light came from two 40 watt bulbs in holders screwed to the floor joists above. No-one came down here. He made sure of that. Outside, the wind whistled around the buildings. Exposed at the top of a rise, it always seemed to be blowing. The rain that had rattled the windows all day had finally stopped. At the bottom of the steps, he paused. Nearby, a train thundered its way past, the floor shuddering beneath his feet. Listening closely, he could tell its direction. Probably on the way to the capital; next stop Doncaster.

Crossing the open space, a cobweb caught his face. Stumbling with his load, he wiped the threads away. She was lighter than the last one and he managed to hold on to her with one arm. Rounding a corner, there was the door. Shifting the position of her body so it rested over his shoulder, he fumbled in his pocket for the key. Only he had access.

The key struggled to turn in the rusty lock, three years it had been. Finally, it gave. Turning his back, he pushed against the solid wooden door. The hinges groaned and the bottom screeched as small trapped stones ground against the floor. With no lights in the room, his eyes had to adjust. Eventually, the shape on the floor could be made out. The musty air hit his nostrils, but the aroma of decaying flesh had long ceased.

Tears began to prick. How did it happen again? Why? They didn't have to come with him. Just because it was raining. Just because they were offered a lift, they didn't have to get in. And then when they came back here, they didn't have to make such a fuss. That's when they had to be shut up. He couldn't have them telling tales. What would folk think? They'd all think he was some sort of pervert. But he wasn't, he knew that. That's why they had to stay here. They'd be safe here.

Placing her gently down on the floor next to the other one, he folded her arms over her chest and smoothed down her dress. Next, the sandals and white socks were carefully removed.

Above, stumbling footsteps on the wooden floor startled him. Instinctively, he looked up and began to panic. He can't be found here. They'd be found. Struggling to get to his feet the shoes and socks were stuffed into his coat pocket. Tiptoeing out of the room, the door was pulled to as quietly as possible. He listened again. The footsteps continued overhead, doors opening and closing as if they were looking for him. The door was locked and the key placed in his trouser pocket before he made his way back to the bottom of the stairs. He waited. Only when the footsteps could be heard to leave did he ascend and make his way out, satisfied his secrets were safe once more.

1
Saturday 2nd September 2000

Susan returned from the supermarket with bags of shopping and stooped to collect the post from behind the front door. Climbing the stairs to her first floor flat, she weighed up the choices she had for her evening meal. Up in the kitchen, bags on the floor, she paused. As a matter of habit, she walked through to the living room and picked up the telephone. With the BT answering service, she would usually hear the normal dialling tone indicating no-one had called. Today though, she heard the dual tone signifying someone had. Pressing 1, the puzzling message began.

"Hello? … Gaz?"

Who the Hell is Gaz?

The male voice continued, *"I didn't know you had this answerphone bollocks. Anyway, this is important. I lifted another one last night… she looks a right goer an' all."* He gave a lewd chuckle. *"I've got her safe in the usual place. I thought you might want to have some fun with her before we have to get rid. So … fancy it tonight?"* The voice sounded youthful but she also thought it had the qualities of a perverted old man. *"Give us a ring back … soon as you can, or I'll call you later."* His excitement rose, *"Can hardly wait."*

At the prompt following the message, Susan dialled 1 to hear it again. Even on the second playing, it didn't make a lot of sense but she pressed 2 to save it anyway. The accent sounded local but she certainly didn't recognise him. A shiver ran through her and she slammed the receiver down. She lived alone, so she knew the message was a mistake.

3

Back in the kitchen, she began the routine task of putting the foodstuffs away. As some went in the freezer, others in the fridge and the tins in the cupboards, she couldn't shake the unnerving voice from her mind. Eventually, she returned to the living room and stared at the telephone. Slowly, curiosity took hold. Snatching up the receiver again, she dialled 1471 and was rewarded, not with a number withheld as she half expected, but the information that a local number had called that day at two thirteen p.m. She made a note of it, broke the connection, then dialled the answering service again, this time to transcribe the message. Her unease grew as she read the transcript, the words in her head uttered by the mystery caller. She began to imagine all kinds of evil scenarios.

Sweeping through to the kitchen once more, she made herself a strong coffee as she tried to get her thoughts into some sort of order. She found herself thinking how her life had changed so dramatically in recent years. When her mother died nearly ten years ago, she'd had to grow up quickly. Her father's health deteriorated, dementia taking hold. Her schooling suffered but since he'd been moved into a home, she'd studied at night school for her 'A' levels and now, at twenty-four, she had accepted the offer of a university place to study journalism. She was excited at that prospect. At last, her life was moving on.

As she sipped her coffee, her thoughts returned to the phone message. Was this an opportunity? This could be a story. She had some dim recall of newspaper reports in the past – young girls working the streets had disappeared without trace. Not exactly headline stuff, tucked away on the inside pages. There had been something about the tone and content of this mysterious message that instinctively told her they could be connected.

Suddenly, the idea came to her. She scrambled in one of the drawers where assorted junk mail was shoved in the unlikely event that it might be of some future use. In this case it was. She pulled out the latest pamphlet BT had sent.

Taking the last mouthful of coffee, she steeled herself and dialled. After two rings she began to hope there was no answer. After four, she considered abandoning the whole idea. It was answered on the sixth.

"Hello?"

She hesitated. There was no mistaking that voice. "Ah … good afternoon to you, this is Linda from BT … just a courtesy call."

"Oh, yes."

"I was wondering if I could have just a few minutes of your time, sir, to let you know about some of our recently introduced services."

"For you, Linda, of course."

She gulped. God, what a creep. "Thank you, Mr … er … I'm sorry, I don't appear to …" she bluffed.

"Chapman. Stephen Chapman, but you can call me Steve."

Can't be too bright, she thought, that was an easy win. "Er … right, thanks … Steve." She composed herself then launched into a convincing display of promoting the advantages of the various features detailed in the BT mail shot, all the while, imagining Chapman leering down the phone at her. "So, Steve," she said, drawing the conversation to a close, "can I send you some of the details we've just spoken about?"

"Yeah, sure, so long as you give me your number."

Shit, she thought. "I'm sorry, but I'm not allowed to do that." She laughed nervously. "Now, I wonder, could you confirm your address for me?"

"I'd have thought you'd know that already."

A moment's hesitation as she thought he might have suddenly become suspicious. "We do normally but my computer's just gone down and it would save a lot of trouble if I could just make a note of your details and log it on the system when it comes back up."

She replaced the receiver and stumbled to a kitchen chair, her legs feeling as if they were about to buckle. She couldn't believe what she'd just done. She felt proud of herself; she'd actually managed to obtain the creep's name and address. Taking a few deep breaths, she studied the note pad with the transcribed message, phone number and now, address written on it.

Checking the address on a gazetteer, she discovered that the street was in an area not far from the centre of Wakefield. Despite a series of low-paid jobs, Susan had managed to acquire three possessions of which she was proud. One was the little six year-old silver Nissan Micra sitting in the street. The second was a pay-as-you-go mobile phone and the third was the second-hand computer and printer which sat on a desk in her bedroom. That would be essential for her to fulfil her dream of becoming a journalist. Grabbing the mobile phone and a jacket she set off in her Micra.

Chapman's address turned out to be a small mid-terraced house in a group of four, built sometime between the wars. It was near dusk and a light was on in the front room. There were cars parked on both sides of the street but she managed to find a space to squeeze into about fifty yards away. She switched off, killed the lights and waited. For what exactly, she wasn't absolutely sure. The initial excitement she had when she made her call to Chapman earlier had begun to give way to the major misgivings she felt now. She could be exposing herself to incredible risk. So? How else was she to get to the bottom of it? Her anxiety grew. Doubting the sanity of pursuing this alone, she pulled the mobile from her jacket pocket, deciding to call the police. Before she could make the final connection she was disturbed.

A white Ford Escort van came down the street from behind and drew to a halt outside Chapman's house, the driver bipping the horn. The light in Chapman's room went out, the front door opened and a man dressed in a dark anorak appeared. Stockily built, he had an unusual bouncy gait as if there were springs in his heels. He paused before opening the passenger door to glance quickly up and down the road. With the benefit of a street

6

light, Susan saw his face. He was clean-shaven with dark hair and looked to be around thirty. As soon as he got in and shut the door, the van drove off.

She started up the Micra's engine and followed. She knew that following someone undetected by car was not as easy as they made out on television and in films. Allowing the Escort to open up a considerable gap before it approached the junction with the main road, she then had no alternative but to come up behind it as it waited for an opportunity to merge into the heavy traffic. Fortunately, from what she could see, the two occupants were engaged in animated conversation and paid no attention to her car behind. Eventually, the van pulled out and headed east. Three cars later, she was able to do the same.

After five or six miles, they were on a minor country road with just one vehicle between them. They had crossed the A1(M) and were somewhere to the north of Doncaster when the van turned off onto a farm track to the left. Susan pulled into a field entrance just beyond and watched the red lights make their way up a hill. The brake lights glared out across the open fields momentarily, then died along with the headlights as the vehicle came to a halt and the engine was switched off. Briefly, she just had time to make out a group of dark unlit buildings. Moments later, a dim glow appeared from a window.

She stepped from the car and pulled on her jacket. She couldn't risk driving up the track, so she set off on foot, reassured that there were bushes and hedgerows on either side so she could hide should another vehicle suddenly appear. As she walked, she heard two trains passing close by, the ground vibrating, and guessed the East Coast main line was on the other side of the rise where the buildings lay. Eventually, she found herself in what appeared to be an abandoned farmyard. The old farmhouse to the right looked derelict. The light she had seen from the road came from a large building opposite. She reached the window and listened. Muffled men's voices but the sill was too high to see in. A quick look round revealed an old bucket. As quietly as she could, she tipped out the stagnant rainwater. Placing it below the window, she steadied herself. Carefully, she stood on it and peered inside.

At last, she could see the object of Chapman and his companion's attention.

Just then, she heard a car crunching its way up the gravel track. She panicked. Looking round, she instantly decided on the old abandoned farmhouse. Dashing into the porch, she squeezed past the front door that hung precariously off its hinges. She turned to watch. The headlight beam swung across the front of the building. She stepped back to avoid it. That's when her luck finally ran out. Her feet met the limited resistance of rotting floorboards before the timber finally gave way. Her legs straddled a joist before that too failed, plunging her into the bowels of the basement. She heard the crack and felt the sharp pain as the bones in her lower left leg snapped. Things seemed to happen in slow motion. As she tumbled into the darkness, the events of the past few hours replayed in her head.

Another London-bound express rattled its way past, the noise drowning out her yell and the sounds of splintering timber. Blackness. Then silence.

2
Monday

Wakefield; eight-thirty in the morning and the city was awake. In the market place, stalls were laden. Above the hubbub of dozens of conversations and yells of greeting, the shouts announcing bargains rang out. Early shoppers, mostly elderly, milled around.

In the bus station, shop and office workers were disgorged and fanned out, some pausing to buy a paper or cigarettes, others rushing to where they had to be. The warm weather of the past fortnight was breaking and large blobs of rain turned the pavements mottled. Umbrellas began to appear.

Nearby, on the second floor of Wood Street Police station, Acting Detective Chief Inspector Colin Strong felt decidedly awkward as he eased his six foot frame into the big leather chair he'd sat opposite many times before. He'd often wondered what it would be like to sit in his old boss, DCI Cunningham's seat but he never expected it would happen; let alone how.

"Who knows," Chief Superintendent Flynn had said, "play your cards right and it could be yours permanently."

But don't hold your breath, Strong had added silently.

On balance, Strong liked Cunningham. True, he'd had a few run-ins with him in the past but he'd always found him to be pretty straight. His part in Cunningham's suspension still felt like betrayal, even though they both knew it was the right thing to do.

Strong sighed, swivelled in the chair and looked round the office. The bookcase was empty and the photographs and trophies marking Cunningham's rugby-playing days had gone. All evidence of the room's previous occupant had disappeared, except for the dent in the wall where he had thrown a glass paperweight at a young Detective Constable. Strong smiled at the memory.

Standing up out of the big chair, Strong swung his briefcase onto the desk in front of him. Opening it up, he took out a framed photograph of the two women in his life and placed it next to the telephone. The picture had been taken on holiday in North Wales five years before; Laura, with fair hair blowing to one side had her arm around a dark-haired twelve-year-old girl. They were standing in the bubbling waters of a river in bright sunshine. Strong loved that photo. For him, it seemed to capture the very essence of his wife and daughter.

He picked up the picture again and studied Amanda's face; innocence personified. Now seventeen and in the throes of 'A' Level studies, she would surely be sensible enough to avoid the pitfalls of modern living. Headstrong and a touch impatient, traits she inherited from him, Amanda could be at once frustrating and inspiring.

He took a second photo from his case, this time a group of footballers laughing at the camera. Elated by obvious success, the captain and the goalkeeper, surrounded by their teammates held a silver trophy between them. Strong studied the picture with pride. His son, Graham, was the goalkeeper, and he'd just made two brilliant saves in the penalty shoot-out that had decided the fate of the schools under-18 knockout cup. There was no doubt about it, he was a useful player but Strong was pleased Graham had decided to go to Hull University rather than try to pursue a career in the game, at least for now. Strong thought back to his own playing days. Never quite good enough himself, like Graham, he'd decided to go to university. That brought his thoughts back to his first meeting with Laura.

Before his mind could wander anywhere else, a knock on the door interrupted.

"Come," he said.

DS Kelly Stainmore entered, closely followed by DC Luke Ormerod. "Guv, good to have you back," she said, with sincerity.

Short blonde hair neatly framed her face which had started to show signs of an unhealthy lifestyle; bags appearing below the eyes and the skin beginning to resemble chamois leather. She was popular with her colleagues, helped, no doubt, by the fact that she could keep up with the best of them in the pub, not to mention tell a good risqué joke.

"Good to be back, Kelly, although I wish it wasn't like this."

"I know," she said, "but he did cross the line."

"Feelings in his trousers overwhelming those in his head," Ormerod suggested, referencing the rumours of the DCI's affair with a female officer. "I've got to say," he continued, grooming his thick black moustache between thumb and forefinger, "she was a looker, though, Kathy Sharp."

No doubt about it, DC Sharp was a very attractive woman and Strong could understand how Cunningham would be flattered by her attentions, assuming the stories of her making all the running were to be believed. He could only think that she had another reason for taking an interest in the DCI. Her swift promotion to DS and transfer to the Met shortly afterwards evidence of that theory.

"Makes you wonder what she saw in him," Stainmore said.

"Built like a brick shithouse," Ormerod added.

"Can you imagine making love with him," Stainmore chuckled, "it would be like having a wardrobe fall on you."

"With the key still in the lock," Ormerod quipped.

Stainmore looked at him questioningly.

"I've played rugby with him and seen him in the showers afterwards."

Strong smiled, enjoying the banter but decided it was time to bring the hilarity to a halt. "All right you two. So, what's been happening?"

"Someone's taking a fancy to some nice motors," Stainmore replied. "Another one knocked off yesterday."

"What this time?"

"A Lexus 400 stolen off the drive of a house up on Princewood Avenue about half-past seven in the morning."

"Expensive wheels."

"About forty grand," Ormerod said.

"How many so far?"

"Four." Stainmore counted off on her fingers. "A Range Rover last month, a Subaru sports a fortnight ago, a Mercedes sports coupé on Friday and this one yesterday."

"All connected?"

"Well - all top of the range, sought-after models and all the same MO, stolen from outside the owners' homes."

"Any leads?"

"Nothing solid yet," Kelly responded.

"A neighbour heard the Subaru being driven away but thought nothing of it," Ormerod said. "Apart from that, nothing. Probably stolen to order. We've got the word out but so far, nobody's heard anything."

"Who's in downstairs?"

"Nearly everyone, guv."

"Okay, Kelly, I'll be down in a minute."

Stainmore and Ormerod departed, leaving Strong alone with his thoughts. The two week break in Italy seemed a distant memory although he'd only flown back to Manchester on Saturday. The Chief Super had told him of his temporary appointment just before he left, so his couple of weeks in the sun was spent getting used to the idea; mulling over the implications. It was a challenge but he knew he had a good team.

A few minutes later, Strong swept into the CID room. "Morning everybody."

Various welcoming responses came from the assembled officers.

Before he could say any more, the door opened and DC John Darby strolled in, index finger of his right hand hooked through the loop of his jacket draped casually over his shoulder. His light blue shirt, taut over his stomach, was spattered with darker spots.

"Either you've just won a pissing highest up the wall contest or it's started raining," Ormerod remarked.

The group burst out laughing.

"Very bloody funny," Darby retorted as he slumped into a chair by his desk. Darby was in his early thirties, divorced, overweight and desperate for a woman. His previous relationship fizzled out a few months ago. His pillow talk was more open than it should have been, jeopardising an investigation.

"What are you up to then, John?" Strong asked.

"I'm looking into this plant scam, guv."

"Plant scam? What sort of plant scam?"

"You know, building plant." Darby adjusted the crotch of his trousers, another habit that did nothing to endear him to the opposite sex. "Some herberts are ordering plant to be delivered to a site, giving a squiggle for a signature and that's the last anyone sees of it."

"What sort of things?" Ormerod wondered.

"So far, three concrete mixers, six transformers, two breakers and a vibrating poker."

"What the hell's a vibrating poker?" Stainmore joined in.

"Thought that'd interest you," Darby grinned.

Stainmore groaned. "P..I..eease!"

"They use them to make sure all the concrete's compacted when they make a pour - you know, like a cake - make sure there are no air pockets in it when it finally sets."

"You seem to know a lot about the subject," Strong surmised.

"Me uncle had a small building business back in Nottingham when I were growing up." Darby's Midlands accent strengthened. "I used to work for him in the school holidays, labouring and that, so I picked a lot up."

"Sounds like we've got the right man on the case then."

A rumble of thunder overhead and a sharp crack of lightning drew everyone's attention to the windows. It looked like a total eclipse outside as the heavens opened and people in the street below scurried for shelter.

Strong turned his attention to his other DS. Jim Ryan was standing by his desk, sheaf of papers in hand, alongside DC Malcolm Atkinson.

"What's keeping you two off the streets then?"

"Misper, guv," Ryan answered. 'Misper' meaning missing person's enquiry.

"You look puzzled, Jim."

"Well, I just don't know how seriously to take this." Ryan handed Strong the file he was holding.

Strong studied the contents for a moment. Helena Cryanovic, he read, asylum seeker from Albania. Twenty-three years old and reported missing by her sister, Magda, on Friday.

"Avoiding the system?" he asked.

"Maybe, but I think there might be something more to it. She had a boyfriend - big sod by the name of Szymanski – Polish, I think."

"Anything on record?"

"No, but he's rumoured to be involved with an Eastern European mob with connections to clubs and the vice trade in Leeds."

"Have you spoken to him yet?"

"We've only just got an address for him this morning, so we're off there now."

"Let me know how you go on."

Strong looked around then focussed on Ormerod. "Where are Sam and Trevor?"

DCs Sam Kirkland and Trevor Newell completed Strong's team.

"Looking in to the case of the dud fivers, guv."

Strong expressed surprise. "Wouldn't have thought it worth anybody's while to forge five pound notes."

At the desk behind them a phone rang; Stainmore took the call.

"That's why they've been so successful. People don't pay too much attention to a fiver. Tens or twenties, yes, fifties definitely, but not fivers."

"I take your point. So where are they now?"

"Interviewing shop staff who've had them passed on over the past week."

"All right. Ask them to give me an update when they get back."

Stainmore put the phone down and looked across at her boss. "Guv," she said, "Chief Super wants to see you."

Strong rolled his eyes and left the room.

3

Angular, and straight from the 1960s school of architecture, the Yorkshire Post building to the west of Leeds city centre was bathed in early September sunshine. That looked to be under threat from the dark clouds rolling in from the south over Elland Road, home of Leeds United football club.

"There's a young … lady in reception for you, Mr Souter." Patricia on the front desk had developed the ability to convey much more in a message than the actual words she spoke.

"Who is it?"

"She won't give her name."

"Well, did she say what she wants?"

"Only that it's important."

Souter sighed. "All right, Patricia, tell her I'll be down in a few minutes."

Bob Souter had just turned forty-three. He'd come down to Leeds from Glasgow to join the staff of the Yorkshire Post a few months before. Although born and brought up in Scotland until he was six when his family had moved south to Doncaster, he felt more at home in the north of England than anywhere else.

Patricia nodded towards the girl sitting on a chair at the far side of the reception area, nervously chewing her nails. Although Patricia's gesture repeated her earlier disapproval, there was the hint of a smile mixed in, betraying her curiosity.

The 'young lady' Patricia referred to wore a cheap-looking, short imitation leather coat over tight fitting jeans and a low cut top. Her white shoes had seen better days, the heels of which were flared out like a rag-man's trumpet. Her bleached blonde hair, parted roughly in the middle, fell over her eyes and straggled down to her shoulders. As he introduced himself, he took in her face, heavily made up to give the appearance of being older than he suspected she actually was. She would only give her name as Sammy. Souter presumed it was short for Samantha but wouldn't trust that it was her real name anyway. He sat down facing her across a low table strewn with that morning's newspapers.

"What can I do for you, Sammy?"

"It's about my friend, Maria." She flicked hair away from her eyes. "She's disappeared."

"So why me? Why not go to the police?"

"Huh," she snorted. "Look at me. They don't take us seriously." She glanced over Souter's shoulder towards the reception desk. "I'm not deaf or blind either. I heard how she asked you to come down and I saw her look at you when you did. She thinks I'm a piece of shit you wouldn't want on your shoe. The police tolerate us, sometimes; nothing more."

"But what makes you think I can help you?"

"I remember how you wrote about that murder a few months ago; Rosie Hudson."

Souter's expression hardened as he remembered the events following Rosie's death. It was one of the first stories he'd written about when he'd started on the paper.

"Most of them loved the chance to slag her off – ex-vice girl, former prostitute – that sort of crap. But you ... you wrote about her as a victim."

He felt flattered. "Well ... I was only doing my job," he smiled.

"Maybe ... but it was how you did it. I liked that."

"All right, Sammy, what about this friend of yours. How long has she been missing?"

"Last night, we worked Wakefield's market square as usual ..."

"Hold on, are you saying she's only been missing since last night?"

Sammy was indignant. "Look, I know what you're thinking but me and Maria, we work together, we look out for each other, we know each other so well. Christ we were in the same kids' home together!"

"All right, Sammy, calm down." Souter glanced round towards Patricia, wondering whether she'd overheard the last part of their conversation, but she was taking a call. "So, you were in the market square, then what happened?"

"She went off with a punter and never came back."

"Did you see who with?"

"Not really. I'd just got into a car with one of my regulars. The last time I saw her was when I turned to put the seatbelt on. She was talking to someone in a small van, white, it was."

"But you don't know if she got in it?"

"Tracey said she had, when I got back."

"Tracey? Who's Tracey?"

"Just one of the other girls."

"So how long had you been gone?"

"Only about fifteen minutes. Like I said, he was a regular."

"And you've checked where she lives?"

"We share a room in a house up on the Woodside estate. She hasn't been back. I'm worried, Mr Souter."

"She wouldn't have done an all-nighter, would she?"

"No, not without telling me."

Souter took a breath and thought for a moment. "Now don't get upset with this, but I've got to ask ..."

Sammy looked straight at him. "Drugs, you mean?"

He nodded. "Was Maria involved with anything?"

"Well, we smoke a bit, maybe some ganja sometimes. Christ, you've got to have something to get you through the day ... or night, if you get my drift ... but nothing heavy."

"I'm not judging you, Sammy, it's just an angle we need to cover. I mean, she's not likely to have taken anything with someone else?"

"No, she wouldn't, not with anyone we didn't know."

"You didn't recognise this white van? Could it have been one you'd seen before, previous client maybe?"

"I don't think so. They are fairly common, though."

"What about this other girl, Tracey, was it? Has she got any idea about this?"

"She said she didn't recognise the van."

Souter leaned forward in his chair. "So what exactly do you think I can do to help?"

"Well, there've been rumours … this might not be the first time something like this has happened."

His eyes narrowed. "What do you mean?"

"I've heard about a couple of girls go missing recently."

Souter looked sceptical.

"Look, I know what you're thinking, street girls just come and go, move on to different territory, whatever. But they were regular girls, worked with mates, kept an eye out for one another, and they just wouldn't have gone off without letting one of the others know."

"Do you know where these others went missing from?"

She looked away for a second. "Not sure. It's just some talk I heard."

"All right, Sammy, let me look into this. I might want to speak to your friend, Tracey."

"She's not really my friend, just one of the girls."

"Well, anyway, could you arrange that?"

"Yeah, I think so."

"So, how can I contact you?"

"Can I borrow a pen?"

Souter pulled one from his shirt pocket and handed it to her. She began writing on a blank margin of one of the newspapers on the table. "Here," she said, tearing off the strip. "This is my address and the number of the payphone in the hallway. You can try that."

"Okay, Sammy, I'll be in touch as soon as I've found anything out." Souter got to his feet and, as he put his pen back, drew out a business card. "In the meantime, if Maria does turn up, give me a call."

"Thanks, Mr Souter." Sammy stood up. "I'm sorry if I caused you any embarrassment." She nodded towards Patricia who was now watching events unfold.

"That's all right. Don't worry about it. You certainly haven't caused me any."

As she disappeared out into the street, the brief smile he gave her dissolved into an expression of concern.

4

Gillian Ramsey replaced the telephone handset on the cradle and stared blankly into the space in front of her desk. She was baffled. No, more than that, she was worried. In all the time since her mother died nearly ten years ago, she'd always spoken to her younger sister at least twice a week. Last Wednesday everything sounded normal. Susan had been so excited at the prospect of starting her university course in a few weeks. Gillian was pleased for her. If anyone deserved some luck it was Susan.

Now, not only could Gillian not get a response from Susan's land line or mobile, despite leaving a couple of messages on each, but their father's nursing home confirmed that she hadn't been to see him all weekend. And that was something she had done religiously since they'd moved him in. Something was wrong, Gillian could sense it. There was nothing for it, she would have to go round to Susan's flat and check for herself. Gillian's mind darted around as if in a pinball machine. Susan could be ill … but surely not ill enough not to be able to let her know. That means she must be seriously ill. She could be lying in that lonely flat unable to get help. She might have been there for days. She might even have been …

"Gill, have you finished those returns yet?" a voice on the edge of her awareness was saying. Before she could reply, the voice went on, "I said, have you finished those returns yet? Mr Adams needs them for this afternoon's management meeting." It was Sally Dobson, the director's PA.

Gillian looked up into Sally's face then down onto her desk and began rummaging through some paperwork in several files. "Yes," she finally responded. "I've just got to finalise the projections and I'm done. I'll …" At that point, her phone rang. "I'll bring them along in half-an-hour." She picked up the receiver.

"Make it twenty minutes," Sally said before flouncing off.

Gillian grimaced behind her disappearing back, drawing a chuckle from a colleague at a work station opposite.

"Gill? Are you there?" came a disembodied female voice from the handset.

"Sorry about that," Gillian said, "Can I help you?"

"Gill, it's me, Alison."

"Oh, Alison, hi." Gillian lowered her voice significantly. "Sorry, I was just in the middle of something with Miss Frosty-Knickers here."

"You sound busy."

"Just got to get something finished before lunch."

"So, not too busy for a bit of lunch and a gossip, then?"

"Well … no," Gillian hesitated. "Actually, there's something I could do with your opinion on."

"Sounds interesting."

"It may be something and nothing but I'm a bit worried about …" Gillian broke off as Sally came back through the office door. "Look, I'll see you in Garcia's at half twelve. Got to go, see you then." Gillian hurriedly put down the phone and busied herself with paperwork as Sally passed by, a scowl on her face.

Garcia's was one of a new breed of trendy wine bars that seemed to have sprung up on every High Street in the land. Situated just off the Bullring, its interior boasted plenty of polished wood, stainless steel and etched glass which gave an almost clinical feel to the place. This was in sharp contrast to the cosy, smoky, town-centre pub it had once been in a previous incarnation.

The bar was buzzing with the incessant chatter of a score of conversations as a broad spectrum of clientele exchanged all the news, gossip and scandal of the day.

Alison Hewitt took her dry white wine spritzer from the bar and found a circular table that had been fixed around one of the retained cast iron columns when the place was refitted the previous year. She placed her drink carefully on a mat on the surface which was just the right height for an elbow and awaited her friend's arrival.

Alison was in her mid-thirties with shoulder length dark hair and dressed in a smart two-piece suit over a sheer white blouse. It was warm in the bar so she unbuttoned her jacket, drawing admiring glances from a group of business men standing nearby. As an attractive woman, she was used to that. However, taking account of their initial reaction, she decided against making any attempt to sit on one of the high bar stools, realising her tight skirt would ride up to reveal what many considered her best feature, a shapely pair of legs.

Just then, Gillian appeared in the doorway, looking flustered, caught Alison's eye and mouthed an offer of some drinks. Alison gestured that she was fine, so Gillian made her way to the bar.

"God, I need this," Gillian said, after weaving her way through the throng to join her friend and taking a sip of her lager. "What a morning."

"You sounded up against it when I called. Are you sure you can afford the time?"

"Oh no, don't worry about that. I just had to get out of there. I've finished what I had to do for that cow anyway."

Alison smiled. "Which 'cow' is that?"

"Sally *'butter wouldn't melt'* Dobson, that's who. The boss's PA. PA, phfaa! That's a laugh. Supposed to be his personal secretary, the only things she's ever filed are her nails. Everybody knows she's shagging him but boy, has she mastered one snooty, aloof expression." Gillian stopped her rant suddenly. "Oh, sorry, Alison, just ignore me. Like I say, it's one of those days."

"No, that's all right," she chuckled, "Don't hold back on my account, you just tell it like it is."

Gillian smiled briefly before looking serious. "Well never mind that, there's something else I want to talk to you about."

Alison leaned forward. "You've got my full attention."

"I'm worried," Gillian began as she related her fears about her sister, Susan. "It's just so out of character," she concluded, "I'm going to have to go round there after work to see what's wrong."

"I'm sure there's nothing wrong."

"But not to visit Dad? That was the clincher for me when I found that out this morning. She's never missed a Sunday."

"Well maybe she's out with a new boyfriend or something."

"No, not Susan."

"It's not so far fetched. She's just about to start a new life with her university course, so why not new friends too?"

"No, I'm telling you, if there was anything like that, Susan would have told me, she wouldn't just disappear."

"Listen, if she's had an accident or something, you'd have heard by now. There'll probably be some simple explanation."

Gillian grew agitated and gulped the rest of her drink. "No … no, there's definitely something not right, I can sense it." She began to shake slightly.

"Well there's no point getting all worked up about it." Alison took hold of her friend's hands in hers. "I'm sure everything's fine." It was no good, despite holding her gaze, she could see Gillian wasn't persuaded. "I'm talking cods aren't I?" she sighed.

Gillian's expression said it all, a slight laugh and then her eyes moistened.

"OK," Alison said, "This is what we'll do …"

5

Souter was intrigued. The call from Alison that afternoon only requested the pleasure of his company at an unfamiliar address just off Flanshaw Lane. There was no explanation as to why she needed him but, no doubt, she had good reason. He'd met Alison Hewitt earlier in the year whilst writing a major story. Despite the circumstances surrounding their first meeting, his relationship with Alison had blossomed.

He was sitting in his car, parked on the fringes of the sprawling council estate, listening to the travel reports, when Alison pulled up in her Saxo behind him. Glad he wasn't on the M1 or M25, he switched the radio off and got out to greet her.

"So what's the big mystery?" he asked, following Alison down the scruffy path to a door on the side of what appeared to be a large semi-detached property.

"There's someone I'd like you to meet." She gave the doorbell two sharp pushes.

Almost immediately, he could hear footsteps descending a staircase on the other side and realised the door would lead to a first floor flat, the building split into four units, two on the ground floor and two on the first.

A woman in her mid-thirties, with blonde hair cut short in a bob and wearing a black mid-length coat, opened the door. She appeared agitated, anxious.

"She's still not here," she blurted out.

"Gillian, this is Bob," Alison said.

Gillian gave him a quick glance before turning her attention back to her friend. "But this is six days now." She seemed close to tears.

Alison took hold of Gillian's hands and guided her inside. "Why don't we go upstairs and talk about this calmly?" She motioned for Souter to follow and close the door behind them.

The top of the stairs opened to a hallway with five doors leading off. Ahead, lay the sitting room, where Alison led Gillian.

The early evening sun was streaming in through the double window. It should have given a bright, cheerful atmosphere but the effect was diminished by the faded and dated wallpaper and the unfashionable furniture that filled the room. Although in good condition, it just seemed to have been lost in some sort of time warp for the past thirty years or so.

"Come and sit down." Alison gently eased her friend onto the green velour settee. "Now, I'd like you to tell Bob here everything you told me earlier while I make us all a drink." Alison then addressed Souter, "Gillian's younger sister, Susan, seems to have gone missing and she's very worried. I thought you might come up with some ideas to help." With that, she disappeared into the kitchen.

A feeling of alarm hit Souter at the news of another missing woman but he hoped his expression didn't show. He made his way slowly round the room, catching himself in the dark-framed mirror above the fireplace. He casually observed the collections of pottery and crystal in the cabinet against the wall behind the settee and scanned the titles on the bookshelves next to it, before settling into an armchair in front of the window. He looked across at Gillian, who was wiping her eyes with a tissue. "From what you said just now, Susan was last seen six days ago, is that right?"

"Well," Gillian said, "it was last Wednesday when we spoke on the phone. I haven't actually seen her since the Sunday before that."

"And when you spoke, everything seemed normal?"

"Yes. She was going into Leeds to have a look round the University Library. She's starting a degree course in September; Broadcast Journalism. She's really looking forward to it. She's done really well when you consider what she's had to cope with, poor kid."

"So how was she getting there? Bus, train or what?"

"She's got herself a little car, a Nissan Micra. She'd probably go in that, I mean, it's not outside." Gillian looked scared. "Oh, God! Supposing something's happened with the car, she's had an accident or something."

"Let's not get carried away, here," Souter said calmly, "I think you'd have heard about anything like that already. We'll take this one step at a time."

He got to his feet. A photograph in a plain frame on the sideboard opposite had caught his attention. He picked it up. Two people were laughing at the camera. A woman with dark hair and sunglasses had her arm around a plain-looking, fair-haired teenage girl.

"Is this Susan?"

"And Mum, yes. That was taken in Scarborough ten years ago on the last holiday they had together before …" Gillian became tearful again then quickly regained her composure. "Sorry, it's just … that was just before Mum was diagnosed with cancer. She died three months after that trip. She was only forty-seven. Susan was fourteen."

"I'm sorry. That must have been hard."

She nodded. "I tried to help out where I could. I'd been married for two years by then. We were living in Dewsbury and I was expecting our Robbie just after. Mum never got to see her grandson."

Souter remained standing, leaning against the wall. "So, just Susan and her dad live here now or …"

"Just Susan. Dad began to show signs of Alzheimer's within a few months of Mum's passing. He's a bit older than Mum. At first, we just thought it was the strain but … things didn't improve. I'd begun to notice he'd repeat himself, asking the same questions, that sort of thing. He'd forget things more and more. I know we're all forgetful as we get older but this was getting serious. Susan would tell me about coming home and finding the front door open; taps left turned on full pelt; saucepans burned dry. She'd sometimes have to search for him; he'd be out and forgotten where he was going.

"With all the strain, Susan's schoolwork suffered and she eventually left at sixteen with a few mediocre GCSEs. She went through a succession of brain-numbing jobs just so she could be around to look after him. I couldn't spend any more time with him than I already did. I mean looking after Robbie was a full-time job."

"I'm not here to make any judgements, Gillian, I'm just trying to build up a picture of Susan's life."

"I know, it's just … it was me who was reluctant to move Dad into a home. Every time I go over those events, I can hear people criticising – you could have done more; fancy leaving a sixteen-year-old girl to cope with that. Not that they were saying those things, it's just … I suppose the hard fact is I feel guilty for not having listened to Susan with all that was going on and spending more time helping her with Dad."

Alison came into the room with a tray of tea and picked up on Gillian's comments. "Come on, now," she said, placing the tray on the coffee table and sitting down next to her friend, "you couldn't have done more. No one has ever said anything remotely like that about you. You had Robbie and your Phil to look after. They were your priority. And anyway, you sorted out the home place for your dad." She handed out a mug to Gillian and one to Souter. "And look how Susan's turned out. She knuckled down, went back to college and got her A levels and she's off to university soon."

"But we don't know where she is," Gillian said, exhaustion evident in her voice.

Alison cast a worried glance to Souter.

"Look," he said, "I think it's time we call this in. From what you tell me, she's a sensible girl, you've not heard from her for nearly a week, no-one has seen her and her car's missing. Now I've got a very good friend in CID. I'll give him a call and see if he can help us." Souter began to dig out his mobile phone from the inside pocket of his jacket, then paused. "Has anyone checked the phone?"

"She's not answering. It's switched off," Gillian replied.

"Not her mobile, the house phone."

The women looked puzzled as Souter scanned the room before spotting the telephone on a small table by the side of the television. He got up and lifted the receiver. As he suspected, the tone indicated messages.

"Has anyone made any calls from here in the past few days?" he asked.

"I rang Phil when I got here this afternoon," Gillian answered.

Souter was disappointed. Now he had no easy way of checking the last call that Susan had made. He dialled 1571 anyway and listened to the three new messages that Gillian had left over the past few days then heard the one Susan had saved prior to setting off on her ill-fated journey. He listened twice, then saved it again before making the call to his life-long friend, Colin Strong.

6

Susan gradually became aware of blackness. Not the big darkness of unconsciousness but blackness due to a lack of light. She'd opened her eyes, she was sure of that, despite the fuzziness. The pain in her head shot through the rest of her system as she moved slightly. That competed directly with the searing pain from her left leg.

Over to her right, she thought she detected something. A movement; a shape, she couldn't be sure. "He... hello?" she hesitated. "Is there anyone there?" She winced as she tried to move. "Please, help me. Please," she said before the big darkness came again. In that big darkness, she was sure she could hear voices. Quiet, soft, young.

"Do you think she's okay," said one.

"I don't know," came the other. "She looks in a bad way."

Then shuffling, like bare feet on bare earth.

"She's bleeding from her head," the first voice said, closer now.

"And her leg looks nasty too."

Susan was in a daze. A conversation was playing out around her and she couldn't join in. But was it around her, or was it only in her head?

"Do you think she's come to take us home?" the first voice said. "It's been ages since anyone came here."

"Not since that ... that man."

"I don't want to talk about him!"

"I'm sorry, Mary, I didn't mean to upset you. But he hurt me too."

Mary? Who's Mary? Susan thought.

"Do you think anyone will still be looking for us, Jennifer?" Mary asked. "It's been a long time."

Jennifer? What's going on? She was confused. If only she could talk to them.

"Someone will come. Someone will find us," the other girl replied, without any real conviction.

"Perhaps that lady was looking for us before she fell."

"I don't know." Susan thought Jennifer was attempting to keep the desperation from her voice.

"Perhaps someone will come looking for her and find us," Mary said, brightly.

"Let's hope so."

There was silence for a while before soft sobbing noises began. Louder, they grew into a loud wail.

"Look, don't cry, Mary," she heard Jennifer say. "It'll be all right, I promise."

Through sobs Mary struggled to speak. "But you've been saying that for ages. I want to go home."

"I want to go home too." Jennifer said.

Susan was terrified but she made a huge effort to open her eyes once again. "So do I," she said.

She heard gasps.

"Please, so do I," she repeated.

Susan blinked and moved her left hand to her face. More pain from her right elbow stopped her using both. She rubbed her eyes; they felt gritty. After a few seconds, she thought she could make out shapes from the direction of the voices. Definitely two forms, one taller than the other but still indistinct. One came closer.

"Have you come to take us home?" the voice she recognised as Mary asked.

Susan was puzzled. The images were speaking to her. "I ... I didn't know you were here," she replied.

The taller shape moved forward to join the other. "So why *did* you come?"

"Well ... I ... I can't really remember," Susan managed to say. The shapes began to take form and she could distinguish two young girls. The taller, the one she took to be Jennifer, had long blonde hair falling down in ringlets over her white smock dress. She was bare footed. The other, Mary, was some six inches shorter with dark hair cut close to her head giving her face a boyish appearance. She was wearing school uniform, a white blouse under a grey pinafore dress. She also had nothing on her feet.

"Who are you?" Susan asked.

"I'm Jennifer and this is my friend Mary," the taller girl said.

"I'm Susan. I can't really see you; it's so dark in here. How old are you?"

"I'm ten," said Jennifer.

"And I'm eight," Mary jumped in. "How old are you?"

"I'm twenty-four," Susan responded. There was silence for a few seconds and she thought the images were fading. Finally, the taller girl asked her if she could move.

"I ... ow!" Susan cried out, trying to shift her position. "My head hurts and I think I've broken my leg."

"It looks painful."

"It is." Susan tried to relax. "It's Mary, isn't it?"

"Yes. My brother broke his arm once when he fell out of a tree," Mary gabbled on. "We had to take him to hospital and everything. He had a plaster on for six weeks. We all drew funny faces on it." She chuckled. "That was around Christmas time. I love Christmas."

"Me too," said Jennifer.

"We're all agreed then." Susan gasped as she tried to move.

"You need to get to hospital," Jennifer said seriously. "Does anyone know you're here? Will someone come for you?"

"I don't know, Jennifer. No one knew I was coming here. I didn't know I was coming here myself."

"What do you mean?"

"I'm beginning to remember now. I was following someone and they led me here."

"Why were you following somebody?"

"I ... well, I was on a case."

"A case?"

"Yes. I'm a journalist. Well, sort of. I'm going to university to study soon."

"Really?" Mary said.

"Yes." Susan paused and raised her hand to her head and felt the dampness in her hair. She rubbed her fingers together. "Well, I've really made a mess of things, landing down here," she said. "This feels like blood."

"It is," Jennifer said.

Susan took a deep breath. "Do you think you could fetch help?"

The girls were silent and again their images became fuzzy.

"Girls? Are you still there?"

"We're here," Jennifer confirmed.

"There's something wrong here isn't there? You wouldn't be here if you could get out would you?"

Again silence.

"What happened to you Jennifer?"

"I ... I don't think I can talk about it."

"Did something bad happen, Mary?"

"Sorry, got to go."

"Go? Go where? Jennifer? Mary? Don't go!"

The basement fell silent and the big darkness returned.

7
Tuesday

Eight o'clock in the morning and Strong's team were assembled in the CID room on the first floor of Wood Street police station. The cacophony of chatter subsided as Strong entered.

"Okay, ladies and gents," he said, "This is what we know: Susan Brown, twenty-four years old, five six, medium build." He placed a recent photograph of a mousy-haired woman on the display board and wrote her name and address below in felt-tip pen. "Last known contact with her sister, Gillian Ramsay, on Wednesday when they spoke on the phone. Susan, for the past four years, without fail, has visited her father in the Riverside Lodge Nursing Home every week." He paused for a few seconds. "Last Sunday, she didn't turn up. That was confirmed by the home manager."

"So, apart from not visiting her dad for the first time in years," Kelly Stainmore said, "she could just be pissed off with the same old routine. Maybe she had something better to do."

Strong shook his head.

"What makes you uneasy, guv?" Jim Ryan asked.

"Besides no sign of her in her flat for the past few days?"

"Boyfriend perhaps?" Stainmore suggested.

"None that we know of. But try this." Strong took a tape from his pocket, placed it in the cassette player on the desk in front of him and pressed the play button. The enigmatic message from Susan's phone began.

The team listened to the voice, the hesitancy then the excitement.

"This was left on Saturday afternoon," Strong told them. "I've got BT producing a proper recording and tracing the number. Luke, can you chase that up?"

Ormerod nodded.

"Next, her car is missing. It's a silver Nissan Micra." A photo of a typical model was pinned up. "This is the registration." More writing on the board. "So far there are no reports of any incidents involving this vehicle but we really need to find it. Top priority, John." Strong looked at Darby. "I've got this out to traffic and uniform so can you keep them focussed?"

"Guv," Darby acknowledged.

"Now we need to narrow down exactly when Susan went missing. Sam, Trevor, organise a couple of uniforms and get down there. See if the neighbours can throw any light on that. Probably last sighting of the car might give us the best idea."

Strong began to pace the room. "At the moment, Gillian was the last person we know who spoke to her. We don't even know if Susan heard that message on Saturday."

He stopped and looked round the room at the various members of the team. Some were writing notes, some looking at the briefing board, others just looking at him.

"Okay, I'm not saying there's any connection whatsoever, we don't take anything for granted but Jim, do you want to bring us up to speed with your Misper enquiry?"

Ryan approached the display board and stuck a photograph of a young blonde-haired woman onto it. "Helena Cryanovic," he said, writing her name below. "Twenty-three years old. Originally from Albania. Arrived here last November with her sister, Magda." He looked round at the assembled officers. "Initially reported missing by Magda on Friday when she failed to return home from visiting friends in Leeds. But, as you know, we couldn't make it official until twenty-four hours had passed."

"These 'friends'," Ormerod commented, "are they part of the Albanian community too?"

Before Ryan could answer, Sergeant Sidebotham entered the room, his eyes searching out the DCI.

"Sorry to interrupt, Colin," he said, "but I've just taken a call from an irate farmer out beyond Pontefract. He's complaining there's a car blocking the entrance to a field he wants to spray."

Groans emanated from the team.

"Go on, Bill," Strong said, "what's the punchline?"

A wry smile spread across the old sergeant's face. "I reckon it's that Nissan Micra you're all looking for. Traffic are on their way."

"Luke, Kelly, Can you get over there and check it out. You know the drill. I'll be along as soon as I can. Keep me informed."

Ormerod and Stainmore gathered their notes and hurriedly left the room.

Strong turned towards the display board, brows furrowed. "Jim, you thought she had a boyfriend?" he asked, bringing everyone's attention back to the missing Albanian woman.

"That's right, guv. Stefan Szymanski." Ryan stuck his photo on the board and wrote the name below. "Thirty-one. Originally from Zakopane near the Czech border. Came here in 1998." He turned to face the room. "Vice have him on their radar. Known to have a close association with this man, Stanislav Mirczack." Another photo, this time a brutal looking bald man in his mid-thirties, was stuck to the board.

"You went to see Szymanski yesterday, didn't you?" Strong asked.

"Malcolm and myself, that's right. He said he'd split up with Helena at the beginning of last week."

Strong's mobile burst into life. Taking it from his pocket, Ormerod's name lit up on the display. He turned away, holding up his hand in apology to Ryan. "Yes Luke." He listened for a few seconds then ended the call.

"Sorry Jim," Strong said, "Traffic have confirmed the car they found is Susan Brown's. I'm going down there now. You and Malcolm stick with your missing person. What's your next move?"

"We're trying to trace the friends she visited," Ryan said. "Magda said she always used buses so we'll see if there's CCTV from any she might have been on. Also see if anyone remembers her on Thursday night."

"All right, let's reconvene at one, unless something develops."

The scene of activity was a fifteen minute drive away. The forecast sunshine still hadn't broken through the morning cloud cover. Traffic's marked Granada was parked nose to nose with the Nissan, the two uniformed officers in conversation with Ormerod. Stainmore's pool car was at the back of Susan's. Behind, a tractor was tucked into the hedge, the large white barrel on the back and folded-up spraying arms evidence of the farmer's intentions.

Strong drew into the lane entrance about fifty yards before them. As he got out, Ormerod approached.

"It's definitely her car, guv," Ormerod said. "Locked up and no sign of her."

"Let's hear what he's got to say." Strong nodded in the direction of the farmer talking to Stainmore.

The man in charge of the tractor was in his mid-twenties dressed in wellington boots, short-sleeved tee shirt and a flat cap. Strong wondered if all farm labourers were born into a flat cap. The radio in the tractor's cab was announcing the nine o'clock news bulletin much to the interest of the black and white mongrel dog inside.

"So when can ah get on wi' me sprayin' then?" the farmer was asking Stainmore. "Ah've got three more fields to do today, you know."

"Mr er ..." Strong said, extending a hand to the young man.

"Clay. Simon Clay." He took Strong's hand in a gigantic paw.

"Simon, I'm Detective Chief Inspector Strong." He hesitated at his first official use of his title, albeit acting.

37

"You do surprise me." Clay responded. "In't thee a bit high-powered for just a bit of obstruction?"

Strong smiled, amused by the incongruous maturity and confidence of the young lad. "We've actually been looking for this vehicle and I happened to be in the area, that's all," he said.

"Ah'd 'ave moved it mesen," Simon offered in his broad Yorkshire accent, "but you lot might 'ave charged me wi' criminal damage or summat."

"Ah, you're probably right," Strong said. "Best leave these things to us. Now I don't suppose you can cast any light on how long this car has been here, can you?"

"Well, it wun't 'ere on Friday. Ah come past about nine on me way to the Black Horse."

"And this is a regular route you take?"

"Once or twice a week."

"Okay, thanks, Simon. I think it's best if you rearrange your schedule and carry on with the other fields you have to spray. We'll get a low loader down here to remove this but it may be this afternoon before that happens. In the meantime, can you give a quick statement to DC Ormerod here?"

Clay shrugged and set off with the detective towards the pool car.

"What do you think then, guv?" Stainmore asked.

"Something's not right, Kelly." He turned to look all round at the horizon. "What's up there?" He indicated the farm buildings at the top of the lane where he'd parked his Mondeo.

"Not too familiar with round here," Stainmore responded.

"Simon!" Strong shouted, as the farmer and Ormerod were about to sit in the car. "Simon, that's not your place is it?"

Clay chuckled. "No chance."

"Any ideas?"

"It's the old Collinson place. Old man Wilf died about ten year since. His lad, Stanley, weird sod, wanted nowt to do wi' it, so it were sold to the Ingleby Estates from

Thirsk way not long after. They farm the land. Buildings are rented off separately but the house were just left."

"Thanks," Strong said.

He scanned the surrounding countryside again then called for Stainmore to join him. "Let's have a look round."

They started up the farm track. The ground was dry and dusty but seemed to have been trafficked recently. All the way up they studied the hedgerow either side for any sign of disturbance or discarded items.

At the top of the rise the old farmyard opened out. To the left was a fairly new metal clad building with a window in the side. Below, an old upturned bucket was conveniently placed. Strong stood on it and peered inside. The building was empty.

Stainmore, meanwhile, wandered towards an older barn with padlocked timber doors. They circled the respective buildings, checking for any sign of forced entry. There was no evidence of any alternative ways in.

Meeting up again in the yard, Strong raised his eyebrows questioningly.

"Nothing," Stainmore said in response. "Just some old machinery and a tractor covered with a tarpaulin. Looks undisturbed for ages."

On the right hand side of the yard stood the old farmhouse, a two-storey Yorkstone building with interesting roof lines and tall chimneys. The windows had rotted, leaving the stone mullions and transoms and in the porch, the front door hung drunkenly on one hinge.

"Let's have a look in here," Strong said. Before they could, his mobile rang. Answering, he looked intently at Stainmore for a few seconds then, with the phone jammed between his ear and shoulder, flipped open his notebook. After making a few notes, he ended the call.

"Developments?" she asked standing by the farmhouse doorway.

"That was Luke. BT have identified the number that left the message. Registered to one Steven Chapman."

"Chapman?"

"Yes, pain in the arse little scrote from a few years back." Strong walked over and joined his sergeant. "Previous for taking without owners consent and other driving offences but I haven't heard of him for a few years now."

"Must be a reformed character."

"Or just more careful."

Strong moved to the porch entrance and peered inside. The floor creaked and he could feel it give slightly with his weight. He stopped and shouted inside. "Hello! Susan! Anyone there!"

All was quiet.

"So, Chapman?" Stainmore said, "You got an address?"

"Luke has. Let's go and have a word with our Mr Chapman. In the meantime, Kelly, get those two traffic officers to check the house out properly."

As they made their way back down the track, the sun finally broke through.

8

Susan woke, aware of a bright light shining on her face. She opened her eyes, blinked and turned her head sharply to one side, immediately regretting it. The dull thudding pain increased as though a bag of marbles was rolling around inside her skull. It took several seconds for her to focus on her surroundings. Shafts of sunlight streamed through the ragged gaps in the floor above. Dust floated through the beams of light. By contrast, dark cobwebs hung down from the joists. The floor on which she lay was compacted earth. Bits of floorboard, edges crumbling away to powder, lay all around.

She had a vague recollection of someone shouting her name. A man, definitely a man. But maybe she dreamt it. After all, she wasn't sure what was reality and what wasn't. But this was real. The pain was real. She had to do something.

A brick wall was about two feet behind her. She decided to try and pull herself towards it to lean against. Checking she could move her arms, she struggled to sit up. Her right elbow hurt but she didn't think there were any breaks, probably just heavy bruising. Her left leg was a different matter. A sharp pain from below the knee made her wince and cry out. Bending her right knee, she pushed herself backwards with her foot and hands. Her left heel dragged against the floor causing the pain to intensify with every movement but she persevered until she was sitting up against the old crumbling brickwork. She was sweating but she felt cold, so cold.

She looked at her watch. The second hand still moving, it showed nine forty-five. But what day? The watch had no date panel. How long had she been here? Phone. Her mobile. Fumbling in the pocket of her trousers, she pulled it free. She tried to switch it on but the battery was dead. Damn! She should have charged it but she had been in such a hurry to pursue Chapman. Should have done a lot of things before she set off on this foolhardy mission. Should have mentioned something to someone, at least left a note. She was about to call it in to the police when the van turned up. But then, who visits her flat? Only Gillian. Oh God, she'll be worried. How long *has* it been?

Staring at the mobile's lifeless display she began to sob. Eventually, she pulled herself together. In her mind she went over the events that had led to her situation; the phone message; her tracking down the creepy Steve Chapman; her surveillance culminating in the dash for cover into the old farmhouse. And, of course, the plunge through the floor. But that wasn't all. What about the two girls? Where were they now?

"Hello!" she called out. "Is anyone there? Jennifer? Mary? Can you hear me?" The only sounds were birdsong. And then the deep rumble of a train passing nearby.

But it couldn't have been. If there *were* any girls, they'd have gone for help. No, she must have been delirious. But her memory seemed so vivid. There again, she didn't actually see them. Not clearly. Although she did recall one had been wearing a white dress and the other a grey pinafore. If she had those images then surely they were real. So where were they now? It didn't make sense.

Another train vibrated the floor and she closed her eyes.

9

Strong and Stainmore drew a blank at Chapman's address. No one was home. As they returned to the car, Strong received a call from Souter.

"Hello, mate. Just wondering if there was any news on Susan."

"Early days yet. But we have found her car."

"Whereabouts?"

"Near a farm called Meadow Woods out on the back roads the other side of Pontefract."

"No sign of Susan, though?"

"Not at the moment. I'll let Gillian know soon as I have anything concrete." With that, he ended the call.

"What now, guv?" Stainmore asked, getting in to the passenger seat.

"Back to Wood Street I think. Do some digging on Chapman. Known associates. Also try National Insurance records; see if he's one of the great employed." Strong was about to start the engine. "And give Luke a call. See if they discovered anything in the farmhouse."

Driving through the mid-morning traffic as Stainmore spoke to Ormerod, his unease grew. He didn't like the way the part of the conversation he could hear was going.

When she finished, Stainmore rubbed her eyes. "Luke waited with Susan's car until a uniformed constable in a patrol vehicle from Pontefract turned up. Apparently, the traffic duo shot off under blue lights about five minutes after we left; accident on the M62, so they didn't get up there."

"Shit! So nobody's checked the farmhouse?"

"He told the uniform to stay with the Micra until the recovery truck appeared then made his way back to Wood Street."

"I'll take that as a no, then."

"He also said to remind you, you have a ten-thirty with the Chief Super before he reports for his meeting this afternoon."

"Bollocks," Strong said, under his breath.

"Promotion brings such a heady lifestyle, guv."

Strong just gave her a disdainful look. "When we get back to Wood Street," he said, "find Ormerod and if you've nothing better to do, get your arses back out there and check that farmhouse. Take some uniforms if you have to but get it checked."

The rest of the journey passed in an awkward silence.

* * *

Souter initiated a search on his computer for Meadow Woods Farm and came up with the details he wanted, including a map and postcode. Ten minutes later, he was slipping on to the M1 prior to picking up the M62 eastbound.

Any doubts he had about finding the location dissolved when he spotted the police patrol vehicle, its blue lights providing a lurid disco effect blending with the orange versions on the flatbed recovery vehicle parked alongside. He pulled his Escort onto the farm track.

As he got out, a young constable approached. "Excuse me, sir. Can I ask your business?"

Souter had to control himself from chuckling at the officious way the question was phrased. "Business? Oh, sorry, you've probably not been told but Detective Inspector, oh," he paused and smiled, "that should be Detective Chief Inspector Strong asked me to pop down and take a look around."

The officer produced a notebook. "Did he, sir. And your name is?"

"Souter. Robert Souter," he said, straightening himself to his full six foot two inches.

The policeman made a note. "Well if you'd just keep clear of the recovery vehicle operations, for your own safety, you understand."

"Sure, no problems." Souter turned away smiling.

He walked up the dusty track as Strong and Stainmore had done an hour before. At the top, he stopped and looked out over the surrounding countryside. Below, Susan's car was on the lorry, being driven away and the police vehicle was about to follow. Elsewhere, open fields rolled out. Unless the car was driven here and abandoned by a third party, this farmyard seemed the most logical place for Susan to have come.

He checked out the newer building, peering through the window. He could see nothing of interest.

Next the house. He pushed the door, testing it wouldn't fall off its one remaining hinge as he stepped past. The wooden floor boards groaned and he could feel the floor give slightly. After the bright sunshine outside, he paused, allowing his eyes time to adjust to the semi-darkness. The central section of the hallway flooring had given way so he kept close to the edge and began to make his way slowly round towards the open door of one of the front rooms. As he moved away from the front door, he allowed sunlight to stream down into the void beneath the floor. He hesitated. A shape could just be made out below. At first he thought it was some discarded rags but then he saw them for what they were; a pair of trouser-clad legs. Kneeling down to look further in, he saw the dust covered body propped up against the brick wall in the basement; the head slumped forward onto the chest.

"Shit," he said softly. "Susan? Susan?" he repeated louder each time.

A low moan came from the body below and the head moved slightly.

"Hang on, Susan. I'll get you out."

He looked round the hallway. There were doors to the right and left, a staircase dead ahead and another door in the opposite wall to the side of it. There had to be access to the basement and he reasoned the most logical point would be below the stairs. Gingerly, he made his way round the edge of the hallway towards the rear. His instincts were correct. An angled door was featured in the timber panelling to the side of the staircase. He slid the bolt and pulled on the handle. It resisted for two attempts then, reluctantly gave with a loud creak; obviously never used for years. Carefully, he tried the steps, one at a time, aware they could be weak. Fortunately, they were sound and he finally stood on the basement floor.

Susan mumbled incoherently as Souter reached her.

"Susan. Susan, can you hear me?" He took hold of her hand.

"I'm, mmm," she struggled.

"Okay, don't try and speak, I'll get ..." he hesitated, his hand touched the matted blood in her hair, "... help."

Pulling out his mobile, he checked the signal. Three bars, good. 999 for ambulance first then he tried Colin. Strong's mobile was switched off but he left a message anyway.

Susan's pulse was slow and erratic and her breathing was shallow. He hoped the ambulance would be quick.

"Come on, Susan," Souter said softly. "Stay with me." He took hold of her hand. "Just squeeze my hand if you can hear me."

He could feel her grip tighten slightly.

"You're doing well. The ambulance is on its way. We'll soon get you to hospital." She gently squeezed again in acknowledgement. "Your sister, Gillian, was worried about you. She'll be glad to know you're okay."

For the next ten minutes, he kept talking to her, kept making her respond. Finally, he could hear a siren in the distance and made his way up the basement staircase and out into the yard to make sure the ambulance crew would know where to come.

They were a good fifteen minutes attending to Susan below before they brought her out on a spinal board. The paramedic seemed concerned for her condition. Souter could hear him radio in and the conclusion reached was that they take her straight to the General Infirmary in Leeds.

* * *

Strong stormed into the CID room just after eleven and discovered Stainmore and Ormerod poring over paperwork.

"Have you two been here all morning?"

"Yes, guv," Stainmore replied.

"We've found out where ..."

Strong interrupted Ormerod. "What did I ask both of you to do? One thing. One bloody thing and you can't even be arsed to do it. You'd rather spend time fucking about with paperwork."

The pair looked shocked.

Trevor Newell was the only other detective present. Strong turned his attention to him. "Did you and Sam sort out some house to house by Susan Brown's flat?"

"Er, yes, guv," Newell replied nervously. "Sam's down there now with a couple of PCs."

"Right, at least there are still some detectives I can rely on. You come with me, forget those dud fivers you've been investigating. There's something far more important." He turned to face Stainmore and Ormerod. "Susan Brown has been found in the basement of Meadow Woods Farmhouse. And before you ask, she's in a bad way; broken leg and a head injury."

Strong turned and left the room with Newell in his wake, leaving Stainmore and Ormerod speechless.

* * *

Souter spotted Strong and Newell approaching the Accident and Emergency entrance and stepped outside to meet them.

"Thanks, Bob," Strong said.

"How come you never found her?"

47

Strong turned to Newell. "Trevor, I'll see you inside." He waited until the detective was out of earshot. "People let me down," he said, in a low voice.

Souter just gave a withering look.

"I know, I know." Strong held up his hands as if in submission. "The buck stops here. If it's any consolation, I feel like shit myself."

"I'm sure Gillian will be relieved."

"Never mind that," Strong retorted, "Don't you dare use me as an excuse for gaining entry to a scene under investigation again."

"Hold on, there was no police tape, only some wet behind the ears plod who asked me some stupid question then gave me some safety advice. Nothing about not being able to wander up to the farm. And don't forget, if I hadn't, Susan would still be there."

"You know what I'm saying."

For a second or two, there was an uneasy silence before Strong broke it. "So how is Susan?"

"She's about to have an operation on her leg. They need to set it and they're worried about the circulation. She must have been down there for three days. I heard mention of infection but I don't know for sure. Also her head injury was being checked out. She was never really conscious from when I found her to getting here. Once she's out of theatre, there'll be a bed in Intensive Care. I think they were talking about an induced coma to give her time to recover, but I couldn't be one hundred per cent on that."

"So no clue as to how she ended up out there?"

"Not really. Like I said, it would appear that she fell through the rotten floor of the farmhouse but why she was there ..." Souter shrugged.

"All right, thanks again. I'll just have a word with the medics." Strong began to walk towards the doors.

"Listen, Col, before you go, have you had any other missing women reported?"

Strong turned.

There was no mistaking the reaction.

"Why?"

"There is something isn't there?" Souter caught up with his friend again. "Is it to do with prostitutes?"

"Prostitutes? What makes you say that?"

"There is at least one other girl missing though isn't there?"

"Well, yes but we've no reason to suspect she was on the game."

"So you know nothing about a street girl going missing on Sunday night?"

Strong shook his head.

"Or any others in recent weeks?"

"No. The only Misper case we have is an Albanian woman who hasn't been seen since Thursday."

"All right, mate. I'll let you get on," Souter said and then, almost as an afterthought, "Listen, don't beat yourself up. At least Susan's safe."

10

"You two. My office please."

Stainmore and Ormerod dutifully followed the DCI.

Strong sat down at his desk. "Close the door will you."

Ormerod did as asked.

"Look, guv, we're really sorry about letting you down this morning but ..."

Strong interrupted Stainmore. "Sit down."

He waited until they were seated across the desk from him. "I'm sorry," he finally said. "I shouldn't have bawled you out like that, at least not in front of anyone else."

"We let you down, guv," Ormerod said. "You asked us to do something and we got distracted."

Strong leaned forward, arms on the desk. "You're right. You did let me down. We've got a young woman in hospital in a serious condition. I don't know if the doctors will be able to save her leg. Minutes might have been vital, never mind the two hours delay it took for someone else to find her."

Stainmore and Ormerod shifted uncomfortably in their seats.

Finally, he judged sufficient time had passed. "Look, you two and Jim Ryan are my best officers. If I can't rely on you, we're all in trouble." Again, Strong let the silence hang for a second or two. "Okay, I think you know how pissed off I am but let's just let it lie.

"Tell me, what have you got?"

"I spoke to the Ingleby Estates Office." Stainmore flipped open her notebook. "And according to their records, the new barn is rented on a six-month lease to Chris Baker."

"What do we have on him?"

"Nothing on record but his younger brother is Gary Baker. Lots of previous for driving while disqualified, no insurance, joy riding and a couple of burglary offences. Known associate of Stephen Chapman. They served two terms in Doncaster Young Offenders Institution together."

Strong stood up and stared out of the window. "Gary," he pondered. "The Gaz on the phone message?"

"That's what I was thinking, guv," Stainmore said.

"And," Ormerod added, "Chapman currently works at Westgate End Garage as a mechanic. So, they're either very understanding or he hasn't exactly given them a full c.v."

Strong turned and faced them. "Have we got an address for Chris Baker?"

"Yes, Outwood."

"Any idea what his business is? I mean, why would he want to rent an industrial shed?"

"Don't know. I'm still looking into that. Do you want me to bring Chapman in?"

"No, not yet, Luke. Let's find out a bit more about the fabulous Baker boys first. At the moment, we're not sure if there's been any offence committed." He turned to Stainmore. "Is this the only building Ingleby Estates rent out?"

"Yes. The house is unfit and the old barn just houses some obsolete machinery."

"Okay. We need to check out the new barn. Let's see if we can find out what it's being used for."

"Barnton Estate Agents in town are handling the rental. They're spare key holders, apparently. I'll get on to them."

"The pair of you get out there and keep me informed."

As they rose and made for the door, Strong thought of something else. "Before you disappear, have there been any reports of missing street girls in the last few weeks?"

Stainmore looked at Ormerod, puzzled. "No, not that I'm aware of."

Ormerod shook his head in agreement. "Why do you ask?"

"Oh, nothing. Just something somebody said to me today. I hadn't heard anything myself. There again I've been away for the past two weeks."

"No, sorry, guv."

After they left, Strong automatically reached into his inside jacket pocket. For years a packet of small cigars would normally be found there. Now it was empty. It had been two weeks, four days and, with a quick bit of mental arithmetic, sixteen hours since his last. Finally, after years of nagging, he'd bowed to the inevitable wishes of Laura. He felt he could do with one now, though. I love them, I could eat them, he used to say. He didn't feel any healthier. Not yet, but he didn't doubt the wisdom of giving up.

Shortly afterwards, he walked into the CID room, hands in his pockets. Jim Ryan was tapping away on his computer keyboard.

"Any news on Helena, Jim?"

"Nothing so far," Ryan said, eyes never leaving the screen. "Malcolm's at the bus station checking possible routes she might have taken; which drivers might have been on duty on Thursday night; seeing who's around who may well remember her."

Strong rested a buttock on the adjacent desk. "Well that's about all you can do at the moment I suppose. Do we know who she visited?"

"She had a female friend who shares a house in Harehills with some other girls. Magda said she was going there to see her."

"Presumably you've spoken to this friend?"

Ryan hit the send button with a flourish, leaned back and turned to face his boss. "Well, that's the thing, Magda has no address, only what Helena told her. We don't even have a street. No telephone number either."

"Does Helena have a mobile?"

"Switched off. That's one of the reasons Magda's fearful. Helena never switches it off. She's always careful to keep it charged up."

"Is there any possibility she might have been on the game?"

Ryan looked surprised. "Never really considered it, guv. I suppose it's a possibility but…"

"You think not?"

"Never say never but no, I don't think so."

Ryan got up out of his chair, walked over to the display board and studied the photograph of Helena. After a few seconds, he turned and faced Strong. "Am I missing something here?"

"Like what?"

"I overheard Kelly and Luke say you were asking about missing street girls."

Strong stood up and began to pace the room. "Have you?"

Ryan blew his cheeks out. "Not since that one from Holbeck. But that was about a year ago."

Strong said nothing.

"Why are you asking, guv?"

"Forget it, Jim. It's just something someone said to me in passing this morning that's all."

Ryan's desk phone chirruped for his attention. Returning to answer the call, he listened for a few seconds then told the caller he'd be down.

"Could be timely," he said. "Magda's downstairs and wants to see me. Want to come along?"

"Sure."

Ryan grabbed some notes in a file and led the way.

Dressed in tight fitting jeans, trainers and a white tee shirt, Magda Cryanovic was an attractive woman of around thirty. At five foot four inches tall, she was slim and her dark hair was tied back. She was sitting at the table in the interview room on the ground floor, nervously positioning and repositioning the polystyrene cup of coffee the desk sergeant had provided for her.

Ryan introduced Strong to her.

"DCI; you very important policeman?"

He smiled, amused by the assertion that a DCI may be perceived as important, but also intrigued by her accent. "Some may say that, but I don't see it that way."

Ryan and Strong sat down opposite her.

"I come to see if you have any news of Helena."

"Magda, "Ryan said, "we're struggling to locate Helena's friend. The one you told us she was visiting on Thursday evening. All we have is an area of Leeds. We're doing some checks but we haven't been able to find an exact address for this Lyudmyla."

"All I know is what I told you. It's all she tell me."

"So we don't even know if she actually intended to visit this friend."

Strong saw a worried look flash over Magda's face.

"You think she could not be telling me the truth? Her older sister?"

"We need to know if it's a possibility," Ryan said. "We need to know where to look."

Magda was silent, staring at her half-finished coffee.

"You think she may not have told you the complete truth, don't you Magda?"

She nodded. When she looked up, her eyes were moist. "She changed. Before, she was always honest."

"Before what?"

"Szymanski."

"Her boyfriend?"

"What he want her for?" Magda became agitated. "I no trust him. I see plenty like him back in Tirana. He bully. I try to get Helena away from him. I tell her what he like but she say he loves her."

"I thought they'd split up."

"Who say that?

"You don't think they had?"

"No. I no hear that."

Ryan looked across at Strong who had been happy to let him lead the conversation.

"Was he ever violent towards her?" Strong asked.

She shrugged.

"Magda," Ryan followed up, "Did he ever hit Helena?"

"I know what violent means," she responded indignantly, sitting back in her seat.

"So, did he?"

She took a moment to consider her answer. "She never say. But I think so."

"Why do you think so? Did she have any bruises?"

She leaned forward again, arms on the table and began to turn the coffee cup around. "Once," she said quietly. "I see marks here, on her arms, as though someone did this." She gripped her own upper arms. "But I never ask."

Ryan opened the file he had brought with him and pulled out a photograph.

"Have you ever seen this man before?"

Magda looked at the picture of Stanislav Mirczack and froze for a split second before turning away. "No," she said.

Strong leaned forward onto the table. "Magda, at the very least, we need you to be honest with us. If you want us to help you find Helena, you need to tell us everything you know."

She sat silently, staring down at the cup.

"You recognised that man, didn't you?"

"Yes," she said, almost inaudibly.

"Where from?"

"He came once. With Szymanski. He evil, I can tell."

"And did Helena go off with them?"

"No, he just come to our flat. He was there with Szymanski when I come home. They left within minutes. I think because I arrive. I ask Helena what they want but she say they just called to see her."

"But you think there was more to it than that?"

"She seem nervous, frightened. Even after they left. But she kept saying there was nothing wrong."

"And you only saw him the once?"

"Yes."

"When was that?"

"About three weeks ago."

"Is there anything else you can tell us about what Helena has been doing in the past few weeks? Any other strange visits or changes in her moods?"

"Only that she has been keeping things from me. I ask but she says there is nothing wrong. Everything fine. But I think she frightened of something."

"Szymanski and this man?"

Again she shrugged.

"Okay, Magda," Ryan said, "if you think of anything else, or if you remember any more about where Helena went on Thursday night, get hold of me immediately." He gave her his card.

Strong waited for Ryan to return from showing Magda out of the station. As they climbed the stairs on their way back to the CID room, Strong asked for Ryan's reactions to the meeting.

"We got a lot more out of her there. I'm not sure I like this Mirczack connection."

"Nor me, Jim," Strong affirmed. "Why don't you get on to Vice and see what they can tell you about his activities."

"Was thinking the same myself, guv."

11

At the hospital, Souter returned to his car, lit a cigarette and listened to the radio on low volume. For what it was worth, he believed that Strong knew nothing of any missing working girls. Chances were, they hadn't been reported. He pulled his wallet from his trouser pocket and removed the slip of newspaper on which Sammy had written her address and phone number. Since she came to see him yesterday, he'd given a lot of thought to the plight of young girls like her and her friend. Girls who had been drawn into that way of life. It had given him an idea for a possible future article on the subject. He stared at the number for a minute then dialled it. He was about to give up when a male voice answered.

"Hello, I'd like to speak to Sammy if she's around," he said.

"Sammy? Ain't no one here by that name."

Before he could speak again, the line went dead.

Just then, he saw Alison and Gillian walk into the A & E Department, passing Strong and his colleague as they left to walk back to their car. He gave it a minute then made his way back inside.

Alison and Gillian were sitting in the waiting area. As he approached, they both stood up.

"Thank you," Gillian said, kissing him lightly on the cheek. She sat back down.

Alison beamed at him. "Well done. God knows how long she would have been there if you hadn't found her. So much for the police, eh?"

"Just good luck, that's all. What news?"

"She's in theatre now. Doctors will tell us more as soon as they can."

"Look, I've got to get back. Give me a call if there's any news."

"Sure." Alison reached for his hand and squeezed it.

He leant forward and kissed her. "See you tonight."

By 'get back' however, Souter didn't mean the Yorkshire Post offices. He made his way out to the address Sammy had given him. Frequently consulting his A to Z, it took him about thirty minutes to find the street and another five to find the actual building. It was a run-down Victorian house that had been split into flats many years before. The windows looked as if they'd never been cleaned in decades and the paint for the most part had flaked off. Filthy net curtains hung in a desperate effort to give some privacy to the tenants, augmented by a variety of clothes pegs, drawing pins and other fixings.

As he approached the building, a youth of about eighteen with greasy hair and severe acne came out.

"Looking for Sammy," Souter said.

The youth looked him up and down. "Oh, yeah."

"She in?"

He smirked. "Room Three." With that, the obligatory hood came up and he was off.

Souter pushed the main door open. The first thing to hit his senses was the smell of stale food. That and dampness. The carpet in the hallway was threadbare and did its best to grip his shoes. It reminded him of a nightclub in Manchester he once visited many years ago. Junk mail was piled on a rickety table in one corner.

Room Three was at the back of the building behind the staircase. He knocked on the door. There was no answer. He knocked again. "Sammy?"

This time, he heard movement from inside.

"Sammy?" he repeated.

"Who is it?" she whispered.

"It's Bob … er … Robert Souter. You came to see me yesterday."

The sound of a chain being removed then a bolt being slid preceded the door's opening.

"Have you got any news? Come in. Come in."

Souter slipped inside and she closed the door behind him.

Dressed only in a man's shirt, she padded back to her bed, jumped in and pulled the covers up.

He averted his gaze. Stripped of the heavy make up of the previous day, she looked much younger and more vulnerable.

He took in the room. Two single beds were side by side next to the window. A bare 40 watt bulb in the ceiling provided a gloomy atmosphere. The curtains were closed, held together in the middle by a couple of safety pins. On the opposite side was a kitchen area with a sink and a small cooker. A few dishes were left out but he was pleasantly surprised how tidy it all seemed. Apart, that is, from the discarded items of clothing on the floor.

"I don't normally do this," she said, seriously.

"Do what?"

"Have strange men in the room." Her face broke into a broad grin.

Souter smiled. "I don't make a habit of it either."

"Going into girl's bedrooms?"

He looked at Sammy as if peering over a pair of reading glasses. "Have you eaten?"

"I'm okay."

"Come on, you need to have some breakfast, even though it's afternoon."

"Oh, all right, do us a coffee then. There's a jar in the left hand cupboard. It'll have to be black. The milk ran out last night."

Souter filled the kettle and found the jar. "There's a couple of slices of bread here. Fancy some toast?"

Sammy pulled the bedclothes over her head in exasperation. "Okay, if it'll shut you up."

Souter switched on the grill, set the bread on the grill pan and slid it underneath.

"So come on," she said, sitting back up in bed, "what about Maria?"

"There's nothing on Maria yet." The kettle boiled and he poured water into the mugs. "I've asked around about any other missing girls like you said but again, nothing."

"So what's the point of coming round here if you've got nothing to tell me? Unless, of course ..." She fluttered her eyelashes.

"Behave! The fact is, if I'm going to help you, I need your help."

"How?"

"Well the girls are hardly likely to talk to me in an open and frank manner, are they? Apart from police, journalists are not the most popular. And I think the answer has to lie with them."

Sammy grew serious. "I'm really worried now."

Souter pulled out the grill pan and turned the bread over. "I know you are."

"So what do you want me to do?"

"First off, I need to speak to Tracey."

"Might not be that easy."

"Why?"

"I don't exactly know where she lives for a start. For another, she works a number of patches."

"We've got to try." He held up a white paper bag. "Sugar?"

"Two."

"Don't suppose you've any butter?"

"Spreadable, in the fridge."

He buttered the two slices of toast, put them on a plate and handed it to her, along with her coffee. He sat on the empty bed, declining Sammy's invitation to sit on hers.

"Now get that down you and we'll get off and see if you can find her."

"Ooh, right away, Mr Souter, sir," she mocked.

"You can knock the 'Mr Souter' bit on the head. Call me Bob. Everybody else does."

She chuckled. "Okay, Bob. Tell me about yourself."

"Not a lot to tell, really."

"I'm not going anywhere."

"Not until you eat that."

"Okay, okay," she said, "but I want to know why you sometimes sound a bit Scottish."

"You detect that?"

"I'm quite good with accents."

"Well, I was born in Scotland," he began. "Lived there until I was six before I came down to Doncaster with my family. And I've just spent nearly four years in Glasgow before I joined the Post in January. So I suppose now and then I slip into the accent."

Sammy laughed. "I was right, then."

"Very good. Anyway, enough of me; what about you and Maria?"

She started on her second slice of toast and slurped her coffee. "We met in St. Benedict's children's home in Otley. Maria's from Manchester. Her mum died when she was ten and her dad began drinking not long after. She was thirteen when she arrived."

"What about you, though?"

"Never knew my dad. He pissed off before I was born. Mum did her best but she couldn't really cope." Sammy stared off into the middle distance. "Succession of blokes. All bastards, except one. Frank. I liked Frank. He was good to me." She smiled and looked across at Souter. Her expression hardened. "Not like the last shit, Roger. Roger by name and Roger by nature. Started getting into my bed when mum worked a shift in the pub. Bastard." Tears began to form and she struggled to keep control. "Fucking dirty bastard."

"Sammy, don't. It's too painful for you. I don't want to know. You don't have to tell me."

Through tears, she said, "But I do. You have to understand. I'm not a bad person just because I do what I have to do."

Souter got up and sat on the end of her bed. "Look, I said when we met yesterday, I'm not judging you. It doesn't matter what you do, you're a young woman, first and foremost."

"I know," she sobbed. "That's why I came to see you. I felt I could trust you."

"And I'll help you if I possibly can. Now," he said rising to his feet, "Get yourself dressed and meet me over the road. I'm in a red Escort."

Souter and Sammy's luck changed at the third venue they tried in locating Tracey. The quiet road flanked by abandoned industrial units awaiting redevelopment provided a perfect stage for the performers. There were about six girls parading the two hundred yards of pavement, eyeing up any passing vehicles.

"That looks like her up there, on the other side," Sammy said.

Before they could reach her a black BMW with heavily tinted windows coming in the opposite direction pulled up alongside the girl. As Souter passed by, he could feel the vibration of the bass line coming from the BMW's stereo.

"Who's that?" he asked.

"That's Winston's car."

"Her pimp?"

Sammy nodded. "Better than some."

"What about you?"

"What about me?"

Souter reversed the car into an entrance, ready to head back down the street. "You know what I'm asking."

Sammy turned her head away. "I have a friend."

They sat in silence for a few minutes, watching Tracey lean in through the BMW's passenger window. She wore knee length black boots, a denim skirt that only just covered the essentials and a low cut blue top. As she tried to move away and straighten up, an arm shot out, grabbed her and pulled her back. Souter tensed.

"Relax," Sammy said. "He's probably telling her she needs to do more business."

A minute later, the BMW drove away from the kerb. But only for fifty yards or so to stop next to a tall dark-haired girl.

Souter pulled back out into the road but not before having to give way to a grey Volkswagen Golf driven by a middle-aged man on his own. It drew alongside Tracey. Souter pulled up behind and Sammy shouted from the window. Tracey was startled. The Golf driver, nervous to begin with, shot off.

"Tracey, we need to talk," Sammy said.

The girl strutted up to the car. "Fucking hell, Sam, you've just lost me a punter. Winston'll be well pissed off."

"Get in will you and stop moaning. My friend here will compensate you."

"Here, you're not in for a threesome are you?"

"Piss off! Just get in."

Tracey opened the door and got into the back seat behind Sammy. "Just fucking drive, will you," she said. "I'll show you where to go."

Five minutes later, they were parked at the rear of an old warehouse building. The detritus on the ground evidence that this was a regular venue.

"This is Bob," Sammy said. "A friend of mine. He's helping me find Maria."

"She still not showed up yet?"

"No."

Souter turned round. "Can you tell me the last time you saw her?"

Tracey shifted in her seat, revealing more than he wanted to see. She blew a bubble of gum and let it crack as she considered her answer. "Sunday. About a quarter to eleven. You'd gone off with that Jerry bloke," she said to Sammy. "Some tosser in a white van pulled up and she got in."

"Did she get straight in or did they talk first? I mean did you get the impression she knew him from a previous occasion?"

"Don't know. I think there was the usual 'want business?' and then she got in."

"Do you remember what kind of van?"

"I dunno, just a white van."

"Big, small, medium?"

"Smallish, like an Escort van."

"And was there anything unusual about it? Any name on the side, different coloured doors, that sort of thing?"

She thought for a moment. "No, I don't think there was any name. But the passenger door was a bit rusty along the bottom."

"That's good, Tracey. It's something, at least."

"What about my money?"

Souter looked at Sammy.

"She's losing business, Bob."

"How much?"

"Fifty," Tracey said.

"Piss off," Sammy responded, "Give her twenty for a blow job."

Souter moved his lips to say something but never quite managed it.

"But my memory might not be what it should," Tracey said.

Souter brought out his wallet and retrieved some notes. "Here. Here's thirty. Now what can you tell me about the man?"

She snatched the money and it disappeared into her small handbag in a flash.

"Only got a quick look." She blew another bubble. This time it cracked back and stuck to her lips. "Fuck." She pulled bits off and put them back into her mouth. "He was quite young, maybe in his twenties with a shaved head. That's all I noticed. It was dark."

"You don't think you've seen him before?"

"Don't think so."

Souter turned to Sammy, checking there was nothing else she wanted to ask, then back to Tracey. "Have you any idea what might have happened to Maria?"

"No idea. Maybe she went down to London. Christ, I don't know. She was your mate, Sam."

"One last thing," he said, "Have you heard of any other girls going missing?"

"Girls get in and out of this game all the time."

"I'd heard there had been a couple go missing in the last few weeks," Sammy joined in.

"Not heard nothing like that."

Souter started the engine. "Thanks for your time."

They drove back and dropped Tracey off where they had picked her up. There was no sign of the BMW or the tall dark haired girl.

"You take care," he said as she got out.

"Whatever."

Souter felt an air of depression as he drove back to Sammy's place. Her road seemed more run down than he'd noticed earlier. Several young mothers were pushing children in scruffy pushchairs, some dragging a reluctant toddler along as well, and all with a mobile phone clamped to their ear.

Sammy made him pull over about a hundred yards from her building.

"I'll walk from here," she said.

"Is my presence a problem for you?"

She paused with her hand on the door handle. "It's just better for me. Thanks for coming round. I'm not sure we're any further forward. Tracey wasn't much help, was she?"

"At least it confirmed what she'd told you earlier – and we now know the white van we're looking for has a rusty passenger door."

"Needle in a haystack, though."

Sammy got out and Souter watched her walk down the road. After a few minutes, she passed two hoodies. One turned to look at her then said something to his mate. They both laughed and Souter tensed once more.

He put the car in gear and slowly set off, passing Sammy about twenty yards from her flat. With a quick glance towards her, he accelerated down the street. The uneasy feeling of hostile eyes on him made him shudder.

12

Four o'clock and Strong was back out at Meadow Woods Farm. The place was buzzing with Scenes of Crime officers in white suits. Stainmore and Ormerod met him in the yard.

"We got the keys from the agents and had a quick look round," Stainmore told him.

"And?"

"A variety of tools, welding equipment and car paints," Ormerod said.

"So, a little car repair business?"

"Maybe, but there's all the materials necessary for producing number plates including a selection of numbers and letters as well."

"Hardly grounds for all this activity."

"It's more what isn't here that struck me."

"And then, of course, there was this," Stainmore said, before Ormerod could add any more. She held up a plastic evidence bag. "In a rubbish bin, discarded items we think came from the Subaru Sports that was nicked from an address in Wooley just over two weeks ago."

"How have you tied that in?"

"When the owner reported the theft, he gave us some fairly detailed information about what was in the vehicle. For instance, he told me that he was virtually addicted to Werther's Originals. Voila, dozens of Werther's sweet wrappers."

"Hardly conclusive. The guys who work here might be big fans."

"He also said there would be three car parking receipts from the multi-storey in town, including the dates and rough times."

"Getting better," Strong said.

"Then the clincher, a parking fine made out in the vehicle's registration number, which he said he'd collected the day before it was nicked, and would be in the glove box."

"Now we're getting somewhere." Strong had a satisfied grin on his face. "At the very least, it looks like the car was cleaned internally here."

"I assume we pull in Chris Baker, guv?" Ormerod asked.

"Oh, yes. But let's have his brother and Chapman in as well. And keep them separate, don't let them see one another. BT confirmed a call from Susan's land line to Chapman on Saturday afternoon. So, for me, that confirms she heard that message and somehow worked out who had left it."

As Stainmore made a call, Strong strolled over to the farm house. He turned at the front door and studied the layout of the yard.

Ormerod joined him. "You think Susan Brown and this little operation might be connected?"

"Not sure yet, Luke. I don't think she was involved with them. But I don't believe in coincidences either. I just hope they weren't responsible in some way for what happened to Susan."

Strong carefully made his way past the front door and stood to one side on a firm piece of flooring. Kneeling down on his haunches, he looked into the gaping hole Susan had made when she'd tumbled through. If only he'd come inside this morning, Susan might not be in such a bad way. He stood up and shuffled back out into the open air.

"She must have made the connection between Chapman's message and this location, guv," Ormerod said when his boss rejoined him.

"Let's not take anything for granted, Luke. It's a theory, but I'd like to hear what the little scrotes have to say first."

* * *

Chris Baker sat at the table in Interview Room 2. About thirty years of age, he was dressed in a suit and shirt but no tie. He was surprised when Newell and Kirkland had turned up at his house just before six but he'd agreed to come to the station with them voluntarily.

Strong and Stainmore were conducting the questioning, Strong happy for Stainmore to take the lead.

"As I said earlier, Mr Baker, you're not under arrest," she said. "You're just here to answer a few questions, help us with our enquiries. You're free to leave at any time."

"So what do you want to know?" Baker responded.

"Can you tell us what line of business you're in?"

"Insurance. I work at the call centre for Olympia. Why?"

Strong made notes as Stainmore continued with her questions. "I understand you rent a small industrial building out at Meadow Woods Farm, the other side of Pontefract?"

"Well … it's to help my brother out."

"Your brother?"

"Yeah, Gary. You lot know all about Gary, seeing as you put him away enough times. I just thought I'd give him a helping hand."

"In what way?"

"He likes tinkering with cars. With his record, he struggles to get a job, so I thought he would appreciate somewhere to do a bit of maintenance work."

"I see. So he's running a small business from there?"

Baker leaned forward, arms on the table. "Look, I told him he'd have to get all the proper paperwork sorted out; insurance, tax, that sort of thing. Now I don't know if he's …"

"Mr Baker," Strong interrupted, "we're not the Inland Revenue. We're not here to look into whether or not he's registered for tax or anything like that. We're just trying to establish what activities were being conducted there."

"Activities? What do you mean activities? Look, if he was up to something dodgy, it was nothing to do with me."

Stainmore took up the questioning again. "When did you last visit Meadow Woods Farm?"

"I've only been there once. When we went to look at it. See if it was suitable."

"Suitable for a vehicle repair workshop?"

"Yes. Look, what's going on here?"

"Simply routine enquiries. So, let me get this straight, you rented the building for your brother to carry out car repairs and you only ever visited the premises once."

"That's right, yes."

"Was the business successful?"

"I don't really know."

"Well, did Gary pay you rent for the property?"

"No. Like I said ..."

"Mr Baker, we know how much the rental agreement is. It might not be a great deal but could you afford it on your salary from the call centre, along with your other outgoings? I mean, you do have a mortgage, don't you?"

"Well, yes. Okay, he did pay me a good bit towards it. I just didn't want to get Gary into trouble, that's all."

"But if it's a successful business and it's making money, how would that get Gary into trouble exactly?"

Baker shrugged.

"Unless, of course, it wasn't successful, not in the accepted sense."

Baker became agitated. "He told me he was doing up cars, that's all I know."

"Okay, Mr Baker, thanks for your help." Strong stood up. "If you don't mind, DS Stainmore here will just take a formal statement before you leave. If we need to talk to you again, we'll be in touch." He paused at the door. "Oh, one last thing ... Gary, has he got a nickname?"

"Nickname?" Baker looked puzzled. "Well his mates call him Gaz."

"Thank you Mr Baker, you've been most helpful."

13

With mail collected from the box downstairs clenched between his teeth, Souter unlocked the door to his flat and struggled inside. He was carrying his briefcase and a fish and chip supper he'd bought on the way home. Two months ago, he moved in to this new one-bed apartment near Wakefield's Westgate station. Alison was a regular visitor but she still based herself in her cosy stone-built terraced house in Ossett. It was still early days in their blossoming relationship and the arrangement suited them both. Souter was as happy as he had been in a long time.

Dropping the briefcase and the post in the lounge, he dived into the kitchen, grabbed a plate, knife and fork, brown sauce from the cupboard and was straight into his food. He'd been looking forward to this since the idea popped into his head around four o'clock. Two mouthfuls in, his mobile rang. It was Alison.

"Hi, gorgeous," he said.

"Not interrupting, am I?"

"No, of course not." Souter stood up, phone wedged between ear and shoulder. "I'm just in."

"I've had Gillian round for the past hour."

"So what's the latest on Susan?" He switched the oven on and put his plate inside as he listened to Alison's response.

"She's obviously worried but the doctor told her Susan is as well as can be expected. They've operated on her leg to set it and there are a few complications they're worried about. Something called compartment syndrome, obviously infection and the chance of a deep vein thrombosis. She's still unconscious but we hope to know more in the morning."

"I knew DVT was a risk, infection too, but I'm not sure what compartment syndrome is. Hopefully, it'll all be academic in a couple of days."

"It's something that causes muscle damage." Alison sighed down the phone. *"But we can only wait. Gillian's just left to go back to the hospital."*

"Let me know if there's any news."

"What I'm wondering is," Alison said, *"what was Susan doing out at that remote spot anyway?"*

"I've a feeling it's all to do with that answer message."

"The one you didn't let us hear."

It was Souter's turn to sigh. "I was only trying to protect Gillian. I didn't want to worry or upset her any more than she already was. It was obviously a miscall. Whoever it was, left it for someone else. I wouldn't mind betting that Susan, pumped full of enthusiasm for this journalism course, thought there might be a good story in it. How she connected that with Meadow Woods Farm, I don't know. But I'll bet Colin does."

"I just hope she wasn't attacked by anyone."

"It didn't look that way. From what I saw, it just looked like an accident. She fell through the rotting floor." He adjusted the temperature on the oven. "Apart from hospital visits, how was your day?"

Alison lightened up. *"Just the usual boring stuff. What about you?"*

"Same here. I did spend most of the afternoon with a prostitute, though."

"You what!"

Souter laughed. "Knew that would get a reaction. No, seriously, this young girl came to see me yesterday about her missing friend." He proceeded to tell Alison about his concerns for Maria before relating the conversation with Tracey.

"It's a murky world," Alison said.

"I know, I've seen my fair share." He switched the kettle on and put a tea bag in a mug. "Anyway, are you coming down tonight or do you want me to come up and see you?"

"I know what you're after Mr Souter, but you'll have to wait," she chuckled.

"You're not turning me down are you?"

"I'm up early tomorrow. I've got to be in Manchester for eight-thirty. One of those waste of time courses we've got to attend."

"I feel rejected."

"Don't worry, big boy, I'll see you tomorrow night. I reckon I'll need some love and attention after Manchester."

The kettle boiled and the conversation drew to a close.

14

In the CID room, Strong and Stainmore were enjoying a coffee when Ormerod and Darby came in. They had been interviewing Gary Baker.

"How did you get on?" Strong enquired.

Ormerod held a video tape in his hand. "Action replay, if you want, guv."

"Let's see it, then."

Ormerod placed the cassette in the video machine, pressed 'play' and sat down.

The tape began with the usual formal introductions of those present, date and time. Baker, with a buzzed head, was wearing a white tee shirt and jogging bottoms. The duty solicitor was seated beside him.

> "So, Gary ... or is it Gaz?" Ormerod began.
>
> He smirked. "It's Gaz to my friends."
>
> "Okay, Gary, let's just start by telling me your connection with Meadow Woods Farm?"
>
> He hunched forward in his seat, nervously playing with his hands. "I do a bit of car repairs and maintenance up there, that's all."
>
> "On your own or ...?"
>
> "Me and Steve."
>
> "That would be Steve Chapman."
>
> "That's right."
>
> "I thought he'd already got a job?"
>
> He leaned back and began to nibble the thumbnail of his left hand. "Well, yeah. He helps me out on an evening, sometimes weekends."
>
> "So it's not a full-time job."
>
> "I'm still building it up."

"And how long have you been working there?"

"About two months."

"What sort of work is it you do?"

"Bit of servicing, small repairs, that sort of thing. Nothing too complicated."

"You got much on at the moment?"

Again, more nail nibbling. "Er ... no, not right this minute"

"That would explain it then," Ormerod said, leaning back in his seat.

"What?"

"Why we didn't see any cars there. I mean, normally you'd expect to see two or three vehicles around the place. Maybe one inside you were working on."

"Well, yeah, things are a bit slow just now."

Ormerod leaned forward. "So what was your last job?"

"What?"

"You know, what was the last job you carried out?"

He paused, looked down in his lap and studied his hands. "Well, I ... er, we serviced my van."

"But that's your own. You didn't make any money out of that."

He perked up again. "Then there was Chris's car."

"Chris? Would that be your brother, Chris?"

Baker slumped in his chair. "That's right."

"But he's renting the place for you."

He stared at Ormerod. "But ... how'd you know ..." Looking away, his voice dropped. "Well, yeah, but it's still a job."

"So how are you making money, then?"

"We do a bit. It's not good but we get by."

Ormerod leaned back in the seat and chuckled. After a few seconds, he continued, "Ever do any work on more upmarket cars?"

"No. We're not equipped."

"Nothing like Mercedes, Range Rover …?"

"Out of my league."

"Or say, a Subaru Sports?"

Baker paused. "Nah."

"Funny that, Gary, because we've found evidence that one has been there within the past two weeks."

"Don't know nothin' about that."

"But there's only you and Steve work there, you told us."

"Well … yeah."

"So if it wasn't you then Steve must have dealt with it."

"Suppose."

"You don't seem too concerned by that." Ormerod turned to Darby. "Don't know about you, John, but I'd be a bit pissed off if my so-called mate was involved in something dodgy on my premises." He turned back to the suspect. "Especially if I'd got a record like yours, Gary."

Baker merely shrugged.

"You know what I think? I think you knew fine what was going on. I think the pair of you have been lifting cars and moving them on."

Baker seemed to relax. "Is that all this is about?"

Ormerod paused the tape. "That response surprised me, guv," he said.

"Yes, it was a bit of a change of attitude. What he's said makes me think we're missing something. Play it on."

Ormerod released the pause.

"Why? What else do you want to tell us about?" Ormerod asked.

"Nothing. Nothing." His hand went to his mouth again, and nails were nervously chewed.

"Okay, Gary. I'm going to hold you for the time being while we continue our enquiries. If you think of anything else you want to tell us, I think it would be in your best interests."

"But ..." Baker looked pleadingly at the solicitor. "They can't keep me in, can they?"

"They've got twenty-four hours, Mr Baker. After that they must charge or release you," the solicitor informed him.

"Unless, of course we successfully apply for an extension from a JP," Ormerod added.

"Shit." Baker muttered.

Ormerod stopped the tape. "Thought we'd let him stew overnight, guv. What about his brother?"

"No reason to detain him at the moment, so I let him go home. Wouldn't mind betting he'll be back once he knows Gary's staying for B & B."

Carrying an audio cassette player, Strong and Stainmore entered Interview Room 3 and sat down opposite Steve Chapman and yet another duty solicitor.

"Mr Chapman," Strong said, "Sorry to keep you waiting."

The suspect grunted.

Strong then went through the required procedures for taped interviews before questioning Chapman about his involvement with Gary Baker and the vehicle maintenance business they allegedly ran at Meadow Woods Farm. The answers were remarkably similar to those extracted from Baker earlier.

"So, it would be fair to say that the business isn't doing too well? You haven't actually got a lot of work on?" Strong concluded.

"Well not really," Chapman replied. "I've got my day job. I mean, I was only helping Gary out evenings and weekends. But, you're right, Gary hasn't got a lot of business drive."

"So you wouldn't deal with any work on higher end vehicles then? Mercedes, Range Rovers, say?"

Chapman's left leg began nervously bouncing on the ball of his foot. "No. You'd need computers and such. Specialised equipment. We can't afford it."

"No Subaru Sports or anything like that?"

Chapman hesitated. "Course not."

Strong bent down and lifted the cassette player onto the table. "I'd like you to listen to something, Steve. You don't mind me calling you Steve, do you?"

Chapman looked at the solicitor, puzzled.

"Chief Inspector, does this have any relevance to the accusations against my client?" the solicitor asked.

"Actually," Strong responded, "we haven't made any accusations yet. But I think this will be of interest to your client."

The solicitor raised his eyebrows.

Strong ignored the interruption and pressed the 'play' button. The answer message left on Susan Brown's phone filled the room. There was no mistaking Chapman's reaction. He was shocked that his words were being replayed here and now.

"That is you, isn't it?" Strong asked when it had finished.

"Well ... I er ... Gary gave you that?"

Strong smiled and waited a few seconds. "Actually, no."

"So ... but where ... I don't get it."

"Do you know a Susan Brown, Steve?"

Chapman appeared totally bemused now. "Susan Brown?" He looked at his solicitor. "Never heard of her."

"Remember I mentioned a Subaru Sports? Would it surprise you to know we found evidence of one having been at the building you and Gary Baker were using at Meadow Woods Farm?"

"Now look here, I told you I only helped Gary out occasionally, evenings and weekends. If there was anything dodgy with a Subaru, it must have been him."

"Who said there was anything dodgy about it?"

"Well, I assumed …"

"And not surprisingly," Strong interrupted, "that's exactly what Gary said. If there was anything dodgy, it would be down to you."

"The bast…" Chapman fell silent.

"And you maintain you don't know a Susan Brown?"

Another puzzled look. "I've told you, I've never heard of Susan Brown. Who is she?"

"But a Subaru Sports, that's a different matter."

"But … what? Look, I don't know anything about Susan Brown or a Subaru Sports car."

"Okay, for the time being, pending further enquiries, we propose to hold you in custody, Mr Chapman."

"But …"

"That's all for now." Strong rose from his seat and left the interview room.

15
Wednesday

"He wants to talk, guv." Ormerod said, as he and Strong made their way along the first floor corridor to the CID room.

"Which one?"

"Gary Baker." He held out a polystyrene cup of indeterminate liquid. "Want a coffee?"

Strong screwed his face up. "No thanks, Luke. You sure that doesn't come with a health warning?"

Ormerod smiled. "Interview Room 2, if you want to join us."

"I'll catch you up in a bit." Strong carried on to his office, and was reviewing his messages when he received a phone call to tell him Susan Brown had regained consciousness. He checked his watch, decided Ormerod and Stainmore could comfortably handle Baker and set off for the hospital to speak to Susan.

Two hours later he left Leeds General Infirmary. Susan was still sedated but she'd managed to confirm most of what he already knew. When he got to his car, he called Ormerod for an update.

"Baker's admitted he stole high value vehicles, changed their identities and moved them on," Ormerod told him.

"You haven't charged him yet, though?"

"Was about to."

"Well, hold fire until I get back. There's a few things we need to clarify."

Just after noon, Strong and Ormerod were seated opposite Gary Baker conducting the third interview. Accompanied by his solicitor, Baker appeared nervous.

"So just to be clear, Gary," Strong said, "you're admitting to the theft of four vehicles as detailed by Detective Constable Ormerod earlier."

"Yes," Baker almost whispered.

"That's fine, as far as it goes, but I need a few more details." Strong sat back in his chair. "For instance, where have the cars ended up?"

"No comment."

"Come on. Other people are involved."

"No comment."

"Steve Chapman must be involved."

"No comment."

A knock on the door and Stainmore appeared. "Guv, can I have a word."

Outside in the corridor, she told him that Simon Clay, the young farmer who'd found Susan Brown's car, had called back to report interesting recent activity at the farm. On a number of occasions over the past few weeks, he'd spotted a container lorry run by a local contractor, Dave Pratt. Normally, the place was deserted. It was only the recent police interest that made him think it might be significant.

"Could be how the cars are moved on, guv," Stainmore said. "I'm going to check it out now."

Strong returned to the interview room and sat down. "Who are you protecting, Gary?" he asked.

"No comment."

"I hope you're not going to do that for the rest of the interview. It's really stupid, you know."

Baker shrugged.

"Do you know a Dave Pratt?"

"Never heard of him." But his face told a different story.

"Where were you on Saturday evening?"

"You know where I was."

"Were you at the barn at Meadow Woods Farm?"

"Yes."

"Alone?"

"No. I'd picked up Steve."

"Did anyone else turn up?"

"No."

"So no other vehicle came up into the yard that evening?"

Baker was beginning to shake and bite his nails. "No."

"You didn't see a dark coloured Mercedes drive up the track?"

"N .. no. There wasn't anyone else."

"Okay, Gary. Let's move on. Why were you and Steve at the barn on Saturday night?"

"We went to look at the Merc."

"That would be the white Mercedes Sports Coupe we spoke of earlier."

Baker nodded.

"For the benefit of the tape, please."

"Yes."

"And you'd stolen the car the day before from an address in the Newmiller Dam area."

Baker hesitated. "That's right."

Strong leaned back, looked across at Ormerod and smiled.

"You know what, DC Ormerod, Gary here is just giving us a whole load of bollocks."

Ormerod smiled at his boss. "And what makes you say that, guv?"

Strong turned back to Baker. "I'll give you one last chance to tell us the truth, Gary."

Baker leaned forward. "Look, I nicked them and took them up to the barn. I only asked Steve to check them over after I'd swopped plates and they were ready to be collected. Steve knew nothing about this."

"That's crap and you know it. Steve Chapman nicked the cars, you changed identities and the pair of you shipped them on."

"No, it was all down to me."

"So how come you hadn't a clue where the Merc was stolen? It was nowhere near Newmiller Dam."

"I got confused, that's all."

"So where did you lift it?"
"No comment."
Strong turned to Ormerod. "Charge him, Luke."

16

Souter walked up from The Post's offices on Wellington Street to Leeds General and passed through the main doors just after two o'clock. Earlier that morning, Alison had called to tell him Susan had regained consciousness. Susan wanted him to visit her so she could thank him personally for finding her. He also suspected Susan wanted to meet him because he was a journalist.

He made his way to ITU and reported to the nurse station. One of them went off and came back with Gillian.

"It's okay," she said to the nurse, "Susan wants to see Mr Souter."

"Only ten minutes, though. We don't want to tire her."

"Thanks for coming," Gillian said as they made their way along the corridor. "I'm sure it'll cheer her up."

At the door she paused. "If you don't mind, I'm just going to nip down for a cup of tea. I've been here since this morning. Is that okay?"

"Sure, we'll be fine."

Susan, head and right elbow bandaged, seemed asleep when he entered. There was a drip up but Souter was pleased to note she didn't appear to be connected to the array of machines behind her bed. A good sign, he thought.

She opened her eyes as the door closed and a weak smile appeared on her face.

"Hello," she said.

"Well you look a lot better than when I last saw you."

"And that's thanks to you."

"I think the paramedics and the doctors had far more to do with it."

"Seriously, though. Thank you." Susan raised her left hand and Souter took hold of it.

"Glad I could be of service," he said.

"How did you know where to find me?"

"I thought you'd still be in ITU so I …"

"No, not here," she giggled, "at that house."

Souter laughed. "Sorry, wasn't on the ball. I have a good friend who's a policeman. He told me where they'd found your car and I decided to have a look round. That deserted farmyard was about the only logical place you could have gone. The alternatives didn't bear thinking about." Souter released her hand and sat in the chair by the side of her bed. "You went there after that answer message didn't you?"

Susan gave a small nod.

"What was that all about?"

She motioned for a glass of water on the bedside unit. Souter helped her take a drink then she began the tale of calling Chapman back and following him and his friend to Meadow Woods Farm.

"So what was in the barn?" he asked when she finished.

"A fancy white Merc sports car."

"Stolen, I assume."

"Don't know."

"That would certainly tie in with the message," Souter considered.

"At first it sounded like … well … this probably sounds daft."

"No, go on, Susan."

"Well, I just had this notion that he was talking about a woman, or a girl … and I thought … I mean, it could have been …"

"You thought Chapman was talking about an abduction?"

"Yes."

"I can see how you might have thought that. It's not so far fetched."

Susan went quiet, as if thinking about what to say next.

"Is there something else?" Souter asked.

"When you found me ..."

"Yes."

"This is going to sound stupid."

"Come on, Susan, if there's something bothering you, just say."

She made a great effort to raise herself up on her good elbow and lean closer. "Well, when you found me, was there anybody else there?"

Souter was puzzled. "How do you mean – anybody else? Where?"

"In the basement."

"No, why?"

"It's just ... when I was there ... on two occasions there were ... no it couldn't be. I was probably just delirious." She lay back down on her pillows.

"Now you've got my interest, don't just leave it there. What?"

"There were two little girls. And that can't be."

Souter leaned forward. "When you say two little girls, what do you mean?"

"Ten and eight."

"That sounds pretty accurate"

"That's because they told me how old they were"

"You spoke to them?"

"See, I told you it was going to sound stupid."

"No. It doesn't. I'm curious now."

Susan then related the details of her encounters with Jennifer and Mary.

Souter's eyes widened.

"And I never saw them again," she concluded.

Souter was about to ask a question when Gillian returned.

"Hi. Everything okay?" she asked.

"Susan was just telling me about her time in the basement."

Before the conversation could continue, a staff nurse entered.

"I'm sorry," the nurse said, "but Susan needs to rest."

"I understand," Souter said. He got to his feet and turned to Susan. "I'll look into it for you and let you know."

"Hey," she called out, "don't forget it's my story."

Souter smiled. "Promise. But we'll work it together."

17

Strong was sitting in the canteen with Jim Ryan drinking a tea when Ormerod spotted them. He bought a sandwich and a coffee and came over to their table.

"Charged Chapman as well?" Strong asked him.

Ormerod sat down beside Ryan and opposite Strong. "Yep. Both released on bail this afternoon. But tell me what was all that about a dark coloured Merc?"

"I saw Susan Brown in hospital this morning," Strong said. "She's regained consciousness, thank God. Anyway, she confirmed what we thought, she'd linked Chapman to the message and followed him when he was picked up by Baker. She saw the white sports car in the barn but panicked when another car came up the track. She ran into the old farmhouse so she wouldn't be seen. Just as she stepped back to avoid the headlights, she noticed the distinctive front end of a large Mercedes saloon. The only other thing she could say was that it was dark coloured. As she took a step back, well we know the rest."

"Wouldn't be a 300SE would it?" Ryan asked.

"Don't know, Jim. It was dark and with the headlights on that's all Susan could tell me. Why? What are you thinking?"

"Probably nothing. Maybe a coincidence, but Mirczack drives a dark blue version."

Strong paused for a second with his drink halfway to his lips. "I thought vice and people trafficking were his forte. Anyway, Susan's description is way too vague. No, as you say, it's probably coincidence."

"Probably." Ryan didn't look convinced.

"At least we know Gary Baker didn't nick the Merc sports car," Ormerod said.

"He didn't have a clue where it came from," Strong agreed. "I doubt if he could tell you where any of them were stolen. No, Chapman, did the lifting. The message on Susan's phone was from him to Gary remember, telling Gary that he, Chapman, had lifted another one. Baker may well have cleaned them out and changed the plates, but who are they working for? They wouldn't have the nous or the contacts to pass them on."

"Mirczack?" Ryan put forward.

Strong puffed his cheeks out and raised his eyebrows. "Bit of a leap, Jim."

"What did Kelly want?" Ormerod asked.

"Ah, that farmer lad who found the car reckons that a local one-man band transport operator by the name of Dave Pratt had his lorry up at the farm on a number of occasions over the past two months. He was coupled to a trailer with a container on it."

"Ideal way of transporting a vehicle relatively unnoticed."

"Exactly."

Strong drained his tea then asked Ryan about progress on the missing Albanian girl.

"No sign of her on any bus CCTV," Ryan said, "and none of the crews remembered her. I'm beginning to think she never took the bus. In fact, I think there's a lot about Helena we don't know."

"I think there's a lot Magda doesn't know either," Strong agreed. "What did Vice tell you about Mirczack?"

"Apparently, he owns three massage parlours in Leeds and Bradford plus interests in two nightclubs in Leeds. They reckon Szymanski manages the parlours for him. At the moment, they're keeping a watching brief. They know what goes on there but as long as it doesn't involve under-age, they'd rather have it off the streets."

"After hearing what Magda had to say yesterday, you don't think Helena was working in one of those parlours, do you?"

"She's an attractive girl and, as we heard, I don't think she was too honest with her sister." Ryan took a drink. "I didn't think so when you asked me yesterday. Now, it could be possible, I suppose."

"We need to get some inside info on these parlours when Szymanski's not around and ask some of the girls if they know Helena. I'll give a contact of mine in Vice a call. I'm beginning to get a nasty feeling about this, Jim."

It was Stainmore's turn to join them, tray in hand. As she sat down next to Strong, she handed him a sheet of paper. "Hot off the press, guv," she said. "Both Gary Baker and Steve Chapman's prints are on the parking ticket."

Strong laughed. "Not the brightest of criminals, are they? How did you get on with that transport lead?"

"According to his wife, he's on his way back from Cardiff. He'd taken a container down to Felixstowe on Monday, picked up a job to Birmingham then Cardiff yesterday and a run back to Leeds tonight."

"Do we know who the Felixstowe run was for?"

"She didn't know. But it's the biggest container port in Europe, so handy to ship a car abroad."

"And you'll be catching up with him tonight?"

"Yes, guv."

"Right," Strong stood up. "I'm off to finish more reports for the Chief Super. This is what real policing is all about."

The others chuckled as he walked out of the canteen.

18

Souter felt a buzz of adrenaline as he walked back down to the newspaper offices. Something in the dim recesses of his memory had been stimulated. He thought there was something familiar about what Susan had told him. He had to check it out. It must have been a good ten or fifteen years ago. Was it when he was on the Doncaster Evening Post or just when he joined the Sheffield Star? He was a sports reporter back then but he had some vague recollection of missing schoolgirls.

"Aah, you're back," Janey Clarke said, as he appeared at his workstation. Janey was a plump but attractive dark-haired girl in her mid-twenties who sat at the next desk. He thought she showed a lot of promise in her junior reporting role. "Chandler's been looking for you," she went on. "Something about the Home Secretary visiting the region tomorrow."

Souter sat down and picked off the three post-it note messages he had on his computer monitor. John Chandler was the deputy editor of the Post and the man who had brought him in. "Oh, yes, he mentioned that last week. I've got to do an interview at the Queens Hotel tomorrow. It'll be the usual old bollocks – 'tough on crime, tough on the causes,' blah, blah, blah."

"Not impressed then?"

"That's politicians for you." He swivelled in his seat to face his colleague, hesitated, then asked, "Janey, how long have you been here?"

She stopped what she was doing and turned towards him. "About three years, why?"

"No, you're too young."

"For what?"

"To remember something from the eighties."

Janey looked indignant. "Try me."

"Sorry, I didn't mean to imply … I suppose they would have been about your age now. Where were you brought up?"

"Darwen in Lancashire. And who would have been my age?"

"You don't remember anything about missing schoolgirls from about ten, fifteen years ago? Maybe more, I don't know."

She looked thoughtful for a few moments. "Nothing rings a bell."

"Mmm. Okay, not to worry."

"You've got something, haven't you?"

"I don't really know. I'll check the archives later." He turned back to his desk and brought his computer to life.

The archives were slowly being transferred to microfiche in the room behind reception on the Ground Floor. Every now and then Phyllis, who seemed to be as old as the paper itself, would transfer another month's issues to film. She used to be a receptionist years ago and did a bit of part-time filling in from time to time. As luck would have it she wasn't in this week so Souter would have to search the files himself.

He discovered the index and saw that she had filed papers as far back as November 1981. That was the year Peter Sutcliffe was convicted. He was sure what he was looking for was more recent than that. He pulled out the film for January 1983 and fitted it into the viewer then spun it through, checking the front pages for anything of interest. By six o'clock, he had made it as far as July of that year. Nothing had jumped out at him. He rubbed his eyes and replaced that month's film back on the storage rack. Tomorrow, he'd start afresh.

19

Chris Baker left the house at ten-fifteen.

His wife was none too pleased about him going out again. "Where the hell are you off to now at this time of night?" She was angry. "You've already been down to Wood Street twice in two days because of that waste of space of a brother of yours." He could also tell she was suspicious.

"I've just got to go out, that's all," he said.

"I hope you're not getting involved in his business."

"Don't worry, I'll not be long."

"Or another woman. I'll kill you if you are."

"Don't be silly." He bent to kiss her but she turned away.

Just off Agbrigg Road to the south of Wakefield, Chris turned into a road with shabby houses on both sides, mostly converted into bedsits over the years. Gary, watching for his brother's arrival from the ground floor window, dashed out to meet him. Over the course of the half hour drive, Chris tried to make sense of the past twenty-four hours.

"What I can't understand," Gary said, "was how they got on to us in the first place. Steve said he'd left me a message on my answerphone last week. They played it in his interview." He paused and looked at his brother. "But I don't have an answerphone."

"Fuck's sake, Gary, I thought he was the brains behind you two."

"But I still don't get it."

"Maybe I was right in the first place. Look it's obvious, he left that message on someone else's phone."

Gary still looked puzzled.

"He misdialled you pratt."

"Oh, right, yeah."

They were quiet for a few minutes before Gary had another thought. "But then they asked me if anyone else had turned up on Saturday night. Someone in a big Mercedes. I mean, how did they know that? How did they know the big man was there?"

Chris flashed a stern look at his brother. "You didn't say he was did you?"

"Course not. I said there was nobody else. Just me and Steve."

"I don't like it. This is getting all too close. I wish I'd never got involved. And I wish I hadn't got you two involved either. This has got to be the last time. I'll just get the money for this last one and that's it. No more."

Five minutes later, Chris pulled in to a remote lay-by, killed the lights, switched the engine off and waited. The adrenaline was pumping round his veins and his heart was racing. This wasn't a usual meet.

The lay-by had been created by a road improvement scheme where the bend had been straightened out. It was now well hidden from the road by a high hedgerow. On the other side, a new hedge and fence separated it from a field. An articulated lorry was parked up about fifty yards away, curtains drawn in the cab, the driver already in the bunk ready for an early drop in Leeds in the morning.

"What time did he say?" Gary asked.

Chris checked the clock on the dash.

"In about five minutes."

"Good. I've got time for a piss."

Gary got out of the car and walked along the footpath for a few yards until he came to a gap in the hedge to the wooden fence. With one hand on a post he vaulted over it.

"Shit!" he cried out, as he went straight down a six foot drop into a ditch.

Chris had watched him disappear. "Fucking stupid bastard," he muttered quietly to himself.

Dropping the window a touch, he lit a cigarette and tried to relax. A half moon gave a little light but clouds kept sweeping across and pitching the scene into darkness every now and then.

He was growing increasingly uncomfortable thinking about the events of the past few months. What started out as being a means to an end, a one-off to avoid any embarrassment, had become a burden. He had told himself he was helping Gary but that was far from the truth. It was bringing his brother back into crime again. And all because of his weakness for the women. If he hadn't spotted the advert; if he hadn't looked for it in the first place. If he hadn't walked in through the door. And Mariana, she drew him in, hook, line and sinker. Like her, he shouldn't have used his real name, shouldn't have told her anything about himself, what he did, where he worked. If he hadn't, none of this would have happened. He would never have been drawn into the whole murky world of car crime.

He never picked up on the car coming in behind, stopping about twenty yards from his. The lights were already off when it left the main road. A figure in dark clothes and wearing a balaclava stepped silently from the car. The figure watched the smoke escape from the driver's window, then looked to the sky. Clouds were just about to cover the moon once more. The figure waited until the moonlight had gone before making their way towards Baker's Rover, pausing to screw the silencer tube to the gun barrel.

Baker drew on his cigarette for the last time. As he flicked the butt from the window, his periphery vision caught movement. It was the last thing he would ever be conscious of. A low crack, then his brains were churned to soup inside his skull. His lifeless body slumped forward, head on the steering wheel, arms down by its side.

The figure turned and walked away from the car, removing the silencer.

Down in the ditch, Gary had finished and was desperately trying for a foothold to get himself back up to the fence. Finally, he managed to grab hold of the bottom rail and pull himself up the last few feet, just in time to see a car drive out of the lay-by and back onto the main road, waiting until the last moment to put the lights on.

"Bollocks," he said to himself. "I've missed the handover."

Climbing back over the fence he scraped as much mud off his shoes as he could. He didn't want to upset his brother any more.

"I suppose you laughed your bollocks off when I went over that fence," he said, approaching the car. "Chris? What the fuck are you fiddling about with down there?" Altering course, he walked up to the driver's door and opened it. "Come on," he said, giving his brother a shake. The corpse rolled to one side and half fell out.

He gasped. "Oh Christ. Oh Jesus fucking Christ."

20
Thursday

It was the early hours of the morning when the phone rang in the house Chapman rented. Veronica had moved in with him about four months previously. She mumbled something incoherent then turned over as Chapman got up to answer it.

He picked up the handset in the living room. "Hello?" he said.

"Oh Christ, Steve, it's fucking terrible."

Chapman recognised the voice of his friend, Gary Baker. "Gaz, calm down," he said.

"What are we going to do, Steve? What the fuck are we going to do?"

"Look, it's half one in the morning. What's so important it can't wait?"

After considerable effort, he managed to get the full story of the tragic events of the past few hours. Slowly it dawned on him what a serious situation they had managed to get themselves into. Not one to easily panic, Chapman began to sweat and shake uncontrollably. In the bathroom, he splashed water on his face in a desperate bid to calm his nerves. His heart rate rose again when he heard Veronica moving around in the bedroom.

She appeared at the bathroom door, bundled past him and sat on the toilet.

"Who was on the phone this time of night?" she asked, pulling toilet tissue from the roll.

"Oh, that. A breakdown." He dried his face on a towel and took a breath. "I'm going to have go out."

She looked at her watch. "At this time?"

"Apparently, he's a good customer."

She splashed her hands under the tap. "I'm off back to bed," she said and padded out.

Chapman got into the garage's van he used and drove out to Garforth railway station. Gaz had managed to get there, that's where he'd called from. Chapman went over the conversation he'd just had with his friend time and again. There was only one reason he could think of why Chris would have been killed. And that involved him … and Gaz. They couldn't stay around here. They would have to get away. As he drove, an idea began to form.

* * *

The wagon driver woke at half past four and began preparations for his early morning delivery in Beeston. He'd noticed the Rover parked further up and wondered when it had arrived. It certainly wasn't there when he'd bedded down.

He completed his checks all round the wagon then climbed back into the cab. By this time, it was fully light and he looked again at the car. There was something about it that didn't appear quite right. The driver's door was open and there seemed to be a bundle behind it. Firing up the engine, he checked his delivery papers and directions but his attention kept returning to the car. He stared long and hard. Putting the lorry into gear, he set off slowly, drawing to a halt alongside the Rover. Shuffling over to the passenger seat, he looked down through the car's sunroof. It was a few seconds before he realised the full horror of what he saw. Reaching for his mobile phone, he made the call that meant the drop in Beeston would be considerably delayed.

Fifteen minutes later, the lay-by was a hive of activity. Police had secured the crime scene, various unmarked vehicles had arrived and white overall-clad personnel were going about their business.

* * *

Ten past eight and Souter was back in the archive room. The previous night, in his mind, he tried to narrow the search field. Over a decade earlier it was hard to pin down exactly what happened when. He tried to pinpoint certain events – 1984 his move to the Sheffield Star; two years later, his marriage to Margaret. 1988, they split up. He didn't remember the name but it was definitely when he was with Margaret he recalled a missing schoolgirl in Yorkshire. On that basis, he decided to resume his search in January 1986.

By ten to ten, he was reviewing April 1986 and had just read reports of the kidnapping of John McCarthy in Beirut on the 17th when his mobile rang. It was John Chandler.

"Bob," he said, *"forget the Secretary of State. He's cancelled his appointments. Something to do with a Commons vote tonight. But something bigger's come up."*

As Chandler was speaking, the front page he had been searching for flashed up on the screen in front of him.

'FEARS GROW FOR MISSING SCHOOLGIRL'

"Shit," he murmured.

"Don't sound too disappointed, there's been a murder, a nasty one too." Chandler went on. *"You need to get onto it now!"*

Souter was silent, staring at the screen in front of him.

"Bob, are you listening?"

"Er, sorry, John. I was just studying something."

"Whatever it is, leave it and get your arse out to Garforth. There's a lay-by on the right-hand side just after the White Lion pub. You should see the activity."

"Okay, got that, John. I'm on my way." He ended the call and studied the newspaper report for Saturday the 19th of April 1986 – 'Fears are growing for the safety of ten year-old Jennifer Coyle from Pontefract who was last seen getting off the school bus at half past four yesterday afternoon.' Souter made brief notes then removed the microfiche, put it back on the shelf and hurried off to Garforth.

* * *

It was half past ten by the time Strong and Stainmore pulled into the lay-by. They flashed their warrant cards and had their details noted by the uniformed constable at the taped boundary to the crime scene. Detective Chief Superintendent Flynn had called Strong earlier to inform him that the Leeds Murder Squad would be leading the investigation but, as the victim was thought to be Chris Baker, he would need to liaise closely and pass on all relevant information from his recent dealings with him. The Senior Investigating Officer was DCI Frank Halliday, an experienced detective, not far off retirement. Strong had come across him several times during his career, one of the old school, a hard bastard. But of more significance for Strong, he had been Cunningham's mentor and, as far as he knew, they were still close.

Halliday, donned in a white SOCO suit, was talking to another officer but broke off when he spotted Strong and Stainmore and came over to speak to them.

"Now then," he said, "I hear you've moved up in the world."

Strong smiled grimly. "Only temporary, Frank."

Halliday hesitated with the use of his Christian name. "Aye, and it will be if there's any fucking justice.

"Sorry," he said, addressing Stainmore, "excuse my language but stitching up a senior colleague then stepping into his shoes isn't something I admire."

"Just ...," she began, before Strong interrupted her.

"It's okay, Kelly, we all know what happened. DCI Halliday here is entitled to his opinion." He could have said a lot more - that he'd done all he could to avoid Cunningham's situation, that he had a lot of time and respect for him - but he could see Halliday had already closed his mind to any alternative view.

Halliday held Strong's gaze for a few awkward seconds before telling the pair to get kitted up and step inside the cordon. "It's not a pretty sight," he added.

Strong and Stainmore fought their way into the standard white suits and overshoes as the conversation continued.

"I hear you've had contact with the poor sod recently."

"We interviewed him on Tuesday night, not under caution, just exploring what involvement he might have had with stolen cars," Strong said. "We were more interested in his younger brother, Gary. He has a lot of previous."

"Well," said Halliday, "he must have been involved in something fairly heavy. This has all the hallmarks of a professional hit. Take a look."

Behind a large green screen, a dark blue Rover was hidden from any possible public view. The driver's door was open and Baker's body was half out onto the footpath. His head was tilted to the right and a small trail of blood had trickled down his neck. When he knelt down to look more closely, he could see the small entry wound in his hair line. He stood up and exhaled.

"You've seen him recently," Halliday said, "I don't suppose there's any doubt about who he is? I wouldn't want to upset relatives unnecessarily ..."

"From what I can see, that's Chris Baker."

"The car is registered to him and I've got officers on their way to see his wife."

"Is there anything unusual in the car? Anything to give a clue as to what he was doing here?"

"Nothing apparent at the moment." Halliday nodded at the black private ambulance reversing towards them. "We're about to have him taken away. We'll have a quick look here but the car will be stripped when we get it back to Leeds." He excused himself to speak to the new arrivals.

Strong turned to Stainmore. "We've got to be missing something here, Kelly." They began walking slowly back to the cordon. "I can't believe involvement with stolen cars would attract a professional hit, because that's undoubtedly what this was."

"I'll chase up that paperwork from Dave Pratt." Stainmore had spoken briefly to the lorry driver the previous evening on his return from Cardiff. He confirmed he had made several trips from Meadow Woods Farm to Felixstowe over the past month or so. He would receive a call from 'Chris at Yorkshire Exports' to collect a container and make the delivery. He promised to forward copies of his invoices which he issued to an address in Outwood. So far, he'd been paid promptly and had no reason to be suspicious.

"What's the betting this ties back to our victim there?" Strong said, as his mobile began to ring. Souter's number came up. He made excuses to Stainmore and took the call.

"Hello, mate," Souter said, *"Are you busy?"*

"I'm a little bit tied up at the moment, why?"

"This Garforth murder, is it your case?"

"Er, no. Why do you ask?"

"Look to your left behind your car."

Strong turned and saw a familiar figure raise a hand.

"Do you know who the victim is?"

"I can't really tell you much at the moment. I'm going to have to go."

"Before you do, I could do with a chat about something else I think might interest you. How about a pint tonight?"

"Depending on how the day pans out, that sounds good."

"I'll ring you."

"So, DCI Strong," Halliday said, pronouncing Strong's new title in a deliberate and somewhat condescending manner. "Just so there's no confusion, this is my case coming under the jurisdiction of the Leeds Murder Squad. Got that?"

"Whatever Chief Superintendant Flynn says," Strong responded, turning away and walking back to his car. "Pompous fucking arsehole," he said under his breath loud enough for Stainmore to hear, then added in mocking tones, "Excuse my language."

*　*　*

Later that afternoon, Souter returned to the archive room and focussed his attention on the disappearance of Jennifer Coyle. The story ran for about two weeks before it appeared to fizzle out with no progress being made in the enquiry, no apparent leads or likely suspects named. He made copious notes of the reporting, details of the family and the investigation. He was now determined to track down the story of the other missing girl, because he felt sure Mary existed also.

It was gone seven and he had fielded two calls from Alison, when his persistence paid off. He could feel the adrenaline surge; was aware of the change in his body chemicals. He'd flipped through reports of various transport disasters; the Clapham rail crash and Lockerbie in December 1988, closely followed by Kegworth in early January 1989 and another train crash at Purley in March. What a dark period those few months were, he thought. Then, there it was, 7th March, a report of missing schoolgirl, Mary Duggan. The eight-year-old was last seen in a park in Pontefract on the Monday afternoon. She was dressed in her school uniform. A picture showed her with short-cropped hair.

"Oh, Christ," he muttered. "Oh, Christ. Oh, Christ!" he said, louder. He felt sick. This was too much of a coincidence for it not to be genuine. But how? How does a young woman falling through a rotting floor come across ... not only come across but actually speak to ... two schoolgirls, one missing for over fourteen years, the other nearer twelve?

He copied the published photos of Jennifer and Mary and made a call to Alison to apologise and tell her he'd be working late. He'd see her tomorrow.

Half an hour later, he rushed into the Intensive Care Unit at the LGI with ten minutes of the visiting time remaining. The nurse told him Susan had been transferred to an orthopaedic ward on the next floor down.

By the time Souter located the ward, it was five to eight.

Gillian was at Susan's bedside when he approached. She got up and looked at him with a quizzical frown.

"Look, I know this is unusual but I need to speak to Susan."

Gillian looked back to her sister.

"Hello, Mr Souter." Susan said.

Gillian sat back down and he made his way round to the other side of the bed.

"Hi. How are you?" he asked her.

"Feeling a lot better, thanks. No grapes then?"

"They'd sold out."

"That's alright, I was only joking."

"Sorry Susan, but I haven't got a lot of time before they'll want me to go. I've been looking into what you told me yesterday." Souter pulled the photocopy sheets from his pocket. "Did you tell Gillian?"

Gillian nodded. "If you mean about the girls, yes. But I think she might have been hallucinating."

"You've found something, haven't you?" Susan asked.

He unfolded the first sheet and held it out to her.

Susan's eyes widened. "I knew it," she whispered. "That's Jennifer."

"Jennifer Coyle." Souter unfolded the second sheet and showed it to her.

"Mary," Susan said, tears welling in her eyes. "I didn't imagine it." She turned to Gillian. "I didn't!" She looked at both girls' pictures, then to Souter. "What happened to them?"

Before he could reply, a bell rang out and a disembodied voice told the visitors their time was up.

"Jennifer disappeared in April 1986 and Mary in March 1989."

"They're dead, aren't they?"

"I don't know, Susan."

Souter emerged into the fresh air, thought about a cigarette but decided against. As he walked past the A & E entrance, a familiar imitation leather coat caught his eye.

"Sammy?"

The girl looked up.

"What happened?"

She turned away. "Sorry, Mr Souter."

He gently held her shoulders and turned her to face him. She kept her head down. "What's all this 'Mr Souter' business? We're friends aren't we?"

"Sorry, Bob."

He lifted her chin and saw her cut and bruised face, several steristrips above her right eye. "Who did this?" His voice firm and even.

"It doesn't matter."

"A punter? Your pimp?"

"I said it doesn't matter." She looked down once more. A rucksack was at her feet.

"Is this yours?"

She gave a small mirthless chuckle. "All my worldly goods."

"Have they finished with you here?" Souter nodded towards the A & E Department.

"All patched up, yes."

"Can I give you a lift back to your place?"

"I don't think that's possible any more." She looked up at him, her eyes watery. "They've chucked me out."

"What do you mean 'they've chucked you out'? Who has?"

She gave no answer and turned her head away.

"So where are you going to now?"

"Don't know yet. I'll think of something."

Souter bent down and picked up her bag which was surprisingly light. "Come on," he said. "I've got a bedsettee. You can park yourself there tonight."

She stood still. "I can't do that."

He turned back. "Why not?"

"It wouldn't be right. What would your girlfriend say?"

He smiled. "How do you know I have a girlfriend?"

"Well you're not married; no ring, or sign of a ring. I notice these things. I can always tell the married ones. You're not bent." Souter grinned at this. "But you have a love interest, so she has to be a girlfriend. Tell me I'm wrong."

"Have you ever thought about studying psychology?"

It was Sammy's turn to smile. "I'll take that as a yes, then."

"Yes, there is someone I'm seeing," he said. "But it'll be fine. I did say a bedsettee and only tonight. And anyway, where else can you go?"

He turned away again and walked towards the car park. After a few seconds, Sammy followed.

21

The dark saloon car drove slowly down Agbrigg Road. There was a high proportion of Asian residents in this part of Wakefield, just off the Doncaster Road. It was dusk and groups of men were gathered on street corners, some in trousers, others in the white thawb, the traditional full-length robe. Two women dressed in black abayas, with a child in tow, were walking past. At the next junction, a shop offering exotic fruit and vegetables for sale was open for custom; on the opposite corner a Chinese take-away vied for business with the fish and chip shop next door. Some white youths were trying to decide between the two. A couple of old men were walking towards the pub about a hundred yards further on. They'd lived here long enough to see many changes in their district. But there was no uneasy atmosphere. This was integrated living in practice.

The driver was looking for the street signs off to the right and the left. Finally, he spotted the road he was looking for and turned to the left. On both sides were large three-storey terraced houses. Eventually, the car drew to a halt outside number 21. He waited until a young white woman of around twenty walked past, dragging strongly on a cigarette.

Reaching into the glovebox, he pulled something out and slid it into the inside pocket of his leather jacket. Stepping out of the car, he cast a quick glance up and down the quiet street. Satisfied no-one was around he approached the front door. Another check to the right and left. A stroke of luck. The main door was ajar. Whoever had last passed through hadn't closed it properly.

In the hallway, all was quiet, apart from the sounds of a television coming from a room upstairs. The room he was seeking was to the right on the ground floor. He put his ear to the door. Silence. The object was retrieved from his jacket pocket. He tried the handle. Locked. Turning and holding the handle, he braced himself and thrust his shoulder to the door, level with the lock. Inside, the keep flew off and the door swung open.

The curtains were open, allowing the only illumination to come from the streetlamp outside. It was obvious no-one was home. An unmade bed was in the middle. Scattered on it were the upturned drawers from the chest against the opposite wall. A table was in front of the window and behind the door, a small wardrobe, its doors open, revealed only empty hangers.

Whoever lived here had cleared out, and in a hurry, by the looks. He swore below his breath and turned to leave. His luck had held. There was still no-one around. Taking a handkerchief from his pocket, he wiped the door handle and pulled the door closed behind him. Back in the car, the gun was placed back in the glovebox. He fired up the engine and made a three-point turn before leaving the area behind.

22

Souter settled Sammy in and told her he couldn't avoid going out again. He knew it was a risk to leave her alone in his apartment, a relatively unknown young woman with a dubious recent past, but something told him he could trust her. He hoped he wouldn't be disappointed. He also hoped Alison would understand.

It was half past nine when he entered The Eagle on Flanshaw Lane. Scanning the interior, he took in the barmaid, perched on a stool behind the bar avidly reading a magazine. Two young lads and their girlfriends were nursing drinks at one table. A man in his sixties with a comb-over that would have done Arthur Scargill proud was standing at the bar, silently whistling accompaniment to the tune on the jukebox. He spotted his friend sitting at a corner table with two pints of John Smiths and a couple of bags of crisps.

"I got you one in," Strong said, "and dinner on me."

"Good man." Souter sat beside him, raised the glass and took a large pull on his beer. "Lovely. I needed that." He looked round the place. "Bloody quiet in here," he said.

"I think it's been going downhill for a while. Beer's alright, though."

Souter opened his crisps. "Bit of a shocker for you this morning, Col?"

Strong shook his head. "Tell me about it. Of all the people, it had to be him."

"Especially just having interviewed him on Tuesday."

"What?" Strong paused and studied his friend busily munching crisps. "I'm not talking about the victim, I mean that shit head Halliday."

"You two don't get on then?"

"He bears a grudge about Cunningham. Blames me, obviously."

"So much for police working together then."

"Anyway, how did you know about Baker being interviewed?" Strong stared at Souter for a second then looked down to open his crisp bag. "I suppose it's your job. Couldn't really keep that under wraps."

"He was involved in the Meadow Woods Farm operation, wasn't he?"

"Exactly what, we don't know. It was more his younger brother and his mate."

"What are they saying about it?"

"Don't know. We can't find them."

"Do you think they had something to do with this morning?"

"Look, I've probably said too much already. But in strictest confidence ... no. I think this has scared the shit out of them and they've decided to disappear."

"Seems there's a lot of disappearances at the moment. How's your missing Albanian girl?"

"Still missing."

"Same with my young street girl. Last seen in the Market Square getting into a white van with rust along the bottom of the passenger door. Not much to go on, is it?"

Strong thought for a moment. "Do you remember a skinny kid with glasses in our class, played football with us for a few games at under 16s, Jeremy Bullen?"

"Did we used to take the piss, call him Jezza?"

"That's him. Not a bad winger, but was too small. Like you say, used to get picked on."

"What about him?" Souter asked, mouth full of crisps again.

"He's not so small and skinny now. He's built like a brick shit house. Must work out in the gym. Doesn't wear glasses either." Strong broke off for a drink, leaving Souter puzzled.

"Was that it, then?"

"I was just going to tell you that he works for the council, quite high up in security. I've spoken to him a few times recently, quite helpful."

Souter was becoming frustrated. "Am I missing something here?"

"Obviously," Strong said. "He controls all the CCTV in the city. Why don't you have a word and see if you can spot anything from the Market Square last week."

"Based at the Town Hall, is he?"

Strong nodded as he crunched some crisps.

"Thanks, I'll do that." Souter licked his fingers, folded up his crisp bag and tied it in a knot.

"So what did you want to speak to me about?" Strong asked. "You said you had something interesting this morning before all this crap broke."

Souter had lifted his drink to his lips but, without taking a sip, put the glass back down, carefully centring it on the beer mat. Now he was about to talk about it, he started to doubt just how sane it would sound. "Do the names Jennifer Coyle and Mary Duggan mean anything to you?"

Strong sat back, brows furrowed for a few seconds. "Schoolgirls from Pontefract way. Went missing back in the late eighties, I think."

Souter pulled the photocopied sheets from his pocket and unfolded them one at a time on the table.

Strong picked up the first one. "Jennifer Coyle … ten years old … yes, I remember now," he said. "And Mary, eight, a couple of years later. Never been found." He looked at Souter. "What are you telling me? You got new information?"

Souter pulled out a packet of cigarettes, took one and lit up, inhaling deeply. Immediately, he realised what he'd done. "Sorry, Col," he said, wafting the smoke away from his friend. "I forgot you'd given up the cigars."

"Nearly three weeks now."

"Sorry, it's just … I don't really know how to relate this." He turned to face Strong. "You visited Susan the other day?"

"Yes. I wanted to know how she ended up where she did." Strong broke into a grin. "Listen, you're not telling me that she's really Jennifer and she'd been kidnapped and brought up by another family?"

Souter leaned back and exhaled, a serious expression on his face. "She didn't tell you then?"

"Tell me what? What are you on about?"

"Okay, this going to sound stupid ... illogical ... any other word you care to use, I don't know but ..." Souter faced his friend again. "When she was in the basement, Susan saw Jennifer and Mary."

"Come on, you're not suggesting ... she was probably delirious. After all, she was down there for, what, three days, her leg was infected, she'd sustained a severe blow to the head ..."

"I know what you're saying but what she told me, *before* I searched the archives ... it all matches. Christ, Mary was wearing what Susan described when she went missing."

Strong stared silently into space for a few seconds. "So where do you think they are? Up at the farm?"

"I don't know for sure but it's got to be worth a look."

Strong slowly shook his head. "Bloody Hell, Bob, I can't just go conducting a full search of Meadow Woods Farm on the strength of a ... an apparition." He held his hands up. "Look, I'm not saying there's nothing in it but I'll need more before I can go off to the Chief Super with this."

"I understand that, Col." Souter finished his pint. "I've got a few more avenues to explore but it's too much of a coincidence." He looked again at Strong. "They're out there, I'm sure."

23
Friday

Sammy had been sound asleep when Souter arrived back the previous evening. Once again, he thought how vulnerable she looked.

Next morning brought a big surprise for him. Activity in his kitchen roused him before his alarm went off. The sounds and smell of sizzling bacon were unmistakeable. Bleary-eyed, Souter, dressed in the shorts he wore in bed, wandered in to discover Sammy in jeans and a loose fitting shirt busily pouring boiling water into the teapot.

"Thought I'd give you a treat by way of saying thank you." She turned round. "I know how important you think breakfast is."

Souter yawned. "There's really no need. But thanks. I don't normally bother with cooked but I appreciate it."

Hands on hips, she made a point of looking him up and down. "Five minutes?"

"Great," he said and set off for the bathroom.

When he returned, they sat down at the small table in the kitchen.

"This is delicious, Sammy. I could get used to this." Souter had his head down shovelling another forkful of bacon and fried tomatoes onto a segment of toast.

She paused and looked at him. "I need to get somewhere sorted out today."

"Where will you go?"

"I've got a few friends I could try."

"Look, give me a call and let me know how things pan out. If you're stuck, I suppose I could put up with you for another night," he said, a smile playing on his lips.

"Thanks Bob, but I do need to get out of your face. You've got your own business to be going on with."

"Okay, but it's no bother."

They ate in silence for a few seconds before she spoke again. "So what big breaking story are you working on today?"

"You heard about the murder in Garforth yesterday?"

Sammy shook her head. "I had other things going on."

"Some bloke shot dead in his car in the early hours. Professional hit."

"Anything to do with these two girls?" Sammy lifted the photocopies from the side of the breadbin. "You left these on the worktop last night."

Souter took a slurp of tea and considered whether to tell Sammy anything about Jennifer and Mary. After a few moments, he decided to give her the edited highlights.

"So," she said when he'd finished, "you think they may be hidden in the farmhouse?"

"Incredible I know, but it needs investigating. But before the police can get involved, I need to check a few more things out. I could do with tracking down their families."

"I could do that for you," she said.

"Thanks Sammy, but you just can't go striding up a path and knocking on the front door. Besides, they could have moved or died or anything."

"I didn't mean go knocking on doors. That's your job. I've got a friend who's a genius on computers and the internet. Leave it with me."

"I thought you had other priorities?"

"Hey, us girls can manage more than one thing at once, you know."

24

Strong had much to mull over on his drive back from Millgarth police station in Leeds. Halliday had called a briefing that morning and brought together his squad officers. Strong had also been invited, reluctantly, he thought. But DCS Flynn had told him to stick with the enquiry regardless of Halliday.

The post-mortem confirmed the cause of death as a single gunshot to the head, 9mm calibre. Nothing too unusual in that. Most weapons of choice used by criminals for this type of operation use 9mm calibre ammunition. The oddity in this instance though, was the use of a semi-jacketed wadcutter round. As the ballistics expert so eloquently put it, 'once the round passed through the skull, the lead fragmented and basically turned the brain to mush.' The fragments were still contained inside the skull, which was why there was no exit wound. He'd explained that it was most likely to have come from the old Eastern Block area, as these rounds are outlawed under the Geneva Convention because of the damage they can do. One other source could be the U.S.A. He was working on piecing the round back together to obtain the forensic evidence to enable comparisons to be made should a suspect weapon be located.

Great play was made of the discovery of Gary Baker's prints on the driver and passenger door handles, as well as in the passenger side interior. There would now be an intensive hunt for him and, by implication, Steve Chapman. The other thing that interested Strong was the discovery in Baker's inside jacket pocket of an invoice from Dave Pratt Transport, made out to Yorkshire Exports covering the latest run to Felixstowe. The address for Yorkshire Exports was Baker's home in Outwood. This tied in with the previous copies Stainmore had obtained from the lorry driver the day before. According to Mrs Pratt who kept the books for her husband, previous invoices had been settled in cash, hand delivered through the letter box in the evenings. She had never actually seen who had dropped the envelopes off.

Baker's wife was distraught. Halliday had allocated a female Family Liaison Officer to the house and his team had conducted several short informal interviews with her. She didn't appear to know anything about transport invoices nor had she heard of Yorkshire Exports. Strong got the feeling that, if anything, Halliday seemed intent on keeping her away from his team.

Strong confirmed he had officers speaking to Baker's work colleagues at the Olympia Insurance call centre. He was pursuing Baker's younger brother, Gary and his associate Steve Chapman, both of whom had not been seen since Thursday morning. He had also outlined his interest in the activities at Meadow Woods Farm which brought his thoughts back to the conversation he'd had with Souter the night before.

When he pulled in to Wood Street car park, he was stlll wrestling with the logic of how Susan could describe to Bob what the girls were wearing. That enigma would have to wait. For now, the priority had to be to establish a motive for the shooting of Chris Baker.

He climbed the stairs to the first floor and walked into the CID room. Stainmore was studying her computer screen and Ormerod was on the phone at the next desk.

"Ah, guv," Stainmore called, as she spotted her boss, "I think we might have something."

Ormerod concluded his call. "That's one more," he said to Stainmore.

"In which case, we definitely have something," she said.

Strong wheeled a chair from a vacant desk nearby and sat down between them.

"When we started talking to Baker's work colleagues," she began, "it started us thinking … where better to obtain details of vehicles than an insurance company."

Strong nodded. "Access through their computer system to registrations, owners, et cetera."

Ormerod flourished the pad on which he'd just made notes. "And this one completes the set."

"Go on."

"That was Mr Jackson, owner of the Mercedes Sports Coupé nicked last Friday. Like all the others, he obtained a quote from Olympia Insurance at some point during the past three months. Not everyone accepted. Only two, the Range Rover and the Lexus owners did."

Strong leaned back, hands on head. "Would have been a bit suspicious if every one of the stolen cars was insured by the same company." He leaned forward again. "So what do we think? Baker knows where top end models reside; younger brother's mate goes round and nicks them; up to the farm for a quick makeover, into the back of a container and off abroad?"

"Very probable, guv," Stainmore said.

"How about," Ormerod suggested, "with access to the database, Baker also comes up with registrations for similar cars, same colour and spec. and younger brother makes up plates for them to put on the nicked one? That way, any PNC check wouldn't register as stolen."

"Cloned, you mean?"

"Exactly."

"Sounds good, Luke. Although I'm not sure how much info an insurance company would have access to." He turned to Stainmore. "What has the paperwork from Dave Pratt told us?"

"Only that he delivered containers to Felixstowe on behalf of Baker. I've got a call in to the authorities down there. I want them to track down their locations and seize any that haven't yet been loaded."

"All right, keep me up to speed with that, Kelly. In the meantime, is there any news on Chapman and Baker?"

"John came back just before you did." Stainmore nodded to where Darby sat at a computer screen some twenty feet away. "He's been down to Chapman's workplace and his house."

Strong stood and walked over to Darby's desk, the detective tapping away on his keyboard.

"John, any signs?"

Darby paused and looked up. "Chapman, you mean? Not a bloody snifter. Seems to have disappeared. His boss at the garage reckons he hasn't made contact and the last time he saw him was when he left work on Wednesday. But he must have left his company van outside the garage with the keys up the exhaust early on Thursday. He's worked there for over a year. Always been reliable up to now."

"What about his address?"

"Girlfriend answered the door. A bit rough."

"Just the facts, John," Strong sighed.

Darby looked indignant. "I meant she looked a bit rough as though she'd been crying. She was worried. My turning up didn't help, especially after we'd had him in here overnight on Tuesday night. Anyway, she said he went out early Thursday morning. I mean like the middle of the night. Said something about a breakdown and not to worry. She went off to work as normal on Thursday and hasn't seen him since. But she reckons he must have come back sometime during the day because a bag and some of his clothes have gone."

"No note or contact since?"

"She said not and I'm inclined to believe her, judging by how upset she seemed."

"And no signs at Gary Baker's address?"

"Been round there too, guv. It's a bedsit in some shit hole of a place just off Agbrigg Road. I only saw one bloke there and he said he didn't know him and couldn't say if he'd ever seen him. It's that sort of place. But the interesting thing is, when I tried the door, someone had beaten me to it. Although the door was closed, the lock had been smashed off the frame. No signs of a disturbance but it looks like he'd left in a hurry. The place was empty."

Strong was thoughtful for a few seconds. "Early hours of Thursday morning you say Chapman went out?"

"Yes, guv."

"With Gary's prints on the driver's door, I think he was with his brother on Wednesday night. How he escaped Chris's fate, I don't know. But I'll lay money he contacted Chapman and the pair of them are frightened of something fairly heavy. I think they've cleared off. I hope they have, anyway. We need to find them before whoever's after them does."

Strong turned round to Ormerod. "Luke, can you go with John. I'd like you to return to Chapman's girlfriend and take a formal statement. Gently probe and make sure she hasn't heard from him. Also see if you can get any idea where he might go if he's in trouble. Try and assure her he's not in any trouble from us, well not any more than we charged him with on Wednesday. In the meantime, I've got another avenue to pursue.

"Kelly, let me know the minute you have anything else from Felixstowe."

* * *

Stella Hunter wore no make-up and looked to be in her mid-forties. Dressed in trousers and a loose jumper, her jacket was on the back of her chair. She was sitting with a white wine spritzer at a table in a quiet corner of the Horse and Trumpet pub near the famous City Varieties Theatre in Leeds when Strong and Vince Denholme walked in.

Denholme sat down with Stella while Strong ordered two pints. He hadn't been in the place for years but was glad to see it hadn't suffered a make-over as some other establishments had. Set into the bar top, it still had a beautiful swan-necked brass water tap and drain. He gathered the drinks and joined them at the table.

"Stella, this is my old colleague Colin," Denholme said. "He saved my life once, you know."

Vince Denholme had become a DC when Strong was a DS at Wood Street in the early nineties. They had worked on a number of enquiries together and Strong held him in high regard, certainly capable of enjoying a successful police career. That had very nearly come to a premature end one night in 1991. They were searching a derelict warehouse building near the River Calder for an escaped prisoner serving a ten year sentence for GBH. Denholme was a little too keen when he opened a door to step into what he thought was an office. Just before he put his weight onto fresh air, Strong grabbed hold of his arm and managed to haul him back to safety. Successfully passing his sergeant's exams, he transferred to Vice in Leeds when a suitable opportunity arose two years ago.

"Don't embarrass me, Vince." Strong took a sip of his beer. "Thanks for seeing us, Stella."

"What's this all about?" she asked. "I've got to be at work in Bradford in an hour and a half."

"Would that be Shangri-La's?"

"That's right. But I only work as a receptionist. I don't do any … treatments."

"That's managed by Stefan Szymanski, isn't it?"

She looked at Denholme. "You know it is. What is this?"

Strong produced an envelope from his inside jacket pocket and took out a 6 x 4 picture of the Pole. "Is this him?"

"Yes," she said slowly.

Strong showed her another photo, this time of Mirczack. "Have you ever seen this man?"

A frightened expression passed briefly over Stella's face. She paused to take a drink. "He's been in a couple of times over the past year or so," she said. "Always with Stefan. I think he's one of the owners."

"*One* of the owners?" Strong queried.

119

"Yeah, I think there's another one but I've never seen him or heard about him. It's just the way they talk. Just an impression I get that there's someone else involved."

"They have two other places, don't they? Over here in Leeds."

"Yes. Sweet Sensations in Chapeltown and Butterflies in Morley."

"Do you ever work there?"

"I do a couple of shifts in Chapeltown now and again but I've done more recently. They've been struggling for staff."

Strong put the two photos away and took out another. "Have you ever seen this girl?"

This time she took the photo from him. "Yes. That's Helena. Nice girl. From Albania she told me. Her English is pretty good. She was close to Stefan for a while."

"But not now?"

"Well she's not been around for a week or so. I think they fell out. That's why I've been doing more shifts at Sweet Sensations. She was receptionist."

"Receptionist? Not one of the girls?"

"No. Stefan took her on."

"So how long was she working there."

"Look, I don't want to get her into trouble. I know she probably shouldn't have been working with her status." She gave the photo back to Strong.

"I'm not interested in that, Stella."

She took another sip of her drink then played with the slice of lemon in the glass before answering. "Well I think she's been there for a few months. She tries to help some of the girls, if you know what I mean." She looked at Denholme.

He turned to Strong. "We think there might be a small problem with trafficking at some of these parlours."

"Girls, you mean?"

"Yes."

"Helena would talk to them and look after them a bit better than Stefan would." Stella finished her drink and began to put on her jacket. "I've got to go or I'll be late."

"Just before you do," Strong said, "Can you take a look at this one and tell me if you've seen him before." He slipped one last picture from the envelope and passed it to her.

"Yes." She stood up. "That's Chris. At least that's what he called himself. He used to talk to Stefan a lot. He's a regular at Sensations. Normally sees Mariana."

"Not any more, he'll not," Strong said, putting the photo away. "He was our victim in Garforth yesterday."

25

About fifty yards from the mid-terraced house Chapman shared with Veronica, a dark saloon car drew into a parking space on the opposite side. Inside, the driver and front seat passenger looked at one another.

"You're sure?" the passenger asked.

"Number 35, my contact said." The driver adjusted the rear-view mirror to take in the house front door.

The passenger reached for the door handle.

"Wait!" The driver placed a hand on the passenger's arm. "Police."

The passenger turned in his seat to see two men leaving the house and walking down the short path. Behind them, the door was closed by a dark-haired woman of around twenty-five. The passenger faced the front again and slouched in the seat. In the overtaking mirror, the detectives' progress was followed as they returned to their car on the opposite side of the street. They got in, and after a few seconds, drove off in the opposite direction.

"Okay," the driver said. "You know what we need."

The passenger hesitated, nodded then got out.

The knock was answered by mutterings from the other side. "What now," Veronica said, opening the door. "Look, I've told you everything ..." Looking at the stranger, Veronica's voice trailed off before she recovered. "Yes?"

"Mr Chapman?"

"He's not here at the moment."

"Do you know where he is?"

"I'm sorry, I don't. Now, if you don't mind ..." She began to close the door.

The man put his foot on the threshold. "Do you mind if I come in," he said, calmly.

"Yes I do. What the ..."

He bundled her back into the house and closed the door behind them.

"I need to speak to Mr Chapman."

"Who are you?" Veronica said, her eyes narrowing.

"Just someone who needs to speak with him." He smiled, but there was no warmth.

She regained her composure. "Join the club. I have no idea where he is, so if you don't mind ..." She made to push past him to open the door.

He grabbed her arm. "I don't think you realise how important it is that I speak to him."

She struggled but his grip was firm. "Let me go, or I call the police."

"You've already spoken to them." He gestured towards the street. "I saw them leave."

Her resistance subsided. She realised this was a serious situation.

He felt her weaken. "I'm sorry," he said. "My people need to find your ... boyfriend." He released her arm.

"Why?" she asked, rubbing her arm.

"He has an arrangement with us and we need to talk to him."

"Look, I'm telling you what I told those two detectives. He left in the early hours of Thursday morning. He said he was called out to a breakdown and that's the last I've seen of him. I have no idea where he is and I haven't heard from him since. If you know where he might be, I'd like to know too."

"But you must have some idea where he might be?"

"As far as I know, he works at Westgate End Garage, try there. The only other friend he has is Gary Baker who lives down Agbrigg way, I believe."

"If you're holding anything back ... Trust me, you don't want to be."

Back in the car, the passenger related the conversation he had just had with Veronica.

"His employers haven't seen him since Wednesday evening. I called them this morning," the driver said. He paused and looked at his companion. "Do you think she was telling you all she knows?"

"Probably not. But I'm assuming we'll be back?"

The driver nodded, started the engine and pulled away.

26

Souter parked in the allocated space outside his block of flats near to Wakefield's Westgate station. The drive home was the first opportunity he'd had all day to give thought to Jennifer and Mary, reporting on the Garforth murder had taken care of that. He also wondered if Sammy had been able to find somewhere to stay, he'd not heard from her.

As he lifted his briefcase out of the boot, she appeared at his shoulder, startling him.

"Christ, Sammy, I thought you were a mugger."

"Sorry."

Souter looked round the parking area. "Have you been waiting for me?"

"About an hour," she said. "I lost your card so I couldn't ring you. I've got some news."

He looked down at the rucksack she was holding. "No joy with any of your mates, then?"

"There's a squat in Featherstone I've heard of. An old pub."

"Have you eaten?"

"I had a good breakfast, remember."

Souter smiled. "Come on, I'm starving. Do you like Chinese?"

She nodded.

"Good. I'll order something and you can tell me what you've found out."

Ten minutes later, Souter was sitting on a chair and Sammy on the settee in the lounge, food ordered and a mug of coffee each on the table in front of them.

"So what have you got?" he asked.

Sammy took a small note pad from her rucksack and flipped it open. "From those newspaper reports, both girls lived in the Pontefract area. Jennifer's dad died about two years after she went missing and her mother moved away. No idea where. Mary's family still live in the same house. She had an older brother, Paul who now lives in Sharlston, and a younger sister, Fay. There's also twin girls who were born after Mary disappeared, all still living at home."

Souter was impressed. "I won't ask where you got all this."

Sammy beamed.

"Don't suppose you have an address for Paul Duggan?"

She held up a finger, flipped her note pad over to another page and ripped it out. "Of course I do," she said.

"Brilliant."

Just then the doorbell interrupted them. "Told you the Chinese would be quick." He got up to answer it.

Opening the door, he found Alison standing there.

"Hi," she said. "Not seen you in days. Thought I'd come and make your evening." She put her arms around him and kissed him. He couldn't disguise his surprise. "What's wrong with you?" She walked past him and into the lounge.

"What's going on? Who's this?" She looked daggers at Sammy.

"Sit down," he said, recovering some composure. "This is Sammy. I told you about her the other day."

Alison remained standing. "But not that she was familiar with your flat."

"Sammy, this is Alison, my girlfriend." Alison gave him a cold look. "Sammy's been helping me track down those schoolgirls' families. Let me get you a drink."

"I'm fine for now," she said.

The doorbell rang again. This time it was the takeaway delivery. Souter paid and returned with the bags.

"Very cosy."

"Come on, Alison, this is all perfectly innocent. Sit down. There's enough food to share."

She slowly sat down on an easy chair.

"I'll stick the kettle on and make us a fresh brew and dish this lot out." Souter took the food into the kitchen, leaving the door open so he could listen to any conversation in the lounge.

After a few seconds he heard Alison ask Sammy what had happened to her face.

"Bob told you what I was doing, right?" There was a pause. "Well the guy that was paying my rent, he got annoyed that I wasn't earning. Well that's what he said anyway, but I think it's because Maria's disappeared. He thinks she's left to work somewhere else. I've been trying to find her and … well, I think the truth is, he has some new girls he wants in the room where we lodged."

"This guy, your pimp yes? He physically assaulted you and threw you out?" Alison asked. There was a slight delay. "When was this?"

"Yesterday."

"So where did you spend the night last night?"

Sammy hesitated before telling her that Souter had put her up on the sofa-bed.

"Christ, this gets worse." Alison stormed into the kitchen. "You didn't tell me this. Working late, you said. You spent the night with her in your lounge. That's if she was in the lounge and not in your bed."

He stopped dishing up. "Don't be ridiculous. Of course she was on the sofa-bed. I couldn't just leave her on the streets."

"Why not? It's where she works."

"Come on, that's not fair."

"Where did you meet? Did she come round here?"

"No. It was after I left Susan last night. She was outside A & E having just been stitched up. She'd got nowhere else to go. She's only nineteen. Her best friend from when they were in the children's home is missing, God knows where. It was only a couple of days ago when you didn't know what had happened to Susan. I'm just trying to help here."

Sammy appeared at the doorway. "Look, I'll go now. I don't want to be in the way where I'm not wanted. I'll check out that squat."

"No wait, Sammy," Souter said.

She turned back into the other room and he could hear her unzipping the rucksack to put her things in.

Souter looked at Alison who shook her head then returned to the lounge. He followed.

"Look Sammy," she said, "Here's the deal. You can stay at mine for a few days, until that face of yours improves. But if anything, anything at all goes missing, I find you smoking so much as a dodgy cigarette, you'll be out on your backside. Got it?"

Sammy put her rucksack back down. "Thank you," she said softly.

Souter smiled. "Thanks, Alison."

"Yeah, well," she replied, "I'm only thinking of your reputation."

"Let's get this food before it goes cold."

As they ate, Sammy told Alison of how she'd met Maria and their lives since.

"So," Alison said as she washed down the last of her meal with a swig of tea, "You've been on the streets for a while now. What about your health? Do you have regular checks?"

"At the clinic you mean? Yeah, of course. And I use protection, always."

"That's not always one hundred per cent though."

Sammy put her plate down. "Look, I don't want to do this. If I could earn a living properly I would. I'd love the chance to leave this life behind."

Alison studied the girl for a few moments. "I know you would," she said seriously before lightening the tone. "Now," she said, opening up her handbag. "Lean back a minute, Sammy."

Sammy looked puzzled until she saw Alison bring out her make-up.

She leaned over and began to apply some foundation to Sammy's eye. "Well if you stay with me," she said, "there will be no evidence of your previous occupation. In fact, I expect you to do a few jobs around the house."

Sammy tried to nod.

"Hold still. These steristrips can come off in a couple of days and that should look a whole lot better. The bruising doesn't look so bad now I've put some of this on. There you go, have a look."

Sammy stood up and checked her face in the mirror behind the settee. When she turned around, tears were welling up. "Thank you," she said.

"Hey, stop that, you'll spoil my handiwork."

"It's just that nobody has shown me any trust before."

"Don't let us down." Souter said.

Sammy stood where she was and looked down at her hands.

"What's up?" Alison asked.

Sammy looked up at her then across to Souter. "I miss Maria. What do you think's happened to her?"

"I don't know, Sammy," he said. "We need to find that van."

"But how? We've no registration number."

"I might have a plan on that. So tomorrow morning, we're off to see a man about a van."

27
Saturday

Strong wasn't planning on working Saturday but events dictated otherwise. Stainmore had received a phone call from the Port of Felixstowe police that morning. They had located two containers from the documents provided by Dave Pratt and currently they were being held dockside pending further instructions.

"All the paperwork seems to be in order, guv," Stainmore said.

Strong, Stainmore and Ormerod were sitting in the DCI's office, coffees in front of them. Hot sun streamed through the window but any chance of enjoying the good weather had evaporated with the events of the week.

"So what does that tell us?" Strong asked.

"Details of a Lexus 400 and a Mercedes sports check out on the PNC database," Stainmore explained. "Not reported stolen, same models as went missing here but the Lexus is registered to an owner in Tewksbury and the Merc in Oxford."

"And those are the only two vehicles recorded? Nothing on a Subaru or, what was the first, a Range Rover?"

"No. They're probably long gone."

"No doubt you're right," Strong said resignedly. "Have you checked to see if those two are due to be shipped out?"

"I've got calls in to both owners. No answer from the Lexus and I've left a message for the Merc's."

"Keep trying, Kelly. We might need to visit Suffolk, though." Strong paused for a slurp of his coffee. "Luke, any developments on Chapman and Gary Baker?"

"John and I went back to see Veronica, Chapman's girlfriend. She says she hasn't heard from him and judging by her reactions I'd say she was telling the truth. She said he'd seemed a bit on edge in recent days but hadn't said why. She appears to be genuinely worried."

"Any ideas where they may have gone?"

"The only thing she could suggest was that Chapman spoke about a cousin he was close to as a kid, used to play together." Ormerod flipped open a notebook. "Name of Barry, Barry Whitefield. She thinks he lives down south somewhere but not a clue where."

"Anything on record?"

"There is a Barry Whitefield with previous for burglary, currently living in Bristol but at fifty-three I think he's too old to be the cousin. I'm checking that out though."

Stainmore's mobile rang and she stood up. "DS Stainmore," she said, walking out into the corridor.

Strong drained his coffee and looked across at Ormerod. "Do we know exactly what you'd need to export a vehicle?"

"I think it's just the vehicle log book and a bill of sale."

"I wonder how easy that would be to forge?" Strong said, more in thought than inviting a response.

Before the conversation could move on, Stainmore came back from the corridor. "That was Mr Morrison in Oxford," she announced. "His pride and joy, a Mercedes SLK 230 Sports Coupe is currently sitting on his drive."

"So, the one at Felixstowe is a clone."

"One more thing, guv," she said, with a self-satisfied grin, "He confirmed that he's insured with Olympia."

"Right, I'm going to see DCS Flynn. Search warrants for both those containers I think. Let me know as soon as you get a call back from the Lexus owner, Kelly."

*   *   *

When Souter collected Sammy from Alison's house next morning, she looked a lot better than even the night before. Although the bruising had started to turn autumnal colours, Alison had done a professional job with camouflage make-up. Hair freshly washed and dressed in her jeans and a tee shirt borrowed from Alison, Sammy looked more like an ordinary teenage girl than the rough provocative woman who had first visited him at the Yorkshire Post offices.

Jeremy Bullen met them in the reception of the Town Hall in Wood Street, opposite Strong's police office. He was certainly different from the spindly young lad Souter remembered playing in their school football team some twenty-five years earlier.

"Bob, good to see you," he said, gripping Souter's hand tightly in his.

"You too," Souter responded. "I'd never have known you though. Colin told me you'd changed."

"Bulked up, you mean."

"Well," Souter hesitated, "the last time I saw you, you'd be about eight stone wringing wet."

Bullen laughed. "I got pissed off being picked on so I did something about it. Not by you lot, I must add, mostly those in my year. Anyway, I went to the gym and started working at it. All legal, none of that steroid shit. I found I enjoyed it and this is the result." He opened his arms wide to demonstrate.

Souter turned to his companion. "Sammy, this is Jeremy. He was a year below me at school. We played in the same football team for a while."

"Look," he said, "call me Jezza. Everyone does. You lot started it." His grin confirmed he bore no malice for the taunting. "So, what can I do for you?"

"Sammy's a friend of mine and I wondered if you might be able to help us. I understand from Colin you have access to the town's CCTV footage. Specifically the Market Square from last Saturday."

"Come down to the office. I'll make us a brew."

Bullen turned and led the way along the ornate corridor of the old Victorian building, stone floors, leaded windows and stained wood panelling, to a staircase dropping down to the basement. Beyond a door proclaiming Jeremy Bullen as Assistant Head of Security, lay his small windowless office.

Flicking the switch on the kettle in the corner he turned to ask the obligatory tea or coffee question. While the water boiled and the drinks were made, Souter outlined what was known about Maria's disappearance.

"We have a problem with prostitution around the Market area," he said, giving Sammy a stare. "Police don't seem too concerned but the Council are getting pissed off."

Sammy was about to respond but Souter put a restraining hand on her shoulder.

"We think there may be something more serious here, Jezza. We're worried about Maria."

Bullen raised an apologetic hand. "Of course. I understand." He stood up. "Now, last Saturday, between eleven and midnight?"

"That's right."

"Okay, let's have a look and see what we've got." Bullen paused at the door. "Remember, you didn't see this."

"Message received," Souter said.

They followed Bullen into the room next door where a bank of television screens was being monitored by a solitary operative.

"Big brother lives," Souter said quietly.

"You'd be surprised how much this benefits the town," Bullen responded. "We're getting more teams of shoplifters coming in, especially in The Ridings shopping centre. They've got their own setup there but we liaise with them and the police. It's estimated it would cost stores around half a million a year without this."

"Listen," Souter said, "if it would help, I could give this operation a bit of a plug, not the sensitive or detailed stuff, but if it puts some of these gangs off and sends them somewhere else it might make your job easier?"

"Thanks. I'll talk to my boss and see if he might want to take that up. But hold fire for now."

"Sure."

Bullen began to peruse the shelves of video tapes along one wall. After a few seconds, he pulled one out.

"Here we are," he said, "Saturday 27th Market Square, 20:00 to 00:00."

He took the tape and placed it in a player at the far end. Fast forwarding it to around three quarters of the way through, he stopped it and pressed play. A grainy black and white image appeared with the time in the corner indicating 23:08. The view was a general one from the bottom end of the square looking towards the cathedral. Four young women were standing on the right hand side.

"That's Maria there," Sammy said pointing to a dark-haired girl dressed in a short, light coloured skirt and dark top, smoking a cigarette.

Souter recognised Sammy with her shoulder length straight blonde hair. "Is that Tracey in the boots?"

"Yea."

"So who's the other girl?"

"Calls herself Bridget but that was the first time I'd seen her. I think she goes off in a big Jag soon."

Sure enough, a dark Jaguar pulled up alongside her, she leaned in towards the passenger window and after a few seconds got in the front seat. The timer read 23:13.

"Is this the only view of here?" Souter asked Bullen.

"There's another camera at the top end but that was out of action for about ten days. Pity, because that's a lot better resolution."

"It must have been about five minutes after this," Sammy said.

A drunk came staggering down the road, gesturing to the girls.

Sammy shook her head. "Forgot about him. Fucking nuisance."

The drunk had moved away when a small hatchback approached the kerb.

"This is Jerry," Sammy said.

On screen, she had just climbed in when a white van came into shot, stopping at the top of the road for a few seconds. As the hatchback pulled slowly away, the van moved alongside Maria and Tracey. Maria exchanged a few words with the driver through the passenger window before getting in. The van then moved off and turned right in front of the camera. The resolution wasn't good enough to read the number plate but the line of dark colour on the bottom of the door, presumably the rust, could clearly be seen.

"Don't suppose you could enhance any of that, Jezza? Any chance of getting the number or closer shot of the driver?"

Bullen puffed out his cheeks. "If it had been the other one, probably, but this is one of the originals. We're due to replace it this year. I'll see what I can do."

The tape played on and about fifteen minutes later Sammy returned. Tracey had gone off about five minutes before in a light coloured BMW. Sammy was on her own until Tracey came back at 23:52. From Sammy's body language she was obviously agitated about Maria not returning.

"How much longer did you wait around?" Souter asked.

"Tracey went off about half twelve and I suppose I must have given it another half hour."

They watched until the tape ended at midnight. "Want to see the next one?" Bullen asked.

"Better check it out if you don't mind," Souter said.

They fast forwarded the second tape until 03:00 with no further activity of interest after Sammy had left.

Back in Bullen's office, he presented them with two A4 stills from the camera, one of the front of the van, zoomed in as far as possible to see the windscreen, an indistinguishable driver and Maria in the passenger seat. The other showed the side detail and rust markings on the passenger door.

"Thanks, Jezza. Appreciate this," Souter said as they made their way back along the ground floor corridor to reception.

"No problem. Only wish I could get more detail for you but if I zoomed in any more, we'd lose any advantage." Bullen shook hands with Souter. "I hope you find her. I have a daughter not much younger than her."

"Thank you," Sammy said.

"You take care," Bullen said with genuine feeling.

* * *

Strong pulled out of the station's car park and was about to turn left onto Wood Street when a familiar figure walked across the road. Souter and a young blonde-haired girl looked up the road before spotting his car. A raised hand then Souter broke into a jog to join him.

Strong dropped the passenger window and Souter stuck his head in. "Now then, mate," he said with a smile in his eyes, "Not like you to put a Saturday in."

"Cheeky sod. Least I'm not bumming a free ticket to a match and calling it work."

Souter grinned and knelt down by the car, Sammy ambled over and stood on the pavement beside him. "Any further forward with Chris Baker's murder?" he asked.

"Halliday's running that but we're still trying to get to the bottom of activities at Meadow Woods Farm."

"Still no sign of his younger brother?"

"Nothing. Nor of his mate, Steve Chapman. Only lead we have is a cousin Chapman was close to as a kid. Some bloke by the name of Barry Whitefield, living down south somewhere, we think. But he doesn't seem to feature on police records. On top of that, I've still got a missing Albanian woman."

"I know the feeling." Souter looked round to his companion. "Sorry, Colin, this is Sammy. I told you about her missing friend."

The young blonde girl bent down, gave a brief smile then stood back up looking disinterested.

"Just been to see Jezza," Souter continued. "What we saw confirmed Maria getting into a white Ford Escort van with rust along the bottom of the passenger door.

Unfortunately, the only pictures we have aren't good enough to get the number plate or a particularly clear view of the driver."

"You got stills there?"

"Yeah, Jezza printed them off."

"Let's have a look."

Souter passed them through the window for Strong to study.

"I see what you mean. How long has this been now?"

"A week."

"You need to make this official, Bob." Strong handed the photos back.

"I know," Souter turned and looked at Sammy.

"No time like the present." Strong nodded towards the station entrance behind his friend. "Ask for DS Kelly Stainmore. She'll be sympathetic, if your friend's not too keen on us."

"I'll do that, Colin. See you." Souter watched as Strong raised the window and set off down Wood Street, turning right on a green light and disappearing from view.

28
Sunday

A short dark-haired stocky man was hosing down his Vauxhall Astra on the drive of the modern semi-detached house in the quiet cul-de-sac in Sharlston. Soap suds had formed a trail into a drain in the gutter.

"Excuse me," Souter said as he approached, "is it Mr Duggan? Mr Paul Duggan?"

The man turned and eyed him suspiciously. "Who wants to know?" He continued to rinse the car.

"My name's Souter, Robert Souter."

"And what do you want, Mr Souter?"

Souter hesitated. Now he was face to face with Mary's brother, things could go one of two ways. "Do you have a younger sister who went missing in 1989?"

Duggan put the hose down and walked over to the tap and turned it off. He sauntered slowly back to face him. "Who are you?"

Souter pulled out a card and handed it to the man. "Robert Souter," he repeated. "I think I might have some new information."

Duggan studied the card. "Yorkshire Post? You're a journalist? What sort of new information can you have that the police haven't already told me?"

Two young children were cycling past on the pavement and a neighbour across the road had stopped cutting his postage stamp of a lawn.

"This is a little unusual, Mr Duggan." Souter looked all round. "Is there somewhere private we could talk?"

Duggan paused, glanced over Souter's shoulder and waved to his neighbour. Quietly, he said, "If you're here to rake up some crap over Mary, I'll lay you out."

Souter didn't doubt the man's sincerity.

"Come in, the wife's taken our young un riding."

Leading the way round the side of the house and into a small kitchen, he indicated for Souter to take a seat at the breakfast bar. "So, what is it that you've got to tell me?" he asked.

Souter took a deep breath. "This might seem odd to you," he said, "but I've spoken to someone who thinks they may be able to help solve Mary's disappearance."

Duggan sat opposite with no intention of offering any refreshment. "Who might be able to help? And how?"

"Can I ask you a couple of questions first?" Souter held both hands up. "I promise you this is no cheap way of trying to dig up a story. That's not my style."

The man studied him for a few seconds. "Go on," he finally said.

"As I understand it, you were the oldest of the family."

Duggan nodded.

"And Mary was, what, seven years younger than you?"

"That's right."

"Can I ask, before Mary's disappearance, did you ever have an accident? One that involved hospital treatment?"

The man looked puzzled, thought for a moment, then said, "Well, yes, I broke my arm when I was about thirteen, just before Christmas."

"And how did you do that?"

"I fell out of a tree."

Souter smiled. "And it had a cast, yes?"

"Of course, it was a broken bone."

"And what did Mary and your friends do?"

"What do you mean, 'do'?"

Souter sighed. "I'm trying not to lead you here, Mr Duggan. You need to tell me what, if anything your friends, and Mary, did with your cast."

"Are you talking about drawing cartoons and signing their names on it?"

"Yes, that's exactly what I meant," he said with a grim smile.

Duggan seemed confused. "What's that got to do with Mary's disappearance?"

"That incident – or fact, whatever you want to call it, as far as I can ascertain was never in the public domain. There were no reports in any of the media. Would that be correct?"

Duggan reached for a packet of cigarettes and a lighter. "Not as far as I know," he said, holding out the opened packet to Souter. "It's so insignificant, I can't possibly see its importance."

He took a cigarette and allowed Duggan to light it for him before replying. "The fact that it wasn't made public and it is so unimportant to you, is its great significance now, because it gives credence to what this witness has to say."

Duggan placed a glass ashtray on the breakfast bar. "Which new witness is this?"

"At the moment, I can't tell you that."

Duggan looked angry.

"But what I'd like you to do," Souter added quickly, "is contact the police – specifically try to see Detective Chief Inspector Strong at Wood Street."

"And say what exactly? That I've had some journalist come and pester me about a new witness?"

Souter exhaled and flicked ash into the tray. "I understand your annoyance, Mr Duggan, but if you saw DCI Strong and told him what you've just told me about your arm all those years ago, it would probably persuade him to take what my witness has said seriously."

"And you think this would help find Mary?"

Souter held his gaze. "I do, Paul. I honestly do."

Duggan stood up and turned away, holding his head in his hands. "Christ, there's never a day goes by when I don't think of our Mary." He turned back again. "She was only eight years old."

"I know."

"Answer me this, Mr Souter. Honestly. Do you think she's alive?"

Souter stood. "No," he said, "I think she's gone a long time ago."

Duggan's eyes filled with tears and he leaned against the bar before sagging back down into the chair.

Souter placed a hand on his shoulder. "I'm sorry, Paul, but you asked me to give you an honest answer." He stubbed out his cigarette and made to leave, pausing at the back door. "You will contact DCI Strong?"

Duggan nodded and Souter departed feeling like shit for knocking the stuffing out of the man.

29

With a towel wrapped around her head, Veronica came into the living room and was about to plug in the hairdryer when the phone rang. She looked at it for several seconds, nervous of who might be on the other end. She'd had visits from the police and then she'd had that thug call round on Friday night. If he'd gotten their address, then he could easily obtain the telephone number. This wasn't right. This wasn't what she'd bargained for when she'd moved in to share Steve Chapman's bed. She knew he was no saint, but she never thought he'd bring her trouble like this. Bad enough the police; she'd never been visited by them before. But there was something threatening, subtle, but still real, about that character looking for Steve.

She snatched the handset. "Yes," she said, as sternly as she could.

"Veronica, it's me. Is everything okay?"

"Steve! What the Hell's going on? You disappear in the middle of the night, don't tell me anything. Where are you?" Instinctively, she looked out the window to see if anyone was watching the house.

"It's best I don't tell you. But I'm safe."

"You're safe. Well that's all bloody right then. What about me? I'm here answering questions from the police about where you've got to."

"I thought they'd be round. What did you tell them?"

"What could I tell them? You'd pissed off and I'd no idea where. Anyway, never mind the police, I had some other man here on Friday, just after the coppers left, asking where you were."

"Who?"

"I don't know, he didn't say. But he frightened me, Steve." She sat down on the sofa. "Said something about an arrangement and needing to talk to you. What arrangement? Because whatever it is, I don't want you to bring me into it. I'm twenty-four years old and this is the first time the police have ever found their way to me. I'm not having it, you hear me?"

"This other man … what did he look like?"

She hesitated for a second, aware he'd just ignored her rant, focussing on her mysterious visitor. "Tall, about six foot, filled out his jacket well enough. Round face and a slight accent."

"What kind of accent?"

"I don't bloody know, do I? … Foreign." She could hear her boyfriend take a deep breath. "Steve," she continued in a level tone, "what have you got yourself involved in?"

"It's just spiralled. I was only helping Gaz. It's all to do with his brother, Chris."

She could feel the colour drain from her face. "You mean …" She hadn't made the connection before. Not paying too much attention to Steve's annoying, slightly simple friend, she never picked up on his surname. "That man who was murdered in Garforth last week?" The question went unanswered. "Oh Christ, Steve."

"Look, don't worry. It'll all blow over. We'll just keep a low profile for a while."

"Don't worry? It's not you here frightened to answer the door. Crapping myself when I hear creaks and groans in the night."

"I'm sorry Veronica. I didn't know this would … Can't you go and stay with your sister for a while? Just while …"

"Why? Why should I?" She stood up. "Just because someone I was stupid enough to … No. You're quite right, Steve. I'm leaving. Don't bother looking for me. I won't be coming back."

"No, listen Veronica, I didn't …"

She put the phone down. A few seconds later, she picked it up again and dialled 1471. Number withheld. She began to sob uncontrollably, letting her feelings gush out. Finally released from her pent up worries about Steve, her relief turned to anger. He'd put her through hell. Not knowing what had happened to him, where he was; that worry had carried her through the visits from the police and the stranger; it had made her stronger. Now the little shit had called. He was safe somewhere, saving his own skin and she would be left to pick up the pieces. Well she wasn't having that. She came to a decision. Wiping her eyes on the towel, hair forgotten, she strode into the bedroom. From under the bed, she retrieved a black holdall then threw open the wardrobe doors. She looked at her collection of clothes and began to carefully fold them up and place them in the holdall. She wasn't going to be beholden to her sister though. She'd sort something out. She'd speak to her friend at work tomorrow. She packed most of her clothes and left the last few bits for when she knew exactly what she would be doing. Finally she zipped up the bag and threw it on the floor by the front door, ready for a quick exit.

30
Monday

Eleven o'clock on a bright sunny morning and Strong caught his first tenuous sight of Felixstowe. Crossing the Orwell Bridge on the A14 at Ipswich, he looked to his right and spotted the dock cranes on the horizon, like some pre-historic arachnid.

It had been late Sunday afternoon before the owner of the Lexus had called Stainmore back. He'd been away in the vehicle for the weekend and certainly had no intention of exporting it. He also told her he'd contacted Olympia Insurance for a quote six weeks ago but had not taken it up.

"Flynn was okay with this then?" Stainmore had asked on the journey south.

"No real objections, Kelly. Even suggested Sarah Wagstaff to sign the warrant."

"Is that the old girl from Sandal, wears her grey hair in a severe bun and looks like she's sucking on a lemon?"

Strong chuckled. "No, Sally's a lot younger, wild blonde hair, looks like Bonnie Tyler on a bad night. Not like your typical magistrate at all."

After a short while, Stainmore had taken up the conversation again. "I had your friend call in to see me on Saturday," she said.

"Which friend would that be?"

"That Yorkshire Post journalist, Souter. The one involved in the Calder Street shooting back in February."

"And did he have a young girl with him?"

"You know about it then?"

"Her missing friend, yes. Any thoughts, Kelly?"

Stainmore considered her response. "First reaction, I'd have said that it was par for the course for young girls to move around in that game."

"But? ..." Strong questioned.

"But the young girl, Sammy, she seemed genuinely concerned. They have a lot of history together and it appears to be totally out of character for her friend, Maria, to fail to return and not make any contact. It's over a week now."

"So a girl working the streets, another involved to some extent in the sex trade ... what's the likelihood of a connection?"

"Too early to say, guv, but I've got Luke instigating another missing persons for Maria."

Fifteen minutes after crossing the bridge, Strong and Stainmore approached the docks complex and realised the enormity their task could have been. Hundreds of containers stacked about eight high and God knows how many deep lined one area visible from the road.

Detective Sergeant James Cowling met them at the dock gates and escorted them to a small portakabin office used by security as a base. Cowling checked the warrant Strong had brought with him and showed them the paperwork accompanying the containers they held in a shed used for routine inspections.

"The lads are still on a high from last Toosday," Cowling explained in his Suffolk burr. He'd amused Strong earlier when he referred to his 'compooter' in the same fashion. "Yes, second biggest haul of cocaine we've ever uncovered," he went on, "Hidden in the hollow sections of the trailer's chassis."

As he was talking, Strong was studying the documents for the two vehicles. "This is good," Strong finally said, indicating the V5 registration for the Lexus. "This is very good, but it's a fake." He was comparing the details with those he'd brought with him in a file. "And so is this," he continued, referring to the Mercedes document. "Whoever's produced these has done an excellent job. They've managed to reproduce the watermarks, all the coloured sections as they should be but the VIN numbers and engine numbers relate to the stolen vehicles which, I'll lay money will be what we'll find on the cars in those containers. The registration marks are from the cloned vehicles, so any checks here would show everything to be in order."

Cowling picked up the vehicle registrations and held them up to the light, turning them over and looking closely at the type. "You're quite right," he said, "these do look genuine." He looked at Strong, then walked to the door. "Shall we have a look?"

Strong rose to his feet and followed the Suffolk man outside, Stainmore close behind.

Gulls screeched overhead in the warm sunshine as they made their way along the concrete road towards the large shed about a hundred yards away. Strong breathed deeply, enjoying the salty, ozone-laden air.

"Get some of that in your lungs, Kelly," he quipped.

Stainmore glanced across to Cowling. "Sorry about this," she said, "my boss doesn't get out much."

Cowling smiled. "We don't do too badly down here weather-wise. Only trouble we have sometimes is if the wind whips in off the North Sea and the cranes have to stop working. Then we have to implement Operation Stack on the A14. Wagons parked up for miles."

They entered the warehouse through a single door, Cowling exchanging pleasantries with colleagues. "Okay, Simon," he said to one of them, "let's open them up and see what we've got."

Inside the large well-lit hangar were a number of articulated lorries and vans in various states of undress. White boiler-suited inspectors, some with instruments and a couple with dogs, pored over them, searching every possible void. Towards the rear stood two maroon-painted containers. They headed in their direction.

Simon released the catches and lifted the levers before turning them to release the door. As the light flooded in, they could see the distinctive rear end of the dark blue Lexus 400.

Stainmore had managed to obtain spare sets of keys from the owners of the stolen vehicles and Strong pulled a set from his pocket and pressed a button. The door locks clicked and the orange indicator lamps flashed several times. He turned towards Cowling. "I'd say that was the one we've been looking for."

"I'll get a forensics officer to check it out." Cowling then addressed his colleague, "The other one now."

Simon repeated the unlocking operation on the second container. Just as the seal broke, it was as if the air was sucked into it.

Strong shivered. He felt his pulse quicken and an unease descend upon him. A faint but distinctive aroma seeped out.

"Oh, Christ," he muttered and began fumbling in his pocket for the other set of keys. "I've got a bad feeling about this, Kelly." He pressed the fob and the indicators flashed on the white Mercedes inside. He put on a pair of latex gloves and slowly stepped into the container. As the others looked on, his hand carefully reached for the boot's catch. He squeezed the button and the lock clicked. Gradually, the lid rose and the odour grew in intensity. Then he saw her, head wrapped in a clear plastic bag, lying on her back. His eyes pricked and he turned away. He answered Stainmore's questioning look with a shake of the head. Taking a deep breath, he strode over to an exit door and burst out into the fresh air.

Stainmore followed a minute later and joined her boss on the dockside.

"It's her," he said, staring out to the North Sea through a gap between two huge ships.

"DS Cowling's arranging for a forensic team from Ipswich."

Strong automatically reached inside his jacket, then patted his side pockets. "Shit," he said.

"Looks like you chose the wrong month to quit smokin'," Stainmore said in a mock American accent.

Strong flashed a quick smile at his colleague, then grew serious. "Helena was a lovely looking girl, Kelly. Not much older than Amanda. Not unlike Amanda to look at too." Stainmore said nothing. "You know I've lost count of the number of bodies I've seen in my career. I used to think it would get easier. But it never does."

"If it did, you wouldn't be able to do your job, guv."

"They come here for a better life, to escape persecution and exploitation by bigoted bastards and hardened criminals in their own country. And she ends up like that. Discarded in a car boot. In a foreign land."

"You want me to let Jim Ryan know?"

"No, Kelly. I'll do that. He'll have the difficult task of breaking the news to her sister. She'll have to come down and identify Helena."

They were silent for a few seconds before Stainmore, sensing her boss wanted to be alone, began to walk away. "I'll just go and check where they're likely to take her, guv."

Strong nodded then turned seaward again before taking out his mobile and dialling a number. After several rings, a female voice answered, *"Dad?"*

"Hi, Amanda."

"Dad, is everything okay?"

"Of course, lovey, I just wanted to hear your voice, that's all."

31

"Mr Souter, it's Paul Duggan here," the voice on the telephone announced.

Souter was at his desk on the first floor of the Yorkshire Post building, drafting a follow-up piece on the murder of Chris Baker, when Patricia on reception put the call through. He'd been trying to gain access to Baker's widow but Halliday's team were keeping her off the radar for now, so he'd had to make do with some neighbour reaction. He was trying to knock the usual, 'shocked that anything like this could happen to someone round here,' and 'he seemed such a nice man,' into something interesting for the readers.

"Paul. Listen, I'm sorry if I upset you yesterday," Souter said.

"It were just a bit of a shock, really. I mean I weren't expecting anyone to come knocking after all this time. I think in my heart I've always known that Mary's gone. It's just, as I said ..."

"Have you spoken to DCI Strong yet?"

"That's why I'm ringing you. Well, one of the reasons anyway."

"Let me guess," Souter interrupted, "One was to see if I was genuine?"

There was a slight pause before Duggan answered. *"I suppose, if I'm honest, yes."*

"Don't worry, Paul, I'd do the same."

"The thing is, I re-arranged my morning so I could go down to Wood Street but they tell me your Inspector Strong isn't in all day and they couldn't tell me when he's back. I just wondered if there's anybody else I could talk to?"

"They didn't suggest anyone, did they?"

"They mentioned a DC Ormerod but with you being so specific, I didn't know if he would know what I were on about."

"All right, Paul. Let me have your number and I'll see what I can find out and get back to you."

After Duggan had given him his contact details, the call ended and Souter dialled Strong's mobile. At first it was engaged, but after a couple of minutes he tried again.

"Bob?" Strong answered.

"Colin, how're you doing?"

"You're quick off the mark."

Puzzled, Souter decided on a guarded response. "You know me," he said.

"It's her."

"Who exactly?"

"Helena Cryanovic. But I don't want that to get out just yet."

"I understand." He was desperately trying to coordinate his thoughts. "That was the Albanian asylum seeker you were telling me about?"

"Yes."

"Whereabouts are you, Col?"

"Felixstowe Docks, why? Wait a minute, I thought … bollocks. You don't know anything about this do you?"

Souter stayed silent, scribbling a few notes on a pad.

"Why did you call?"

"I just wanted to know when you'd be back because there's someone I need you to see."

"Who's that?"

"Paul Duggan, Mary's brother."

"You're not still on about that, are you?"

"It's important. You should hear what he has to say."

Strong hesitated and Souter could hear him take a deep breath. *"I'll probably be back tomorrow sometime",* he finally said. *"But listen Bob, don't report any of this until we have a chance to inform the sister."*

"Okay Col, I understand." Souter then pressed the red button.

He was thoughtful for a moment before checking his computer for another number. He found it and dialled, this time from his land line. After the receptionist on the East Anglian Daily Times answered, he asked to be put through to the newsdesk. Eventually, a male voice came on the line.

"Is there a breaking major incident at Felixstowe Docks, do you know?" he asked.

"Er, not that we know of at the moment. Is there some information you have, sir?"

"Not to worry, my mistake." Souter replaced the handset.

32

Cowling organised two rooms at the Novotel in Ipswich for Strong and Stainmore. After checking in and freshening up, they all met up in an Italian restaurant nearby that the Suffolk detective had recommended.

"You've spoken to your colleague back in Yorkshire then?" Cowling asked, as the waiter fussed around bringing bottled water and a carafe of house red wine.

Strong waited until they were on their own once more before responding. "About the sister?"

Cowling nodded.

"DS Ryan broke the news this afternoon. He's bringing her down first thing in the morning."

"The PM's scheduled for nine tomorrow, so give us time to make her presentable, she could make the identification around one, say?"

"That should be fine." Strong offered round the bread sticks. "Any thoughts from your forensic people as to cause of death then, James?"

"Ah, you probably didn't see it when you opened the boot but there was a gunshot wound to the back of the head."

Strong looked sharply at Stainmore.

"I steered clear after I spoke to you on the dockside," she responded. "I thought it best to let them get on with it, so it's the first I've heard too."

Strong turned back to Cowling. "Any idea what kind of weapon was used?"

"At first sight, probably a small calibre weapon but, I must admit, I've not seen too many shootings."

"Tell me, I didn't see one, was there an exit wound?"

The Suffolk man thought for a second before shaking his head. "No, I don't think so."

Strong was lost in thought and the conversation stalled as the waiter brought the starters.

Cowling sampled some of his minestrone, then spoke. "We've had the press sniffing round."

Strong swallowed some garlic mushrooms before responding. "Who exactly?"

"East Anglian. Heard we'd found a body at the docks and wanted some details."

"No mention of Yorkshire connections then?"

"Not as far as I've heard but we've got the press officer dealing with it. There'll probably be a press conference tomorrow."

"Not till after Magda's identified her sister though?" Strong said.

"Of course."

"Have we got any other forensics from the car?" Stainmore asked.

"I spoke to my colleagues just before I came out and they told me the car was fairly clean. Nothing on the handles, steering wheel or gear stick where you'd expect."

The waiter returned, collected the plates and topped up their wine.

"Probably wiped thoroughly before it was put in the container," Strong suggested.

"But they did get some from inside the glove box and a couple of partials from under the bonnet – screen wash filler, that sort of thing."

They were silent again as their main courses arrived, chicken in a spicy pasta sauce for Cowling, a pepper steak for Strong and a pizza for Stainmore.

"They probably belong to the rightful owner," Stainmore said. "I'll have to organise his for elimination."

Cowling took up his knife and fork. "In the meantime, we'll run them through the system. Just in case we get a hit."

Strong nodded. "Thanks. Let me know as soon as you get anything."

Cowling took a sip of wine. "We also got some fibres from the boot and on her clothes, so we'll see what that shows up."

"Any indication of time of death?"

"The pathologist reckons at least a week but he'll have a better idea in the morning once he's completed a few tests."

"That figures. I mean it's unlikely anyone's tampered with the container since it arrived at the docks so she was in the boot when it left Yorkshire."

"That's what my boss reckoned too, so he's happy for me just to assist on this one until the coroner releases the body."

The rest of the meal passed without any further revelations. Cowling spoke of some of the investigations he'd been involved with and picked Strong's brains about some of his cases in Yorkshire. With coffees to round off, Strong thanked his host and walked back to the hotel with Kelly Stainmore.

"It got to you today, didn't it?" she asked.

Strong sighed. "Must admit, I'm not looking forward to tomorrow."

"Do you think this is linked with the Baker case?"

"Let's just see what the PM throws up. Might be an opportunity to piss Halliday off, though." He stepped aside to let Stainmore through the hotel's revolving door first.

"Fancy a nightcap, guv?" she asked, nodding towards the bar.

"Not this time, Kelly," he said, "I'm knackered. You carry on, though."

She did and Strong went to his room.

He switched on the television and began to undress, making use of the wall-mounted trouser press. Trevor McDonald was just rounding off the news bulletin with a light-hearted item but he wasn't paying any attention. He wasn't in the mood. He went into the bathroom, rinsed his face then cleaned his teeth. He'd have a shower in the morning. Back in the room, he lay down on the bed and decided the TV was irritating him. With no real interest in the latest C list celebrity's upcoming true story about how having breast implants was the key to making her feel a complete woman, he switched it off with the remote. A complete airhead, he thought.

Lying back, he went over the events of the past few days. He was annoyed with himself for not taking the missing person's report more seriously when Jim Ryan discussed it with him. There again, he did have the Susan Brown report to deal with. At least that ended better than Helena. And what of Bob's friend? Another missing young woman. The image of the open car boot in the container flashed into his mind yet again. Helena, such a lovely looking girl treated like that; wrapped in plastic. Was her death connected to Chris Baker? No exit wounds in both cases. What had she got herself into? She was obviously involved with Szymanski and Mirczack. Was she just a receptionist as Stella had said or had she been working as a masseur in the parlours? Or some other role? Questions, all these questions. But the most important question of all, who was the lucky bastard next door making the bedhead bounce off the wall?

God, he missed Laura.

33

The bus dropped Veronica off at the end of her road. It had been another unremarkable day in the shoe shop where she worked in the Ridings Centre in Wakefield. There had been no further unpleasant visits. She also felt relieved by her decision to leave and her girlfriend's offer to let her rent the spare room in her flat. With just the last few things to pack, she'd be ready when her friend called to pick her up shortly. And then, they would discuss where they would be going in town tonight. Beginning to feel more relaxed already, she wasn't paying much attention to anything in her street.

The big car was squeezed into a space opposite her house. The two men inside had followed her progress since she'd come into view. The driver nodded in her direction. "She must know something."

The passenger zipped up his jacket and placed a hand on the door handle in anticipation. "I'll find out," he said.

She walked up the short path to her front door, put the key in the lock and turned. As she opened the door, she felt the palm of a hand push her inside.

"What the ..." She tripped over the holdall that had been beside the door since Sunday.

The door slammed shut and the big foreign man bent over her. "You need be careful," he said with a smirk.

"You again."

He offered a hand to help her up but she refused, getting to her feet herself.

"Just get out. Get out!" she screamed.

He held both hands up. "Look, I have no wish to hurt you. I only need to know where Chapman is."

"I told you last week, I have no idea. Now, get the fuck out of here."

He tutted calmly. "Really, that is no way for a young woman to talk. I'll bet you don't talk to Steve like that. Unless …" He looked down to her breasts, then her legs and finally, the black holdall. "This is a very stupid place to leave a bag. It could cause an accident."

He bent down and began to unzip it.

"Leave that alone. It's nothing to do with you."

He let her snatch it from him and stood up. "Why don't you tell me what you know? He isn't worth it."

"For the last time, there's nothing to tell. He left here early hours of Thursday and I haven't seen him since."

"But you've heard from him."

"No."

"Have it your way. But my people will not be pleased when they find out you have been lying to me."

She pulled herself up to her full height. "You don't frighten me."

His smile only registered on his lips. "You have been warned," he said, turned and let himself out.

Veronica leant against the back of the door and burst into tears.

"Well?" the driver asked, once his passenger had returned.

"She says the same as before. She doesn't know where he is, that she has not heard from him."

"You believe her?"

"There was a bag of clothes behind the door. I think he has been in contact and they are ready for him to collect."

"You must return." The driver checked the street and pulled away from the kerb. "For now, we have another matter to attend to."

A few minutes later, Veronica's friend drove down the street and pulled into the space left by the big car. Veronica had completed packing and was watching from the window. She dashed out and slammed the door, shoving her keys through the letterbox. As she strode down the path, the telephone rang inside.

34

Ten to seven in the evening and the sun was dropping behind the trees at the end of the road. The stone buildings radiated the heat of the day and it still felt warm in the street. Souter knocked on the front door of Alison's terraced house. After a few seconds, the door opened.

"Hi," he said.

Alison smiled. "Hello you. I was wondering if I'd see you tonight." She swung the door open allowing him to step straight into the living room.

"Sammy not around?"

Alison closed the door. "Gone to see Susan, would you believe."

He looked surprised. "Those two a bit chummy, then?"

Alison walked through to the kitchen and he followed. "They were chatting away like old friends when we went in to see her the other night. I think they've both got interesting life stories to exchange. Both had difficulties to overcome in different ways."

"True, I suppose." Souter leaned against a worktop. "How's Susan doing?"

"I spoke to Gillian this afternoon and she's due for another operation tomorrow morning. They've got to clean out the leg wounds. It's routine for that type of injury apparently. That's why Sammy went in to see her tonight, to wish her well."

"If everything goes okay, I'll try and pop in to see her tomorrow."

She pulled a bottle of Chianti from the wine rack. "You staying?"

"Mmm, looks good." He put his arms around her and bent his head to kiss her. "Have you eaten?"

"Sammy and me had something when I came in. Why, are you hungry?"

"Just thought we might eat out but ..."

"I can knock you something up if you like."

He produced his best lecherous expression. "Best offer I've had all day."

"Behave and open this." She smiled and thrust the bottle into his chest.

He found the corkscrew and began to open the wine as Alison opened and closed several cupboards in search of something suitable. Eventually, she looked in the freezer and pulled out a flat cardboard box. "Pizza all right for you?"

Five minutes later, back in the living room, the margarita warming in the oven, Alison was snuggled up next to him on the sofa, a glass of wine in her hand.

"So how are you two getting along?" he asked.

"She's okay." Alison turned to look at him. "She's a good kid really. God knows what she's been through in that short life but ... so far so good."

"She could do with a job but with her past, it might not be that easy."

She turned back round and tucked herself under his arm. "You're right. But did you know she's a whizz on the computer?"

"No. She told me she had a friend who was."

"Well, she sorted mine out here yesterday. I've been having real problems, running slow, crashing regularly. I thought I'd got a virus."

"And Sammy's fixed it?"

"Yeah. Running perfectly now, and as fast as I remember when I first got it."

Souter leaned his head back into the sofa. "Well if she's good with the new technology, it'll help getting a job." He took a sip of his wine and gently stroked Alison's hair. "How long have we got?" he asked.

"Pizza should be ready in another five minutes."

He chuckled. "No, I mean ... how long do we have ... you know?"

161

"Like I said, another five minutes."

"Cheeky sod," he said and playfully hit her with a cushion.

They were back on the sofa, relaxing in the afterglow of their earlier energetic activities upstairs. Alison was wrapped in a pink dressing gown, Souter back in his trousers and a loose shirt. The television was quietly reporting the ten o'clock news. At times like these, he would have previously enjoyed a cigarette. Losing interest in the latest inflation figures, his thoughts wandered and he realised that since he'd met Alison, his craving for nicotine had subsided. Since Colin had given up his cigars, he'd begun to think it was really a crazy habit and perhaps he should go the whole hog as well and give up completely.

From outside in the street, running footsteps could be heard approaching. A second later, a key was hurriedly inserted in the lock, two attempts before it engaged and then the door flew open. Sammy rushed in and slammed it shut behind her. She was breathing fast and appeared close to tears.

"Sammy, what's wrong?" Souter jumped up from the couch.

"Bob! Sorry, I didn't expect ..." Sammy took a deep breath. "I'm being stupid. Don't bother about me."

"Nonsense. Come and sit down. Something's obviously bothered you."

Sammy sat on the armchair. "It was just ... well, now I think about it ... probably just my imagination."

"Sammy, let's hear it."

"Okay." Another deep breath. "I got the feeling I was being followed."

"What made you think that?"

"I dunno. It was ... well, I thought I spotted a car when I was waiting for the bus outside the hospital." She looked at Souter. "You know I went to see Susan."

He nodded.

"It was a dark Merc. I mean it looked like it was just parked up but I got the impression there were two people inside – just sitting there."

"But you couldn't see them clearly?"

"No. But when I got off the bus here in Ossett, I'm sure it was the same car that pulled up behind it. Only this time some bloke got out. He didn't look at me or anything. In fact he slowly walked off in the opposite direction."

"So just a coincidence then?"

"Except when I turned into Station Road he was coming towards me."

"Then what?"

"I turned and ran. But don't worry, I didn't come straight here. I doubled back through a few side streets before I came in from the opposite end."

"And you didn't see him again?"

"No."

Souter got up, opened the front door and looked up and down the street. "Nothing," he said when he sat back down.

Alison looked nervous. "Who do you think it might have been?"

"No idea."

He leaned forward. "How old was the man? Could he have been a punter?"

Sammy shook her head. "He didn't look familiar. In his thirties, I'd guess."

"Possibly an associate of your pimp?" he went on.

"Look, forget it. It's just my imagination, okay?" She looked at Alison. "Can I have a drink?"

"Help yourself."

"Thanks." She walked off into the kitchen as Souter and Alison exchanged glances.

Sammy returned with a glass of Coke, her mood lighter. "I haven't told you, have I?" she said to Souter as she sat down in the chair again. "I've got some news for you."

"What's that then?"

"You know your friend, the detective?"

"Colin, DCI Strong."

"Well, he's looking for someone, isn't he?"

"He's probably always looking for people."

"But when you spoke to him on Saturday after we came out of the Town Hall he mentioned somebody could have gone off to stay with their cousin, Barry Whitefield."

"You heard that?"

"As well as knowing what to forget, I've also learned to remember things that could be of use."

"So what about this Whitefield character?"

"I think I've got five or six possibilities."

Souter looked at Alison, surprised, then back to Sammy. "So how have you done that?"

She smiled. "The internet's a mine of information, if you know how to use it. You can trace families and all sorts, but this search still needs a bit more work to refine it. I need to check things like the electoral roles."

"So this friend of yours who's a 'genius on the computer' as you told me, they don't exist, do they? It's actually you, isn't it? You tracked down Paul Duggan?"

"It's only what I've picked up from other people. It's quite easy really."

"Go on then, tell me what you've found out so far."

35
Tuesday

When Magda returned from the viewing room she looked as if she had no more tears to cry. DS Ryan, who had accompanied her, nodded the confirmation Strong already knew. She looked at Strong, her expression asking the question before she spoke. "Why? What she done to anyone here?"

"I will find out, Magda. And I will find whoever did this."

"That bastard Szymanski ... and Mirczack. They did this. We were okay till they ..." Her eyes blazed. "Why don't you arrest them mister important policeman."

"We need to talk properly," Strong said, leading her down the corridor to the mortuary office Cowling had arranged for them to use.

After some coffee had been brought in, Strong, Ryan and Cowling sat down in the cramped office to talk to Magda. Stainmore was chasing up feedback from the pathologist and ballistics reports on the bullet used in the murder.

After she officially confirmed that the body was that of her sister, Strong began the questioning he hoped would tease some important information from her.

"First of all, Magda," he said, "we are all truly sorry for your loss. The last time we spoke when you came in to see us, we were looking at a missing person's enquiry. We're in a different situation now, so I'd like you to be absolutely honest with us – not that I thought you weren't before – but forget anything else you may think you might be in trouble for, the only thing that interests me is finding out what happened to your sister and who is responsible."

Magda slowly nodded.

"So can you tell me exactly when was the last time you saw Helena?"

"On Thursday, a week ago. She tell me she was going to visit some friend."

"I know that's what you told me before but that friend doesn't appear to exist." He sat back in his seat. "Now, my turn to be honest. I know that Helena worked at a massage parlour, Sweet Sensations, in Chapeltown." A shocked look passed over Magda's face. "But from what we can tell, she was only employed as a receptionist, she didn't do anything unsavoury."

The woman looked down.

Strong leaned forward, arms on the table. "Again, Magda, I'm not interested in anything else other than finding Helena's killer. Now, did you know, or did you suspect she was working in some capacity?"

Slowly, she looked up at him, held his gaze for a second then said, "I know not what she do but I did think she do something."

"What made you think that?"

"She go out on certain nights and come back around eleven. Each time she tell me she visit friend in Leeds. But one night I see her getting into his car at end of street."

"And whose car would that be?"

"Szymanski's."

"What kind of car does he have?"

"I think a BMW, black, but it was him driving."

"When was the last time you saw Szymanski?"

"It was then, the week before she disappear, the Tuesday, I think."

Strong gave a wan smile. "You're doing really well, Magda. Everything you can remember, no matter how small it may seem, will help us."

For the first time since she sat down Magda took a drink of her coffee.

"So, just to recap, the last time you saw Helena was a week past Thursday, that would be the 1st of September?"

"Yes."

Strong made a brief note before continuing. "When you came to see us last, you mentioned you'd come home and found Helena with Szymanski and Mirczack on one occasion."

"Yes."

"Can you tell us again what happened?"

"I came home and they left quickly."

Strong sighed deeply. "There must be more. Did they say anything? What were they doing? Anything you can remember, however small, may be vital."

"They no expect me to come home. They all look surprised when I came in. Szymanski and Mirczack were both standing." Magda swallowed hard and fought back tears. "Helena was sitting. I could tell it was not relaxed. They quickly finish what they say."

"Could you tell what they were talking about?"

She looked over Strong's head and into the distance for a second or two, as if trying to recall something. "I got impression Mirczack was warning Helena not to do what she had done before. He say something like 'Make that the last time. You know what happens.' Then he say to Szymanski, 'Let's go.'"

"You're sure that's what he said, 'Make that the last time. You know what happens.'?"

"I think so. He was speaking quietly. Then he put his finger up like this." Magda held up her forefinger at an angle. "He raise his eyebrows then he pushed past me and left."

"What about Szymanski? Did he have anything to say?"

"He just say to Helena, 'Be careful,' then he follow Mirczack. But then he turn round and look at Helena, holding a finger to his lips." She mirrored the action.

"Okay Magda, DS Ryan will take you back to Wakefield."

"What about Helena? When can ..." She became tearful again.

"It'll all depend on when the coroner releases ... her." Strong stopped himself from referring to Helena as 'the body'. "I'll try and find out as soon as I can. But for now, thank you for your help."

She slowly rose to her feet. "You will get them?"

"I will do my very best," he promised. "In the meantime, when you get back home, I'd appreciate it if you would let DS Ryan have a look around Helena's room. There may be something that might help us."

Magda looked as if she was about to say something, but just nodded, turned and left the room with Ryan.

As they departed, Stainmore appeared, acknowledged the woman and Ryan, closed the door behind her and sat down.

"What news, Kelly?"

"Pretty interesting, I'd say, guv. Cause of death, as we already know, confirmed as a single gunshot to the back of the head. Initial estimate of time of death given as between seven to twelve days ago. That's between a week ago Wednesday and last Monday. He's conducting more tests, you know the usual thing with insect life, to refine that. But I did say, she was last seen on the Thursday." She pulled out her notebook. "However, the fascinating thing is, the bullet that did the damage, and it did do some damage internally, was one of these semi-jacketed wadcutter rounds you mentioned had been used against Chris Baker."

Strong leaned back and looked to the ceiling. "Shit," he said. "I've not come across too many shootings in my career ... but two using this same ammunition in such a close period of time. They've got to be connected."

"You suspected that last night though, didn't you? That's why you asked about an exit wound."

He nodded and sat back up straight. "When I saw her in the boot, there was no obvious sign. So how soon before we can get something?"

"I've arranged for the fragments to be sent to the firearms lab in Leeds," Stainmore answered.

"Good. That's where Baker's evidence has gone. I'll chase that up when we get back to Yorkshire."

Strong stood up and held out his hand to Cowling. "James, thanks for all you've done for us."

The Suffolk man shook hands with him. "No problem. Only wish I could help more."

"I'd appreciate it if you could let me know as soon as the coroner can release the body. And anything else your forensic team might uncover. But for now," he glanced towards Stainmore, "I think we've gleaned as much as we can down here, Kelly. Time to rattle a few cages back north."

36

Sammy was in the kitchen, hand washing a couple of tops when the knock came from the front door. Drying her hands, she made her way to answer it, knowing Alison was in the bath.

As she opened the door, it was pushed wide.

"Hello, Sammy," the man said, taking a step into the room, hand on the door.

She tried to close it but he stepped forward and pushed Sammy back into the room.

"That's no way to greet me. Especially when you're in my debt."

She regained her balance. "You need to get out."

"I'll go when I get what you owe me."

"What the hell's going on?" Alison appeared down the stairs, dressing gown around her and a towel on her head. "Who are you and what do you think you're doing, barging your way into my house?"

The man looked shocked to see Alison. He obviously was expecting Sammy to be in on her own. "I've come for my money."

"What money?"

"Perhaps your ... friend here should tell you."

Alison tensed. "No. You tell me."

"She owes me rent. All £800 of it for her and her scabby mate."

"Right. I don't know who you are but you do *not* force your way into my house demanding money from anyone. You will leave now or I call the police. If you think anyone owes you money, there are proper means to go about it. And this isn't one of them. Understand?"

The man smirked at Alison. "Got to give it to you," he said, "you've got some spunk." He walked back to the door, paused and looked at Sammy. "Now, I'll be back tomorrow to collect. Like I say, £800." Finally, he stepped out into the street and was gone.

Sammy dived for the door and slammed it shut.

Fifty minutes later, Alison let Souter in to the house, a stern look on her face. He'd made the dash down the M1 to Ossett from his Leeds office.

"What happened?" he asked once inside.

Sammy was sitting in an armchair, eyes red from crying. "I'm sorry," she whimpered.

He stood, looking from Alison to Sammy and back again.

"We had a visitor," Alison said, "and not a welcome one at that." She sat down in the other chair while Souter sat on the sofa. She folded her arms. "Why don't you tell him, Sammy?"

Sammy looked up briefly at him then down to her hands in her lap. "I thought I could handle it. I didn't want you to be involved. You've done so much for me – had faith in me and I've let you down."

"So," Souter said, "from the beginning."

Sammy wiped her face then took a deep breath. "Me and Maria, we've been renting our room from a scumbag by the name of Jed Robinson. He knows what we had to do to earn the money. That's why the rent was so high."

"How much?"

"£200 each a week."

"Each!" Alison exclaimed. "Bloody Hell."

"Pimping by any other word," Souter added. "Go on."

"When you saw me outside A & E, he hadn't thrown me out. We'd rowed."

"He hit you?"

Sammy hesitated. "Yes. He wanted two weeks money. With Maria missing, I'd got no chance. He said it was a warning. Something to help me focus and he'd be back." She sniffed and rubbed her nose with the back of her hand. "When you took me in, he thought I'd run off. I went back next day when I knew no-one would be about and grabbed the rest of our things." She looked up again. "But that little shit in the room upstairs must have seen me. He also saw me with you that day we looked for Tracey."

"And this mystery car last night?"

"His brother, Phil. They're partners, renting properties."

"And you recognised him, didn't you?"

Sammy nodded. "I did try to avoid being followed and I honestly thought I'd done enough."

"But?"

Alison unfolded her arms and took up the story. "I was upstairs. My day off this week and I don't think he was expecting anyone else to be in, was he, Sammy?"

She shook her head. "It was Jed. He pushed me back inside."

"That's when I heard the commotion and came rushing down the stairs." Alison then related the rest of the events.

"So how much was he after?" Souter asked.

"£800," Sammy said in a quiet voice.

"Eight hundred," he exploded. "How the … No I'm not having that. I've been there. It's a shitty little room in a scruffy rundown house. I wouldn't pay twenty quid a week all in." He took his mobile out and began scrolling down his contact list.

"What are you doing?" Alison asked.

"I'm going to sort it." He put his mobile to his ear for a few seconds then cancelled the call. "Shit, it's switched off. I forgot he's probably still down in Suffolk."

"Who?"

"Not to worry," he said, "there's always plan B. So, how's it been left?"

"He said he'd come back tomorrow, and he's expecting his money," Sammy trembled.

"Oh no he's not," Souter said. "I'm not having him here again."

"And neither am I," Alison joined in, "I'll get my brother Mark and his rugby club mates down here."

"No. I'll sort this once and for all. Have you got some way of contacting this Jed?"

"I've got a mobile number," Sammy responded.

"And have you still got a key to get in?"

She nodded.

"Good. Leave it with me for now." Souter rose to leave. "And try not to worry. I'll give you a call later when I've got the details worked out."

37

Strong paused in the car outside the neat semi-detached house in the quiet street in Outwood.

"How does a bloke like Chris Baker get himself into a situation like this? On the face of it, a decent man, good job, wife, house, albeit with a mortgage." He wasn't looking at his colleague sitting beside him, he was staring at the house.

"God knows how he got sucked in, guv," Stainmore responded, "But it'll be down to money and sex."

Strong turned to her. "I think you're right, Kelly. But she must have known something was wrong, wouldn't you say? I mean, you're a woman."

"Glad you noticed."

"You know what I mean. If your bloke was visiting massage parlours, having it elsewhere, you'd pick up on that, wouldn't you?"

Stainmore puffed out her cheeks and exhaled. "Difficult one, guv. Can't say I've ever been in that position. But … depends how long they've been together. Things could have gotten stale over the years. Slowly, things change."

"Do we know how long they've been married?"

"Not sure. He was thirty-one, but no kids."

Strong was silent for a few seconds before taking the keys from the ignition. "Alright, Kelly, let's see if we can fill in some gaps."

Their knock on the door was answered by the female FLO Halliday had stationed in the house. She introduced herself as DC Rebecca Walters in response to Strong and Stainmore displaying their warrant cards.

"We'd like to have a little chat with Mrs Baker, if that's okay," Strong said.

"Janice is still upset about what's happened to her husband and DCI Halliday has told me ..."

"Don't worry about DCI Halliday," he interrupted, "this is in connection with another enquiry."

DC Walters looked put out but, faced with a DCI and a DS, she stood aside.

Janice Baker was in the lounge, in one of two easy chairs, part of a three-piece leather suite. An unlit gas fire stood in a stone surround where sympathy cards festooned the mantelpiece. The room was warm but Janice was wearing a thick cardigan and trousers, legs tucked underneath she appeared to be hugging herself. Scents from three separate floral arrangements placed around the room were almost overpowering. The large screen television in one corner was switched off.

As Strong and Stainmore entered the room, a grey-haired man arrived behind them carrying a mug of tea.

"Not more questions," he said, as he gave the mug to Janice. "She's answered all she can."

Strong introduced himself and Stainmore once again. "And you are?"

"Robert Baker. I'm Chris and Gary's dad."

"Well, Mr Baker, as I'm sure you'll understand, we need to find whoever was responsible for what happened to Chris and to do that, we need to have as much information as we can."

Baker nodded. "Of course. But Janice has told all she knows to the other officers already." He looked down at his daughter-in-law and squeezed her shoulder. Janice looked up briefly through swollen eyes then back to the mug of tea she was cradling.

"If we could just go over a few things ..."

"It's alright, Robert," Janice said, then turning to the detectives, "You can sit down, you know."

Strong and Stainmore sat on the settee, Robert on the arm of Janice's chair and the FLO took the other seat.

"We're extremely sorry for what happened to Chris," Strong began. "Can you tell us what happened the night he went out?"

"Look, we've been over this several times," Baker responded.

"I'd just like to hear it again. From Mrs Baker, if you don't mind. There may be a small detail she's remembered since. I take it you weren't here that evening, Mr Baker?"

"No. I live in Ripon. I'm here to support Janice. I need to do something useful. I've lost a son too."

"Of course. In fact, could I have a word with you separately?"

Baker looked surprised initially. "Well alright, if it'll help. We can talk in the kitchen."

"Thanks, Mr Baker, my colleague can chat to Janice in the meantime." Strong looked at Stainmore as she produced a notebook from her handbag.

"We just need a little more background, Janice," she said.

Strong followed Baker into the kitchen and closed the door behind them.

"Is there no Mrs Baker?" he asked.

"My wife died three years ago."

Baker took a seat on one of the bar stools at the island unit. Strong sat at another opposite. "I'm sorry," he said.

"Probably just as well. This would have broken her heart." He made to stand. "Where are my manners? Would you and your colleague like a tea or a coffee? The kettle's just boiled."

Strong held up both hands. "No thank you, Mr Baker, we're fine. Please, sit down."

Baker slowly resumed his seat.

"There are a few questions I'd like to ask you, and there's no easy way of putting things."

Baker looked puzzled.

Strong drew a breath. "How well did you know your son?"

"What are you getting at Inspector? We all know what's happened with Gary in the past. He got in with some unfortunate company when he was younger, but Chris was trying to help him."

"Do you think there might be a connection with Gary and what he was involved with?"

Baker took a deep breath before answering. "I don't know. I just don't know."

"Have you any idea where Gary might be?"

"I can only think he's gone off somewhere with a mate. You know they were trying to make a go of a little business, him and that guy Chapman he spent time with inside. And you know Chris was trying to help them?"

Strong nodded. "We also think Gary was with Chris the night he was shot. Now, personally, I don't think Gary had anything to do with it. Whatever happened that night, we'll only find out when we can talk to him."

Baker slumped forward, put his head in his hands and rubbed his face. "It's bad enough having lost a son. I don't think I could cope if anything happened to Gary too. I only think I'm staying strong for Janice." He looked up at Strong. "You know she has no living relatives?"

"I didn't."

Baker seemed to recover. "But why are you here Inspector? What else has happened? I heard you at the door with Becky, Rebecca."

"That's why I asked you how well you knew your son." Strong paused. "Are you aware of any problems he might have been having?"

Baker looked indignant. "What sort of problems?"

"Money for one."

"No more than any married couple their age with bills to pay and a mortgage. Anyway, he knew he could always come to me. I'd have helped him."

"How would you describe the state of Chris and Janice's marriage?"

"What do you mean 'state'? I don't think I like the way this is going."

"I'm sorry, Mr Baker, it's just that some other developments have occurred which mean I have to look into all aspects here. That's why I asked to speak to you away from Janice."

Baker frowned.

"I have evidence that Chris was in the habit of visiting a massage parlour."

Baker looked angry. "You what? Evidence? What evidence?" He stood up and turned to look out of the kitchen window.

"This would be a surprise to you would it?"

When Baker turned back to face Strong, he seemed to have regained control of himself. "Well, yes. I don't know anything about that. It's hardly the sort of thing he might tell me." He looked incredulous now. "No. No, I can't believe that."

Despite the protestations, for Strong, there was something about the reaction he got from the man that didn't ring true. "So you would be surprised to hear that he has been identified as a regular customer of such an establishment?

"Which 'establishment'?

"We understand he visited Sweet Sensations in Chapeltown on a number of occasions."

"In Leeds? That's a bit of a rough area. I wouldn't have thought ..." Baker trailed off.

Strong produced some photographs from his inside pocket. "Have you ever seen either of these two men before?" He passed across pictures of Szymanski and Mirczack.

Baker took them and studied both before slowly shaking his head. "No. Never seen them before. Don't know if I'd want to, especially this one." He pointed to Mirczack.

"Do the names Szymanski and Mirczack mean anything to you?" Just a slight reaction in the eyes but, again, a shake of the head from Baker. "And you've never heard either of your sons mention them?"

"That's who these two are then?"

Strong ignored the question and showed one more photograph to Baker, that of Helena Cryanovic. "Have you ever seen this girl?"

"She's pretty. Is she the one who's saying Chris visited this place?"

"She's not actually saying anything, Mr Baker. Not any more."

Back in the car on the return journey to Wood Street, Strong asked Stainmore how the conversation with Janice had progressed.

"Still deeply shocked, guv," she replied. "He'd gone out a few times before at night. He never said exactly where. She assumed, or he led her to believe, he was having a pint with a work colleague, or his brother, Gary. Then, on that last night, she upset herself remembering the last words she ever said to him, *'If you're going to see another woman, I'll kill you.'*"

"Hmm. That might have been prophetic, Kelly."

"Well that gave me the opportunity to ask how their marriage was."

"And?"

"She said they'd been married for over ten years. The 'no kids' thing was down to her. Apparently she can't have any. And for the past three years or so, they've just been going through the motions."

"So to speak," Strong added, drawing the car to a halt at red lights. "Does she think he's been having an affair?"

"I didn't ask directly but she said she wouldn't have been surprised if he was, hence the last comment to him. Now, of course, she's not so sure."

"But we suspect differently, albeit of a professional nature. What does she do, by the way?" he asked as the lights changed to green and he set off again.

"Works in a store in Leeds."

"Did she say if they had money worries?"

"Chris looked after that. He hadn't mentioned anything to her about being short or cutting back or anything. In fact, he'd talked about a late holiday."

"So if anything, he had a bit spare? Anything strike you as odd in there, Kelly?"

"How do you mean, guv?"

"Well, the father-in-law. He tells me he's a widower and Janice has no living relatives."

"You don't think old man Baker's sniffing around his daughter-in-law, surely?"

"No." Strong hesitated, "No, forget that. I suppose if he's on his own and she has nobody, it's natural for him to be sharing the grief with her. Do we know what he does?"

"From what Janice said, I think he's retired. But what he did for a living, I don't know. I can find out."

38

Billy Wilkinson was a photographer with The Post. Souter had worked with him many times. Passionate about his job, it also seemed to be his hobby and he was up to speed with all the latest technology. This was now the twenty-first century and, even in the past few years, amazing advances had been made. Wilkinson had set him up in the past with recording devices for sensitive interviews. But, more importantly for Souter, he was built like a brick shithouse.

And so it was that the pair of them were now sitting in Wilkinson's battered old Toyota across the road from the house where Sammy rented her room. Having been spotted previously, Souter thought it best not to turn up again in his Escort.

"You absolutely sure this'll work, Billy?" Souter asked.

"Relax, man. Have I ever let you down? Listen." Wilkinson twiddled a knob on the small receiver he was holding and muffled breathing sounds could be heard. "This is good for a hundred metres. If I turn it up any more you could hear her stomach rumbling."

Sammy was wired up and Wilkinson had connected it to a small transmitter. The sounds from inside the room were being picked up by the recorder they held in the car. Sammy had checked earlier that the tosser in the room upstairs who'd reported back to the Robinson brothers was out before letting them inside. Wilkinson had taken photographs of the state of the hallway and the room. Backup Souter had called it. Hopefully, they wouldn't have to use it.

"Here we go," Souter said, nodding to the black Mercedes that drew to a halt outside the house.

Jed Robinson looked up and down the street before pressing the key fob in his hand. The car squelched and the hazard warning lights flashed quickly three times, confirming the central locking had engaged. Satisfied, Robinson walked up the path and let himself in through the main door. Moments later, the room door could be heard opening through the receiver.

"Don't bother knocking, then," Sammy said.

"You get your privacy when you pay for it. You got my money?" Robinson asked.

"I've got what it's worth."

"I hope you're not pissing me about. I told you what would happen. Now, as I see it you and that other tart owe me eight hundred exactly. And that's what I mean to have."

"Well, I reckon we owe two weeks rent on this … this room. And by my reckoning that's worth about a hundred tops."

Robinson sniggered. "I really didn't think you were that stupid." He took a step closer to Sammy. "Now, we have an agreement – two hundred a week each and that's eight hundred by anybody's reckoning." Another step closer. "So, for the last time, have you got it?"

Sammy pulled some notes from her jeans pocket and threw them on the bed. "There's a hundred. And I quit."

Robinson grabbed her by the throat as she tried to rush past him. "Well that's just not good enough. I've invested in you and that scummy little mate of yours. You owe me." He looked down at her then slowly raised his eyes, all the while, a tight grip on her throat.

"You're hurting me," Sammy struggled to say.

He looked down again and squeezed her breast. "There again, I'm willing to take a payment on account. You were always the sexier one."

As her knee smashed into his groin, the door burst open and Souter and Wilkinson rushed in to witness Robinson rolling around in agony on the floor, unable to speak. Wilkinson began taking photographs. Souter bent down and grabbed Robinson by his jacket lapels and pulled him into a sitting position with his back leaning against the bed. Robinson's eyes were tight shut and both hands never left his crotch. Souter picked up the money and held it in front of Robinson's face. "You see this," he said. "You see this, Mr Robinson?" he repeated, this time forcing the man's eyes open. "This is all you're getting. And if it were up to me, you wouldn't even get half of that. Now you listen good. Your business with Sammy and her friend is finished. You ever try and make contact again, we've got some interesting information that will be all over the newspapers and in the hands of the police. Have you got that?"

"Who the hell are you?" Robinson struggled to ask.

"I said, have you got the message?" Finally, Robinson nodded. "Good. Let's go."

Sammy, Wilkinson and Souter left the room and closed the door. In the hallway, the same pimply youth Souter had spoken to when he first visited looking for Sammy appeared.

"Got a problem?" Billy asked him.

"Didn't hear anything," he responded, turned and rushed up the stairs.

As they walked across the street to the Toyota, Sammy turned back. "Just one last thing I need to do," she said. From the front garden, she lifted half a brick and lobbed it through the Mercedes windscreen. As the alarm sounded, she ran to Wilkinson's car, jumped in the back seat and they sped off.

39

The mobile rang in Strong's pocket just as he was bringing Detective Chief Superintendent Flynn up to speed with developments in Felixstowe. He had also reported on his visit to Baker's widow and father. He pulled out his phone and saw the number on the display. "DCI Halliday, sir," he said to the Superintendent.

Flynn nodded and Strong pressed the green button to take the call.

"DI Strong, what the fuck d'you think you're doing conducting an interview with Baker's family without my say so?"

"It's DCI, Frank, and it wasn't an interview, more of an informal chat. Certain information had come to light concerning the murder of Helena Cryanovic, which is my enquiry," he retorted.

Halliday spluttered at the end of the line. *"It's only Acting DCI and when I tell Flynn how you're fucking up my enquiry, he'll have your bollocks."*

"Well, I can put him on now if you like, I'm sitting in his office."

There was a pause on the end of the line. Flynn nodded for Strong to pass the phone to him. "Frank," the DCS said, "we've got to work together on this. Now DCI Strong had a positive connection between his case, the murder of the Albanian girl, and your Baker murder."

Flynn paused and Strong could hear Halliday whinging through the mobile, but not exactly what was said.

"So how is the Baker enquiry coming along?" Flynn asked.

Again, Strong could hear the voice at the other end, quieter now, so impossible to make out the response.

"Well, what I can tell you Frank," Flynn cut in, "is that DCI Strong has my full backing on this. I can clear it with the ACC if you like but ..."

More chatter from the other end.

Finally, Flynn wound up the call. "Just remind me again, Frank, when are you due to retire?" After a pause, "It would be a shame if it left a sour taste... Of course, I'll make sure Colin keeps your boys in the loop. And, no doubt, your team will do the same."

Flynn pressed the red button and handed the mobile back to Strong. "He's upset about what's happened to Jack," Flynn said. "He was Frank's prodigy in a way and I know he blames you. Personally, I don't know anyone else who does. Just try to work with him on this one, Colin. You heard my side of the conversation there."

Strong stood up. "Thanks, sir. I appreciate that."

"'Night, Colin."

"Sir," he said and left.

40
Wednesday

It was a bright sunny morning when Souter and Sammy approached Leeds General Infirmary. The news the day before was encouraging. Everything seemed to go well with Susan's operation. Souter had intended to visit yesterday but with the events of the day, time ran out.

They squeezed some antiseptic gel onto their hands from the container that had newly appeared at the ward entrance, rubbed them together and made their way in.

"Hi, Belinda," Sammy greeted one of the nurses at the desk.

She looked up from her paperwork and smiled. "Hello, Sammy. Back to see your friend?"

"If that's okay."

"'Course it is, love. She'll be delighted to see you. She seems a lot better today. She was even complaining of being bored."

"Operation went well, then."

The nurse lowered her voice. "Can't really tell you 'cause you're not a relly. But yeah, doctor thinks she'll be fine. Probably out in a day or two."

"That's great," Sammy said, and was off into the ward, Souter following.

Susan was propped up against her pillows reading that morning's Yorkshire Post.

"Now this is more interesting," she greeted them, folding up the newspaper. "Sammy, Bob, good to see you. Nothing much exciting in here."

"Nothing much going on," Souter replied. "Anyway, how are you? Still lolling about in bed, I see."

She grinned. "I'm hoping to go home tomorrow. Well, I say 'home'. I'll actually be staying with Gillian for a while. I'm being sorted out with crutches this afternoon."

"That's great," Sammy said. "Here, I got you some Jelly Babies." She put a bag of sweets on the locker by the side of the bed.

"Oooh, lovely." Susan then looked at Souter.

"Ah," he said, "and I got you these. A brand new reporter's book and fancy propelling pencil. So you can start your articles."

Susan chuckled and shook her head whilst Sammy and Souter drew up chairs on either side of the bed and sat down.

"So what made you decide on doing a journalism course?" he asked.

Susan raised her eyebrows. "Well, there's a question. I was always interested in reading. You probably saw the bookshelves when you met Gillian at the flat."

He nodded. "I noticed some interesting stuff, yes. That was you, was it?"

"Mum read a lot too, so all the classics were hers. I quite like mysteries, so things like the Sherlock Holmes compendium were mine. I've always been interested in finding things out – nosy little kid, I suppose." She laughed, then her face grew serious. "But there was one defining incident, if I'm honest. After Mum died, it hit me hard and I basically pissed about at school."

"I can understand that," he said. "It must have been traumatic."

Susan looked to Sammy and back to Souter. "It was, yes. So I left school when I was sixteen and got a job, well a series of jobs. As time went on, we had to rely on my input more and more. Dad became ill. You know about that?"

Again, Souter nodded, content not to interrupt and let Susan continue.

"It was when I was working in a petrol station on Leeds Road. I was on my own one afternoon when these two sods came in shouting they wanted money and fags.

One of them jumped the counter. I didn't get paid enough to be a hero, so I moved out of the way and let them get on with it. It was very frightening. Fortunately, the CCTV footage was good enough to get useful images and they were soon caught. But that was also my first encounter with the press. The reporting was creative to say the least. But it brought home to me that I didn't want to spend a lifetime in dead-end jobs. They say that if you read, you can write. And English was my favourite subject at school, so I looked into doing a GCSE at night class. Then I started looking at how I could become involved in journalism. But I want to report accurately. I think that's what the media *should* do."

Souter smiled. "That's what the vast majority of us try to do, Susan, I can assure you."

She brightened. "Anyway, what about the girls?"

He hesitated. "You mean…?"

"Yes."

"Well, I saw Mary's brother, Paul on Sunday."

"I tracked him down," Sammy put in.

Souter carried on, "And what you said about the cast on his arm … it was true."

Susan's lip began to tremble and her eyes moistened. "They're down there," she said quietly, "I'm sure of it. Lying here, I've had a lot of time to think. It was so real."

Souter and Sammy exchanged glances.

"They were frightened. They just wanted to go home." She looked earnestly at him. "Did I tell you they were both bare-footed?"

"No you didn't."

"Have you ever had any experiences like this before?" Sammy asked.

Susan looked off into the middle distance for a moment. "My mum … just after she died. I thought I heard her voice one night. I was in bed. I thought I was asleep but … She just asked me to look out for Dad. And a few years later, I knew what she meant." A tear trickled down one cheek.

Sammy took hold of her hand.

Susan turned to Souter. "Are the police going to search? I mean, what Mary's brother said ... it all adds up."

He shook his head. "Paul's been trying to see Colin, DCI Strong, but he's tied up at the moment on a murder case where a body was discovered down in Suffolk."

"But there must be someone else he can speak to. Mr Strong can't be the only detective in Yorkshire."

"No, but he would be the best one because of how this has come about. I had a big enough job trying to convince him you weren't delirious in the first place. And there are inexplicable elements to it all."

"If I could get out and about, I'd search the place myself. Why don't you look?"

"I'll come with you," Sammy added.

"You've got your interview to prepare for, young lady," Souter said.

"But ..."

"No buts. Alison's gone out on a limb to get you this opportunity."

"What's this, Sammy?" Susan asked.

"Alison's managed to get me a meeting with her boss to see if I'd be suitable for a junior post in their office. Secretarial type stuff but using computers too."

"Sounds good, especially after all that's ... well ... Good luck for that. When is it?"

"Twelve o'clock."

"I'll keep my fingers crossed."

"Sorry to interrupt you guys," the nurse from the ward station said, approaching with a medical trolley, "but I need to attend to the patient."

"That's okay," Souter said, "we need to be off anyway."

"Yep, I'll see you later." Sammy gave Susan a hug.

"Look after yourself, and do what they tell you," he warned.

"Best of luck." Susan held up both hands with crossed fingers. "And you get back out there," she said to Souter.

41

Souter stood in the middle of the farmyard and looked up at the dilapidated stone-built house. This was the first time he'd been back since he had found Susan. The day was overcast but bright. A warm breeze blew a plastic bag around the abandoned yard. Thoughts of spaghetti westerns and tumbleweed drifting down the main street passed through his mind.

The house had once been a substantial home on two floors. Intricate stone details to the windows and door openings combined with the porch and bay window above gave a pleasant symmetrical look. Substantial chimney stacks adorned each gable with a red tiled roof between. Some of the tiles were missing and the lead had long since been stripped by some enterprising thieves. Walking around the side, there were more vacant windows, guttering hanging down and buddleia growing out of the stonework in several places where the downpipes had fractured. At the back, a flat-roofed, single-storey extension to the kitchen marred the building's appearance. Chunks of render had spalled from the grey blockwork and the back door was missing. Completing his circuit revealed similar deterioration to the other elevation. Finally, standing back outside the front porch, he checked his torch and took a careful step inside.

The building was exactly as he'd last seen it when the paramedics brought Susan out. He bent down and peered through the large void in the hall floor to the basement. Carefully retracing his steps of a week ago, Souter made his way around the perimeter to the open door leading to the basement. As he ventured down the stairs, a musty, stale aroma permeated the room. He stood and looked up at the gaping hole in the floor above and wondered how Susan's injuries hadn't been more severe. It was a drop of over six feet and he could only think that the way the timbers had failed, in a slow progressive manner, had saved her from a more catastrophic result.

As his eyes got used to the darker conditions, he began to gauge the position of the external wall at ground floor level relative to the front wall of the basement. So far as he could tell, they lined up. He walked over and stood with his back to it before switching on the torch. Straight ahead was the wall Susan had ended up leaning against. Taking his bearings through the gap in the floor above, he estimated this to be in line with the back wall of the hall. Panning the beam to the right, he picked out the side wall, more or less where he expected it to be, below the outside wall. To the left, another brick wall ran across, in line with the dividing wall between the hall and a front room above. In the middle of this, was a panelled door that he hadn't noticed before.

He walked over, turned the handle and pushed. After a bit of resistance, it opened. The room behind had the benefit of some light from a small grille that had probably been a coal chute when first built. This also allowed a slight breeze to waft through, bringing with it an odour of dust and decaying timber. With the benefit of his torch, he could see that the room ran the full depth of the house front to back. This left the area behind the room where Susan fell and the rear of the house, assuming the basement ran below the total footprint of the building.

Then the beam picked it out. A doorway, or it had been a doorway, now closed up with grey blocks and rough mortar. This was in stark contrast to the other brick walls.

He walked around the room, empty apart from the dust of decades and an array of spiders' webs. In the room where he'd discovered Susan, he looked all round. Apart from the stairs, no other way in to that level and no signs of any other blocked up doorways. There must be another room to the rear, he thought.

Making his way back through the doorway, he approached the blocked up opening and began to examine it. He took a key from his pocket and scraped at the surface of one of the blocks. It seemed relatively soft, like those used more for insulation than solidity. He'd need something bigger.

He returned from his car with a screwdriver. It was the largest he had with him. He began to scrape away at the surface of a block at eye level. It would be a slow process, but it was working. After a few minutes, he'd excavated a pit the size of a golf ball, after five, beaded in sweat, a cricket ball could have been forced into the void. Finally, after about ten minutes, he'd broken through, a hole about two inches in diameter. He raised his torch and peered inside.

*　*　*

In the front interview room on the ground floor of Wood Street Police station, Strong and Souter sat either side of the table.

Half an hour earlier, Souter had finally tracked him down by phone. "We need to talk," he'd said. "This is important." Souter appeared agitated.

"So what's so urgent, Bob?"

"Did you ever manage to speak to Paul Duggan?"

"Not yet, I've only just got back from Suffolk. Things are moving fast."

"Any further developments you can tell me about the Albanian girl, then?"

Strong paused and looked at his friend. "I told you more than I should have the other day. Look, I'm up to my armpits with what's now a murder enquiry ..."

"Well things are going to get a whole lot busier for you."

"What do you mean?"

"If you'd seen Paul Duggan, he'd have told you that he broke his arm when he was thirteen."

Strong was puzzled.

"You didn't get back to speak to Susan either?" Souter rolled his eyes then took a deep breath. "Okay, this is what Susan told me when I saw her in the hospital." He proceeded to relate Susan's encounter in the basement, this time including the comments from Mary regarding her brother's broken arm, the cast and what they'd done to it. "And when I spoke to Paul on Sunday, without leading the witness, your honour, he confirmed he had indeed broken his arm and that Mary and her friends had drawn funny faces on the cast. That's what I wanted him to tell you. As far as I can ascertain, that bit of trivia had never been reported in the media."

Strong was silent for a few seconds. "Okay, I'll take a couple of officers with me and have a look round the old farmhouse myself."

"Already done it."

He shook his head. "Bob, you haven't been interfering again. You know it makes ..."

"They're there." Souter interrupted. "Like you, when something nags at me ... I couldn't let it go any longer. I went there this afternoon. There's a blocked up room. I scraped through one of the blocks, shone a torch in and ... well, you need to see it."

An hour later, Meadow Woods Farm was a busy scene. The whole farmyard area was taped off, white suited SOCOs were coming and going and specialists were setting up lights from a hastily installed generator. A mobile toilet unit was making its way slowly up the track. Strong and Detective Chief Superintendant Flynn were standing by the side of Strong's car where the track joined the road.

"This Souter character Colin, I don't want any of this in the public domain yet."

"He'll keep the confidence, sir. All I've said is that he'll get priority when we can announce this."

"We need to be sure. It'll take some time for these boys to work their way through to gain as much forensic evidence as possible."

"I was talking to them before you arrived," Strong said. "They reckon it'll be tomorrow morning before they can remove the bodies."

"You reckon it's them?"

"Seems so."

"So how did this Souter fellow know?"

Strong looked over the fields into the distance as he considered his answer. "This isn't a conventional one, sir. And I'm not even sure I believe it myself."

"Try me."

He puffed out his cheeks. "The young woman who fell into the basement, Susan, Susan Brown ... she had an encounter."

Flynn looked puzzled. "Are you trying to tell me she saw their ghosts?"

"I'm not sure what happened but the trail of events led Souter here."

"How old is he? He couldn't be considered a suspect?"

"No sir." Strong turned away.

By way of timely intervention, trundling onto the scene at that point, Strong was pleased to see a familiar pair in the cab of a green tractor. He held up his hand. "Excuse me, sir," he said, turning back to his boss. "I just need to have a word with this lad."

The black and white dog was jumping around excitedly in the cab. Simon Clay, still below the flat cap but dressed in a different tee shirt, ordered it to calm down. "Now then," he said through the cab window. "Tha's back then."

"Something else has come up," Strong said.

"I 'eard about young lass that fell through t'floor. Bloody lucky she were found."

He winced. "Er yes she was, Mr Clay."

DAVID EVANS

"Must be summat serious now." The farmer nodded up the track. "All them white suits. Tha dun't bring them out for nowt."

"When we spoke here last time, you told me about the last occupants of Meadow Woods Farm."

"Aye. The Collinsons. But best person to talk to would be me Dad. He knew all about them goin' way back."

"And where could I see your father?"

"'e's up in Twenty Acre Field ploughin' at moment. But 'e should be back in for 'is tea about seven, unless 'e's carryin' on wi' lights t'gerrit finished."

"Whereabouts is home, Mr Clay?"

"About two mile up here." The farmer pointed up the road. "The farm's on the right. Moorends Farm. Tha' can't miss it."

"Alright, thanks. I'll probably pop up myself later."

Strong walked slowly back to rejoin his boss. "Local farmer, sir. His father knew the previous tenants," he said, nodding towards the farm.

"I've spoken to the top brass, Colin and I'm bringing in another team from Leeds on this one. You've got your hands full with your Albanian murder."

"What about Halliday? You know what he's like. And I'm sure Helena's murder is linked with the shooting of Baker."

"I'll speak to the ACC. We can't be working against one another here." DCS Flynn walked back to his car.

Strong watched him get into the Jaguar and drive off. He had turned towards his Mondeo when his mobile rang.

"Bob," he answered.

"It's them, isn't it?"

"Can't say, yet. Forensics will take some time. Listen, you're going to have to answer some questions on this."

"I know," Souter sighed. *"You will let me know when I can report this?"*

"Flynn said so and I'll try and let you know but it'll be a separate team investigating, not me directly."

"Appreciate that, mate. In the meantime, what's happening with your murder enquiry?"

Strong thought for a second. "Well, you probably know she was found in the boot of one of the stolen cars Baker and Chapman knocked off."

"So there's a connection between Baker's murder and this Albanian girl?"

"I'm treating it that way."

"No sign of those two yet?"

"Gary Baker and Chapman, you mean?"

"Yes."

"No. Wherever they are they're doing a good job of lying low."

"Don't suppose there's any chance of getting an interview with Baker's widow? Halliday's team are keeping her under wraps."

"I had to endure the bastard's wrath when I went round there yesterday," Strong chuckled.

"How's she doing?"

"In bits. She's got her father-in-law stopping with her, Robert Baker."

"Very cosy. Listen, something else I wanted to ask. Have you come across some scumbag by the name of Jed Robinson?"

Strong's brows furrowed as he trawled his memory. "Robinson? Are there two of them? Couple of small time pimps, if I recall correctly. Why?"

"Just wondered. The name came up recently. Have they got a violent reputation?"

"Not sure, mate. Not that I know of, but probably to the girls they run. You haven't upset them, have you?"

Souter laughed nervously. *"No, don't worry. Anyway, don't forget to keep me up to speed with developments out there."*

"See you, Bob."

42

Mrs Clay bid Strong sit down in one of the solid kitchen chairs placed around the old pine table. The Yorkstone floor, white painted rendered walls and wooden furniture gave the room a friendly, warm atmosphere. Adam Clay was in his fifties, around five foot ten inches and solidly built. His face was deeply lined and tanned through long hours spent outdoors. He was scrubbing his hands in the Belfast sink, rinsed them then turned, drying them on a white towel. "Must be summat serious," he said. "Simon told me you were all up there this afternoon. The full team; boiler suits, lights, the lot."

Strong was intrigued that, although Clay senior had a distinctive local accent, it wasn't nearly as pronounced as his son. "It is, Mr Clay, but for reasons I hope you'll understand, I can't reveal any details at the moment."

Clay nodded as his wife pulled the source of the delightful aroma from the Aga. "Are you sure you don't want some?" he asked, "There's enough to go round."

Strong was sorely tempted. The lamb casserole that now sat on the hob looked every bit as tasty as it had smelled when he first entered the farmhouse kitchen. "That's very kind of you, Mr Clay but I've got a meal waiting for me at home."

"Please, call me Adam," the big farmer said, sitting down next to his guest. "Now, how can I help you?"

"I'll try not to take up too much of your time, Adam, Mrs Clay, so please carry on with your meal, don't mind me."

"Call me Jean, please." The farmer's wife wiped her hands on her pinny front and began to dish up the meat and vegetable gravy into two bowls along with mashed potatoes. "Mrs Clay sounds so formal."

"I was wondering what you could tell me about the last residents of Meadow Woods Farm."

"Simon said you were asking about the Collinsons," Adam said. "Wilf and Enid. You used to get on well with Enid, didn't you, love?"

"She were lovely," Jean replied, placing the two bowls on the table. "We used to go out together, maybe three or four times a year – to the pictures or the theatre if there was something good on. She was good to have a laugh with." She stared into nowhere for a split second before continuing, "But then the cancer came. Two years she lasted. She was in a dreadful state at the end. It was a blessing when she were finally took."

"When was this?"

"Ooh, let's see," she pondered, "It must have been '84 or '85."

"It was 1985, Jean." Adam broke off some bread and buttered it. "It was the year Simon did his GCSEs."

"Yes, that's right," Jean agreed.

"So after Mrs Collinson died, what happened then?"

"It hit him hard, old Wilf." Adam said. "He was about ten years older than Enid. I think he just gave up. Stopped looking after himself. He tried to keep up with the farm but that lad of his, he weren't interested."

"That was Stanley, wasn't it?"

"That's right."

"Did they have any other family?"

"No, just the one lad," Adam replied. "He was about twenty-six when his mam died."

"What was he like?"

The farmer smiled and shook his head. "He seemed all right growing up but he became more and more odd after Enid had gone."

"How do you mean, odd?"

"He just seemed to laze about the place, not that he was ever much of a help to his dad. He'd dress scruffy, let his hair grow for months on end. I used to call on old Wilf from time to time, try and keep him going but ... I don't know, like I said, he seemed to give up. After a year or so, he'd resent me going."

"That's a bit unfair, Adam," Jean interrupted. "Different people handle grief in their own way."

"Well at the end, he told me not to bother wasting my time calling again. So I didn't."

"And how long after Mrs Collinson did Wilf die?" Strong asked.

"He finally went in 1990. Just about this time of year."

"And from what you said, young Stanley wasn't interested or possibly capable of carrying on?"

"Couldn't wait to get out of the place. Their rent was due in the October and Stanley was gone by then. After that, the Ingleby Estates bought it and have farmed it ever since. They wanted the land but had no use for the house, so it's been allowed to go to rack and ruin."

"Any idea where Stanley moved to?"

Adam shook his head. "Sorry, no."

"Was there ever any girlfriends?"

Again the farmer shook his head.

"Boyfriends?"

This drew a loud chuckle from Adam. "Never seemed to have any friends at all. Not that I'd ever seen visiting, but there again, we're not past the place very often to notice."

Strong stood up. "Okay Adam, Jean, thanks for your help." He took out a card and placed it on the table. "If you think of anything else, like where Stanley might have moved to, give me a call."

Adam began to get to his feet.

"It's okay." Strong put up a hand. "Enjoy the rest of your meal. I'll see myself out."

43

It was nearly half past eight when Strong drew to a halt on the driveway of his modest detached house five miles from Wood Street. Mrs Clay's casserole smelt delicious and it had been a difficult refusal to make. He was ravenous, it had been a long day and he wondered what might be on the menu. He waited until Rod Stewart's *Maggie May* finished on the radio. For once, it wasn't cut short, spoiling the mandolin solo.

He got out and was just about to lock up when his mobile rang. A number he didn't recognise flashed up on the LCD display. "Strong," he said.

"Colin, it's Jack," came the response. He didn't need to be told. He recognised the baritone voice of his old boss, DCI Jack Cunningham.

"Jack, you know you shouldn't be contacting me while you're still under suspension."

"I don't blame you, Colin. I knew you took some risks trying to keep some of my ... well, my situation quiet. I appreciate that. That's why I'm using this mobile that no-one knows about."

Strong turned and walked back down the drive. "I said at the time you were a good officer, Jack. I still think that. But I had to get to the truth. And Paul Summers didn't deserve that." Paul Summers, the unfortunate individual who'd spent four years in prison for a crime he didn't commit.

"I know, Colin. I'm sorry you put yourself in a difficult situation with those photos."

"A pity your mate, Halliday doesn't agree."

"I've had a word. I only just heard he was giving you a hard time. I think you'll find him a bit more ... accommodating."

"Thanks."

"But listen, the reason I thought I'd call you – I hear you were the one to discover those missing schoolgirls' bodies?"

Strong looked up the road and noticed two pink bicycles belonging to his neighbour's children propped up against the wall by their front door. How ironic, he thought, they would have been riding up and down the pavement earlier, both around the same ages as Jennifer and Mary. "Not exactly, but we've yet to confirm identities. How did …? Never mind, I'm not surprised that word is leaking out."

"The thing is, I was involved with the original enquiries. Jennifer Coyle back in '86, I was a detective constable then, and two years later, I was a DS when Mary Duggan went missing. I just wondered if I could be of use to you, unofficially like, now that it looks like you've probably found them?"

Strong walked back up his drive and leant against the bonnet of his Mondeo. "I don't know, Jack. Flynn is bringing in a separate murder squad team from Leeds. I'm only going to be liaising with them as far as anything else I'm involved with."

"But, like you said to me many's the time, you need to know the truth. If I feed in what I remember from our enquiries back then – not everything might have been recorded correctly."

"Christ, Jack, you're not telling me proper records weren't kept?"

"No, I don't mean that, Colin, but if I just throw in some things I remember from the time, maybe a different slant on something, you know what I'm saying."

"Okay. Thanks, I appreciate that." There was a short silence before he continued, "Listen, Jack … how's things? I mean, with you?"

"I'm okay, Colin. Don't worry, I'm not about to stick my head in a gas oven or jump off the Humber Bridge. I'm fine."

"And Kathy?" he asked, referring to Kathy Sharp with whom Cunningham had had a relationship.

"With a DCI in Bow. Doing well for herself. I always knew she would. But it was good while it lasted." A soft chuckle followed.

"Look after yourself, Jack."

"Thanks, Colin. Oh, before I forget, I don't know how much of it you'll find on the records but what came back to me when I heard the news was that during the search for Jennifer, several witnesses reported sightings of an old maroon pick-up, one of those Japanese things, spotted in the area of Pontefract where she was last seen getting off the school bus. And when we got involved in the search for Mary Duggan, a similar vehicle had been seen around the park where she was last seen. As far as I know, despite an intensive search, we never did trace that vehicle – assuming they were one and the same."

"Thanks for that, Jack. If I need to get in touch with you, is this the best number?"

"Yes. But don't log it as me, just in case someone checks your phone contacts."

"See you," Strong said, ending the call. He straightened himself up and stretched. It *had* been a long day. He walked to the front door, turned the key in the lock and opened it. The welcoming smell of beef stew drifted out to greet him.

44
Thursday

Chapeltown, Leeds. A once prosperous area when the industrial revolution was in full swing. Now an area with a disreputable reputation, it had become squalid.

The street they were on bore an air of decay at one end. Some of the brick-built terraced houses looked abandoned but as they drove along, signs of regeneration were evident. Some properties were undergoing renovation, the obligatory white van and skip left outside. Elsewhere, scruffy cars were parked, leaving only a few spaces available. The unit Strong wanted had once been a corner shop. Now, the windows either side of the doorway had been replaced with solid black panelling and, out of hours, a roller shutter would protect the door from any vandalism.

Stella looked up from the magazine she was reading when Strong and Stainmore entered the small reception area of Sweet Sensations. She was seated behind a glazed screen and small counter. Recognising him, she moved a hand towards a button to the side.

Strong held up a hand in an emphatic 'Stop' command then put a finger to his lips. "Szymanski?" he whispered.

She held up four fingers and he nodded towards the door into the place itself. Slowly and deliberately, she reached for the button she had gone for before, mouthing, "Okay?"

The electric lock clicked and both officers stepped into a short dimly-lit corridor. It opened out into a lounge area where two sofas were placed against opposite walls. Immediately, a young dark-haired girl dressed only in bra, pants, hold-up stockings and high-heeled shoes stood up from the right hand one and approached Strong. The broad smile on her face melted into a look of concern as Stainmore appeared behind him.

Moving quickly past him, she ushered the girl back down onto the sofa, motioning her to keep quiet. "Police," she said quietly, flipping out her warrant card. "You have nothing to fear. You understand?"

The girl looked frightened but nodded.

"Room 4?" Strong asked.

She pointed to the corridor to the right of a wall-mounted flat screen television which was showing a large-breasted blonde girl being taken from behind by a black man over a kitchen table. The moans and groans from the soundtrack didn't match the action and seemed to have been added later.

"Can we kill that?" Strong said, thumb towards the screen. He set off down another dingy corridor. Halfway towards the emergency exit at the very end, doors led off both sides. Behind door 3 to the left, the familiar rhythmic creaking accompanied by moans that did sound genuine, could be heard. Door 4 to the right seemed quiet. Putting his ear to it, he thought he could hear a male voice speaking quietly.

Taking hold of the door handle, he slowly turned it. Slight pressure revealed it was locked somehow from inside. He took a deep breath and hoped Stella hadn't let him down. Shoulder to the door, he burst in. Szymanski was sitting on the side of a massage couch, trousers at his ankles whilst a skinny blonde girl was in the middle of performing oral sex on him. She jumped back and began to scream hysterically.

"What the fuck ..."Szymanski began.

"Stefan Szymanski," Strong stated, holding up his warrant card, "I'm DCI Strong and I'd like to have a word with you."

"Shut the fuck up, Nadia," he said to the still screaming blonde.

Almost instantly, she did.

"If you'd care to join your colleague in the lounge," Strong told the frightened girl, "my fellow officer will take care of you."

"You mind if I get myself dressed, officer," Szymanski said.

"Be my guest." Strong then escorted Nadia out of the room.

As he did so, Szymanski, trousers quickly back up, barged past Strong and bolted for the fire exit. He shook his head as the Pole burst through the door and out into the daylight. The sounds of a brief scuffle could be heard before Ormerod, a broad grin below the familiar thick black moustache, appeared, dragging a now handcuffed Szymanski back inside. "Lost something, guv?" he asked.

Darby strolled in behind them, hands in his trouser pockets. "Always wanted to see what one of these places looked like from the inside," he commented. Strong and Ormerod exchanged looks of incredulity but said nothing.

The overweight middle-aged bald bloke who had been humping the young girl in Room 3 gave his name and an address in Huddersfield. Strong gave him five minutes to get dressed and told him they'd be in touch – which they probably wouldn't, unless something more sinister surfaced – but it would make the bastard sweat a bit. Darby saw him off the premises by the fire exit and made a note of the details of the car he drove off in. The PNC check revealed it was owned by a stationery wholesaler in Manchester.

Ormerod meanwhile sat on one of the sofas in the lounge alongside Szymanski. The television had been switched off. Nadia, the girl from the lounge and the young girl from Room 3 had been taken into the reception area by Stainmore.

Strong walked up the left-hand corridor and found two more rooms. The door to Room 2 revealed another grubby massage couch in a darkened room. The other door, marked Room 1, was locked but he was satisfied there was no other person on the premises.

Back in the lounge, he slowly paced the room, saying nothing for several minutes. Eventually, he spoke. "Why did you make a run for it, Mr Szymanski?"

"I didn't know who you were, you could have been anybody," the Pole replied with only a slight accent.

He stopped and turned to face him. "After I told you who I was and showed you my warrant card?"

"Could have been false."

"Cut the crap," Strong snorted, "You knew perfectly well who I was." He began to pace again.

Ormerod was studying Szymanski all the while, but he appeared to be relaxed and gave nothing away.

"Are you in charge of this … establishment?" Strong asked after another few seconds pause.

"I manage it, yes."

"For Mr Mirczack?"

"He owns the place, yes."

Strong stopped and faced Szymanski. "Room 1, what's in there?"

"It's another massage room but we don't normally use it. The girls use it to get changed."

Stella had put up the 'Closed' sign, locked the door and set the telephone on answer machine before sitting with the three young women in the reception area.

Stainmore took out her notebook. "I'll need some details from you ladies," she said.

Before any of the others could say anything, Stella cut in, "I'm Stella Hunter, receptionist here today. Can I have a word in private?"

Stainmore regarded the girls briefly and decided that they were unlikely to run out into the street dressed the way they were, even if they could unlock the door. She was led to a toilet behind the reception desk.

Stella produced a card from her handbag. "Can I suggest you give Vince, Detective Sergeant Vince Denholme a call. Your DCI Strong knows him and knows we have … an arrangement."

Stainmore studied the card. "You're an informant?"

Stella shrugged. "Sort of. Mr Strong was interested in Helena, the Albanian girl who worked as receptionist here." She paused.

"Go on."

"He was also asking about a punter, Chris, who used to see Mariana." Again a pause before she continued, "Mariana is the dark-haired girl in reception."

"Thanks." Stainmore gave her the card back, turned and made her way to rejoin the other women.

Darby returned down the corridor from the fire exit, having seen the punter off the premises, then sat on the opposite sofa.

"I think we can lose the cuffs, Luke," Strong said to Ormerod as he sat next to Szymanski. Strong reached into his jacket pocket and produced a photograph. "Do you recognise this girl?" he asked.

Szymanski took hold of the picture, looked at it for a few seconds then handed it back. "That's Helena," he said, "used to work here."

"We know that already. But she was a bit more than that though, wasn't she?"

"I don't know what you mean."

"She was your girlfriend for a while."

"She had a silly infatuation, that was all."

"Is that why you used to visit her?"

He smiled. "Aah, her sister, Magda. She told you that?"

"When did you last see her?"

Szymanski sucked in air through his teeth in an exaggerated gesture of giving the question some thought. "Ooh, let's see … it must have been at least two weeks ago. The Tuesday, I think."

"So she wasn't here on the Thursday evening?"

"No," Szymanski said sharply. "She was supposed to but she didn't show up."

"And that didn't concern you?"

"I just thought she'd decided to stop coming."

Strong looked round the room. "You have CCTV here, don't you?"

"Only in reception. In case we have an awkward customer."

Strong got to his feet. "I'd like to see it for last week."

"Ah, I'm afraid I can't help you."

"Not going to make me go through the motions of obtaining a warrant?"

He smirked. "No. More simple than that, they were wiped on Sunday ready for the new week."

"Stay with our friend," Strong said to Ormerod before walking through to the reception area.

Stainmore sat next to Nadia. "I need to have your name and address."

Nadia looked nervous. "I not sure what's happening," she responded in a heavy accent.

"There's nothing to worry about," Stainmore said, with a smile. "We only need a few details in case we need to talk to you again."

"Don't worry, Nadia," Stella reassured her, "You haven't done anything wrong."

Nadia looked from Stainmore to Stella and back again. Quietly, she began, "My name is Nadia Petrov and I come from Estonia. I come to work as nanny but ..." Her response tailed off.

"And where do you live?"

"I stay with the other girls in a house."

"And where is that exactly?"

"It's called Harehills I think, but I not know the address. Szymanski or one of the others, they bring us."

Stainmore looked at the other girls. "All of you? You all live in the same house and you're ferried in?"

They both nodded.

"What about you, Mariana is it?" she asked the dark haired girl.

"I only call myself Mariana here. My name's Lyudmyla Butkus and I come from Lithuania."

Again Stainmore looked at all the girls. "Do you all use false names."

"Nadia is my name," the Estonian girl said.

"I'm Katarina, Katarina Kazlauskas, also from Estonia, but in here they call me Lucy," said the girl from Room 3.

Stainmore paused taking notes. "Although you don't know the address where you stay, do you think you would be able to find it if we took you there?"

The girls looked at one another, then Lyudmyla spoke. "Yes, of course."

Strong came into reception at that point, taking in the assembled group. He approached Stella. "I'd like to see the CCTV," he said.

Almost imperceptibly, she indicated for him to follow her and went behind the counter to slide open a cupboard beneath. "When from?"

"How long do you normally keep them?"

"If it's like the other parlours, usually two weeks. I think the idea is that it gives us time if we've been passed some dodgy money, we can try and trace it back."

"How about two weeks ago today, Thursday."

She bent down and beckoned Strong to join her. "That girl," she whispered, "the dark-haired one, she's Mariana, the one your victim used to visit. I've told your colleague."

He nodded. "Thanks," he said, straightening up again.

Stella came back up with a cassette bearing the date, put it in a player behind her and pressed play. The monitor flickered from snowy to blank grey and stayed that way.

"That's funny," she said, "there's nothing on it. It seems to have been wiped."

"And that's unusual?"

"Well, yes. As I said, they're normally kept for a fortnight and this wouldn't be recycled until tomorrow. Let's try another."

She ejected the cassette and dug out another, this time bearing a more recent date. The result was the same.

Strong scooped up the tapes and returned to reception. "Can you bag these up, Kelly," he said. "We'll see if our experts can retrieve anything from them," then quietly added, "although I doubt it." With that, he disappeared back into the parlour.

Stainmore produced some plastic evidence bags from her jacket pocket and began to feed the cassette tapes into them. "Have you got other clothes here?" she asked the women, "I assume Szymanski doesn't bring you in dressed like that."

"There's a room at the back," Stella held up a key. "Room 1, where the girls change."

"Just wait here a minute." Stainmore got to her feet and headed towards the internal door. "I'll just check with my boss."

Strong returned to where Ormerod was sitting with Szymanski.

"Very convenient of you to attempt to wipe the tapes, Mr Szymanski," Strong said, standing in the middle of the room. "Still, I'm sure our experts will be able to recover the images," he bluffed.

Concern showed on Szymanski's face for the first time. "But it's just routine, they're always wiped at the end of a week."

"I think we'll continue this conversation back at Wood Street."

"But what about this place?"

Strong looked at Ormerod as he turned to lead the way. "I'm sure the ladies will appreciate an early night."

Just then, Stainmore appeared. "Is it alright to bring the girls through to get dressed, guv?"

"Good idea, Kelly. We're just about to leave." Strong turned to Szymanski. "Just sit there a minute," he said.

"All right, ladies, come and get changed please." Stainmore led the way through the lounge area. Stella, with the key, and the three girls overtook her and disappeared down the left hand corridor, much to Darby's amusement.

Szymanski tried to look hard at the girls as they passed. Nadia and Katarina kept their heads down but he fixed Lyudmyla and she momentarily froze.

Stainmore caught the exchange. "I hope that's not an attempt to intimidate, Mr Szymanski?" she said.

Ormerod cuffed the Pole again and dragged him to his feet. He pushed him in the back towards reception, Darby following behind.

Strong hung back to speak to Stainmore. "Have you shown them the photos of Helena and Baker yet?"

"Not yet, guv."

"You know the dark haired one is Mariana who Baker used to see?"

"Her real name's Lyudmyla."

Strong looked surprised. "Lyudmyla? I'm sure that was the name of the friend Helena was supposed to have been visiting. I need to talk to her. What are you doing with them now?"

"Apparently, they all lodge together in a house in Harehills. They can't give an address but Ludymila, that's Mariana, can take me."

"Harehills? That was where Helena was supposed to be visiting friends when she disappeared." He scratched his head. "Are they all from Eastern Europe?"

"Lyudmyla's from Lithuania and the other two are from Estonia."

Strong checked his watch. "Look, I'm going to get Szymanski back to Wood Street. I think we also need to talk to the girls, as witnesses for now. See what they can tell us about Helena. If you go back with Mariana or whatever she calls herself, check out the house, I'll get Luke to take the other two back with him to the station. He can bring Stella in too, at least for appearances. John and I'll make sure Szymanski gets there safe and sound. We need to keep them separate though. See what you can find out in Harehills then bring her back with you."

Five minutes later, Stella had locked up the unit and the place was lifeless.

45

As Souter walked into the Archive Room behind the reception in the Yorkshire Post's offices, Phyllis looked up from the latest batch of newspapers she was working through.

"Ah, Mr Souter. I heard you'd been rummaging through my files."

"Yes, Phyllis, and very useful they were too." He sat opposite the slim, neatly dressed, grey haired woman. "How far back are you now?"

"I'm back to 1980, love," she said. "I don't know how much longer they'll want me to do." She turned some pages over. "Here, can you believe it'll be twenty years this year since John Lennon was murdered?"

"Twenty years? It doesn't seem that long." Souter looked off into an unseen distance.

"I liked a lot of his songs. *Imagine* was beautiful. But there was some rubbish among them as well." Phyllis looked at him. "Do you think they would have got back together if it hadn't happened?"

"That's certainly one to ponder."

"Anyway, anything particular I can help you with?"

"Just wanted to have a look through the last couple of years, see if anything catches my eye."

"They're all up there." She indicated the rows of shelving on the back wall. "If there's anything you want, just ask."

"Thanks." Souter selected the microfiche from 1999 and fed it into the machine.

After about half an hour's trawl, looking for any background he could find on the Baker family, he'd only come across some small reports of Gary's appearances in court for various motoring offences. Sentenced to six months in April. Mention was also made of previous offences for burglary. He rubbed his eyes as Phyllis, hair back-combed and lacquered to within an inch of its life, placed a mug of coffee in front of him.

"So, how are you settling in?" she asked. "It must be, what, six months now?"

"Thanks," he said, taking a sip. "Yes, it's okay."

"What do you reckon to young Janey?"

Souter paused before answering. She probably thought he was considering his reply. In fact he was trying to determine what the black specks were in her hair. "She'll be good," he said, "She's writing some good stuff." Flies. The specks were small flies he realised, trapped and killed by some form of human fly-paper.

"That must be contender for headline of the year last week."

"Which one was that?"

"When she was reporting from the courts, *'Flasher Told He Must Keep His Trousers On'*, I nearly wet myself."

He chuckled, surprised at her turn of phrase. "Yeah, she had some fun with that one."

Phyllis took her drink back to her desk and resumed her work.

Souter returned his attention to the viewer and began spinning through the microfiche once more. Five minutes later, something caught his attention. Bringing the page back to the viewer, he saw an article on the retirement of a senior printer for the company, De La Rue. A photograph depicted a group of men and women surrounding a grey haired man accepting a silver tray from a distinguished looking bald man, all with broad smiles on their faces. That headed a quarter page article. The caption read, *'Managing Director, Mr George Aspinall presents a silver salver to Mr Robert Baker to mark his retirement after thirty-two years employment with De La Rue.'* he began to read the article. *'Latterly, Mr Baker was a senior designer at their factory at Team Valley near Gateshead and had been responsible for the design and printing of currency notes for a number of countries as well as various forms for the British Government.'*

He read through the article, wondering if this was the same Robert Baker Strong had mentioned. Towards the end, he was quoted as a widower, looking forward to his retirement, enjoying golf and time with his two sons.

"Here, Phyllis," Souter said turning round to face her, "Is that printer over there online?"

"Should be," she said.

Page printed, he got up and replaced the microfiche on the shelf, collecting the printout on the way. As he left, he said his thanks and goodbye to Phyllis, unable to resist one last glance at her hair.

46

Now casually dressed in jeans, tee shirt and a jacket, Lyudmyla sat in the front passenger seat alongside Stainmore and guided her to the house where the girls lodged. Devoid of the heavy make-up, she looked healthier, more wholesome somehow, Stainmore thought. Initially, she had seemed suspicious that her two friends were driven away separately.

"It's just routine," Stainmore told her. "We need to take statements and establish your identities and status."

"They are frightened," Lyudmyla said. Her accent was pronounced but her command of English seemed good. "They have a lot to lose."

Stainmore was puzzled. "But not you?"

"I have no family back home." The girl took out a packet of cigarettes. "Can I?" she asked.

Stainmore preferred not to have smokers in the car but considered leniency may help build a rapport in this instance. "No, it's okay," she said, and dropped the passenger window a touch.

Lyudmyla took out a cigarette, lit up, then exhaled sharply. "My mother, she died when I was ten. My father, he drank himself to death last year. Turn here, by these shops."

Stainmore followed the instructions. "No brothers or sisters?"

Another deep draw on the cigarette. "I had a baby sister but she die after a few days."

"Sorry about that." Stainmore glanced across but the girl was nervously looking out of the window. "What about your two friends, Nadia and Katerina?"

"They not really friends. I only meet them here in Leeds. Back home, they both have families. Next turn here."

Stainmore indicated left and made the turn into Luxor Grove off the Harehills Road. It was even more run down than the street where Sweet Sensations was situated. Several of the three-storey houses were boarded up but, unlike Chapeltown, there were no signs of any reinvigoration.

"It's this one here," Lyudmyla said, pointing to the right, "the one with the brown door."

When they pulled up, Lyudmyla explained that she didn't have a key to get in.

Stainmore looked hard at the Lithuanian girl. "Why only tell me now?"

Lyudmyla smiled. "Don't worry," she said, "I have a way in at the back that Szymanski not know."

"If this is some kind of try on ..."

The girl turned to face Stainmore, looking serious. "There is a small road at the back. We can go round the next corner and park."

Stainmore took a breath then set off as directed. She was paying attention to the girl. Perhaps she should have been more aware of her surroundings. The dark blue Mondeo parked on the corner with two men inside went unnoticed.

Stainmore suddenly felt vulnerable. She was on her own with a young woman who, despite what she said, may have something to lose, but more importantly, nothing to be gained by helping the police. She would have preferred to have been in the company of a colleague but it was too late for that.

The girl opened the car door and Stainmore went to do the same.

"Please, give me two minutes," Lyudmyla said. "I can get in through the basement, then I open the door for you."

Stainmore studied her for a few seconds then nodded. "I'm trusting you," she said.

Inside the Mondeo, a digital camera fired off a colonnade of shots recording the scene. A telephone number was dialled on a mobile and Stainmore's car, description and registration number related.

She watched as Lyudmyla walked down the narrow street and turned in through a gate on the right. Six stone steps led up to a rear door but the girl disappeared around the far side of them.

Stainmore got out of the car, locked it and began to follow. She began to panic when she couldn't see the girl and hurried her pace. As she approached the gate, the door at the top of the steps opened and Lyudmyla's head peered out. Stainmore's feeling of panic slowly subsided. The girl waved her hand quickly to beckon her inside.

"I not sure who keeps watch on this place," Lyudmyla said, closing the door behind them. She led Stainmore up the creaking staircase to a first floor room facing Luxor Grove itself. "This is mine," she said, sitting down on the made single bed.

"Is there a bathroom here?" Stainmore asked.

"Just outside there," the girl said, waving an arm towards the door. "Why, you want to go?"

Stainmore chuckled. "No, it's just you have black streaks on your face, you might want to wash them off."

"Sorry, it is very dirty in the basement. I check."

While the girl freshened up, Stainmore looked around the room. It seemed very tidy. Apart from a single wardrobe in one corner, there was a small table and two chairs by the window. Stainmore sat on one of them.

The girl returned. "Better?" she asked.

"Yes." Stainmore nodded. "Lyudmyla, I need to show you some photographs. Could you take a look for me, please?"

The girl sat down opposite the detective, nervously playing with her hands.

Stainmore held out a photo to her.

Lyudmyla recognised the subject immediately. "This is my friend, Helena," she said. "Is she in some sort of trouble? I not see her for some time." Her expression told

Stainmore that she could instantly tell there was something wrong. "What has happened?" she implored.

"Why do you think something has?"

"She was coming to see me, two weeks ago, but she didn't come. It was the first time she doesn't come. Also, she stopped working at Sensations," adding quickly, "as reception. She not do massages."

"When was the last time you actually saw Helena?"

Lyudmyla thought for a moment. "Two weeks last Tuesday. He bring her in to work."

"Who?"

"Szymanski. They used to be … you know, friends."

"Used to be?"

"Yes. But that last night. The big man come. Stan the Man, they call him."

"Is this who you're talking about?" Stainmore produced a photo of Mirczack and handed it to her.

Lyudmyla seemed to shudder, looked away and gave it back straight away. "Yes," she said. "He horrible man. Szymanski, he frightened of him too."

"So this man Mirczack, he is the top boss? The owner?"

"I think so."

"And what happened that last time you saw her?"

"Mirczack, he take Helena and Szymanski into Room 2, the spare massage room. I hear some shouting. Then it goes quiet."

"If they were shouting, could you hear what was said?"

"Not really. The only one shouting was Mirczack. He said something like, 'I told you before … but you still not listen.' Something like that."

"And what happened afterwards?"

Lyudmyla took the pack of cigarettes from her jacket pocket, shook one free and lit it. Blowing the smoke out, she finally answered. "Mirczack, he storms out. I know he's not pleased."

"And Helena and Szymanski?"

"When they come out, they're very quiet. There's, you know … an atmosphere, yes?"

Stainmore nodded. "But you don't know what Mirczack was annoyed about?"

"No." Lyudmyla drew on her cigarette. "Then Szymanski leave and Helena goes on reception. I try to ask her what is going on but she says it is nothing."

"When did Szymanski come back?"

"About three hours."

"But she did arrange to see you on the following Thursday?"

"She said she would call round here."

"But she never turned up?"

"No … well … I don't know. They take us to Sensations that night. It was supposed to be our night off but Szymanski tell us we have to work." Lyudmyla looked out the window, gazing over the rooftops opposite. "We miss her. She helps the girls here. When we are here, we are not allowed out but she come and bring cigarettes for us, some food items we cannot get."

"Let me get this straight, you're saying that you girls are left locked in here when you're not working at the parlours?"

"Well, yes, unless he organises private parties."

Stainmore was shocked. "Lyudmyla, are you prepared to make a statement covering what you've just told me?"

"I worry for the others. Me, I not too bothered, I will claim asylum but the others, they have families back in their home country. Police there cannot protect them. Mostly they are corrupt too."

Stainmore didn't respond immediately, taking a few seconds to absorb all she'd been told. Finally, she said, "Can I see the other rooms?"

"Sure."

On the floor they were on, there was a small kitchen with some dirty crockery and cutlery awaiting washing up. A smell emanated from the bin where the remains of take-away meals had been discarded. There was also a bathroom, with a bath and shower over, toilet and wash hand basin. On the second floor, were Nadia's and Katerina's rooms. Both were unlocked and very much like Lyudmyla's but some underwear was scattered around Nadia's while Katerina's had washed clothes drying on the backs of the two chairs and off the table. There appeared to be no personal photographs or other items you would normally associate with girls of that age living in a foreign land.

"You mentioned a basement – and the ground floor. What happens there?" Stainmore asked.

"I show you." Lyudmyla led the way back down to the ground floor.

"Here, there is another bathroom." She opened a door to a room similar to the one on the first floor. The door opposite she threw open to reveal a smaller kitchen which was clean, neat and tidy. "We are not allowed to use this." The girl pointed to a door to the left of the front door and said, "That is a spare room for another girl, but we don't have at the moment."

Stainmore opened the door to reveal a small room with a bed with a bare mattress, an old wardrobe and an easy chair in the corner. She turned around and walked towards the door opposite. "And this one?" she asked, turning the handle but finding it locked.

"This is the room where they sometimes bring men for parties. It is always kept locked. In the basement there is another room but I have not seen inside."

"These 'parties' you talk about, have you been involved?"

Lyudmyla looked away.

"Look, I only want to help you. If you want to apply for asylum, I'll do what I can to assist you."

When the girl looked back, there were tears running down her cheeks. "Twice," she said.

"Who brings these men for the parties?"

"Him. Stan the Man."

Stainmore couldn't help herself. She put her arms around Lyudmyla and gave her a hug. "You've been very brave," she said. "I think we'll go back to Wakefield now – to the station and see what we can do to help you."

The girl nodded. "I have to leave by the same way I got in. I meet you back in the car."

Again, Stainmore had to trust her but from what she'd been told in the house, she felt more confident. Once outside the door, she heard it being locked from the inside, then footsteps. On her way back to the car, she considered there had been enough revelations for now. She had held back the photo of Chris Baker. Once they got to Wood Street, she'd open up that line of enquiry.

The blue Mondeo was a flurry of activity as a camera recorded Stainmore returning to her car. Just as she reached to put the key in the lock, behind and to her left, a car alarm announced its presence. She turned to see two youths run off down the street, away from an old brown Rover, the hazard warning lights flashing. "Little shits," she murmured to herself, before turning back to unlock her own pool car. As she did so, her eye caught the blue Mondeo with two men inside, attempting to look inconspicuous. In the twenty seconds it took Lyudmyla to join her, she angled the overtaking mirror to focus on the car and discreetly made a note of the number. She'd check it out when she got to the station. Finally, Stainmore saw the tell-tale glint of a camera lens as Lyudmyla got back into the passenger seat beside her. She drove off, checking in the rear view mirror that she wasn't being followed.

47

Whilst Stainmore took Lyudmyla to the lodging house, Strong drove Szymanski, handcuffed to Darby, back to Wood Street. Ormerod followed close behind with Stella and the two Lithuanian girls. It was risky but with the resources they had available it was the best solution he could come up with. He left Szymanski in Interview Room 2 alongside a uniformed constable, and took the opportunity to catch up with Luke Ormerod.

On the first floor corridor, Ormerod was coming out of the soft interview room when Strong spotted him.

"How was it on the journey?" Strong asked.

"The receptionist didn't say much. She sat in the front. The two girls in the back exchanged a few words on the way, all in a foreign tongue. Seemed a bit frightened, to be honest, guv."

"Not surprising. Your Estonian not good enough to understand what they were saying then?"

Ormerod smiled. "I've got a female uniform to sit in with them for the moment."

"That's good. Offer them some coffee or something, will you? I want them to settle in for a bit before we have a chat. What about the receptionist, Stella?"

"In Interview Room 4 downstairs."

"Right. Heard anything from Kelly?"

"Not yet, but I'm sure she won't be long. Might be an idea to get together before we move things on. I'll give you a shout."

On the way back down to join Szymanski, Strong's mobile rang.

"Colin, it's Vince."

He recognised the voice on the other end of the line as his ex-colleague, Vince Denholme from Vice. "Hello, mate," he responded, "Have I trod on your toes?"

"Not exactly but I'm assuming it was one of your team that took a young woman back to an address in Harehills?"

"You know about the house?"

"We've had it under surveillance since the beginning of the week."

"I didn't know."

"No reason why you should. I'll put my boss on, DCI Holmes. He'll explain."

Strong heard the muffled sounds of the handset being transferred.

"Colin, is it? It's Geoff Holmes here," came the older-sounding voice with a distinct Lancashire accent.

"Hello Geoff."

"Look, we might have a bit of a problem. This house in Harehills came to our attention this week when we received reports that it was being used for sex parties and that there might be some under-age activity going on."

"Well, my officer was DS Kelly Stainmore and she was taking one of the girls from Sweet Sensations back to where they were lodged. But, so far as I know, she's over eighteen and we haven't any reasons to suspect any under-age activity."

"So what happened today, Colin?"

"As part of my enquiries into the murder of a female Albanian asylum seeker, we visited the massage parlour. I wanted to speak to Stefan Szymanski who had links with the victim. He tried to make a run for it and was being unhelpful so I made the decision to bring him in. We're also bringing in the three girls who were working there. I know Vince has connections to Stella Hunter, the receptionist. I had to bring her in too, so it looked convincing."

"No sign of Mirczack?"

"Not yet. Have you any idea where he might be?"

"He has one of those fancy new apartments in Leeds near the railway station but we haven't seen him for several days."

"What put you on to this place in Harehills?"

"Phone call. Anonymous. Said we should be aware that there were special parties taking place there, disgusting sex with young girls."

"The call, was it recorded?"

"We always try to, yes."

"So was it a man or a woman?"

"A young girl's voice, foreign accent." Holmes took a breath. *"Look, you're interviewing Szymanski and the girls from the parlour. I think it would be a good idea if Vince joined you. He could fetch a recording of the call. To be honest, if none of the girls are under age and you're investigating the place already in connection with your murder case, we've got plenty of other things we can switch resources to, but Vince could liaise."*

"I'd have no objection to that, Geoff. But tell me, what brought Szymanski to your attention before now? And Mirczack, for that matter."

"Obviously Szymanski for his involvement in managing the parlours. As for Mirczack, there've been rumours for the past couple of years that he's been involved in trafficking. The parlours would be a good outlet for that, if you follow. Also, he's got interests in a couple of nightclubs in Leeds. He's got some fairly dubious connections in London too. And, before I forget, property. When we checked on the house where those girls are kept, we find it's owned by Balkan Investments, and guess who's principal shareholder in that?"

"All right Geoff, that is interesting. How soon can Vince get here?"

"I'll send him off now."

"Thanks, I'll wait till he arrives to brief the team."

Instead of going down to the interview room with Szymanski, Strong went back to his office to check on any messages. DCS Flynn had left a memo on his desk giving details of the murder team allocated to the schoolgirls' enquiry and inviting him to a briefing in Pontefract where they were setting up the incident room.

Just then, Darby knocked and addressed his boss from the doorway. "Guv, I've got a Jim Marshall downstairs. He's a bus driver in Leeds. He's only just heard we were enquiring into the missing Albanian girl."

"Come in a minute, John."

Darby took a couple of steps into the room. "Apparently he's been away in Lanzarote on holiday. He recognised the photo in their canteen and one of the other drivers told him about the reports in the papers yesterday."

"Where is he now?"

"Front interview room."

Strong rose and made for the door. "Okay, let's see what he's got to tell us."

Jim Marshall appeared to be in his mid-thirties, deeply tanned with a buzzed head, dressed in a white tee shirt, jeans, trainers and a denim jacket. He was nursing a Styrofoam cup of coffee.

"Jim," Darby said, "this is DCI Strong, the senior investigating officer in charge of the Helena Cryanovic murder case."

"Mr Marshall," Strong said, "thanks for coming in. I understand you may have some information that might help us?"

The detectives sat down opposite the driver.

"Well I didn't know till I got back." Marshall began, looking from Darby to Strong. "I've been away you see, ten days in Lanzarote. Bloody hot. Anyway, it's first day back, early shift, and I spotted your poster on the canteen wall. And I thought, I recognise that face. Pretty girl, foreign accent. And then I find out she's dead, murdered. So I thought it best to come in after I finished work."

Strong nodded and flipped open his notebook. "What can you tell us?"

"Well, I've seen her. Maybe two or three times, on my bus."

"When did you last see her, Mr Marshall?"

"It was that last night, Thursday, 1st September. We flew out next day on the 2nd. I was on the 49 to Monkswood Gate. She boarded on The Headrow."

"What time was that?"

The driver thought for a moment. "It must have been about half six," he said.

Strong made a note. "And how was she dressed?"

Marshall finished his coffee before replying, "Black short jacket, jeans and trainers, I think."

Strong moved in his chair to avoid anyone noticing him shudder. The image of Helena in the boot of the car in Felixstowe flashed into his memory. She was dressed as the bus driver had just described. He struggled to shift the recollection of her head, as if shrink-wrapped in that clear plastic bag. "Where did she get off?"

"It was up the top end of Harehills Road, just before the lights where we join Roundhay Road."

Strong turned to Darby. "Have you got a Leeds street map there, John?"

Darby stood up. "I'll get one," he said and left the room.

"I appreciate you coming in, Mr Marshall."

Marshall nodded.

"Tell me, was there no CCTV on your bus that night?"

"There was a fault. On that vehicle it hadn't been working all week. I'm not sure if it's been repaired yet."

"Must have been a worry on the late night services for you, not that CCTV in itself is a deterrent."

"You'd be surprised how many of them don't work. I suppose the fact that the cameras are there is deterrent enough. It's the same with speed cameras. I mean you tell me, but they reckon not all of them work. The fact you don't know which ones mean you slow for them all."

"I suppose that's true."

Darby returned, clutching a gazetteer. "Ah, thanks, John."

He opened the street plan at the appropriate pages and placed it on the table in front of his boss.

Strong traced Harehills Road with his finger and followed it up to the junction with Roundhay Road. "So she got off here?" he asked.

"That's right. The stop's about a hundred yards before the lights."

"And that would have been, what, around a quarter to or ten to seven?"

"About that, yes," the driver agreed.

"Was she the only one to get off there?"

"Er, no, I think there was an old woman with one of those shopping bags on wheels and a couple of young lads."

"Don't suppose you saw where she went?"

"I had one man get on and by the time I took his fare and began to set off, when I checked my mirror, she'd gone behind the bus and crossed the road."

"One last thing," Strong said, "you said you'd seen her two or three times."

The driver nodded. "That's right, yeah."

"Always on this same route?"

"Yep, gets on on The Headrow and gets off where she did on Thursday."

Strong closed his notebook and the gazetteer before getting to his feet. "Well thanks very much for your help, Mr Marshall. DC Darby here will take a formal statement from you. You've been most helpful."

When he left the room, his mobile rang again. This time, Souter's name came up.

"Look mate," he said, "I'm a bit busy at the moment. Is it quick?"

"Sorry, Col," his friend said, "just wondering if you fancy a pint tonight. Bit of a catch up. There's a couple of things I wanted to run by you."

Strong blew out his cheeks and checked his watch. "I might need one after today. I'm not sure how the rest of it'll pan out yet. Can I give you a call later?"

"Yeah, sure."

"Where were you thinking of?"

"How about The Redoubt at the end of Westgate?"

"Just after the church?"

"That's right. He keeps a decent pint and it's on your way home."

"I'll call you."

Finally, when Strong returned to his office he found Kelly Stainmore waiting.

"Ah, Kelly," he said, "anything interesting at the house."

"You could say that, guv. I've just done a PNC on a suspicious Mondeo with two blokes taking photos of us and guess what?"

"Vice."

"They've spoken to you?"

"Vince Denholme is on his way to join us for a briefing." He checked his watch again. "Should be here anytime. They've had the house under surveillance for a few days. What have you done with the girl?"

"Interview Room downstairs. Seems we're running out of space. I've got a female constable sitting in with her but I don't want to leave her too long. I think she's trusting me."

"That's good. But before you talk to her again, I think Vince might have something interesting to say when he arrives." He opened the street map where Jim Marshall had told him Helena had stepped off the bus. "Now, exactly where is this house?" he asked.

Stainmore leaned forward in her seat and studied the map. "Here," she said, pointing a finger, "Luxor Grove, number 57."

Strong smiled grimly. "So if I tell you Helena got off the number 49 bus here around 6:50 on Thursday evening, 1st September, last seen crossing the road, where do you think she was heading?"

Stainmore nodded. "Plus, Lyudmyla tells me she was expecting her that evening but Szymanski changed their night off and sent them off to do a shift in Sensations."

He was thoughtful for a few seconds. "How did the house look?"

Stainmore described what she'd seen inside the girls'
accommodation, including the locked ground floor room
where Lyudmyla stated that special parties took place.
She also mentioned the mystery room in the basement.

"Right," Strong said, "I'm going to see Flynn. We need
a warrant and get SOCO round there. All the evidence
points to Helena heading for Luxor Grove and never seen
since. Round up the troops for …" He checked his watch.
"Fifteen minutes. Vince should be here by then."

48

The CID room was buzzing when Strong and DS Denholme walked in. Kelly Stainmore, Luke Ormerod and John Darby were relating the events of the afternoon to Jim Ryan, Sam Kirkland, Trevor Newell and Malcolm Atkinson. Ormerod was regaling the others on Darby's assertion that it was the first time he'd been in a massage parlour.

"It's true," he protested, adjusting his crotch and drawing more laughter from his colleagues.

"Okay, everybody, listen up," Strong announced. "We've got some work to do now."

The conversations quickly died and attention focused on the latest arrivals.

"For those of you who don't know, this is DS Vince Denholme." Strong held out an arm indicating the new man. "DS Denholme is from the Vice Squad and here to liaise and give us the benefit of his knowledge."

Strong turned to the whiteboard behind him with various photos stuck to it. Writing and lines in felt-tip pen connected text boxes and some of the pictures. "Helena Cryanovic," he began, pointing to her photo on the board, "last seen, as we now know, getting off the number 49 bus on Harehills Road, near the junction with Luxor Grove, on Thursday 1st September at approximately 6:50pm. Her body was found last Monday in the boot of a stolen Mercedes SLK 230 Sports Coupe which was in a container at Felixstowe Docks. Estimated time of death, Kelly?"

Before Stainmore could respond, DS Ryan interrupted, "Sorry, Kelly, I took a call for you this afternoon. The pathologist in Ipswich had results from the tests he was running and he's refined his estimate to between Thursday and Saturday which would be between the first and third of September."

Strong wrote a note on the board. "That's good, so now we've got a smaller window to work with. The Merc was stolen from an address in Crigglestone on Friday evening, that's the second of September. We know this car was in the barn at Meadow Woods Farm on Saturday the third because it was seen by Susan Brown and it had been stolen by Gary Baker and Steve Chapman – current whereabouts unknown. Any news on that anyone?"

A few mumbled responses of, 'No, guv,' greeted this request.

Strong gave a frustrated sigh. "Moving on, we know Helena was involved with this man, Stefan Szymanski." He pointed to a photograph of the Pole. "Earlier this afternoon, we brought Szymanski in for further questioning. We tracked him down to the massage parlour, Sweet Sensations, in Chapeltown. We also brought in the receptionist and the three girls working there, one of whom we suspect could be Helena's friend, Lyudmyla, who she was supposed to have been visiting on the evening she was last seen. Kelly, you accompanied her to the house in Luxor Grove where they've all been staying. What can you say about that?"

Stainmore described the house, the various girls' rooms, a couple of Spartan kitchens and bathrooms before mentioning the locked ground floor room where she was told special parties took place. "Lyudmyla also mentioned a locked basement room as well," she continued. "And, on the Thursday night Helena was last seen, Lyudmyla tells me that Szymanski made them work when it was supposed to be a night off."

"And I've just been to see DCS Flynn," Strong came back, "he's agreed we get a warrant to search the house. So, Jim," he turned to DS Ryan, "I'd like you out there with the SOCO boys and see what they can turn up. Take Malcolm with you. I know it's a long shot some two weeks on, but see what the neighbours recall. Probably all flats or bed-sits, but, you never know, you might come across some observant soul who remembers something around that time." Strong then turned to Denholme. "We'll come to Stella in a minute, but anything you can add to that, Vince, bearing in mind we now know you had the house under surveillance."

"That's right. We had an anonymous call telling us that there were sexual parties being held there. I've got a tape of the call here, so if there's a player I could borrow …?"

"Try this," Kirkland said from the back, picking up a tape player and passing it forward.

Denholme put the machine on the table in front of him, placed the tape inside and pressed play. A young female voice with a distinct Eastern European accent began to speak:

> *"You need to know,"* she said, *"house on Luxor Grove, number 57, men come there for … for disgusting sex. And the girls, they are young and are made to perform everything. You need to stop this."*
>
> *"Can I just take your name, please?"* a male voice asked.
>
> *"No,"* she replied, *"no names. Just stop it."*

A dialling tone interrupted, indicating the call was over.

"Can you play that again," Stainmore asked.

Strong nodded to Denholme, who rewound, then pressed play again.

"You got something, Kelly?" Strong wondered when it had ended.

"Make your mind up for yourself, guv," she replied. "Come and have a word with Lyudmyla."

"You think it's Lyudmyla?"

"Ninety-nine per cent. I've just spent most of the afternoon with her."

Denholme raised his eyebrows. "Makes sense, I suppose."

"She was also lying when she said she didn't know the address. I think she wanted to separate herself from the other girls. She kept saying she had nothing to lose but they did. Families back home, she was talking about."

"You've had Szymanski on your radar for some time, Vince. What can you tell us about him and his connections with this man?" Strong pointed to another photograph on the board, "Stanislav Mirczack."

"Stefan Szymanski," Denholme began, "born in Zakopane in the Tatra Mountains in 1969. Arrived here, we believe, nearly three years ago. He first came to our notice when he was employed by Mirczack to manage the massage parlours; Shangri La in Bradford, Butterflies in Morley and Sweet Sensations in Chapeltown. In conjunction with the local authorities we do some spot checks to make sure there are no under-age activities, drugs, anything like that, health and safety checks.

"Mirczack himself became known to us in 1996. Originally from Yugoslavia. As well as the three parlours, we believe he has interests in two nightclubs in Leeds and property through a company known as Balkan Investments – including 57 Luxor Grove."

"But you've no evidence of any criminal activities?"

"We know he has connections with some heavy operators in Eastern Europe and is associated with an Albanian crew in London, but nothing we can tie him down to here so far."

"Is he running the other parlours with Eastern European women?"

"No, the others are mostly staffed by English girls. Sensations seems to be the only one of its kind. But bear in mind, the girls you've brought in are only one shift at Sensations. There must be another group of girls who do the days this lot don't."

"Of course," Strong said. "They weren't working seven days a week. Have the girls said anything about any others, Kelly, Luke?"

"No, guv," Stainmore replied. Ormerod shook his head.

DAVID EVANS

"So trafficking, then? Is he involved with that?"

"We're not sure," Denholme responded. "We're working with the London boys and the Greater Manchester force because we suspect these girls may be sold and shipped around the country between establishments but it's early days, we're still looking for links."

Strong exhaled deeply. "So any idea where he is now?"

"We think he may be out of the country. We've got a watch on all air and seaports to let us know when he passes through."

"All right. Kelly, you speak to Lyudmyla again. She's obviously not telling you everything – that phone message for a start, and any other girls and where they might be."

"What about the other two, guv?" Ormerod asked, "Nadia and Katarina."

"Who's the officer sitting in with them at the moment?"

"Kath Milner."

Strong nodded. "She's pretty experienced. See if she can tell you how they've reacted while they've been kept waiting. Keep her with you when you talk to them in the light of what Kelly's told us. You know what to look for."

"Right, guv."

Strong turned to Denholme. "Vince, can you find out a bit more about Mirczack's whereabouts? I wouldn't want him walking in on our search party at Luxor Grove. And we could do with getting a formal statement from Stella too. She must know something about another shift of girls. Can you and Sam conduct the interview?"

"No problems. I'll get on it."

"Trevor, can you chase up the ballistics reports for me on Helena?"

Newell nodded and walked back to his desk.

"John," Strong addressed Darby, "You come with me. I want you to sit in on our next little chat with Szymanski."

Lyudmyla sat nervously nibbling the skin at the side of her thumb when Stainmore returned to the ground floor interview room carrying a brown file. She looked up expectantly. The female uniformed officer acknowledged the detective's nod and left the room.

"Would you like another drink?" Stainmore asked, indicating the empty styrene cup on the table between them.

The young woman shook her head. "Thank you, no."

"I don't blame you." Stainmore smiled and studied her for a few seconds. "Lyudmyla," she finally said. "Why did you let me think you didn't know the address of the house?"

She looked indignant. "I didn't."

Stainmore raised her eyebrows in a gesture of disbelief.

"I didn't," the girl repeated. "It was Nadia you asked and she wasn't sure. Then you ask something else."

"But you wanted the others to think you didn't know too."

She shrugged. "Maybe."

"What shifts do you and the other two actually do?"

"We work from eleven in the morning until ten at night."

"I mean what days do you work?"

"Usually Tuesday, Wednesday, Friday and Sunday."

"So what happens on the other days."

"They have other girls but I don't know who."

Stainmore raised her eyebrows again. "Come on Lyudmyla, you must know."

She exhaled heavily. "I don't know. Helena, she tell me there are more girls in another house, but I don't know names or where they are."

Stainmore paused for a few seconds, then opened the file she had brought with her. "Okay. One more picture for you to look at." She pulled out a photograph and passed it across to Lyudmyla. "I think you know this man."

The girl took hold of it then immediately put it face down on the table.

"Be honest with me."

She looked at Stainmore, eyes moist. "Yes," she said.

"Can you tell me who he is?"

"You know who he is. It's Chris. He come regular to see me. And now he's dead. He was in the paper. Shot, they said."

Stainmore picked up the photograph and placed it back in the envelope. "What was your relationship?"

She looked puzzled. "Relationship? He come for sex. We have good sex."

"Nothing else?"

"Like what?"

Again Stainmore paused. "Was that why you telephoned the police?"

Lyudmyla looked puzzled.

"To report 57 Luxor Grove. 'Disgusting sex parties'?" Stainmore quoted.

She looked away.

"It was you wasn't it?"

Finally, she looked back at Stainmore. "They will kill me too."

"Who will?"

The girl remained silent.

"Seeing the reports in the paper of Chris's murder, you think you know who was responsible?"

"Can I have that drink please? Coffee, black with sugar."

Stainmore held her gaze for a second. "Okay," she said with a grim smile. "But if you want me to help you, you'll have to help me."

With the female uniform back in the room alongside Lyudmyla, Stainmore went upstairs in search of her boss. She found him coming out of Interview Room 2 with Darby.

"How's it going, guv?"

"It isn't," Strong responded, thrusting his hands deep into his trouser pockets. "Clammed up, demanding a solicitor. You?"

"There is another house but she claims not to know where or the names of any other girls. She reckoned Helena knew, though. She got a bit emotional when I showed her Baker's photo. Reckons they used to have 'good sex', whatever that was." Stainmore glanced at Darby who was smirking but ignored him and looked back to her boss. "Anyway, she's spooked. I think she has an idea who shot him. It definitely shook her up when she saw it splashed all over the papers and I think that's why she made the call to Denholme's mob."

Just then, Newell strode up the corridor. "Guv," he said, "just got hold of the scientist at the ballistics lab. The bullets recovered from the bodies of Chris Baker and Helena Cryanovic were fired from the same gun.

Strong pulled his hands from his pockets and clenched his fists. "I knew it."

"So all we've got to do is find the gun," Newell suggested.

"Easier said than done. Have you seen Vince?"

"He was in the CID room on the phone."

"Right. Let's go see what he might have for us."

"I'll get Lyudmyla a coffee and see what else I can tease from her," Stainmore said, heading for the stairs.

In the incident room, Denholme was replacing the receiver when Strong, Darby and Newell entered.

"Any news on Mirczack, Vince?"

"According to our boys, he's out of the country. We talked to Immigration and he took a flight to Riga from Leeds/Bradford on Tuesday. There's a flag on him so as soon as he's checked in on a return, they'll let us know."

Strong thought for a moment. "Riga, that's Latvia isn't it?"

"That's right. We think he has connections there."

"That's where the containers were headed from Felixstowe. What about Stella? What was she able to tell you?"

"Got her statement here." He held up some sheets of paper. "Basically, she worked only one shift with the other team. From what she can remember, there were four of them. She could remember three of their names, all presumably false, and struggled to remember the fourth. As with the Luxor Grove team, Szymanski brought them in and took them back. But she never heard where they lived."

"Shit, we need to find them. If they're locked in like the others, well … You sure Stella didn't have a clue?"

Denholme spread his hands wide. "I tried all sorts to see if she could remember the minutest detail; had they mentioned anything they passed, a shop, a building site, but there was nothing."

"Have you released her?"

Denholme nodded. "Thought it best. I can always get hold of her again if I need to."

"Colin," DCS Flynn appeared at the door. Strong walked towards his boss and followed him out into the corridor.

"The warrant's been signed for Luxor Grove and the team are on their way. How're things progressing?" Flynn asked.

"Slowly, sir. Szymanski's not saying a word now."

"What about the women?"

"Kelly's back in with Lyudmyla. She's the one that Baker used to visit. She obviously knows more than she's already told us. Luke's speaking to the other two."

"You know we're going to have to get Immigration involved?"

Strong leaned back against the wall then looked away from Flynn for a second. "I know. But once we do that, we won't get much more from them. They're definitely frightened. From what Kelly said, Nadia and Katerina have families back in Estonia, which, if my 'O' Level Geography serves me well is right next door to

Latvia which is where we think Mirczack is at the moment."

"I can probably delay Immigration until the morning," Flynn offered.

"In the meantime, what do we do with them? I can't let them go back to the house. They're not technically under arrest."

"We haven't got a budget for a B&B. Besides, you won't want them disappearing into the night. You're going to have to do the best you can in the soft interview suite."

Strong looked heavenward as he pondered this. Before he could respond, Ormerod appeared.

"I'll leave that with you, Colin," Flynn said, turning on his heel and walking off in the opposite direction.

"Thank you, sir," he said quietly to his retreating back. Looking to his DC, he sighed, "Tell me you've got something positive to tell me."

As Strong walked back into the CID Room, Ormerod began to report, "From what Kath Milner told me outside, they're both pretty scared. When she was alone with them they weren't talking much to each other but when they did, obviously it was in Estonian. From their mannerisms and body language, they seem dazed by their situation, they don't know what will happen next. The blonde one, Nadia, seems the most upset. She was tearful and Katerina was trying to console her. They did get animated at one point, Kath said. That was when they mentioned Mirczack's name a couple of times."

"How did you get on with them?" Strong asked.

"I took it gently. I think it helped having Kath there as you suggested guv. They confirmed Lyudmyla's story that on the Thursday in question, Szymanski changed their night off and took them in. Helena had been on the scene for about three months. She seemed close to Szymanski but that had cooled about two weeks ago, around three or four days before she was last seen."

"What about other girls and other houses?"

"They claim to know nothing. Never seen anyone who might work different days to them and have never heard of another house. Seems like Szymanski and Mirzcack kept the two teams completely separate,"

"What about Baker? Did they recognise his photo?"

"Yep. Said he was a regular with Mariana, I mean Lyudmyla. But something else, they said he would often be in conversation with Szymanski. It didn't seem to be just small talk type of chat. Sometimes they were discussing things intensely. Baker seemed uncomfortable at times, they thought. Quite observant, those two."

"Did you bring up the subject of the parties at the house?"

"Briefly. They coloured up when I mentioned them. Seemed nervous and embarrassed."

"Did they say who organised them?"

"Mirczack."

Stainmore appeared at the door at that point. "Guv, I think you might want to hear this," she said.

"Lyudmyla?" Strong enquired.

Stainmore nodded and disappeared back into the corridor.

"You'd best start getting formal statements from those two," Strong said to Ormerod as he picked up a notebook and made to follow Stainmore out into the corridor. "Gently does it. They may be hungry too."

"Right."

Strong hesitated at the door. "Oh, nearly forgot with all this going on, Luke, but any news on that other Misper, Maria Brownlow, the streetwalker from the market place?"

"Nothing, guv. I've been over to the CCTV centre to see if we could get better stills from the cameras but nothing that would allow us to zoom in on the van's number plate or get a better shot of the driver."

Strong left and followed Stainmore down to the Ground Floor Interview Room. "She was talking a bit more about Baker," she said. "Turns out she knew quite a lot about him."

Lyudmyla was smoking a cigarette when Stainmore returned to the room with her boss.

"You shouldn't be doing that in here," Stainmore told her, looking at the female uniformed constable.

"I did tell her," the constable said.

"Don't worry about it." Strong looked to the ceiling then took a seat. "There's no smoke detector in here."

Stainmore sat down at the table. "Lyudmyla," she said, "you remember DCI Strong from earlier this afternoon?" The girl nodded. "Can you run through what you just told me, for Mr Strong's benefit?"

"Sure." She blew out smoke then dropped her cigarette into one of the polystyrene cups on the table. It hissed as it was extinguished by the coffee dregs. "Chris, he comes to see me, first time, three maybe four months ago. He was very nice, not like some of the men. He also use his real name. Not many do, I think. But also we talk about his work. He tells me he works for big insurance company. A bit later, Szymanski, he talks about his car insurance to be renewed. I tell him Chris works here and maybe he might get a good deal. That's what starts all this."

"Go on," Strong encouraged, jotting down a few notes.

"I don't know details but I think Szymanski gets information from him. Mirczack then wants to know from Szymanski."

"What sort of information?"

"I can't be sure but I think they blackmail him for names and addresses. I think to do with cars. They say they know where he lives and they will tell his wife he comes to Sensations if he don't tell them."

"So Mirczack is pressurising Szymanski to get information from Chris. From his work you think?"

"Yes."

"When was the last time this happened?"

Lyudmyla furrowed her brows as if in thought for a few seconds then said, "That week when we see Helena for the last time. He came in that night, the Tuesday, I tell you about when Szymanski bring her in. Chris came in that night also. He give Szymanski a piece of paper with some writing. He'd gone when Mirczack came later. I told you they had big argument – Szymanski, Mirczack and Helena."

Strong looked at Stainmore who nodded confirmation before he turned back to the girl. "Do you think this argument was something to do with Chris?"

She shrugged. "Maybe. I tell you I could not hear."

Strong leaned back in his seat and studied the girl. "Lyudmyla, how did you come to be here?"

"You mean here," she pointed to the table. "Or in this country?"

"In Yorkshire."

She looked all round as if avoiding any eye contact then reached into her jacket pocket. Pulling out her cigarettes, she looked enquiringly at Strong.

"You're not supposed to but ... go on," he said.

She lit up and blew the first drag fiercely away. "I come through agency in Vilnius. They say for 5,000 Litai, that's about £1,000, they can get me visa and job in UK. I can come to work as waitress to start. I can pay back over time. I want to make a good future for myself. I think I cannot do that in Lithuania. But when I come I'm told I have to work to pay for the rest of the fee. I say, 'what rest of fee?' and they say I owe another 5,000 Litai. They take my passport and put me in house in London. They bring men to house and say if I don't satisfy them, they will harm my family in Estonia. I say I have no family, so they say they will kill me."

"So they forced you to have sex with these men against your will?"

She flicked her ash into the polystyrene cup. "Yes."

"So how did you get from London to Leeds?"

"Mirczack. He come one day, not to have sex, he come to look at the girls. I think he choose me because next day, Szymanski drive me to Leeds."

"How long ago was this?"

"About six months."

Strong made some more notes then resumed, "You mentioned parties at the house. Can you tell me about them?"

"Sometimes Mirczack bring men to the house. Sometimes one but mostly two or three."

"Are they different every time?"

"Mostly. But once or twice I recognise one from before."

"Any from those who visit Sweet Sensations?"

"No, never."

"Are these men from this country, do you think, or are they from abroad?"

"Mostly English, I think."

"These 'parties', they involved Nadia and Katerina too?"

"Always."

"And they took place in the ground floor room you showed DS Stainmore?"

"Yes."

"And only girls from the house, or did they ever bring in girls from outside?"

"Only us," she confirmed.

"You also mentioned a locked room in the basement. What can you tell us about that?"

She looked puzzled and shook her head. "Nothing. I have never been there. It is always locked."

Strong paused and looked to Stainmore then back to the girl. "What would you like to happen to you now, Lyudmyla?"

"I would like to be free. I like to stay here but to work at a proper job, not this."

He nodded. "What I'd like you to do is to give a formal statement to DS Stainmore here, just covering all we've spoken about. Is that okay?"

"Will you help me?" she asked looking from Strong to Stainmore and back again.

"I'll do what I can for you." He stood and picked up his notepad. "You must be hungry?"

She nodded.

He then turned to Stainmore. "Can you sort something out, Kelly?" He turned and left the room.

Strong rubbed his eyes as he sat in his office and considered the events of the day. It had been fast moving. Flynn had backed his decision to hold Szymanski overnight to see what the search and forensic teams discover at Luxor Grove. The girls had been fed and were being made as comfortable as possible in the soft interview suite which was kept for dealing with children, rape and other vulnerable victims. Nothing they'd found out so far could shed any light on the second house and other girls. Tomorrow, he hoped something would materialise from Luxor Grove, plus he had the briefing at Pontefract with the Meadow Woods Farm Murder Team.

He was just about to put his jacket on when his mobile rang. Bob.

"Hello, mate," Strong said.

"Still there?"

"Just about to leave."

"Good. See you in The Redoubt in fifteen minutes."

"I don't know, I'm feeling a bit …"

"Like you need a pint?" Souter interrupted. *"Fifteen minutes. See you."* And the line went dead.

49

It was ten past eight when Strong pulled into the car park at the side of The Redoubt. The other elevation proudly announced that this was the start of the famous Westgate Run – a line of pubs along Westgate leading into the city. The aroma from St. Michael's Fish and Chip shop over the road reminded him he hadn't had much to eat all day. He entered through the side door by the toilets and cast glances into the two rooms at the back of the pub. Moving through to the bar, he found Souter already there, a pint of Tetley's ready for him.

"What a day," Strong said.

"Big developments then?" Souter took a pull on his pint.

"Yes and no." Strong lifted his beer. "Come on, let's sit down."

"They're in the middle of a quiz night in here."

Strong rolled his eyes. "Great. That's all I need."

They walked towards one of the back rooms and stood in the doorway. To the left, a group of three women and two men were huddled around their answer sheet on the table. To their right, two seriously overweight men were chatting and opposite them another group of two men and two women were drinking and talking. Just as Strong was about to walk to the far end and sit down, the landlord made another announcement over the PA. "The next round is a music round. Question eleven; what was the name of Elvis Presley's backing band? The name of Elvis Presley's backing band," he repeated slowly.

Strong hesitated. A blonde woman in the group of five, in a stage whisper offered her suggestion to the rest of her group. "Was it The Tourettes?" she said.

As one, the rest of her friends, as well as the two men at the adjacent table turned on her. "No it fucking well wasn't!" they exclaimed, then burst into laughter.

Souter nearly spilt his pint and Strong had to turn away.

"Let's have a look in the front," Strong suggested, a broad smile on his face.

As they passed the bar, the landlord, microphone in hand, looked puzzled. "No fuckin' idea why that question was so amusing," he said.

The snug was empty, apart from a middle-aged couple sitting on bar stools, leaning against the counter with a half of bitter and a glass of white wine in front of them. They nodded as Strong and Souter entered and sat down at a table in the corner.

"So what's been happening today especially that's made you feel so knackered then?" Souter asked.

Strong shook his head. "You know, looking back, this morning seems a long way off now." Souter waited for his friend to carry on. "I only wanted to speak to a suspect and we end up bringing him into custody, along with the three Eastern European women he's had working for him in a dodgy massage parlour. That'll mean Immigration will get involved. No doubt, Inland Revenue. Times like these, I could do with a cigar."

Souter chuckled. "How long now?"

"Three weeks, five days and ..." he glanced at his watch. "Twenty-two minutes."

"Good man." Souter took a drink from his glass. "Is this massage parlour business connected with your Albanian girl?"

Strong leaned back in the seat. "Yes. And the guy I brought in was her supposed boyfriend."

"A serious suspect?"

"Not sure. There are other parties involved. At the moment I need some hard evidence, which I haven't got."

"What about these other two herberts you've been looking for? Any joy tracking them down? Who was it now ... Baker and Chapman?"

Strong put his head back and closed his eyes for a few seconds. "Disappeared off the face of the earth."

Souter was even more impressed with Sammy. If the police were struggling to track down this mystery cousin but she had at least narrowed the field, he wasn't going to pass that on. "Talking of disappearances, have you got anything for me on Maria? Sammy's bound to ask."

"She still lodging with you?"

"No, she's staying at Alison's."

Strong shook his head. "You found yourself a diamond there, mate."

"I know. It was a bit awkward at first when she found out I'd let her stay at mine for a night but ... we're solid."

"I'm glad for you. But no, nothing on your Misper. I asked the officer in charge today. He'd been back to see Gazza I think, but he doubts he could get any better images of the van."

The sirens of an ambulance disturbed the conversation and Souter followed the flashing blue lights' refraction through the pub window as it passed by. "It doesn't look good, does it?" he said, after a brief pause. "I mean, it's been too long. I know you get these girls moving on, drifting through life, but when Sammy tells me how close they were ... she would have been in contact with her somehow." He looked at Strong who nodded understandingly. Souter finished his beer. "One more?"

"I'll get these," Strong said and got to his feet. "I'll only have a half, I'm driving and I haven't had anything to eat since a sandwich at lunch time."

At the bar, Strong was served by a pimply youth of about twenty. He bought a couple of bags of crisps, a pint of Timothy Taylor Landlord for Souter and a half of Tetley for himself. He also learnt that the answer to question eleven was The Jordanaires.

"So," he said, settling himself back in his seat, "what did you want to run by me?"

Souter looked puzzled.

"When you rang this afternoon," Strong reminded him, "you said there were a couple of ..."

"Oh, yeah, sorry." Souter lowered his voice and leaned in across the table. "Well, I nipped in to see Susan today."

"Oh yeah, how is she?"

"They let her out this afternoon. Gillian collected her. Alison and Sammy have popped over to see her tonight. But she wants me to keep her up to speed with the events at the farm. I was just wondering when I could report on the schoolgirls' discovery?"

Strong opened one of the crisp bags and offered some to Souter, who declined. "You know there's reporting restrictions at the moment. The families need to be informed first and the forensics team needs to carry out their work with minimal distractions and interruptions. I've been invited to a team briefing in the morning in Pontefract so I would expect you'll know shortly after that. I think they're planning to move the bodies to the mortuary in the morning." Flynn had told him as much. "And there'll probably be a press conference in the afternoon."

"I'd better get a head start on the rest of the pack." Souter looked concerned.

"DCS Flynn said you would." Strong offered the crisp bag again. This time Souter took a couple.

"It'll have taken them a while to move the bodies."

Strong finished some crisps before he answered. "I think they want to gather as much evidence in-situ. You know what these scientists are like."

Souter crunched his crisps and washed them down with a gulp of beer. "The other thing was Baker's father."

"What about him?"

"It's Robert, isn't it?"

Strong was curious now. Souter knew something and he seemed to be testing the water. "What do you know?"

A loud cheer and laughter drifted through the bar from the other side. Souter reached in for another crisp. "No, nothing really," he said in an innocent tone. "It's just this afternoon, I came across a report on his retirement last year in the archives, that's all."

"Retirement? If it hit the Post, he must have had a fairly decent position then. What did he do?"

"Worked at De la Rue, you know, the printers."

"The bank note specialists. What as?"

"Some sort of designer, I think."

Strong felt the familiar effects of an adrenaline rush. "Like I said, it must have been a senior position to warrant a report in the papers." He took a drink of his beer, hoping he didn't make any obvious reaction to what Souter had just told him. His mind was buzzing. If Baker senior had the skills and knowledge, he would be the obvious source of good quality fake documents, like those registration papers accompanying the stolen vehicles. He thought again of Baker's reaction to questions about his son, Gary, and Chris's visits to the massage parlour. He definitely knew more than he had told him. He needed to speak to him again.

"Thought that would interest you," Souter said with a grin. "That's why I thought you might like to see a copy. Here." He took a folded up piece of paper from his pocket and handed it across.

Strong opened it and read the article. When he'd finished, he folded it back up and put it in his jacket pocket. "Thanks for this," he said, "Interesting that from a fairly normal, reasonably wealthy family, a scrote like Gary Baker can emerge. Plus his brother, of course, involved in something so wrong, he gets himself topped." Strong rubbed his eyes.

Souter smiled to himself. What Robert Baker had done for a living certainly caught his friend's attention, no matter how he tried to cover it.

"Sorry, mate," Strong said, "I'm going to have to go. I'm starving and I'm knackered. Laura's got some shepherd's pie to heat up for me, and I can hear it calling me." He stood up to leave. "Listen, why don't you and Alison come round for something to eat, sometime soon? Laura only said this morning how she hasn't seen you for ages."

"Sounds good to me. I'll check with her and give you a call."

"See you." With that Strong left the way he'd come in, got into his car and drove home. First thing in the morning, he'd get one of the team on Baker's case – address for one thing. For now, he was looking forward to some food.

* * *

Laura was sitting at the dining table going through some paperwork when Strong arrived home. He took off his jacket in the hall and looked in at the doorway.

"Hi," she said. "Hungry?"

"Starving."

"Hi, Dad," Amanda called from the lounge, the sound of the television in the background.

He walked to the lounge doorway. "Hi, sweetheart. Got your shortlist for universities sorted?"

"Not really. Still working on it." She turned on the settee to face him. "God, you look knackered."

Strong lifted a finger. "Hey. Enough of that sort of talk."

She smiled and turned back to her programme.

Laura came up behind and put her arms around him. "She's right, though, you look tired. Your tea's in the microwave. I'll warm it up." As she went into the kitchen he took off his shoes and put on some slippers. When he joined her, he sat down at the kitchen table.

"Had a busy day?" Laura asked.

"There's just so much going on." He rubbed his eyes with the heels of both hands. After a pause, he looked up at his wife. "Jennifer would have graduated by now and Mary probably looking forward to her second year, if they'd been clever enough."

"Those two schoolgirls?"

Strong nodded. "I know they're not my case, but I can't help being interested."

"Is that what's taking up your time?"

"No. It's the more seedy side of life."

"Your Albanian girl?"

"She got involved with some nasty people – sex trafficking I suspect now."

The microwave pinged, prompting Laura to walk over, test the food and set it going again. She leaned against the worktop.

"We're really lucky here in Britain, aren't we?" Strong looked off into space for a second before focussing back on his wife. "She reminded me a lot of Amanda, you know. Imagine if she had to leave England just to get a basic standard of living; risking all sorts of exploitation. I know there is some poverty here, but nothing like some of the conditions in countries like Albania, Estonia, Latvia and the other former Russian satellite states. Nobody here feels compelled to travel abroad for a better life.

The microwave pinged again and Laura dished up.

"Wow, we are in a melancholy mood aren't we?" she jibed.

"No, it's just … do you know, this is delicious," he said, taking the first mouthful of food.

"Do you want something to drink?"

"I'll have a mug of tea later. I nipped for a pint with Bob on the way home. He seems to be settled."

"At the moment," Laura added.

Strong laughed. "Yea, I know. His track record isn't the best but Alison seems good for him."

"She's got that young girl staying with her now, though, hasn't she?"

"Sammy, yes. There's still no news on her friend either."

"How long is that?"

"Must be ten days." He paused to eat more of his shepherds' pie. "I was thinking, what are we doing Sunday? Maybe ask them round for lunch. You were only saying, you hadn't seen him for months. And I don't think you've met Alison yet."

"I haven't, no. Sunday? No, nothing planned. That'd be nice."

"Okay, I'll call him tomorrow."

50
Friday

By contrast to the impressive Victorian stone building housing Pontefract Magistrates Court, the Police Station behind it in Sessions House Yard was the epitome of the architectural carbuncle that had once exercised Prince Charles so much. Brick ground floor elevations between concrete columns with precast concrete panels above did nothing to inspire visitors, not that most visitors would be looking for inspiration, certainly not of the artistic kind. At least there were a couple of traditional Police blue lamps either side of the public entrance.

Strong parked in one of the bays to the side and, after announcing his presence at the front desk, was buzzed through to make his way upstairs to the murder room that had been set up in one of the larger first floor offices.

Before he could enter, DCI Walker strode up the corridor to greet him. "Colin, glad you could make it," he said, offering a hand. "I hear you've got your hands full yourself."

Strong knew that he and Peter Walker were about the same age, but balding, being shorter and heavier set, gave Walker the appearance of being much older. He'd met him a couple of times over the years on various courses and thought he was a straight talking 'what you see is what you get' sort of copper. "Good to see you again, Peter," he said, shaking hands. "Yes things have been hotting up back at Wood Street. I don't know if I can add much to your enquiry but I appreciate the invite."

"Well, I'm just about to bring everyone up to speed, so if there is anything that springs to mind, just join in." Walker opened the door and ushered him into the room where around ten CID officers and a couple of uniforms were assembled.

Over the course of the next fifteen minutes, the history of the disappearances of Mary Duggan and Jennifer Coyle were reprised. Various items of clothing found on the bodies clearly identified them as belonging to the girls. Memories of Strong's mother ironing name tags onto the collars of his school shirts were dredged from his subconscious. The families had been told, and the bodies were being removed that morning. A press conference was being called for three o'clock but, with a nod towards Strong, Walker indicated that the Yorkshire Post would be reporting the find in their earliest evening edition, ahead of the pack.

"Is that for the benefit of the journo that found the bodies?" a voice from the front asked.

"It is, Dean," Walker responded.

"But is he not considered a suspect?"

"Technically, I suppose, but it would seem unlikely. Jim, Paul, you interviewed him yesterday, didn't you?" Walker addressed two detectives standing beside Strong. "What did you make of his story?"

"Bit unbelievable, sir," one said, "but then the girl, Susan, said exactly the same thing. The two girls just appeared to her when she fell into the basement."

"Colin, can I bring you in at this point?" Walker said. "Gentlemen, for those of you who don't know, DCI Colin Strong is leading another murder investigation which seems linked to the discovery of our two bodies. In fact, their find was reported to him in the first instance. Colin, what do you make of this?"

Strong decided there was nothing to be gained by recounting the tangled tale of events which had led to the discovery of Susan in the basement of the farmhouse and the subsequent investigations into the use of the new barn building by the Baker brothers and Steve Chapman. "The only link between my investigations and your enquiry is purely location," he said. "For what it's worth, I wouldn't consider Robert Souter a suspect. He was acting on what Susan Brown had told him. In fact, I hold my hands up here, he'd actually come to see me before to report what Susan had told him. Like you, I thought it sounded a bit far-fetched and I didn't think I could spend precious resources to investigate, not when we'd got other aspects unfolding. To be fair, he trawled the newspaper archives to check what he'd been told and came to the conclusion that there was no way Susan could have known some of the things she said without the experience she had. Eventually, he decided to have a look for himself."

"Okay, so moving on," Walker said, "any forensic evidence we can consider?"

A tall detective standing near the front flipped open his notebook and took up the discussion. "Early indications seem that both girls had been strangled, sir. The small bones in the neck were broken. Jennifer was wearing the white smock dress she wore to school the day she went missing. Mary was also wearing her school uniform. Both girls were missing socks and shoes. We'll know more once they've had a chance to get them back to the mortuary."

"Thanks, Tim," Walker acknowledged. "What about the search of the buildings? Anything there?"

Another detective on the far side of the room reported that the house was in a poor state, windows had disintegrated, the lead had disappeared from the roof years ago and there were signs of numerous leaks. There were no personal possessions inside and nothing of any interest to their enquiry so far. "The building had been unoccupied for ten years, we understand," he explained. "In the new barn, we found some tools and materials that looked as though the place had been used for vehicle repair."

"That's right," Strong interrupted. "The property was used by the group we suspect of changing identities of stolen cars. Two of the vehicles we traced to Felixstowe Docks where we discovered the body of my murder victim."

"Did you search the other buildings there, Colin?" Walker asked.

"We didn't. All indications were they'd been locked up and left for years."

"That would seem so," the detective resumed. "There was an old barn padlocked up which we forced. Inside we found some rusty farm machinery and, under some tarpaulins an old tractor and a maroon Mitsubishi pick-up."

Strong pricked up his ears. "Was there any registration plates on that?" he asked.

The detective looked round. "No, probably taken off years ago. Seemed to have bits missing off it, as though it had been raided for spares at some point. Same with the tractor."

Strong walked towards the front. "Should still be able to identify it through chassis and engine numbers though, provided the engine's still there."

"Yeah, it's still there."

Walker joined in. "What are you thinking, Colin?"

"Just something someone said to me … rings a bell. Can you check back through the original files when these girls went missing? There might be mention of a maroon pick-up seen in the vicinity of both disappearances."

"Frank, can you follow up on that?" Walker instructed. "What do we know about previous owners of the property?"

"Last tenants by the name of Collinson, sir," one of the officers who'd interviewed Souter replied. "They were there when both girls went missing. Both dead now, though."

"I can help you there too, Peter," Strong offered, "You might want to talk to the Clay family who work the adjoining farm. They gave me some background when we were looking into the stolen cars. Apparently the Collinsons had a son, Stanley."

"Thanks for that, Colin," Walker said. "Jim and Paul, can you get out there and take statements from the Clays? And see if we can trace this son." He tidied up some notes he'd brought with him. "Right, Tim and I are off to the mortuary. Everyone else, you know what you're doing?" Acknowledgements were mumbled. "Good." He turned to Strong. "That was really useful, Colin. Thanks for coming."

"Glad to be of help. I'd be interested to hear how it goes."

"I'll keep you informed,"

Strong walked down the stairs and back to his car, thoughts returning to Szymanski, Mirczack and most interestingly, Robert Baker.

On the way back from Pontefract, Strong called the station and asked for Kelly Stainmore. "How are the guests?" he enquired.

"Spent as comfortable a night as possible, guv. They're obviously concerned at what's going to happen to them."

"I'll speak to the boss when I get there. Should be about twenty minutes. He is in by the way, isn't he?"

"So far as I know. I saw him in the corridor first thing, unless he's gone out, but I don't think so."

"Okay, thanks. Can you do something else for me?"

"Sure."

"Robert Baker. Can you get a home address for him. Also, see if you can find out if he's still comforting his daughter-in-law."

"You think he might be involved?"

"Just covering all the angles."

"I'll see you when you get in, then."

Strong ended the call then dialled Souter's number. As he travelled through Featherstone, he confirmed what he thought the previous evening, that the girls' bodies would be removed this morning, and let him know that the Post would be reporting the story in their first evening edition, ahead of the opposition, DCI Walker would be contacting his Editor to confirm.

He felt depressed when he finished his conversation; nothing to do with anything Souter had said. He'd been passing numerous derelict businesses, boarded-up pubs, houses and demolished commercial sites. It seemed as if the place was closed for business.

He snapped himself out of it and made good time the rest of the way, hitting the only real traffic coming up Doncaster Road as he passed the site of Wakefield Theatre Club by Trinity's Rugby League ground.

As he parked up, Jim Ryan pulled in. Strong waited.

"Tell me they found something useful at Luxor Grove, Jim."

Ryan locked up his car and walked in to the station alongside his boss. "They had to break down the door to the ground floor room."

"So what did they find?"

Ryan paused as they passed through a set of double doors to the stairs. "Big double bed, just a bare mattress, mirror on the ceiling, shackles on the wall, large wardrobe with mirrored doors and all sorts of fantasy uniforms inside. Also in the bottom, a large bag of mixed condoms, all sizes, all flavours." He smiled at Strong and opened the door onto the first floor corridor.

Strong passed through first. "But any forensics of any use?"

"Definite signs of sexual activity. Various semen stains and blood spots, mostly on the carpet but some on the walls, not evident to the eye but picked up by their instruments."

"That'll take time to run through the system." They paused outside the CID Room. "Anything from any of the neighbours?"

"Nah. A lot of foreign residents, some students, one elderly lady who said she couldn't keep up with all the comings and goings, but nothing of any use."

Strong frowned. "What about the basement?"

"We had to break that door down too. Smaller room than upstairs, windowless and airless. Just a mattress on the floor, no other furniture. I left them checking for fibres, fingerprints and any other stains or forensic evidence."

"Colin," DCS Flynn called along the corridor. "I need a word."

"I'll be back in a bit, Jim." Strong said to Ryan, "We'll catch up on things then."

Strong turned and followed his boss to his office.

Once there, Flynn closed the door. "I've spoken to Immigration this morning. I had to."

Strong nodded. "I understand. I'd like to bring the troops up to speed with all that's gone on before we hand the girls over, if that's okay."

Flynn checked his watch. "Better hurry, the Immigration team should be here any time now. Have we got anything from Luxor Grove?"

He repeated what Ryan had told him. "It'll be a little while before they confirm any findings we could use."

"In the meantime, what about this Polish bloke, Szymanski, you have in custody?"

"He wants a solicitor, so we'll have to arrange that, but I want to have another go at him."

"You've still got some time left to hold him."

Strong checked his watch. "About five hours."

"I can authorise a further twelve and we can always get a warrant from a magistrate for a further thirty-six."

"Thanks, sir."

"All right, keep me informed."

51

The bottom of the gravel lane was as close as they could get to the farmyard. Police tape fluttered across the entrance and a marked car stood guard. They'd arrived in time to see two black private ambulances waved through and guessed the forensics team were ready to move the bodies of Jennifer and Mary.

Susan had called Souter earlier. Once he'd told her that the bodies were being moved, she'd insisted that Gillian drive her there. Gillian was reluctant to comply but Souter persuaded her, saying he understood how Susan felt and offered to meet them at the scene.

Initially, they sat in Gillian's car, near where Susan had left her Micra on that fateful evening, parked facing the track end. Susan sat in the front, seat fully back and leg in a cast stretched straight out. Souter sat behind Gillian.

Susan studied the activity that could be seen in the farmyard. "Mary has twin sisters she knows nothing about?" she said, almost to herself.

"I believe so," Souter responded.

"What about Jennifer's family?"

"Her mother's still alive and living in Cheshire. She moved away after her husband died in a crash on the M62. No other vehicle involved."

Susan struggled to turn round and looked questioningly at Souter.

"Maybe," he said. "I don't know. Grief can take many forms. Accidental death was the coroner's verdict. Anyway, Mrs Coyle moved away shortly after that."

"And so the torment continues," Susan said quietly to herself.

They were silent for a few minutes. Eventually, it was Gillian who spoke. "You need to get home now, Susan. Remember what the specialist said. That isn't a straightforward break. We could be here for hours waiting. You need rest."

"I just want to ..." Susan broke off as movement appeared at the top of the track. "Help me out, Bob," she said, opening the door, manoeuvring her crutches and trying to swing herself out.

Souter could see one of the two ambulances begin to move away from the clutch of vehicles by the farmhouse. He got out and went round to help Susan up onto her crutches. Gillian appeared at their side. Together, they made the short journey to the track end. The first private ambulance with blacked out windows approached the police tape. Susan bowed her head as the uniform released the blue and white plastic to allow the vehicle to pass and make its way to the mortuary. A minute later, the second ambulance followed.

Souter thought he heard Susan say a prayer before she raised her head again. "I'm sorry," she said quietly, a tear falling from her chin.

"Come on." Gillian put her arm round her shoulders and gently turned her back towards the car.

Before they'd gone a few steps a red Vauxhall Astra approached at speed. They turned back to see it slithering to a halt by the track. Souter recognised the driver who jumped out, leaving the door open and engine running.

The man shouted at the uniformed constable, "Is that them?" and pointed after the last ambulance. "Is that my sister?" the man continued.

"Calm down, sir," the officer responded.

"I need to know." By this time, the man had grabbed hold of the policeman with both hands on his arms.

"Sir, if you don't calm down, I'll have to arrest you."

"Paul," Souter said quietly, approaching the pair. "Paul, come away. This isn't helping."

Paul Duggan dropped to his knees, tears streaming down his face. He looked up at him. "It's Mary," he said, spittle around his lips. "You knew?" He buried his face in his hands and began to sob.

"It's okay, officer," Souter said to the policeman, putting an arm round the distraught man. "Come on, Paul, come and sit with us a while."

Slowly, Paul got to his feet. Dazed, he half stumbled, half walked with Souter's help, back to Gillian's car. He guided him to sit sideways on the rear seat behind Susan.

The police officer got into Paul's car and pulled it into the side of the road and switched off the engine before returning to his watching brief.

Paul pulled out a handkerchief and began to wipe his face. "They told me this morning," he said. "Two detectives - not your DCI Strong, they came while I was getting ready for work. Said they'd found bodies. They couldn't be sure but they thought one was Mary." He looked up at Souter. "It is her, isn't it?" he pleaded. "You knew when you came on Sunday."

Souter shook his head. "Not exactly. I'm sorry, Paul. We all are."

Susan and Gillian had watched events in stunned silence.

Paul looked round, puzzled, seeing the women for the first time. "Why are you all here?" he asked. "Did you all know?"

"I knew, Paul," Susan said, through tears. "Eventually, I knew."

"Susan, we need to get you home," Gillian said. "You shouldn't be out like this, it's too soon, you know that."

"But wait." Paul stood up and leaned in. "What do you mean, you knew eventually?" He studied Susan. "And what happened to you anyway?"

"Can we go somewhere?" Souter asked. "Paul deserves to hear Susan's story."

Susan looked to her sister. "I know it's a bit of an ask," she said, "but he could come back with us?"

Gillian was indignant. "Just a minute, what do you mean inviting a perfect stranger back to my house?"

Susan put a hand on her sister's arm. "You said I need to get home. But Paul needs to hear what happened to me in there."

Gillian held her stare for a few moments, then relented, realising what had to be done. "Okay," she finally said.

52

Vince Denholme was in the CID Room when Strong returned from Flynn's office. "Right. Nothing for it but to have a real go at Szymanski. I want you in with me, Vince." He turned to Stainmore. "Anything on Robert Baker, Kelly?"

Stainmore looked up from her desk. "Yes, guv. Home address in Ripon, Studley Road. Quite posh apparently."

"We'll pay him a visit later. In the meantime, have you got witness statements from all the girls?"

"Got them last night. Nothing more significant than what you already heard. I don't think they knew anything of any other girls. They were kept totally separate."

"Immigration will be turning up any time soon, so have another word before that happens, just to see if there's anything else they can add. Oh, and nearly forgot, did we get anything from those video tapes from Sensations reception?"

"Sorry, guv, nothing."

Szymanski was sitting at the interview table, arms folded looking sullen. The assigned duty solicitor, a balding man with glasses dressed in a shiny suit, was sitting to his left, a notebook in front of him, clicking his pen.

"How much longer do you intend to keep me here?" Szymanski protested.

Strong ignored him to begin with, placing blank tapes into the recording machine, pressing the record buttons then going through the procedure of introductions of those present, date and time.

"I said, how much longer do you intend to keep me here?"

"Until I get some proper answers, Mr Szymanski." Strong responded.

"I don't need to say anything."

Strong leaned across the table so his reddening face was inches from the arrogant Pole. "We have an innocent girl dead, a bullet in the brain, who used to be your girlfriend. Doesn't that concern you?"

"Just a minute ..." the solicitor began.

"I told you, she just had a silly infatuation," Szymanski answered.

"That's not what witnesses have said."

Szymanski shrugged.

Strong sat back down opposite, and the solicitor relaxed. "We know you bring Mariana ... well, let's use their real names, shall we? Lyudmyla, Nadia and, of course, your favourite, Katarina, from the house where they, shall we say lodge, for want of a better word."

Szymanski leaned back and made a facial expression of indifference.

"Those girls worked normally on Tuesdays, Wednesdays, Fridays and Sundays." Strong looked directly at Szymanski. "You're open seven days. Who works the other nights?"

"It depends."

"On what?"

"Who's available."

"Mr Szymanski, we know you drive the other girls to and from Sensations as well. Now where do you collect them from and where do you return them to?"

"I meet them in town, near the railway station."

"Stop feeding me a load of crap. There's another house. Where is it?"

"I don't know what you're talking about."

Strong sighed heavily, looked at Denholme to his right, then opened up the file he'd brought with him. "Okay, let's go back to Tuesday 30th August." He shuffled through some papers. "Do you remember what happened that day?"

Again another shrug. "It's a Tuesday, I collect the girls and bring them in to Sensations."

"That would be from 57, Luxor Grove?"

"You know this."

"I'm just making sure that *you* do. You see, those girls were kept in that house which was locked."

"I was only concerned for their security."

"I'm sure Immigration will be delighted to hear you had their best interests at heart, especially when we discuss their status." Strong isolated a photograph in the file. "But what I want to know is what happened after you all got to Sensations."

"We open up, there is nothing to tell."

"Did this man come in as a customer?" Strong passed the photo of Chris Baker across the table. "For the benefit of the tape, I'm showing Mr Szymanski photograph P2."

He gave it a cursory glance. "I can't remember."

"Your security tapes confirm he did," Strong bluffed.

Szymanski looked alarmed. "They were wiped. There was nothing on them."

"That's a common misconception. I told you our experts can recover information that most people think is lost forever." He moved a few papers around in his file, allowing the Pole time to consider his answer.

"Yes, I think he did come in," he finally responded.

"He came in because he had some information for you, didn't he?"

"I don't know what …"

"Information you wanted to pass on to your boss, Mr Mirczack."

Szymanski looked flustered.

"Where is he, by the way?"

"I don't … He's away on business."

Again another shuffling of papers. "And that would be Riga, wouldn't it?"

Szymanski coloured. "How …?"

"When is he coming back?"

"Su… I'm not sure."

Strong and Denholme exchanged glances.

"You're not sure when, or you're not sure if, he's coming back?" Strong leaned forward on the table. "You see, Stefan ... if you don't mind me calling you by your first name ... you see, if Mirczack doesn't come back, you're going to be the one carrying the can, if you're familiar with that expression." Strong leaned back again, looked over to Denholme then back to Szymanski.

He looked worried, bowed his head and studied the table.

"Now, let's start getting some straight answers here. Once more from the beginning; where do you bring the other girls from? The ones known as ..." he turned to Denholme.

"Sylvia, Janice, Crystal and one other, not their real names, of course," the Vice Squad detective offered.

Szymanski looked to the solicitor who raised his eyebrows.

"I think, gentlemen," the lawyer said, "if I could have some minutes with my client."

"Interview suspended at twelve-fifty-two pm." Strong got to his feet. Before leaving with Denholm, he turned and addressed the solicitor. "I'd advise your client to think very carefully. There are some serious matters here and his cooperation could make a vital difference to all concerned."

53

Sitting in Gillian's living room, Susan told Paul all that she could remember from her time in the basement. He asked a few questions and she gave answers as best she could. He listened to all she had to say, then put his hand on hers. "Thank you," he said. He looked dazed. Souter couldn't imagine what it must be like for him; to have to take all this in. Bad enough to be finally told his sister had died all these years before, he always suspected that, but now, to have it confirmed and to have some indication as to what had happened to her, he was distraught.

He stood up. "I have to go," he said, "I have to be with Mum and Dad. They're devastated." Souter got to his feet as Gillian accompanied him to the door. He watched from the window as Paul got into his car and slowly drove away.

"Can we report this now?" Susan asked as Gillian returned to the room.

"Susan, I want you in bed. You need to rest," Gillian said.

"I'm okay. We need to write this. Bob, you promised."

"I did," he said, "But Gillian's right. You've only just been let out of hospital."

"But …"

"And that's a serious leg injury," Souter interrupted. "They only let you out because Gillian said you'd be looked after here."

"I know …"

"And she'll be in a lot of trouble if you have to be re-admitted because you've been ignoring advice and overdoing it."

Susan sulked. "All right, all right. But here's my take on the story." She held out the notepad he had given her in the hospital. "Promise me you won't change it."

"Well, it won't be down to me ..."

"Promise me."

"Susan, I said we'd work this together. I'll look at this and do what I can. But all reporters are subject to the vagaries of our editors, you know."

Susan held his gaze.

"I'll do what I can," he said softly.

By the time he got into his car, his mobile was ringing. It was John Chandler, the deputy Editor. *"Bob,"* he said, *"we've got the go ahead to report on those schoolgirls. I need something within the hour."*

Souter flipped open the notebook Susan had given him and quickly scanned what she'd written. "Already started," he responded.

54

When Strong and Denholme came out of the interview room, Flynn called down the corridor to him.

"Colin, can you spare a minute?"

While Denholme made his way to the CID Room, Strong followed his boss upstairs.

"Immigration have just turned up and want to remove the women to Morton Hall, their detention centre in Lincolnshire," Flynn said. "I couldn't put them off any longer."

"That's fine, sir. I don't think they have much more to tell, unless we get a surprise from the forensics at Luxor Grove."

Flynn paused at the top of the stairs. "In the meantime, I've got an old friend of yours in my office. And he's none too pleased."

Strong was puzzled.

"Frank Halliday's come in complaining he wanted to interview Szymanski and Mirczack in connection with Chris Baker's murder and you've shanghaied him."

"Should have got his arse into gear earlier then, shouldn't he?" Strong grinned.

Flynn looked serious. "Colin, you should have kept him in the loop with your progress on that massage parlour." He held up both hands. "I know. It took him some time to make the connections but ... play it down eh? And share what you know."

Strong shook his head resignedly and followed Flynn into his office.

Halliday was standing by the side of Flynn's desk, arms folded and face flushed. When he saw Strong, he launched into a verbal onslaught. Flynn cut him short.

"Frank, you're not doing your blood pressure any good."

"Fuck the blood pressure."

"Sit down, Frank. DCI Strong will bring you up to speed with progress from his side of the enquiry. Then, I'm sure, he won't object to you sitting in on his next interview with Szymanski." Flynn looked at Strong for confirmation as Halliday slowly sat down.

"I've got no problem with that, sir. We're just giving him ten minutes with the brief. He's considering his position on the whereabouts of a second house." Strong took the other seat in front of Flynn's desk, next to Halliday. "We know there's another location where a separate team of girls are housed. Our information is that Mirczack is currently out of the country but we should be notified as soon as he checks in for return."

"That's if he comes back," Flynn added.

"That, of course is what I suggested to Szymanski. The implications for him are what he's giving thought to now."

Over the course of the next ten minutes, Strong outlined all that had happened in the previous twenty-four hours, after which, Halliday seemed calmer.

Strong collected Denholme from the CID Room and, along with Halliday, walked into Interview Room 2. Szymanski appeared more contrite.

"My client will be able to provide the information you require, Chief Inspector," the solicitor announced.

"Thank you." Strong restarted the recording machine. "Interview with Stefan Szymanski resumed at thirteen fourteen pm. Joining us in the room is Detective Chief Inspector Halliday from Leeds CID who is investigating the murder of Chris Baker."

Both detectives sat down as Szymanski glanced across at the new arrival.

"So, Mr Szymanski," Strong resumed, "you've obviously given some thought to our previous conversation." The Pole nodded. "The other girls, where are they?"

"I had nothing to do with any murders."

"Where are they?"

"They should be at 47 Back Cooper Street. It's off Chapeltown Road. You took the keys from me when I came in."

Strong looked to Denholme. "Can you fetch Mr Szymanski's possessions from Custody?"

Denholme got up and left as Strong made the announcement for the tape. A few minutes later, Denholme returned with a brown envelope and tipped the contents onto the table.

The keys are on here." Szymanski picked up a bunch of keys and isolated a Yale key and one for a deadlock. "These are for the front door."

"Get these down to the team. You know what to do," Strong said to Denholme.

The Vice Squad officer picked up the keys, returned the rest of Szymanski's possessions to the envelope and left the room, Strong making another tape announcement.

"Now, before you took a break to consider your position, I showed you a photograph of this man, Chris Baker." Strong placed the photograph on the table once again. "You confirmed that he had visited Sweet Sensations on Tuesday 30th August." Szymanski nodded. "For the benefit of the tape, Mr Szymanski has nodded confirmation. My colleague, DCI Halliday would like to ask you more about this."

Halliday leaned forward, barely acknowledging Strong. "Was this the last time you saw Chris Baker?"

"Yes."

"Sure about that?"

"I told you, yes."

"And he was a regular customer here?"

"He liked Mariana … I mean Lyudmyla."

"But he also visited for another reason, didn't he?"

Szymanski shrugged and looked down.

Halliday leaned forward, closer to him. "He was providing confidential information from his workplace, wasn't he, Mr Szymanski?"

The Pole never looked up from the table. "Yes."

Halliday sighed. "So can you tell me exactly what that information was?" His voice grew louder.

Finally, Szymanski looked up at Halliday. "He was passing on details of vehicles, their owners' names and addresses."

Halliday's voice became softer. "And why was he doing that?"

"It wasn't my idea," Szymanski protested. "I didn't want to get involved."

"Again, why did Baker provide information to you?"

"We had threatened to tell his wife he visited Lyudmyla."

"That's another aspect of interest, thank you for that, but what I meant was, what were you going to do with these details?"

"Mr Mirczack wanted them."

Halliday rubbed his face with both hands and exhaled. "Mr Szymanski, your solicitor here stated just a few minutes ago that you were willing to provide us with all the information we require. I have got other things to attend to. I would appreciate if you could just answer each question as fully as possible without holding back. That way, we can sort this mess out sooner rather than later." Halliday studied Szymanski for a few seconds. "So, why did Mirczack want this information and what was he going to do with it?"

"I think you know this already. But I tell you, I had nothing to do with it. I think he wanted details of certain types of vehicles located nearby so he could steal them. I only picked up bits of information and worked things out for myself. Once he had these cars he would swap identities with similar vehicles from other parts of England. I think he was shipping them out of the country where he had a market for them."

"Thank you Mr Szymanski. It wasn't that difficult was it?"

"But I wasn't involved in any of that."

"I think you'll find that by the very fact that you passed the information from Mr Baker to your boss, you are involved," Halliday concluded.

Szymanski looked down and shook his head.

"Is that why Mirczack is in Riga?" Strong asked. "Latvia is one of the markets for these stolen luxury vehicles?"

He looked across at Strong. "I'm not sure, but I think so."

"Who actually stole these cars and who changed their identities?"

Szymanski looked across to the solicitor who gave a slight nod. He took a deep breath then answered. "I believe one was Chris Baker's brother. I think he had been in trouble before to do with cars. The other was a friend of his. I'm not sure who."

"That would be Gary Baker then?"

Szymanski nodded.

"For the benefit ..." Strong was interrupted.

"Yes, I believe his name was Gary."

"Would the name Steve Chapman mean anything to you?"

"I think I heard talk of someone called Steve, so that may be him. But I told you, I was not involved with cars."

Strong looked to Halliday to seek confirmation that the questioning was at an end for now.

"Do you own a gun, Mr Szymanski?" Halliday asked.

The denial came as Strong knew it would. He thought Halliday was just making a point.

"No. I have no use for guns."

"Thank you for the moment. We'll be back to ask you some more questions later. In the meantime, interview terminated at thirteen thirty-one."

Outside in the corridor, Strong confronted Halliday. "Look, I know you're pissed off about what happened to Jack

Cunningham and somehow you blame me for his situation …"

"He's an excellent officer," Halliday interrupted. "He doesn't deserve what's happened."

"Come on, even he sees that what he did resulted in an innocent man being sent to prison for four years. And all because of a bit of rumpy-pumpy with a junior officer. He doesn't bear a grudge. Why should you?"

Strong waited as Halliday fixed him with a stare, then decided to take a chance. In a low voice, he said, "Do you want to ask him yourself? Here," Strong took out his phone and sought the Call Log page on the menu and scrolled down to the number Cunningham had called him from on Wednesday. He held it out to Halliday. "Recognise this?"

Halliday nodded.

"He called me the day we found the schoolgirls' bodies up at the farm. He wanted to give me the benefit of what he could remember when he was involved in the initial investigations when they went missing. Call him. Ask him. That wouldn't be the actions of someone who blamed me now would it?"

Halliday hesitated, visibly sagged, then looked up and down the corridor. "Where can we get a cup of tea in this place?"

By the time they reached the canteen, Strong thought Halliday was more conciliatory, so he let him buy the teas. It was quite busy at this time of the day and Strong was lucky to find a free table in a corner. A few minutes later, the Leeds man joined him.

"Jack Cunningham was a DC when I first knew him," Halliday began. "A year later, he was my DS when I became a DI. I saw a lot of me in him. He was a good copper, a good solid detective."

"He still is," Strong put in.

Halliday shook his head. "No, this thing's finished him. He'll take his pension and drop out." He looked straight at Strong. "I know Jack doesn't blame you for any of this. But I do. I detested what I saw as an officer dob his colleague in it. He told me you were a straight up sort of bloke." He looked around to see if anyone else was near enough to hear. In a quiet voice, he continued, "But he also told me about the incident during your drugs raid."

Strong's heart rate increased as his thoughts returned to the discovery he'd made of compromising photos of Cunningham and DC Kathy Sharp. He'd tried his best to keep them discreet but, with the successful appeal of a young man wrongly convicted of sexual assault, the whole sordid tale had come out.

Halliday saw Strong's expression. "The problem's mine, not yours … or Jack's. I suppose I'm old school. But don't worry, I was told in the strictest confidence and that's where it'll remain. He said you had tried to protect him. He also knew how difficult things were for you at the time and how he must have put you in a terrible position."

Strong relaxed slightly.

"He stressed you did everything for the right reasons. You're a detective who has to know the whole truth, not just what's happened but all the whys and wherefores."

The two men looked at one another for a few moments.

"What I'm trying to say is," Halliday reflected, "I'm sorry if I caused you unnecessary grief."

"Forget it."

Halliday held out his hand and after a moment's hesitation, Strong shook it.

"So what finally led you to Szymanski and Mirczack?" Strong wondered.

"We did a check on Baker's finances. Until about six months ago, everything seemed normal. We'd also been talking to a lot of his work colleagues at the call centre. Had his behaviour changed recently? Did he talk about his marriage? Did anything seem to be worrying him? That sort of thing." Halliday took a drink of his tea. "Again, things seemed to have changed about six months ago. From what we've learned since, that was about the time he discovered the massage parlour. One advantage of placing an FLO in the house has been the odd snippet

DC Walters has picked up. At times, Janice and Robert have not been the most discreet. During one frank exchange between the two, Janice had told Baker senior that his precious son hadn't been near her for over a year, if you know what I mean?"

Strong nodded.

"She began to wonder if he'd been seeing someone else, someone from work maybe. However, our investigations at Olympia Insurance came up with nothing."

Strong leaned forward. "But how did you make a connection to Sweet Sensations?"

"Ah, that was thanks to you. After you'd spoken to Robert, he was keen to find out if Janice had any inclination. So, as I said, Rebecca, DC Walters, kept her ears open and heard him ask her if the name Sweet Sensations meant anything to her. It didn't and he had to do some quick thinking to put her off. So, I thought I'd do some digging around with that place myself and came across the names Szymanski and Mirczack."

"What was unusual about his finances then?"

"Up until around six months ago, everything was as you might expect for a married couple of their age, mortgage, two salaries, a few hundred quid on credit cards that they never seemed able to pay off, that kind of thing. But then regular cash withdrawals of a hundred pounds from a number of cash machines between here and Leeds began to appear."

"About the time he discovers Sensations," Strong added.

"So it would seem. Then, about six weeks ago, they stop. On his credit cards, there's all the usual items; petrol, weekly supermarket shop, etcetera. Then again about six weeks ago, they disappear. Yes, there's still the big one offs, I think he renewed the house insurance on his card. But nothing for the day-to-day items that were there before. And he's managed to clear them for once."

"About six weeks ago is when the first of the cars were knocked off. So if he was paid for his involvement in that, with cash, that would explain how suddenly, petrol and food bills were paid for, in readies," Strong considered.

"Exactly."

Strong's attention was caught by Ormerod approaching from the other side of the room.

"Ah, Luke, have you met DCI Halliday from the Leeds Murder Squad?"

"Sir," Ormerod acknowledged.

"What news from the front?" Strong enquired.

"We've been to Back Cooper Street and now have another four young women in the interview rooms."

"Did you get anything from them on the way in?"

"Not a great deal. Same story as the others. Came here on the promise of a proper job. Szymanski drives them in and out of Sensations."

Strong looked across at Halliday. "Do you want to sit in when we interview them, Frank?"

Halliday shook his head. "Can't see the point. Can't think they'd have much to add to what the others have already told you. Until Mirczack shows up, there's not a lot more I can do." He stood up. "Thanks, Colin. Keep me informed please." He held out his hand once more.

Strong shook it again. "Sure."

When he'd left, Ormerod looked back at Strong. "Did I just see what I think I saw," he said.

"Don't worry about it Luke." Strong rose and the two walked out of the canteen.

"As Frank says, I can't see that these other women can add much more. I'll let you, Kelly, John and Vince interview them. If anything interesting does come up, let me know."

"So what are you doing now then, guv?"

"I'm behind with my reports, Luke," Strong smiled. "You know how it goes. And no doubt Immigration will be glad to have to come back and collect another four women."

As he got back to his office, Flynn followed and closed the door. "Made your peace then?"

"I think we're looking at things from the same angle now, sir."

"Good." Flynn walked over to the window and looked out. "He's not a well man, you know?"

"I didn't." He hid his puzzlement.

"This will be his last case. He's retiring at the end of the month."

"Sorry to hear that."

Flynn turned round and gave Strong a look that said, no you're not. Aloud, he said, "Carry him through, Colin."

Strong opened his mouth to reply but Flynn was half out the door. "Thanks."

55

"Look, John. I'm closer to this story than any reporter has been to any I know. If it wasn't for Susan, they'd still be lying in that cold, damp basement. She's off to Leeds to study journalism as soon as she's back on her feet. She's a bright girl; woman really."

Souter was in Chandler's office. He'd been called up to go through what was going to form the front page of the first evening edition. He'd had a good run up the M1 from Gillian's house and was back to the office within twenty minutes. He'd read through Susan's draft and thought it was a good attempt at a report. A few minor adjustments here and there and some additional information that Souter had gleaned, and it was submitted to his editor.

"This is all well and good, Bob," Chandler retorted, "But I decide how we're going to present the stories. And …"

"I promised her," Souter persisted.

The heated debate surrounded the headlines which were normally the domain of the editor. In this instance, Souter thought Susan had come up with exactly the right words to describe the mood and feeling. He'd also insisted Susan was given part credit. Chandler had reluctantly conceded that. But only on this occasion.

He waited as his boss stared from the window over the construction sites that stretched back to the old Wellington Street railway station. Finally, he turned round. "Okay, this one time. And only because we've known each other so long. Go with it."

"Thanks, John."

Chandler nodded and Souter left the room.

An hour later, he picked up a copy of the first edition of that night's Yorkshire Evening Post. Under an 'EXCLUSIVE' banner, he read:

TORMENT
The torment for the families of two schoolgirls missing for over ten years continued today with the discovery of two bodies in a derelict farmhouse near Pontefract.
Report by Robert Souter
Crime and Home Affairs Correspondent
and
Susan Brown
Guest Reporter

He smiled as he read the opening again. Yes, Susan would like that, he thought.

56

"Hi Bob!" Sammy shouted from the kitchen as he came through Alison's front door.

Alison was sitting on her legs on the settee, glass of white wine in hand. "Sammy's cooking a chilli," she said. "Got something to celebrate."

"Oh, yes." Souter removed his jacket and sat down next to Alison.

"Yes." She gave him a kiss. "I'll let her tell you."

Sammy appeared at the kitchen doorway. "I got the job," she beamed.

Souter jumped up. "Well done you." He gave her a hug. "When do you start?"

"Monday. And I'm cooking a meal for you both to say thanks for all you've done for me."

"Aw, thanks, Sammy. I'm really pleased for you. You deserve a break."

"And, I've got something else for you. But that'll have to wait until we've eaten." Sammy turned back into the kitchen.

He sat back down with Alison. "I'm intrigued."

"She's done well. They liked her."

The chilli was a success. She served it with rice and hot crusty bread.

"So where will you be working exactly?" Souter enquired between mouthfuls of food.

"From what I can gather I'll probably be spending a bit of time in most departments. A bit of filing and photocopying to start with but Alison reckons they'll give me something more interesting once I've settled in."

"They should do," Alison agreed. "I'm sure you'll impress."

"Well I couldn't have done it unless you'd put in a word. And I would probably be in some squat somewhere if you hadn't had faith in me, Bob." She was struggling to keep her emotions in check.

"You'll do well, Sammy," he said. "You've got a personality and a lot of balls."

Sammy wiped a hand over her face and chuckled. "I wouldn't go that far. Anyway, I thought Susan's debut in print today was excellent. They were her words, weren't they?"

"Yes it was her headline idea, although I did have a job on to convince Chandler not to change that. All I did was beef up some of the body of the article, but mostly it was her writing."

"I'm sure she's delighted with it. Probably frame it on her wall."

Souter smiled. "I know. So what else have you got for me then, Sammy?"

"Barry Whitefield," she said with a grin. "I've found him."

"You have? How the ... You're a genius, Sammy."

"You've just got to know how to conduct a logical search, that's all."

"So where does this Barry reside?"

"Jaywick."

"Where?"

"Jaywick. It's just outside Clacton."

"Clacton? That's Essex, isn't it?"

"Yep. I looked it up. On the coast, just beyond Colchester. Did you know Colchester was Britain's oldest recorded town?"

Souter laughed. "Full of information, aren't you."

"It's interesting." Sammy began to clear their plates to the sink, squeezed washing-up liquid from a bottle and ran some hot water.

"But anyway," Souter thought aloud, "I'm not even sure that's where these two characters are."

"They are still missing, aren't they?"

"As of last night, yes."

"Well, if they'd been seen off like that Chris Baker, they'd have turned up somewhere by now, wouldn't they?" Sammy began to wash the plates and cutlery.

"Unless they were disposed of where they would never be found." Souter picked up a tea towel, lifted a plate from the draining board and began to dry. "I mean, maybe when they topped Chris, whoever it was, was disturbed and they had to leave him there?"

"No, you said that had all the hallmarks of a professional hit. He was left to be found."

"Look, can we talk about something a bit more pleasant?" Alison put in. "I've just eaten and I don't want to discuss gory details about any of this."

Sammy grinned. "Sorry."

"But can I just ask you one last thing," Souter persisted, "how do you know this Barry Whitefield is Steve Chapman's cousin?"

"Ah," she said, "I trawled through all sorts of records. Chapman's mother and Whitefield's mother are sisters."

"I'm impressed," he said.

Kitchen left tidy, they made their way back into the living room.

"So what are you going to do?" Sammy wondered. "Are you going to pass that information on to your friend?"

"Colin? No, I don't think so." Souter was thoughtful. "I think maybe a trip to Essex might be on the cards. If I get in early on Monday and finish what I have to do, I could take the rest of the day off and head down there."

"You just be careful, Bob Souter," Alison warned. "These guys could be desperate."

Souter and Sammy exchanged glances and smiled.

57
Saturday

Baker's detached property on the Studley Road in Ripon lay hidden from view behind trees. A sweeping tarmac drive led up to a pair of garages attached to the house. Strong looked at Stainmore as they turned off the road and up towards the house. They stepped out of the car. He took in the property while Stainmore's attention was caught by the slightly open garage door. Slowly she walked towards it. Strong saw her and strolled over to join her as she bent down to lift the door open.

"Shit," Stainmore gasped as she saw the hosepipe leading from the Jaguar's exhaust to the driver's window. There were no fumes and the engine wasn't running. Strong bent down and looked through the rear window. The car appeared empty. Stainmore walked up by the side of the car, and with a puzzled expression, shook her head in confirmation. She rejoined her boss and they made their way to the front door.

Strong raised his hand to ring the bell but paused. The door was ajar. Again, they exchanged concerned glances. He pushed the door open and stepped inside. The hallway was wide with an elegant timber staircase leading up to a galleried landing. A few steps in to the left, an open door led to a lounge.

A still figure sat in an armchair.

"Mr Baker," Strong said quietly.

Baker sat motionless, staring through the broad window looking out over the front lawn. "I was expecting you," he finally said. "Not sure when, but I knew you'd be here."

Strong walked over to the settee opposite him, Stainmore close behind. "Can we?" he asked.

Baker nodded and they sat down.

"I couldn't do it, you know."

"The car?"

Again Baker nodded. "If it was only me … but … Gary's still missing." He looked at Strong, eyes moist. "He is still missing, isn't he?"

"We haven't been able to trace him. Have you any more ideas?"

Baker shook his head. "He must have found somewhere to lie low. You'd have found him by now if anything had happened to him the night Gary … well."

Strong interrupted his melancholy. "You know why we're here, Robert?"

Baker wiped his face with the back of his hand, then pinched his nose and sniffed. "I thought it would only be a matter of time before you joined the dots, unlike that other lazy bastard. Just marking time for retirement that one." He pulled a handkerchief from his trouser pocket and blew his nose.

"Halliday?"

"Acted like he couldn't find his arse with both hands." Baker glanced at Stainmore. "Sorry." He looked back to Strong. "The questions you were asking at Janice's, I knew you'd be back."

"So what can you tell us about Chris and Gary? What had they got themselves into?"

Baker put his head in his hands, rubbed his face then sat back in the chair. "I was only trying to help Chris. Stupid idiot, letting his … well, getting involved in that place." He drew a deep breath. "They'd been having some problems, Chris and Janice." He looked up at the detectives. "You know she couldn't have kids?"

They both nodded.

"He told me he had been bored for some time. I did ask if he was seeing someone else but he said he wouldn't want to do that. A little later, he told me he'd been tempted to try one of those massage parlours. He thought he could enjoy different women with no guilt. However, he developed a favourite."

"Mariana?" Strong asked.

"Yes."

"Although, you know that's not her real name."

"I never thought it was. A pity the idiot didn't do the same. For some strange reason, he told her a lot about himself, including the problems he was having at home, where he worked, Gary's wayward path and other stuff. The next thing, what started out as doing the manager of the place a favour with an insurance quote leads onto something else."

"Szymanski?"

"He never said a name. But when you showed me those photos and mentioned them, I knew who they were." Baker sighed and altered his position slightly in the chair.

"So knowing where Chris works, he gets requests for information from Szymanski regarding certain makes and models of car and their owners' details, yes?"

Baker nodded. "That was bad enough, but the next thing I knew, he'd involved Gary. Him and his mate, Steve. They were paid to rent that barn, you know? Chris's name was on the contract but it was those other men who funded it. He'd be asked to match up vehicle identities. One local and one the other side of the country. Always top models. Then Gary and Steve would have to lift the local one."

"Up to Meadow Woods Farm, switch identities and into a container then shipped to Felixstowe, job done." Strong continued.

"Yes," Baker said quietly, looking down onto his lap.

Strong studied him for a second or two. "Except there was something you contributed to the whole set up, wasn't there Graham?"

The man seemed suddenly older. Slowly, he looked up, tears streaming down his face. "Yes."

"Do you want to tell me about it?"

"Thirty-two years I'd worked for them. Thirty-two years. A lifetime. I'd seen all that currency pass through the system. I'd even been involved in the design of some of the notes. All I wanted was for Alice to be able to enjoy life without any worries."

"And Alice was your late wife, was she, Robert?"

Baker nodded and wiped away the tears.

Strong waited while the man composed himself.

Finally, he continued, "Inoperable brain tumour." He looked across at Strong. "She was only fifty-nine."

He suspected there was more Baker was about to reveal and he'd distracted him. "I'm really sorry to hear that," he said. "But you were telling us …"

"Over the last few years there, I managed to obtain various papers. Specialist papers. I didn't know what I'd do with them, I suppose I thought of them as souvenirs at first, but Chris is … was quite good with computers. And well … do you want to see?"

"Please, Robert. We need to clear all of this up." Strong glanced at Stainmore.

Baker wiped his face with his handkerchief, then slowly rose to his feet. "I only did it to help Chris," he pleaded.

Strong put a hand on his shoulder. "I know."

Baker turned and led the way out of the room to the front door. Outside, he shuffled over to the second garage, the first one still with the door open and the rear end of the Jaguar on view. He turned the handle on the second garage door and lifted it open. Inside, at the rear was another door. He rummaged in his pocket for a set of keys, selected one and unlocked. With the door open, he switched on the light to reveal a complete office set up; desk with keyboard and computer screen and chair and along one wall a professional looking printing and copier machine.

Strong looked all round. "What are we likely to find on the computer then, Robert? Draft vehicle licence documents? Invoice letter headings in the name of Yorkshire Exports?"

Baker filled up again. "All of them," he said. "And these." He opened one of the drawers in a desk and pulled out a wad of mint condition five pound notes.

"Are these what I think they are?" Stainmore asked.

"Looks like we've solved Sam and Trevor's case for them too," Strong said.

Baker had been taken back to Wood Street, charged and was languishing in a cell until his appearance in the Magistrates Court on Monday morning. Strong was in his office checking through his messages when the phone rang.

"DCI Strong."

"Colin, it's Peter Walker here, over in Pontefract," came a familiar voice.

"Hello, Peter, how's the investigation?"

"Steady progress. Just thought I'd keep you in the picture with events."

"Appreciate that."

"The DNA tests the boffins carried out confirm they are the bodies of Jennifer Coyle and Mary Duggan. They also found some other samples which we're running through the databases to see if we get any sort of hit."

"Sounds promising."

"Well, we'll see. That's only any good if they've got form and had a sample taken in the past. The other thing was your tip about the pick-up."

"Oh, yes."

"Yes. We've been in contact with Swansea and they tell us the tax expired in 1990 and was registered to a Mrs Enid Collinson, address ..."

"Meadow Woods Farm, I know," Strong interrupted.

"That's right. You'd spoken to the farmer neighbours, hadn't you? Anyway, from DVLA records, Enid Collinson first bought the vehicle second-hand in 1980. She died in 1985."

"The Clay's told me that."

"And her husband passed on in August 1990."

"So the pick-up has been in that old barn ever since?"

"Seems like it. We've taken it off to the SOCO garage. They'll pick it apart. If there's anything to connect that vehicle with the girls, they'll find it. We've gone back

through the original witness statements from both missing person's cases and you were right, there was mention by a couple of witnesses in both cases of a maroon pick-up seen in the vicinity of where we knew the girls were last seen. It might just be a coincidence but …"

"I know what you mean, Peter, there are no such things as coincidences."

"Not generally in my book. Anyway, thanks for that little steer, I thought you'd be interested."

"Always. Let me know how things go, and if I hear anything else like that, I'll be on to you straight away."

"See you, Colin."

Strong replaced the handset and stared at it for a few seconds.

58
Sunday

"Hello, Bob," Laura greeted, hugging him and giving him a kiss. "Haven't seen you since that little scare at Calder Street." She turned to the woman with him. "And this must be Alison. I've heard so much about you." The two women embraced.

"All good I hope?"

"Of course," Strong replied. "Go through to the lounge and let me get you a drink."

Souter followed Strong into the kitchen. They helped themselves to a beer from the fridge, got a white wine for Laura and a glass of red for Alison then joined the women. There was a good twenty minutes of general chit-chat before dinner was ready and seats were taken around the table in the small dining room.

They were onto the main course before the subject came up.

"I hear you've adopted a teenage girl, Bob." Laura said.

"Sammy, you mean? Oh, well …" Souter stumbled.

"She's a good kid, really," Alison said. "She certainly seems to have bonded with Susan. You know, Gillian's younger sister who had that terrible accident out at that remote farmhouse."

"Yes, Colin told me. A good job you found her, Bob."

Souter just shrugged, Strong kept his head down.

"How is she, by the way?" Laura continued.

"Came out of hospital on Thursday afternoon." Alison paused for a sip of wine. "She's staying at Gillian's for a while. In fact, Sammy's gone over there to see her this afternoon."

Souter turned to Alison. "Did you know they might look to get a flat together when Susan's back on her feet?"

"When did she say that?"

"This morning when you were in the bathroom."

"Would make sense, I suppose. Susan's probably been lucky to hold on to that flat since her dad went into care."

"I don't think she told Housing. But yes, especially when she finally gets to start her course. And I think Sammy's the sort of girl who needs company. I don't think she handles being on her own too well."

"It was great you could get her that job interview, Alison," Strong said.

"She still had to impress, though. Is there any news on her friend, Maria?"

"Not a thing. I wouldn't say it to Sammy but, it's not looking too good. In cases like these, if they'd just gone off of their own free will, we'd usually have found them by now."

"And no sign of that white van?" Souter asked.

"As you saw yourself, Bob, no chance of getting an enhanced image from the CCTV footage that would be good enough to read a number plate."

"She hasn't mentioned Maria for a few days though," Souter said.

"Nor to me," Alison added.

"Sounds like she's had an awful lot to put up with in her short life," Laura said.

"I also think Susan has in her own way." Souter offered.

By the time Laura brought in her home-made apple crumble and custard, Souter was asking Strong about another subject.

"How are things progressing with your Albanian murder case?"

"We're getting into all sorts of dark corners."

"Sounds interesting."

"But you know I can't talk about it."

"And that other murder, Baker. Are you still looking for his brother and his mate?"

"Not a sign of them. They've got to be lying low somewhere. We thought Chapman had a cousin he was close to growing up but, so far, we've not been able to trace him. Still, they'll no doubt reappear at some point."

"I thought Sammy ..." Alison began, looking to Souter.

"So how's your dad these days, Colin," Souter interrupted. "I haven't seen him in ages. Still going to Belle Vue regularly?"

"He seems fine," Strong said. "Although I don't think he's as keen on seeing Rovers these days, not since they dropped into the Conference. That and I think standing on a draughty terrace isn't his idea of entertainment at his age."

"You know I can't believe Doncaster are still playing at that run-down ground. But what about Amanda?" Souter followed up.

"We're trying to get her to select which university open days she wants to go to," Laura answered. "Before you know it, the deadline for applications will be here."

"She's a bright girl, she'll do well."

Before the conversation could move on, the phone rang.

Strong jumped up. "That'll probably be Graham. He usually calls on a Sunday."

When he returned a few minutes later, Souter thought he had something on his mind.

"I assume that wasn't our Graham, then?" Laura said. "They'd normally be chatting away for half-an-hour."

"No, it was a colleague. I might have to go out later tonight."

"Fresh developments, Col," Souter asked.

"Hopefully." Strong got to his feet. "Now, who wants a coffee?"

The telephone call Strong had taken had been from Vince Denholme. Stanislav Mirczack had checked in on the flight from Riga, due into Leeds/Bradford at eight thirty-five that night. Immigration officers would be detaining him on arrival and Denholme, Stainmore and Ormerod would accompany the suspect back to Wood Street for questioning. The promise of a period costume drama on the television for Stainmore and a darts match in the local for Ormerod would have to be forgone.

At eleven o'clock that evening, Strong got his first sight of the big Yugoslav. He watched as Ormerod led him into Interview Room Three. He was six foot three and looked as though he would weigh around twenty stones. And it was all solid. The flippant thought crossed his mind that he would have been upset if he'd had to sit next to him on the flight from Riga. He would have had no chance trying to get his arms up to eat an in-flight meal. He quickly focused on the reason he'd had him brought in, the image of Helena in the boot of the car in Felixstowe did that.

Stainmore and Denholme joined Strong in the corridor outside.

"How was he?" Strong asked.

"Angry," Denholme responded. "Resentful that we should interrupt his travel plans back to Leeds."

"Any sign of a car?"

"No sign of a car park ticket in his possession," Stainmore said.

"Hmm. So are two taxi fares cheaper than leaving your car in the car park for five days, or was he expecting Szymanski to pick him up. He certainly knew Mirczack would be back today, he let it slip when we spoke to him, if you remember, Vince?"

"That's true," Denholme confirmed.

"The other thing, guv," Stainmore said, "he was banging on about his brief. I doubt you'll get anything from him until he turns up."

"Okay, well let's see what he does say." Strong opened the door and joined Ormerod in the interview room.

"Good evening, Mr Mirczack. I'm Detective Chief Inspector Colin Strong."

"So you the man in charge, yes?"

Strong sat down across the table from him, next to Ormerod. "As my colleagues have no doubt informed you, I wish to speak to you in connection with a number of serious incidents that have occurred in the past few weeks."

"I say nothing without my solicitor," Mirczack responded, in a voice that seemed to come from the soles of his shoes.

"I believe you are the owner of a massage parlour in Leeds that is known as Sweet Sensations. Is that correct?"

"No comment."

"A man by the name of Stefan Szymanski works for you as parlour manager, does he not?"

"No comment."

Strong and Ormerod exchanged glances.

"Do you own a car, Mr Mirczack?"

"No comment."

"Has your solicitor been called?"

Mirczack smirked. "No comment."

Strong stood up, exasperated. "Escort Mr Mirczack back to the cells, DC Ormerod."

When he walked into the CID Room, Stainmore and Denholme looked up. "Any joy, guv?" Stainmore asked.

Strong shook his head. "No commenting everything. Even when I asked about his solicitor. I'm assuming he has been contacted?"

"Yes."

"Which delightful overpaid, obstructive arse-wipe are we looking forward to doing battle with then?"

Stainmore chuckled. "Our old friend Peter Atherton, if you remember. Legal advisor to the stars."

"Great," Strong sighed. "When's he likely to waft in on a cloud of expensive aftershave?"

"Tomorrow morning. Apparently, he's in London today."

"Right, I'm off back home for a decent night's sleep. You need to do the same." Strong turned and left.

59
Monday

Despite the previous late night, Strong was at his desk early the following morning catching up with paperwork. He'd spoken to Flynn regarding events surrounding the detention of Mirczack. Halliday was on his way to sit in on the interview once Atherton turned up and had the opportunity to be briefed by his client.

Ryan knocked on his door and he beckoned him in.

"Got some initial results from the basement room in Luxor Grove. They're checking the DNA database for matches from the ground floor but they have a match with Helena from samples in the basement. Also, fibres from her jacket she was wearing when she was found were discovered on the mattress. Nothing on the ground floor."

Strong leaned back in his chair. "So Helena was definitely in that basement room, and probably on the day she disappeared." He rose and walked to the window. The morning sun was showing the town hall off to its best advantage. Another fine September day beckoned.

He turned and rested his backside against the window sill. "Has that smarmy sod, Atherton arrived yet?"

"Not heard, guv."

He pushed himself away and strode towards the door. "Right, let's catch up with the troops."

At the door, Halliday appeared.

"Ah, Frank, good timing. We're just about to have a little review of where we are before we face Mirczack."

In the CID Room, the main players were assembled. Stainmore and Ormerod were studying their respective computer screens, Denholme was drinking a coffee and sifting through paperwork whilst Darby and Atkinson were discussing the weekend's football results.

"Okay everybody," Strong said, "this could be an important day today. For those of you who don't know, this is DCI Frank Halliday from Leeds. Frank has been investigating Chris Baker's murder. Now, as it appears this murder is linked with that of Helena Cryanovic, it makes sense we work together on this."

Strong walked over and stood in front of the whiteboard. "As you all know, we will be interviewing this man shortly, Stanislav Mirczack." He pointed to the Yugoslav's picture. "Once his brief deigns to turn up. He was detained last night at Leeds/Bradford on his return from Riga in Latvia. We know he owns three massage parlours in and around Leeds, including Sweet Sensations where we found seven Eastern European girls working for him and living in two properties which his company, Balkan Investments, own." He went on to explain where investigations were in relation to Szymanski, who was still in custody, and the latest forensic evidence surrounding Helena and also events on Saturday resulting in the arrest of Robert Baker for his involvement in the theft of the stolen cars.

Stainmore answered the phone which interrupted Strong's recount. "Atherton is here, guv," she announced.

Strong checked his watch. "Right, we'll give him time to talk to Mirczack and aim to start the interview at nine-thirty. Frank will obviously be in there with me. And Kelly," he turned to Stainmore, "I'd like you in there too. You spent a lot of time with the girls, especially Lyudmyla. You might spot something if he starts talking. We'll be video recording the interview so the rest of you can observe."

Atherton greeted Strong, holding out a freshly manicured hand. "Congratulations, Chief Inspector."

"It's acting DCI, Mr Atherton," he replied, shaking hands.

Atherton shook his head, "A mere formality, Mr Strong, I'm sure." He turned to the Leeds detective. "Mr Halliday, an unexpected pleasure."

Again the offered hand. As Halliday shook it, Strong thought he noticed the Masonic grip.

"And this is DS Stainmore." Strong gestured towards his colleague. "I believe you've met before."

"DS Stainmore, a very pleasant surprise." Atherton offered her his hand as well.

She shook it reluctantly, not impressed by his smooth manner.

All this time, Mirczack was sitting impassively at the interview table. The others joined him as Strong placed fresh cassettes in the tape machine before making the statutory announcement of those present, date and time. Strong also informed them that the interview was being recorded on video.

"First of all Mr Mirczack, I'd just like to establish that you are the owner of the establishment known as Sweet Sensations located in Chapeltown," Strong began.

"I have an interest, yes."

"You also, as I understand it, have an interest in a company known as Balkan Investments."

"Yes."

"You will also be aware of the people working at Sweet Sensations."

Mirczack waved a hand. "The day-to-day management is handled by the manager."

"And that would be Stefan Szymanski?"

"It would."

"But you would be aware of the women who work there?"

"I have seen them, yes."

"And these women are ... accommodated in two properties owned by Balkan Investments?"

"If you say so. I have no input into the letting of these properties."

"Mr Mirczack, do you honestly expect us to believe that you had no idea who lives in these properties,

301

especially when we know they also worked for you at another of your businesses?"

"That is why I employ a manager."

Atherton stirred. "Mr Strong, my client has made it clear he may have interests in businesses, but would not expect to be involved in some of the more mundane matters that might entail."

Strong's eyes never left Mirczack. "Those 'mundane matters', as your solicitor puts it, include the employment of women we suspect of being illegally trafficked into this country."

"I am shocked that my manager would allow such a thing."

A slight hand movement from Strong was picked up by Halliday.

He took up the questioning. "Can you account for your movements on the night of Wednesday 7th September between the hours of ten pm and three am the following morning?"

Mirczack furrowed his brows. "A Wednesday, nearly two weeks ago? I was probably at home."

"Probably?"

"I think I was, yes."

"And can anyone corroborate that?"

"Excuse me?"

"Was anyone else with you?"

Mirczack smirked. "Not that night, I think not."

Strong joined in. "How about Thursday 1st September between six pm and eight am the following morning?"

Mirczack shrugged and looked to his lawyer. "I can't remember."

"It isn't that long ago."

"Thursday? I think I may have had a business meeting in Leeds. I would have to check."

Strong opened one of the files they had brought with them and produced a photograph of Helena. "Have you seen this girl before? Photograph identified as P1."

Mirczack took hold of it and studied it for a few seconds. "She's very pretty girl. Is she one of these women who work at Sweet Sensations and have rented property from me?"

Strong smiled sardonically. "Look again please, Mr Mirczack. Are you sure you haven't met this girl?"

"Oh, wait. Is she one of the receptionists?"

"Do we take it that you do recognise her?"

"Yes, I seem to remember her there."

"Hardly surprising since you were heard rowing with her and your 'manager' in one of the rooms at Sensations on Tuesday the 30th of August."

"I don't remember that."

"Or what it was about?"

Mirczack shook his head. "No."

"We have a witness who says you were shouting at both of them in a room at the parlour."

"It can't have been important, I can't remember."

Atherton interrupted again. "My client has told you he doesn't remember, Mr Strong."

"Did you ever visit her at home?"

"Home? How could I? I don't know where she lives."

"You were never taken there by your ... manager, Mr Szymanski?"

"No."

"Your memory must be failing Mr Mirczack, because we have another witness who saw you there."

"She must be mistaken."

Strong let the silence stretch for a few moments. "I didn't say it was a woman," he said, before glancing at Stainmore.

"Do you own a car Mr Mirczack?" she asked.

Mirczack leaned towards Atherton and whispered into his ear.

"My client would like a comfort break, gentlemen ... and lady." Atherton said. "And I would like a few words alone with him too."

Strong sighed, made the announcement to suspend the interview, gathered up his files and walked out.

Back in the CID Room, Strong began to pace. "He's going to pass all responsibility on to Szymanski," he said, to no-one in particular.

"Could see that coming," Halliday chipped in. "Apart from statements from Szymanski and the women, there's nothing substantial to tie him in. He'll even try and side-step anything to do with employing those girls."

"We could do with finding his car." Strong looked round the room, before settling on Ryan. "Jim, what kind of car did you say Mirczack drove?"

"Dark blue Mercedes 300SE, guv."

"I might be wrong but I think he wanted time to think on that question, Kelly. My guess is that he's got that garaged somewhere and won't want us to find it. Probably because there'll be some forensic evidence … I don't know. Jim, see if you can track down the details. It may be registered in his name, or Balkan Investments or any other company he's involved with." He turned to Denholme. "Vince, can you help with that?"

"Sure."

Darby entered, a broad grin on his face.

"What's with you?" Ormerod asked. "Just got your leg over?"

"You may mock," he said, "but I've just arrested three likely lads from the Warwick Estate in Knottingley, caught in the act of trying to remove plant from a building site in Wrenthorpe." He pretended to lick a finger and mimicked marking a figure one on a board. "Chalk one up to me," he said.

"You realise it'll cost you a round of drinks tonight," Ormerod said.

Darby ignored him, adjusted the crotch of his trousers and sat down at his desk.

"Right," Strong said, "we'll give them ten more minutes and back in for round two. I'm off for a pee."

In the toilet, Strong's mobile rang. Souter.

He checked there was nobody else in the place before he answered. "It'll have to be quick, mate, I've got my hands full at the moment."

"You're in the bog, then?" Souter quipped.

"Seriously, I've got to go back to an interview as soon as."

"Okay. Are you still trying to trace Chapman's cousin?"

The question took him by surprise. "Well, yes. I still need to speak to Baker and Chapman. They'll have information we need to find out who killed Chris Baker. Bob, do you know where they might be?"

"Maybe."

"I can hear you're on the move. Tell me you're not going there now."

"Sorry, the signal's breaking up."

"Don't give me that bollocks. This is serious. We need to know who they were nicking the cars for, and how Helena's body ended up in one."

"I'll call you later, the traffic's getting heavy."

"Bob? Bob?" The line was dead.

When the interview resumed, Kelly picked up where she had left off. "So, as I asked before the break, Mr Mirczack, do you own a car?"

"Yes," he responded.

"What type of vehicle is it?"

"Well, I say, yes, but I don't know where it is. It was stolen before I went to Riga."

"Have you reported it?"

"No. I don't think it's worth it. If I do find it, it will probably be burned out somewhere."

"Where was it stolen?"

"Outside my flat in the centre of Leeds."

"When exactly?"

"Monday. I came down and it was gone."

"And it's a dark blue Mercedes 300SE, is that correct?"

"You know the details?"

"Of course we do. And you didn't think it worth reporting."

"Insurance pay nothing. Police don't do nothing. Waste of time."

"I'm sure my client will make a formal report of the matter before we leave here today," Atherton said.

It was Halliday's turn to pick up the mantle. He selected the photo of Chris Baker from the file and placed it on the table. "Do you recognise this man? For the benefit of the tape, I'm showing Mr Mirczack photograph P2."

Mirczack glanced down then across to Halliday. "No."

"If you could take a proper look."

Mirczack let out a breath, leaned forward and picked it up. "No, I'm sure."

Halliday looked to Strong. "Strange," he said, "I thought you said he was a regular client at Sweet Sensations?"

"Oh, there's no doubt about that, Frank," Strong said. "We have witnesses to support that."

"I said before, I leave business to the manager. I don't see the men who visit."

Strong knew he had nothing to place Baker and Mirczack in the same place at the same time. Lyudmyla said that Baker had left before Mirczack turned up on the night of the argument. It was only Szymanski's statement that linked the information provided by Baker to Mirczack. What if Szymanski was organising the car thefts? And yet, it was Mirczack who had the connections in Latvia, where the cars were destined.

"So you've never seen this man before?" Halliday persisted.

"No."

Strong tried a different tack. "Do the names Gary Baker and Steve Chapman mean anything to you?"

He thought he detected a glimmer of a reaction from the big Yugoslav.

"I'm sorry but I never heard of these people."

"Have you ever had dealings with Yorkshire Exports?"

Mirczack shrugged. "I do not recognise the name but …"

The interview continued for some time with the same negative or nondescript responses. Strong knew they needed something more substantial to link Mirczack to the car thefts, the Bakers, Chapman and Helena. As it stood, Mirczack would hang Szymanski out to dry, claim innocence of all that went on at the parlour and even accuse Szymanski of organising the vehicle exports. As Halliday had surmised, he would even side-step the sex-trafficking accusations and leave Szymanski to take the blame for that. Eventually, Strong suspended the interview.

Atherton was his usual smooth-talking self. "Obviously, my client wishes to help with your investigations Mr Strong but I think he has told you all he can. I would like you to release him now. Should you wish to …"

"I don't think so just yet," Strong interrupted. "We still have questions to put, and we will need to take a statement. We'll take a break for now."

Gathering up their files, Strong, Halliday and Stainmore left the room.

60

Jaywick. The place sounded … well Souter didn't really know how it sounded. Possibly as if it belonged in a Hans Christian Anderson fairy story. But then again, it could have been a children's TV series. This was just one of his trains of thought as he sat nursing a tea in a café in Clacton. He'd treated himself to some seaside fish and chips after the four hour journey south from Yorkshire. Spoilt for choice in the resort, he decided against the Essex specialities of jellied eels or pie and mash complete with liquor, a strange green parsley and garlic sauce.

"Everything all right for you?" The waitress collected his empty plate and cutlery from the table. "Can I get you anything else?"

"No. No thanks, love."

"Just here for the day or are you staying longer?"

"Me?" Souter was surprised by her interest. "I'm not sure. It just depends." She stood for a few seconds before he spoke again. "Listen, I'm looking for a friend of mine I think might be in a place called Jaywick. Have you heard of it?"

She smiled. "Oh yeah, I've heard of it. It's unique."

"What way?"

"You need to experience it. There's nowhere else like it in the country, I'm sure. I always take my visitors there. There and Dedham – Constable country. Chalk and cheese."

He looked at her. She was quite attractive for her age, he thought. "You do realise," he said, "you've said quite a lot but told me nothing."

She laughed. "That's the secret," she said before walking back to the kitchen.

An elderly couple at a nearby table got up and left. The café owner came from behind the counter to clear their crockery away and wipe the table.

The waitress reappeared minus her apron with a jacket over her arm. "See you tomorrow, Tommy," she said to the man with the cloth, then to Souter, "Still here?"

He held up his hands in mock surrender. "Don't worry, I'm leaving. As soon as I work out the way to Jaywick."

She smiled. "I'm finished now, so I can point you in the right direction. I live just off Jaywick Lane."

He stood. "That's very kind of you …"

"Carol," she offered. "And I'm just off for the bus."

"I'm Bob," he responded. "Listen, if it's on the way, I could give you a lift." Hands up again. "I'm just parked round the corner. And I'm perfectly safe."

Carol looked at him seriously for a second or two, then grinned. "But I'm not," she said. "I teach Karate to black belt standard."

"She does an' all," Tommy confirmed.

Fifteen minutes later, they were in Souter's car cutting through some back streets heading for the sea front.

"I sometimes walk the dog on the beach at Jaywick," Carol said. "The beach is lovely. It's just some of the houses, well shacks really, that exist down there, you wouldn't think people live in them."

He was finding it hard to concentrate. He'd just seen some apparition appear from a flat. Heavily rouged face, bright red lipstick, red housecoat, white scarf and slippers, she must have been at least seventy-five years old. Around the corner, walking casually down the street, was a man who looked to be in his late forties dressed in full cowboy outfit; black trousers, waistcoat, boots and Stetson, the only things missing were chaps and six-guns!

Carol caught the focus of his attention. "I know," she said, "There are probably more characters per square mile in Clacton than any other place in Britain."

Souter just shook his head. They drove past the hospital and turned right onto the seafront. It was a fine sunny late afternoon and a lot of people were walking along the greensward, some motorhomes were parked up and children were playing in the playpark, watched by smiling parents. Out past the golf club, Carol pointed to the opposite side of the road. "Clacton International Airport," she said.

"Really?" Souter looked surprised.

She laughed. "No, only kidding. Just light aircraft, but there is a brilliant airshow around August Bank Holiday."

They were approaching a mini-roundabout opposite The Three Jays pub.

"Turn left here and just drop me off. I'm only up there," she said, indicating the other side of the pub.

He pulled in to the side and she opened the door. "Might see you later if you're still down there. It looks a fine evening. Me and my boy might take the dog down after tea. Thanks again, and I hope you find your friend."

"No problem," Souter said.

She closed the door and made her way carefully across the road and cut through the pub car park. Nice legs, he considered, then shook that thought from his mind and set off on his way.

* * *

In the CID Room, you could almost cut the air of frustration with a knife.

"He's going to walk out of here, Colin," Halliday said. "The smarmy Atherton will see to that."

Strong, hands in his trouser pockets, was staring out of the window as if seeking divine inspiration. "The fact that it's Atherton won't have much to do with it. Even a junior solicitor would push for release." He turned around. "And when he does go, he'll most likely simply evaporate and never be seen again."

"We haven't even found any forensic evidence to connect him with Luxor Grove," Ryan said.

Strong strode towards the door. "I'm going to have another word with Szymanski. He's being hung out to dry on this. He must know about Mirczack's car. No way would he just dismiss a Mercedes, eleven years old or not."

"I'll come with you," Halliday said.

Bill Sidebotham was acting as custody sergeant and opened the cell door to Szymanski.

"Stefan," Strong began, "we wanted to have another word with you."

The Pole looked frightened. "Where's my solicitor?"

"This is unofficial. Just between us." Strong leaned against a wall, Halliday stood by the open door.

"Is this where you beat the shit out of me?" Szymanski wrung his hands.

Strong smiled. "You've been watching too much telly. Look, I think you should know that Mirczack has denied any involvement in the car thefts, the sex-trafficking, in fact anything at all and is blaming you as his manager for absolutely everything."

Szymanski sat on the bed with his head down.

"You told us you had nothing to do with stealing and processing the cars," Halliday said. "Unless we get something tangible on him, Mirczack will walk, leaving you to rot in prison."

He eventually looked up, the fear evident on his face. "I've told you all I can."

"Mirczack owns a car," Strong stated. "A Mercedes. Quite a nice one, we understand. It seems to have disappeared. He says it was stolen. Ironic really. He claims it wasn't worth reporting. We think it's in storage somewhere. Have you any ideas on that, Stefan? Just between these four walls, of course."

Szymanski shook his head. "You have no idea what he's like. I would be dead."

"We could help you," Halliday said.

"In prison? I don't think so. I'm sorry, I can't help you."

"Come on, Stefan," Strong persisted. "He wouldn't know you told us anything."

Szymanski lay down on the bed and turned to the wall.

As Strong and Halliday made their way back upstairs, Sidebotham locked the cell door.

"I'll see you back in the Incident Room, Frank," Strong said. "I just want to make a quick call."

Outside in the yard, Strong dialled Souter's number. It wasn't picked up and went straight to voicemail. He hesitated, then decided to leave a message. It was a big risk but he thought he could trust his friend not to use any information he gave him inappropriately. From their last conversation, Strong knew he was on to something. At a time like this he needed something, anything that might give him another chance with Mirczack.

* * *

Jaywick itself didn't seem too bad. It was noticeable as Souter made his way down the road into the community that the bungalows became progressively shabbier, but it compared favourably with some parts of the north he was more familiar with. The road continued past some shops and a pub with the odd name of 'Never Say Die'. A little further on, he passed an open concrete car park area next to a run-down amusement arcade. From here, the road ran parallel to the concrete sea wall with small bungalows on the opposite side. The accommodation began to take on more the appearance of a shanty town. The weather was warm and sunny and the car's windows were down. He drifted past a brightly painted bungalow with a donkey and flowers cast into the gable end. What one of his colleagues at the Post would have referred to as 'diddly–eye' music was blasting out to the obvious delight of the elderly gent sitting in the small front yard, shirt off, smoking a cigarette.

Eventually, he spotted the street he was seeking. All the roads in this area were named after classic British cars of the forties and fifties. Names like Alvis, Humber and Standard harked back to a time when this development was a weekend escape for people from London some seventy miles away. That was also before the great disaster of 1953. An unusually high surge tide running down the East coast combined with severe low pressure, high winds and heavy rain, led to the sea sweeping in behind the poor sea defences that existed then. Some 37 people lost their lives.

Jaguar Avenue led off to the right. If he thought the buildings on the sea road were in a poor state, these looked positively dilapidated. Some were on stilts, making him think he'd crossed the Atlantic and was somewhere in the Mississippi River delta. The road was unmade, full of pot holes and strewn with rubbish. Various cars, the odd headlight missing or jacked up on bricks, made it difficult to negotiate. Number ten was one of those raised about four feet above the ground with a wooden veranda in front. He glanced towards the building as he drove slowly past but could detect no signs of activity. Managing to turn at the end of the road, he drove back down and pulled up behind a white van. Just before he wound up the windows, a young girl passed by, heavily pregnant in a short skirt and a top that left the bulge exposed. She was dragging a toddler by her tattooed left arm.

"Get a fuckin' move on, Conner. I ain't got all day for you ya little sod." It was only after she spoke again that he realised she was also holding a mobile phone to her right ear conducting a conversation at the same time. "Yeah, we're on our way back now, Mum."

His phone vibrated in his pocket. A voicemail. He dialled and listened to the message Strong had left him. A tinge of conscience pricked that he hadn't told him what he was up to exactly. He'd try and put that right, if he got the chance.

As he got out of the car and locked up, he could feel numerous pairs of eyes on him. Dressed in jeans and a tee shirt, he hoped he didn't stand out. But a stranger still elicits interest in a place like this. He opened the gate and climbed up the five steps onto the timber deck.

As he knocked on the door, a woman in her seventies called to him from the veranda of the adjacent property. "I doubt you'll find them in, darlin'," she said in a cockney accent. "Not at this time of the day."

Souter turned, walked across towards her and leaned on the balustrading. She was sitting at a table with a man he took to be her husband. They had mugs of tea in front of them and both were smoking. "Do you know who lives here?" he asked.

"Young Barry," the man replied. "Well I say young, they're all young to me." He broke off into a chuckle which developed into a hacking cough.

"That was until about a week ago when two other lads appeared," his wife added.

"Two of them?"

"Yeah that's right. Northerners like you. That's their van there." She nodded towards the Escort van parked in the street.

Souter looked round and froze. He hadn't paid any attention to the vehicle before, his focus was on finding Gary Baker. But there on the bottom of the passenger door was that distinctive outbreak of rust. It can't be, he thought.

"Fancy a cup of tea, son?" the man asked, "You look like you need one."

"Er, yes. That's very kind of you, thanks."

When he'd made his way round to the couple's table, the woman added, "We're not all rough as arseholes round here, you know. Would you like some cake?"

He struggled to keep a straight face. "No thanks, I had something in Clacton not long ago."

The woman introduced herself as Beryl and her husband as Tom.

"How long have you two lived here?" Souter asked.

"Used to come down here before the war with our parents. Lots of us did then. Have you seen the beach? It's as good as you'll get anywhere in this country, bloody sight better than Southend. That's just a mud flat," Beryl said.

"So, have you found the right place?" Tom asked. Souter was puzzled for a second. "Next door?"

"Oh, sorry," he hesitated, "I'm not sure yet. I'm looking for friends of mine, Gary Baker and his mate Steve Chapman. I'd heard they were staying with their cousin, Barry."

"You might have found them," Tom said. "I've heard Barry call the taller of them Steve and the lad with the shaved head Gaz."

"Yeah, Gaz, that's right. That's what we call him." Souter finished his tea. "I don't suppose you know where they might be now?"

"At this time," Beryl checked her watch, "they'll be down the boozer. You must have seen it on the way in."

"I know where you mean." He stood up. "Listen, Beryl, Tom, good to meet you and thanks for the hospitality."

"You're welcome, son," Beryl said.

"If you miss them, who should I say was looking for them?" Tom asked.

"I'd appreciate it if you didn't say anything for now, I want to surprise them, they don't know I'm down south," Souter smiled.

He walked slowly past the white van on the way back to his car, taking in as much of the detail as possible. Before setting off, he took the CCTV stills from the glovebox and studied them carefully. He was in no doubt that this was the van that Maria got into that Saturday night, but whose van is it?

He drove back up towards the pub and parked a little way beyond on the opposite side. He crossed over and decided to have a quick look at the beach. The sun was still warm and he wondered if Beryl had been exaggerating. A small unmade road ran between two houses where steps led up to a wide footpath. The concrete sea wall separated the pathway from the beach. When he could finally see over the wall, he realised the old girl was right. You could go a long way to see a better beach in Britain. The contrast between where he'd just enjoyed some pleasant hospitality and the glorious sandy beach could not be more marked. What an incongruous place this is, he thought. Carol was right, this is unique.

Outside the pub, a few couples with young children running around were enjoying the evening sun at several picnic tables in the small forecourt. The remnants of pub meals, overflowing ashtrays and half empty glasses covered them. Inside, a hubbub of conversation, jukebox music and cigarette fug enveloped him. As he made his way to the bar and ordered a pint, he casually took in the other customers. He had to identify Baker, Chapman and the cousin as inconspicuously as possible. It was as he took the first sip of his fizzy lager that he realised he didn't actually know what they looked like. He had some rough idea yes, but he'd never seen photos of any of them. Unless, of course, you counted the grainy image of the driver of the white van he got from Jezza.

A group of four lads in their twenties were engrossed around the pool table, two middle-aged couples were in deep conversation at one table and four men in their forties were at another. There were two possibilities, as far as Souter could ascertain. Three men were standing at the far end of the bar talking to two women and a further three men were sitting silently at a table near the rear door. Both groups featured one who might fit the vague description of Gary Baker. He would have to get close enough to catch the accents. Since coming south, he hadn't heard another northerner talk. There were two other pairs of men standing around chatting and smoking but none of them appeared to fit Baker's profile.

Pulling out a packet of cigarettes, Souter patted his pockets and looked round the pub before heading over to the three men by the back door.

"Excuse me lads," he said, "but could I cadge a light?"

"No, sorry mate, we don't smoke," the one with the buzzed head said in a southern accent.

"Thanks anyway." Souter shrugged and walked over to the group at the far end of the bar.

"Sure," one said in response to his request before offering his lighter.

"You on holiday here?" the blonde women asked.

"I'm just down for a couple of days, staying with a friend in Clacton," Souter answered.

"From Yorkshire?" the dark-haired woman joined in.

"Er, yes," he replied.

"We love it up there, don't we Jeff?" She looked at the balding man next to her. "North Yorkshire, we've had a few holidays in Pickering and Scarborough."

Definitely southerners, Souter decided. "It is nice," he agreed.

Out of the corner of his eye, he caught sight of a man in his twenties with very short hair returning from the gents to join two others standing around a column in the middle of the room.

"Thanks," Souter said to the man who'd lit his cigarette, "I'm just going to get some crisps."

He took a slow wide berth around two older men, trying to pass close enough to the trio around the column to pick up some of what they were saying.

"Who? Veronica? Naw, last few times I tried to ring, there was no answer. I think she'll have pissed off. Anyway, cheers Barry," the young man with dark hair said to the oldest one as Souter drifted by, "you can get us another in."

No mistaking the Yorkshire accent. In fact, he was sure it belonged to the voice on Susan Brown's answer service. He'd found them. This was Steve Chapman talking to his cousin Barry Whitefield.

He stood at the bar and observed. Now he was here, he wasn't sure what his next move should be.

Chapman drained his glass but Baker's was still half full. Judging by his body language, Baker didn't seem too comfortable. He'd obviously refused another drink and Whitefield was asking him again. Another refusal and Whitefield picked up Chapman's glass and his own and strode up to the bar. Souter turned away as Whitefield approached and ordered two more pints. He returned with the drinks and Baker hung around for a further five minutes whilst he finished his lager. He took his leave alone and, hands in his jeans pockets, disappeared outside.

Thirty seconds later, Souter left the pub. Baker was heading down the road in the direction of Jaguar Avenue. Walking, it would take him a good ten minutes to get back to where he was staying. Souter got back to his car, started the engine and turned around to follow him. About three hundred yards from the pub, the road split to form a one-way system, fortunately, the shortest route was the one he had to follow. Souter pulled alongside Baker and dropped the passenger window.

"Excuse me," he said, "I'm looking for Jaguar Avenue."

"It's down here, mate, about half a mile on t' right." He chuckled, "Mindst if you turn t' left you'd be in t' sea."

"You from up north?"

"Aye. Wakefield," Baker answered.

"Thought I recognised the accent. I'm from Leeds myself," Souter said. "Can I give you a lift?"

"Aw thanks, I'm actually stopping on Jaguar Avenue."

Baker opened the passenger door and got in. As Souter pulled away, he coughed loudly to disguise the clunk as he switched the central locking on.

"Been down here long?" Souter asked.

"Not really. We're just stayin' with my mate's cousin for a bit. What about you?"

"I've come down to help you, Gary." He pulled off to the right and on to some waste ground. "I think you're in a bit of trouble."

As the car drew to a halt, Baker grabbed the door handle but it wouldn't release. "What the fuck d'you think you're doing. Let me out, you crazy bastard."

"Calm down. I know you're scared and I know why." Souter turned to face the young man. "But I'm not out to get you. I want to help."

"Help? Help? What d'you know?"

"I know your brother was murdered and I think you know who did it and you're shitting yourself they're going to find you and Steve."

"Wha.." Baker stopped mid word, his face a mixture of bewilderment and alarm. "Who are you? What do you want?"

"My name's Souter. I'm a journalist. But don't let that put you off," he added quickly. "I really am here to help you."

"How? How can you help me? How do you know I need help?"

"Look, I know what Chris was into and that he was involved with some heavy people and I know you were with him the night he died."

"But... how? I mean, how can you know that?"

"I've got some good connections." Again, Souter saw the expression on Baker's face. "No, not with the people who're after you."

"Oh, no. Not the police?"

"You see, Gary, they're struggling to pin down those responsible. You do know who was responsible, don't you?"

Once more the terror returned to Baker's face. "I can't. I just can't. They'll kill us too."

"Not if they're sent down."

"They'd know it was me."

"But they're free to walk about and you're scared shitless now. How do you know they'll not find you anyway?"

"But we've got a plan. Steve and me, we're gonna lie low for a bit. We'll get a job. A proper job. We can do up cars. We'll get something down here."

"But I found you. And you'll always be looking over your shoulders."

"I'm no grass."

"That's a pity, Gary." Souter pulled out a packet of cigarettes. This was only his second one since leaving Wakefield. He was almost ready to give up completely, but he felt it was a timely distraction. He offered one to Baker who took it, produced a lighter from his shirt pocket and lit up. "You see, they've got some evidence, mostly circumstantial, but they need something concrete."

"I don't know nothing."

Souter lit his own cigarette, then dropped his window a touch. "That Saturday night, when you had that Merc sports car up at the farm..."

"How do you know about that?"

"I also know what was found in the boot when they opened it in the container at Felixstowe docks. Now that's not so very far from here, is it?"

"Me and Steve ... and Chris, we'd got nothing to do with that."

"So you do know what was in the boot?"

Baker went quiet and examined his fingers, then began to nibble his nails. "He'll kill me," he said quietly.

"Who will?"

"That big bad bastard. He's crazy."

"Who?"

"Some foreign bastard. Mirczack. Even his sidekick, some Polish guy, Szymanski, he's scared of him."

"This Mirczack, did he kill Chris?"

"I think so." Baker nodded, transferring his attention to the other hand.

"Did they put the girl's body in the boot?"

"Him and Szymanski. We didn't want anything to do with it." He looked at Souter, pure terror on his face. "We're not into violence. He told us we had to get it into the container and it would be shipped out on the Monday. And then Chris called me to say he was getting the last payment – for the cars I mean. That's why I put my hands up to the police for lifting the cars. I thought they'd been shipped out of the country by then." Baker was talking quickly, as though a boil had been lanced and he was desperate to squeeze all the poison out. "We got to the meet, in that layby and then I had to go for a piss and ... when I got back ... he was ... I mean ... if I hadn't needed to go..." Baker looked intently at Souter. "It could have been me too." The tears were flowing down his cheeks.

"Did you see who did it?"

Baker drew long and hard on his cigarette. "No. There was just a car driving away from the layby when I got back over the fence."

"You see, Gary, that's why you've got to tell the police."

"No. No, I can't."

Souter let the conversation stall for a few seconds. "Is that because of the other thing?"

Baker wiped his face with the back of his hand. "What other thing?"

"What happened to Maria?"

Puzzlement appeared on Baker's face. "Maria? Who the fuck's Maria?"

"About twenty, five foot six, dark hair, short light coloured skirt and a dark top."

Baker began to colour.

"You picked her up in Wakefield's market square on a Sunday night about two weeks ago."

Baker's mouth opened and closed like a freshly caught fish.

"Have a look in the glovebox," Souter said.

Baker did as asked and took out the photographs.

"That is your van, isn't it Gary? I mean, the rust along the bottom of the passenger door is a bit of a giveaway."

"I... I... You can't tell that," Baker stumbled.

"No, you're right. You can't see it too clearly on those copies but with all this new technology, they can enhance these, no problem. In fact, that one of you driving, they can probably see the blackheads on your nose," Souter lied.

Baker had flushed. "I didn't ... I don't ... I mean, I've no idea."

"Come on, don't give me that shit. You were the last person seen with her. That's you driving her away in that van of yours. Where did you go? What did you do?"

"Nothing. We didn't do nothing."

"Bollocks. You've just picked up a young prostitute, driven her away in your van and you didn't do 'nothing'?"

His eyes were wet when he looked across at Souter. "Honest. We didn't actually do anything." Another drag on his cigarette. "Look, this is the truth, right? She took me to this old warehouse place. There was a door that had been forced. She led the way inside. There was this room where the street light shone in through the broken window." A big drag then a sharp exhale. "I thought she was going to do … well, the business, you know. The next thing, she starts shaking like some loony. Her eyes are in the back of her head, half closed, she's frothing at the mouth and then she's on the floor trembling like she's havin' some almighty fucking orgasm. I thought to myself, she's on drugs."

"So what did you do?"

"Do? I fucked off quick. I mean, I hadn't paid her any money or anything. I thought, fuck that, I'm not getting involved with no junkie."

"And you left her there?"

"Yeah. I thought she'd come round and have to make her own way back."

Souter looked hard at the man. "Where was this warehouse? I mean exactly."

"We went down Thornes Lane. Down by the side of the river. Just before The Jolly Sailor. On the opposite side, there was a gateway. We pulled in there and went through a small door in the gate into the old yard. There was a door to the right into the building."

"You didn't touch her at all?"

"No."

"And she just collapsed?"

"Honest."

He held Souter's gaze for a few moments.

"Okay, Gary, I believe you. But," he held up a finger. "For me to sort this for you and keep you out of it, I'll need you to give me something on this Mirczack character."

"Like what?"

"I don't know, they're struggling for evidence. The gun would be good. That Saturday, they turned up in a Mercedes didn't they?"

"Yeah, Mirczack's."

"And was the girl's body in that. Is that what they brought her in?"

Baker nodded.

"If he wasn't using it, where would he keep it?"

"What do you mean?"

"Well, it's not outside his flat in Leeds, so it must be somewhere, unless he got rid of it."

"I don't think so. He loves that car."

"So where might it be?"

Baker looked down into the floorpan.

"Come on, Gary, if you know something ..."

"Okay. He has a lockup under the arches near the station."

Souter took out a notepad and jotted down the details Baker gave him.

*   *   *

"We've got nothing on the bastard, and he knows it, sir." Strong was standing in front of DCS Flynn's desk in his second floor office in Wood Street police station.

The boss was sitting with his elbows on the desk, fingers entwined and chin resting on his upward pointing forefingers. "I know it goes against the grain, Colin," he finally said, "but unless we have something more solid, we're going to have to let him go."

Strong looked out of the window and across to the Town Hall. He imagined the office staff sitting at their computer terminals or walking to the photocopier, totally oblivious to the nasty specimens of humanity they had to deal with on this side of the street. At the same time, he was turning everything over in his mind to see if he'd missed something vital. It was true, he needed a bit more than the circumstantial evidence he had against Mirczack. With Szymanski's statement, it would be his word against

Mirczack. Although, judging by his reaction in the cell, he wouldn't be surprised if he withdrew that. The girls' statements all helped but, in isolation, were nowhere near enough. And he wasn't about to use them without something more substantial. That would expose them and their families to great risk.

"Right, I'd best get it over with," he said.

On the stairs down to the Incident Room, Strong ran into Luke Ormerod.

"What did the boss say?" Ormerod asked.

"What we expected. Got to let him go."

Ormerod sighed and shook his head. "I'll fetch him down then."

"Thanks, Luke."

Five minutes later, Mirczack and Atherton, Strong and Ormerod were finalising the release process with Sidebotham, the custody sergeant, when a text message announced itself on Strong's phone. Opening it up, he read, *'Don't ignore next call – IMPORTANT INFO'.* It was from Souter.

There was a smirk on Mirczack's face as he gathered up his personal belongings from the desk and followed Strong through to the public area. "Thank you for wasting my time," he said.

Strong ignored the jibe and his phone rang.

"This had better be good," Strong said to Souter, whose name came up on the display once again.

"I've got something on Mirczack. Are you still looking for more evidence?" Souter asked.

Strong turned away to speak in a low voice. "We're just releasing him," he said, "so anything you've got, let's hear it quick."

Souter related what Gary Baker had just told him about Mirczack's Mercedes, the sighting of the gun in the glovebox and the location of the lock-up in Leeds. *"You might find nothing, but it's worth a try,"* he concluded.

"Thanks," Strong said, ending the call. He turned as Mirczack and Atherton were halfway through the door into the street. "Oh, Mr Mirczack," he said, stepping towards the two. "One last thing. Can you tell me what I might find in a certain lock-up in Brussels Street in Leeds?"

The colour drained from the big man's face. "You know nothing," he said, taking a stride nearer.

Strong held his stare for a moment. "About number 23A, you mean?"

Strong didn't get a response, at least not one that he heard. His lights went out suddenly as Mirczack threw a fist into his jaw and dashed out into the street, bustling past a bewildered Atherton. There was a moment of disbelief before Ormerod made sense of what he'd just seen and bounded out after the Yugoslav.

Outside, Mirczack turned left, leapt down the steps, bundled two men out of the way and ran off down Wood Street towards the traffic lights opposite The Black Rock pub. About half way down he dived off to the left into Cross Street.

John Darby had taken advantage of the chance to nip out to Morrison's in The Ridings to buy an individual meal for one, some washing powder, a bottle of red wine and four cans of beer. On the way back to the station, he needed to get some cash. He was removing the receipt for the fifty pounds he'd just withdrawn from the cash machine when he heard footsteps running from the other end of Cross Street. That was quickly followed by shouting as the short stocky figure he recognised as Luke Ormerod came into view. About fifty yards ahead of him, the unmistakeable bulk of Stanislav Mirczack was thundering down the street in Darby's direction. A young mother pushing a buggy and holding a young girl's hand screamed and pulled the child in close as he stormed past. A middle-aged woman jumped into the doorway of a restaurant to avoid being knocked over.

For a big man, Mirczack was surprisingly quick. Ormerod was shouting after him, the thought flashing through his mind that there was never a policeman around when you needed one.

Darby gathered up his plastic carrier bag and faced the cash machine, pretending still to be carrying out his business. But he was glancing up the street, keeping an eye on developments. Mirczack was approaching fast. Timing was going to be everything. Then he saw Mirczack half turn to see how much of a gap he had on Ormerod. That was just before he passed by. Darby turned and threw his carrier bag towards the big man's legs. Mirczack stumbled and tripped over, crashing to the ground. Unable to get his arms out quickly enough, his face struck the road. Darby immediately jumped on his back, grabbing his arms. Ormerod, struggling for breath, joined in and between the two of them, they handcuffed the big Yugoslav.

Two burly uniformed constables caught up with them at that point and dragged Mirczack to his feet. Blood poured from his nose and a deep gash above his right eye. A police transit van, blue lights flashing and sirens blaring, came down the one-way street towards them and another two uniforms got out. Between the four of them, Mirczack was bundled into the back. Ormerod leaned against a wall, hands on his knees, getting his breath back. Darby looked forlornly at the plastic carrier bag trampled onto the tarmac, red frothy fluid seeping from it.

"I wouldn't mind but I specifically bought a more expensive bottle of Chianti as a treat," he said quietly, to no-one in particular.

Ormerod pushed himself off the wall, stood up and walked over to his colleague. He put his arm around his shoulder. "I'll buy you another one, John," he said. "I don't think I could have chased him much further at that speed."

Darby picked up the bag, pulled out the four battered but intact cans of beer and placed the dripping remains into a nearby bin as the police van set off back to Wood Street.

"Come on," Ormerod said, "best get back there too. I want to see how the guv'nor is. Last I saw he was out like a light."

Darby looked puzzled and as they set off up Cross Street, Ormerod told him what had led to the chase.

By the time Ormerod and Darby arrived back at the station, a crowd had gathered around the public entrance. An ambulance with blue lights flashing was in the middle of several police vehicles in the street. Strong was being brought out on a patient chair, looking grey and holding a compress to his jaw.

"How is it, guv?" Ormerod asked.

Strong managed to nod and give a thumbs up to Darby.

"I thought you'd gone all Columbo on me in there," Ormerod said, dropping into character, "You know, 'Just one more thing, Mr Mirczack ...'"

Strong tried to smile, then winced. Ormerod patted his shoulder as the paramedics took him down the ramp and into the ambulance. They watched as the ambulance drove off with sirens on and people started to disperse.

Back inside, Flynn greeted them. "Well done you two," he said. "I've spoken to our colleagues in Leeds and they're organising a SOCO team to conduct a search of that lock-up. Judging by Mirczack's reaction, we should find some strong evidence there. How did Colin pull that one out of the hat, do you know?"

Ormerod shrugged. "All I know is he took a phone call just as we were releasing him from custody."

"Excuse me, Luke," the desk sergeant said, apologising to Flynn, "I've got a call for you, says it's urgent."

"Go on," Flynn said, "I'll see what the doc says about our prisoner's injuries. He's seeing to him in the cells at the moment."

"Thanks, sir." Then to the sergeant, he said, "I'll take it upstairs."

In the CID Room, when Ormerod took the call, Souter introduced himself.

"I remember," Ormerod said, "you were involved at Calder Street earlier this year, an old friend of the guv'nor."

"That's right. But listen, what's going on? I spoke to Colin about fifteen minutes ago. Since then, I've tried to get hold of him again and it's ringing out and going to answer machine."

"Did you just give him some information about someone we had in custody?"

"Mirczack? Yes."

Ormerod hesitated. "Well, he's not available at the moment. Is there something else I can do for you?"

"You're dealing with the Maria Brownlow disappearance, I believe?"

"That's correct."

"Well I've got something for you. You need to check it out as a matter of urgency …"

61

Ormerod took Darby with him when he set off for Thornes Lane. They found the building that Souter had detailed fairly easily and pulled into the entrance, almost opposite the pub. The sun had just dropped over the horizon but there was still a bit of daylight left when they stepped out of the car and studied the abandoned warehouse building. Since Baker had last been there, someone had secured the gates with a chain and padlock. Ormerod checked that there was no other means of entry.

"Get the bolt croppers," he instructed Darby, who opened the boot and grabbed the tool.

Across the street, on their way into the pub, two men stopped to study the activity.

Ormerod pulled his warrant card from his pocket. "It's okay," he said, "Police business."

The two shrugged and turned into the pub, a beer more interesting than what was happening over the road.

Darby cut the chain, put the croppers back in the boot and locked the car.

Ormerod opened the gate and they marched into the yard. A door on the right into the building, Souter had said. Up three steps, a set of timber double doors could only be what he meant. They made their way across to them. The doors were closed and when Ormerod tried, appeared to be locked.

"You sure this is right?" Darby asked.

"Only one way to find out, John. There's a crowbar in the boot, fetch that will you."

As Darby walked off to the car again, Ormerod walked down the side of the stone-built building. Most of the windows had been smashed and some graffiti adorned the walls. It was a good few years since this was a bustling hive of activity.

Darby returned with the crowbar and jemmied the doors. He pushed them open and, taking a torch from his pocket, stepped inside, Ormerod just behind. They were in what had once been a reception area. Ormerod flashed his torch around to reinforce what little natural daylight was now coming through the windows. The parquet floor was covered in dust and stones and broken glass. Some sections had lifted and oblong pieces of timber were scattered around. There were also some discarded needles. "Careful where you stand," Ormerod warned.

"What's that smell?" Darby asked.

Ormerod's torch beam scanned the floor to the sides and picked out three piles of shit.

"Dogs? In here?" Darby queried.

"I don't think so."

Overhead, the light fittings had been ripped out and wires dangled down, catching Darby unawares. "Fuck," he said, "That could have been live."

"Not very likely," Ormerod chuckled.

They made their way past the reception desk, thick with dust. A calendar on the wall announced that it was still July 1995. Ormerod pushed open a door to the left and carefully walked into a corridor. There was a different aroma here. Only slight at first, but definite. On up the corridor, they proceeded carefully. A door to the right was open. There was enough daylight coming in through the window, augmented by the street light outside, to see it was empty. Yet more stones and broken glass. The next door to the left was closed. Ormerod paused and pulled on some gloves before opening it. This had been the gents' toilet. It stank of stale urine and excrement. A quick flash of the torch indicated it was empty, apart from the smashed basins, urinals and cubicle partitions. He closed the door.

"It should be the next room on the right," Ormerod said, carefully picking his way along the corridor. The aroma was strengthening. "I don't like this, John," he said. "I've smelt this before."

"Smells like something's died," Darby offered.

Ormerod ignored the remark and walked to the next door. It was partly open. Shining the torch around the floor, he found what they'd been looking for.

Outside in the fresh air of the yard, Ormerod made the call that would bring reinforcements. Darby struggled to keep his last meal down, but he did, the colour slowly returning to his face.

Within fifteen minutes, Kelly Stainmore and Trevor Newell had arrived with Scenes Of Crime officers turning up about five minutes after that. Dr Andrew Symonds, the duty medical officer, pronounced life extinct and emerged into the yard for a cigarette.

Standing next to Stainmore and Ormerod, he said, "Poor kid."

"Any initial thoughts, doctor?" Stainmore asked.

"I'll need to check toxicology, of course. It wouldn't surprise me if she'd taken something but I would say, unless any other injuries become apparent when I get her back to the mortuary, it looks like she probably had a fit and choked on her own vomit."

Ormerod looked at Stainmore then to the doctor. "If there was someone with her, do you think she could have been saved?"

Symonds exhaled some smoke. "Usually in these cases, simply putting them in the recovery position and keeping their airways clear, and getting help of course, means people suffering a fit, survive. But, like I say, I'd like to check to see if there was anything else going on before I can say for definite."

Doug Norris, one of the senior SOC men joined them in the yard with something in a plastic evidence bag. "Thought you might want to see this as soon as," he said. "A small clutch handbag with two twenty pound and one ten pound notes inside and some loose change."

"So she wasn't robbed," Ormerod concluded.

"But more importantly," Norris continued, "a Matalan card in the name of Maria Brownlow. I think you have your missing girl."

Ormerod turned away and walked to the far side of the yard. Taking out his phone, he dialled a number.

"Hello," Souter answered.

"We found her. She's dead."

Souter exhaled. *"How?"*

"Choked on her own vomit, we think, but won't know for certain until the PM."

Souter was silent for a while. *"Thanks,"* he eventually said, *"Appreciate the call."*

62
Wednesday

Two days later, Strong in DCS Flynn's office was sitting opposite the man himself.

"Are you sure you should be back so soon, Colin?" Flynn asked.

Heavy bruising coloured his jaw and his speech was slightly affected. "I'm fine, sir. Nothing broken, just a bit sore for a while that's all."

Flynn nodded approvingly.

Strong gingerly nursed a cup of coffee to his lips. This was a rare treat; coffee from his boss's personal percolator. "Besides, there seems to be a lot that's happened in the last forty-eight hours."

"Certainly has." Flynn was relaxing in his chair hands clasped over his stomach. "You'll be pleased to know that your assailant is safely locked up," he continued. "He's been charged with the murders of Chris Baker and Helena Cryanovic plus a number of other charges related to sex trafficking and offences associated with the girls and the parlours." He leaned forward and grinned. "Where did you pull that rabbit out of the hat? They found his car in the lock up in Leeds and the handgun in the glovebox. Forensics are having a field day. Lots of trace evidence to substantiate that the girl was in the boot."

"It was just good timing of information received."

"Good work though, Colin."

"And Szymanski?"

"He's been charged too. So overall a good result." Flynn paused a moment, growing serious. "But tragic news about your other Misper."

Strong nodded grimly. "Maria Brownlow. Yes, Luke told me last night."

"Sad end to a sad life, I gather. The PM Results confirm natural causes but she might have been okay if she'd had help at the time. And then Essex police tell us they'd detained our two likely lads, Baker and Chapman down in Clacton of all places. Anonymous tip off apparently."

"They're back here now aren't they?"

"Kelly and Luke are conducting interviews," Flynn confirmed. "I expect they'll be charged in connection with the vehicle thefts later today."

Strong tensed. "A pity we can't do that little shit for leaving Maria to die."

"I know."

"On that subject, sir." Strong stood up and placed his coffee cup onto its saucer. "I said I'd be at the mortuary this morning."

* * *

Half an hour later, Souter and Alison were standing alongside Sammy as they waited in the designated area of the Mortuary when Strong entered.

Souter stood and the two men hugged one another. "How are you feeling, Col?" he enquired.

"I'll be fine."

Alison looked up at his face. "It's certainly colourful," she commented.

"Honestly, I'm okay." Strong shook her hand then looked to Sammy. "Are you sure you can do this?" he asked.

Sammy, eyes red with crying, nodded.

Souter knew they'd made Maria as presentable as possible but it would still be another traumatic event for Sammy to experience in such a short life.

After Sammy had formally identified Maria, all four went to a nearby café. Strong bought them coffees.

"Thank you, Sammy," Strong said, as he stirred some sugar into his drink. "I know it's never easy."

"At least I know what happened to her. It must have been terrible for the families of Jennifer and Mary to go years before finding out. Some families never find out."

Alison gripped her hand.

Sammy looked at her then to Souter. "The only way I can think of it is, that it's the end of a chapter. And I hope … I'm sure, the next chapter will be much better."

"I'm sure it will, Sammy," Strong smiled, then flinched.

"How is it?" Souter asked.

"I was lucky, I suppose. No break just bruising and gave my teeth a good rattle."

Sammy chuckled and the mood seemed to lighten.

63
Tuesday 4th October 2000

Strong was at his desk working on some paperwork when the phone rang.

"Colin, it's Peter, Peter Walker in Pontefract."

"Hello, Peter."

"How's the jaw?"

Subconsciously, his free hand rubbed the spot Mirczack had caught. "Still aches on a night but it was a lucky punch. No real damage."

Walker chuckled. *"When's the trial?"*

"Early December." Strong sat back in his seat. "Anyway, how are your investigations coming along?"

"That's why I wanted to talk to you. You'll remember I told you we'd sent Enid Collinson's old pick-up for forensic tests? Well, we got some interesting results."

"Go on."

"They found trace evidence in the rear seats matching the remnants of both girls' clothing."

"So they'd both been in the vehicle."

"At some point. But also, I said we'd sent off samples taken from the bodies to the DNA lab, we got a hit on that too."

"Did you now? Anyone we know?"

"Not directly. What we got was a familial match against a sample taken from a drink driver four years ago."

"Meaning it's not them but someone closely related."

"Correct. And that driver is Stanley Collinson. So the samples from the girls could only have come from Collinson senior, Wilf. There are no other family members we can find."

"You got an address?"

"Sure have. According to our investigations, Stanley now lives in Rotherham, quite near the town centre. We're heading off there now and I just wondered, seeing as you were in at the beginning so to speak, if you wanted to come along."

Strong checked his watch. "Give me forty minutes?"

"Perfect. We'll pick you up at Wood Street, it's on our way. See you then."

Strong got into the rear seat of Walker's Volvo. DS Tim Miller was driving with Walker himself in the front passenger seat. On the way down the M1 Walker and Strong talked about various criminals they'd come into contact with over the years and some of the stupidity they'd displayed, much to the amusement of Miller. Eventually, the conversation drifted to Strong's most recent case.

"So with this court case against Mirczack and Szymanski coming up in December," Walker commented, "how did you manage to get them to drop that smooth-talking poncy bastard Peter Atherton from their defence team?"

Strong smiled as he remembered the telephone conversation he'd had with Atherton a week ago. Being the sort of high-profile, publicity seeking individual that he was, Atherton had taken part in some television news item earlier in the year about the taking of DNA from anyone charged with an offence. Although speaking out against the routine taking of samples, he'd agreed to put himself up as a guinea pig to show how it would be done. The samples were supposed to have been destroyed afterwards. Unbeknown to most, they hadn't, but had found their way onto the national DNA database instead. Strong was shocked when Jim Ryan had told him that the forensics team had discovered some interesting matches from the ground floor room of Luxor Grove where the sex parties had taken place. One of those belonged to Peter Atherton. Naturally, because the original sample hadn't been taken in accordance with correct procedure, nothing further could be done with it. It did, however, provide him with a satisfying encounter with the solicitor, culminating in his agreement to drop Mirczack and Szymanski as clients.

"Oh, just got lucky, I suppose," Strong responded.

Collinson's house was a brick-built mid-terraced house about half a mile from the railway station. Although cars were parked both sides, surprisingly there were spaces. Miller pulled the Volvo into a gap opposite the house they wanted. After about twenty seconds delay, their knock on the door was answered by man Strong assumed was Stanley Collinson. He was forty-one, according to the file but looked older. The balding pate with a dark-haired comb-over didn't help. He wore thick-rimmed spectacles, a grubby pullover and dark trousers. His feet were in slippers.

"Mr Collinson? Stanley Collinson?" Walker began.

"Yes," he replied.

"I'm Detective Chief Inspector Peter Walker from Pontefract CID. This is my colleague DS Tim Miller and from Wakefield CID, DCI Colin Strong. We'd like to talk to you about your time at Meadow Woods Farm, if we may. Can we come in?"

All three held up their warrant cards for a second.

Collinson seemed shell-shocked. After a moment's hesitation, he opened the door wider to allow the detectives to enter.

"Two DCIs? That's a bit heavy isn't it," he pondered as he closed the door behind them.

Like many terraced houses in the area, the front door led straight into the sitting room. The room itself was furnished with what Strong guessed was furniture he'd inherited from his parents. A solid wooden table was by the front window and a dresser in matching dark wood stood by the wall opposite the fireplace. A well-worn three piece suite filled up most of the room and what could be seen of the carpet would have been fashionable in the seventies. A brown rug lay by the hearth and an unlit gas fire was in the old tiled surround. The only nod to the present day seemed to be the large television sitting on a media unit in one corner. Surprisingly, from Strong's experience of talking to people in their own homes, Collinson switched it off with the remote control.

"May we sit down, Mr Collinson?" Walker asked.

"Er, sure."

Walker and Miller sat on the settee with Strong on one of the easy chairs, allowing Collinson to sit opposite the television in the remaining one which seemed moulded to his shape.

Before Walker could say any more, Collinson spoke. "I've been expecting you. Well, not you specifically, but someone. It's about them little girls isn't it?" He looked pale and his hands were beginning to shake.

Walker was leading the interview with Miller taking notes. "You've seen the newspaper reports?"

Collinson nodded. "Yes."

"We understand you were the last resident of Meadow Woods Farm?"

"Lived there most of me life. I was born in York and me Mam and Dad had a farm near Beverley. Then when I were five, we rented Meadow Woods."

"And it was just you and Mr and Mrs Collinson?"

"That's right."

"Until your mother died in ..." Walker flipped open his notebook. "1985, is that correct?"

"October 24th. She were only fifty-two." He looked up and Strong thought his eyes were moist.

"You were close to her weren't you?"

"She were a lovely woman until the cancer came. At the end she were in a terrible state. She wasn't me Mam by then." Tears began to streak his cheeks.

"Tell us what happened after she'd gone."

"It hit me Dad hard. He was sixty-four at the time. While me Mam were alive, he'd struggled on with the farm. I did try to help him but farming weren't for me. I could see it were a struggle to make a living. It's alright for those as has their own land but when you were a tenant farmer like he was ..." He wiped his cheeks with both hands. "Any road, we did carry on for another five years until he died in 1990. Then I moved on myself."

"Did your father own a Mitsubishi pick-up at any time?

"It were me Mam's. When she became ill, me Dad used it."

"Did you ever drive it, Mr Collinson?"

"Now and again, yes, but I had my own little Ford Fiesta."

"And do you know what happened to the pick-up?"

"Before me Dad died, it'd clapped out. The clutch finally went in the winter before he passed on. It were due an MOT and taxing in the new year. It were knackered, so it were left in one of the old barns. Probably still there now."

"It was," Walker confirmed. He paused for a second as he studied the man. "When was the last time you used it?"

Collinson puffed out his cheeks. "Oh, I don't know, maybe that last summer, 1989. I had my own car, as I said. Me Dad were the one who always drove it after Mam died."

"When was the last time you went into the basement, Mr Collinson?"

Walker's question had an instant reaction on Collinson, not just the unexpected change of direction. Strong saw him colour up and appear to shake nervously. He looked down onto his lap. "That's where you found them isn't it?"

"So when was the last time you were in the basement?"

"He changed after Mam went. He was all withdrawn like." He looked at Walker, tears back in his eyes again. "I'm sure he didn't mean them any harm."

"Who Stanley?"

"Me Dad." He rubbed his palms nervously on his trousers. "After he'd gone, I was clearing out his stuff. And I found them." Collinson stood up and went to the door leading to the back of the house. "I'll show you," he said.

Miller stood but Walker raised a calming hand and he resumed his seat. They heard Collinson's footsteps on the stairs then into the room above them. After some shuffling around, he returned.

"I think you might be interested in these," he said, placing two pairs of children's shoes and four white socks carefully on the table.

All three detectives rose and surrounded Collinson to look more closely at what he'd brought downstairs with him. Strong felt a knot form in the pit of his stomach.

"Are these what I think they are?" Walker turned to the man.

Collinson nodded, then went back to his seat.

"Where did you get them?"

"I found them in a drawer in me Dad's bedroom. They were at the back, hidden under his pyjamas. It puzzled me at first. I began to wonder if they'd had a child that had died before I came on the scene."

"Bag these up," Walker instructed Miller as he sat back down opposite Collinson.

"I'd never heard Mam and Dad talk about a sister, but I did wonder. Although once, when he'd had a drink one night, he started talking about how he wished he'd had a daughter. And then, I began to realise ..." He looked across at Walker, eyes wide behind his glasses. "And I remembered how me Dad never used to like me going down the basement. So I went down there and had a look. There was no-one to stop me now."

"And what did you find, Stanley?"

The atmosphere in that terraced house living room was electric. All three officers held their breath, waiting to hear what Collinson would say next.

"There were one or two old tea chests," he continued. "My old bike I hadn't seen for years, I thought he'd thrown it out ages before. It was dusty down there and smelled a bit but nothing else really, apart from a locked door. At first, I wondered if it was just an outside door, but then I had a second look, started working out where everything was compared to upstairs. That's when I realised there must be a room behind. But it were locked. So I went back upstairs and started searching through me Dad's things. And then I found this old key. I went back down again and it fitted the lock. It were a bugger to turn, but it finally did. The door was stiff but I gave it a hard shove and it opened. I remember the terrible scraping sound these small stones made that had been trapped under the bottom edge. There were no lights in there, only a couple of dim lights outside. Slowly, my eyes adjusted and I could see them. I didn't know what they were at first, I thought they were just a couple of manikins perhaps me Mam had years ago. But then I looked closer ..." The tears were streaming down his cheeks by now. "And I realised what I were seeing. I didn't know who they were but I knew what they were." Saliva was dribbling from Collinson's mouth as he struggled to keep control. "I'm sorry. I'm sorry," he managed to say before removing his glasses, pulling out a handkerchief and burying his face in his hands, sobbing uncontrollably.

Walker looked across to Strong then to Miller. "Why don't you have a look in the kitchen, Tim?" he said, "and make us some tea. I think we need that."

All were silent before Miller came back after a minute. "Kettle's on," he said.

"Mr Collinson? Stanley?" Walker quietly prompted. "We will need to take a formal statement from you. You do understand that, don't you?"

Collinson nodded, pulled a handkerchief from a trouser pocket and began to wipe his face.

"You will need to accompany us to Pontefract Police Station to do that."

"Are you arresting me?"

"We would like you to come with us. But first, can you tell us what you did next?"

He put his glasses back on and his handkerchief back in his pocket. "Next?"

"Yes, Stanley, after you discovered the bodies."

"Well I ... I didn't know what to do. I panicked. I ran back up into the living room. And then suddenly, I remembered the disappearances; earlier the year before and one about three years before that. I couldn't remember their names but I knew they must be them little girls. I started to think about me Dad's behaviour. When was it he first went off on one because I went down there? I tried to tie it back to events that were happening at the time. And I remembered it were just before Wimbledon got promoted to the First Division. That was 1986. I always took an interest in non-league teams when I were growing up. And a couple of years later, in 1988 when they won the Cup. I wished I'd placed a bet years before about a non-league team winning the Cup, and there they were, in the top division and Cup holders."

Walker took a deep breath and sat forward on the settee. "Look, Stanley, this is all very interesting but what I want to know is what did you actually do about your find."

Collinson looked slightly confused. "Oh, sorry, I ... Well, after I thought for a bit, I decided the best thing to do would be to block the room up completely. That way, anyone else taking on the farm wouldn't discover them. I mean, I didn't know it were going to lie empty and go to rack and ruin after I left."

Walker looked to Strong and Miller then back to Collinson. "So, just to be clear, Stanley, you took out the door and frame and blocked up the opening? With blocks?"

He nodded. "That's right. There were some left lying around the yard and I used them. I've done a bit of building work before, so I left it neat and tidy."

Walker glanced down at Miller's notebook to make sure he had everything written down. "I don't think we'll bother with that tea now, Tim. We'll have a drink back in Pontefract." He rose to his feet and asked Collinson to do the same.

"Stanley Collinson," he said, "I am arresting you on suspicion of perverting the course of justice. You are not obliged to say anything unless you wish to do so but whatever you say will be taken down in writing and may be given in evidence."

Collinson looked shocked.

Walker looked around the room. "Is there anything we need to do to make the house safe before we leave?"

Collinson put his hand in his pocket and pulled out some keys. "Just need to lock the front door."

Five minutes later, all four were in the car on their way back to Pontefract, with a small detour to drop Strong off in Wakefield.

64
Monday, 25th December 2000

Souter was in the front passenger seat of Strong's Mondeo as they followed Susan's Micra. She was on a mission, Sammy with her. For Strong, the conversation was becoming awkward.

"But how the Hell did you get Mirczack to plead guilty?" Souter looked intently at his friend.

"I didn't have any influence on the decision. That was down to his legal team. They obviously considered it was his best option." Strong concentrated on his driving. He was uncomfortable with some of the facts that weren't revealed in court because the guilty plea avoided a trial.

"So there was no pressure from elsewhere?"

"No idea what you're talking about." Strong knew that Souter suspected something. The establishment, whoever they were, definitely had influence on the defence team.

Souter took in the view of the surrounding countryside, the fields' bare earth, the trees barren in the depths of winter. "There are rumours, you know."

Strong had not only heard them, he was probably one of the few who knew some of the key facts. He wasn't party to everything, he was sure of that.

His old boss, Jack Cunningham had called him a few weeks earlier and they'd met for a quiet pint in a pub well off the patch. He'd been allowed to take his pension and retire from the force. He told Strong he had a few irons in the fire as far as future work was concerned. He also spoke of Halliday. He'd retired immediately after Mirczack was charged and was in hospital a month later. The cancer was inoperable and the medical staff had given him three months. The main purpose of the meet was that

Halliday wanted Strong to know some of the pressure he'd been under during those last few weeks. All he told him was in the strictest confidence. Strong was correct when he thought he'd seen a masonic handshake between Halliday and Atherton. But the lawyer's position was only the tip of the iceberg.

The forensic findings at Luxor Grove had caused shock waves. Mirczack was certainly well-connected. Of the DNA samples that provided a positive match, several surprises had come to light. Apart from Peter Atherton, there were two prominent business men, a retired judge and an MP at least; all attendees at the special parties the girls spoke of. No names were given but Strong had a pretty good idea who they were. The MP would announce early in the New Year that he wouldn't be seeking re-election. There were also photographs which Mirczack's defence team used to good effect. Neither Halliday nor Cunningham had been allowed to see those.

"There are always rumours. But that's all they are."

"Phaw, right. And that's why they got such light sentences."

Strong didn't respond.

"Come on, twelve years for two counts of murder? Compare that to the six they gave that sad bastard Collinson for perverting the course of justice. No, there was something else going on. You know there was."

"Look, I can't say I'm happy about it, but that's where it is."

They were silent for several minutes before they reached their destination.

Driving up the gravel track towards the farmyard, Susan swung her car round and drew to a halt in front of the new barn. The building where, some months ago, she had peered in through the side window. The rain had stopped but the wind buffeted the cars. Strong pulled alongside. All police hazard tape had been removed but the farmhouse was fenced off. Signs on the fencing panels advertised the services of a local demolition contractor. The farmhouse was due to be obliterated in the New Year. The old barn had already gone, a pile of ash residue from a bonfire the only evidence.

Susan was free of her plastercast but still having physiotherapy. She had won the argument with the medics that she could now drive her automatic. Stepping out into the biting wind, she drew her coat tightly around her neck. Sammy joined her. Strong and Souter did likewise. Susan opened the boot and took out the two teddy bears she'd bought earlier in the week. A label was tied around the arm of each one. She stood for a moment and studied the old decrepit building. Apart from the wind, there was no sound. No trains pounded their way past on the East Coast main line; being Christmas Day, there was no service.

Sammy linked arms with her friend and Susan blinked back a tear. Susan glanced up at Souter as he put his arm around her shoulder. Strong looked on. This was a time for Susan. This was something she had to do.

Once she was ready, Susan walked towards the fence, Sammy and Souter supporting her. On her own, she took one further step, bent down and carefully placed both bears in front of the house as near as she could get. With red ribbons, she tied both bears in place. She stood again and bowed her head. Strangely, the wind dropped as she said a silent prayer and wiped away a tear.

After a minute, Souter and Strong stepped up on either side of her. "I'm sorry," they heard her say softly.

"You did everything you could, Susan," Strong said. "If it hadn't been for you, they would still be undiscovered and no one would ever have known what happened to them."

She turned to look at him. "Why doesn't that make me feel any better? What did really happen to them anyway?"

"You were there, at the trial. You heard Stanley speak about what he discovered when his father died. The forensic evidence supported the theory that Wilf Collinson abducted the girls, brought them here and strangled them. It was only after his father died that Stanley discovered their shoes and socks in one of his father's bedroom drawers."

Susan wiped her face with the back of her hand. "They were barefoot."

"Stanley still held on to them, probably in some twisted sense of loyalty to his father. But he'd also discovered them down there." He pointed to the farmhouse. "And instead of reporting it then, he blocked up the doorway, hoping to conceal them. I suppose we'll never know for sure, but Stanley has admitted everything else, so I tend to believe him when he says he had no idea what his father had done … until the day he made his discovery."

They stood in silence for a few more seconds.

"I love Christmas," Susan finally said. "That's what Mary told me. And Jennifer too."

"Come on, let's get back." Sammy took hold of her arm and turned back to the car. "Gillian will have Christmas dinner ready for us."

Strong checked his watch and looked at Souter. "Laura's expecting us at two and we've got to pick up Alison on the way."

"Thanks for coming with me, Bob," Susan said, as she opened her car door.

"Enjoy the rest of your Christmas."

As the cars fired up and disappeared back down the gravel track, the farmyard fell silent and peaceful once more. The wind picked up again, fluttering the labels on the bears.

"To Jennifer, Happy Christmas, love from Susan XXX", read one, and on the other, *"For Mary, Happy Christmas, love from Susan XXX"*; along the bottom of both, *"Sleep well, your torment is over."*

THE END

Enjoy TORMENT?

Then please review on Amazon, Goodreads etc.

Have you read more in the series?

See the next few pages …

Book 1   TROPHIES

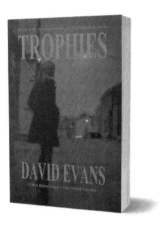

By the turn of the millennium, memories had dulled. But the discovery of a trophy case at the scene of a murder leads to the realisation that a series of attacks on women over the previous twenty years had gone unconnected. DI Colin Strong is convinced there is also a link with one other notorious unsolved crime. His best friend from schooldays, journalist Bob Souter, has returned to Yorkshire and begins to probe. Working separately and together in an awkward alliance, they seek the answers.

Available through Amazon:

Getbook.at/Trophies

Book 3   TALISMAN

A man's body found naked and shackled to a frame in a house fire; a body lying undiscovered in a bath for over a year; massive European funding for a controversial construction project. Is there a link between the bodies and the business deal? And what exactly is the Talisman Club?

In the third instalment of the Wakefield series, DI Colin Strong and best friend, journalist Bob Souter must work together to bring the guilty to justice before time runs out.

Available through Amazon:

Getbook.at/Talisman

Book 4　　　　　　　TAINTED

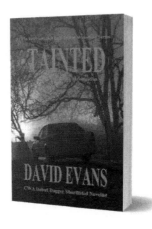

A botched attempt to extort money has tragic consequences.

An embarrassing DNA match to an unsolved rape and murder twenty years before means DI Colin Strong has to use his best diplomatic tactics.

Simultaneously, journalist Bob Souter is tasked with writing about that same case to re-focus public attention. Will the newspaper's actions help or hinder the police?

Meanwhile, Strong's team has two separate murder enquiries to run.

Available through Amazon:

https://getbook.at/Tainted-DavidEvans

Printed in Great Britain
by Amazon